Wicked, MY Love

SUSANNA IVES

sourcebooks
casablanca

Published by Sourcebooks Casablanca, an imprint of Sourcebooks,
Inc.
P.O. Box 4410, Naperville, Illinois 60567–4410
(630) 961-3900
Fax: (630) 961-2168
www.sourcebooks.com

Printed and bound in Canada.
MBP 10 9 8 7 6 5 4 3 2 1

i14077048

To Cathy Leming (w/a Catriona Scott) for your kindness, encouragement, and wonderful insight through the years. My books would not have been born without your help.

Prologue

1827

NINE-YEAR-OLD VISCOUNT RANDALL GAZED TOWARD the Lyme Regis coast but didn't see where the glistening water met the vast sky. He was too lost in a vivid daydream of being all grown up, wearing the black robes of the British prime minister, and delivering a blistering piece of oratorical brilliance to Parliament about why perfectly reasonable boys shouldn't be forced to spend their summer holidays with jingle-brained girls.

"You know when your dog rubs against me it's because he wants to make babies," said Isabella St. Vincent, the most jingled-brained girl of them all, interrupting his musings.

The two children picnicked on a large rock as their fathers roamed about the cliffs, searching for ancient sea creatures. Their papas were new and fast friends, but the offspring were not so bonded, as evidenced by the line of seaweed dividing Randall's side of the rock from hers.

"All male species have the barbaric need to rub

against females," she continued as she spread straw-berry preserves on her scone.

She was always blurting out odd things. For instance, yesterday, when he had been concentrating hard on cheating in a game of whist in hopes of finally beating her, she had piped up, "Do you know the interest of the Bank of England rose by a half a percentage?" Or last night, when she caught him in the corridor as he was trying to sneak a hedgehog into her room in revenge for losing every card game to her, including the ones he cheated at. "I'm going to purchase canal stocks instead of consuls with my pin money because at my young age, I can afford greater investment risks," she'd said, shockingly oblivious to the squirming, prickly creature under his coat.

Despite being exactly one week younger than he was, she towered over him by a good six inches. Her legs were too long for her flat torso. An enormous head bobbled atop her neck. Her pale skin contrasted with her thick, wiry black hair, which shot out in all directions. And if that wasn't peculiar enough, she gazed at the world through lenses so thick that astronomers could spot new planets with them, but she needed them just to see her own hands. Hence, he took great glee in hiding them from her.

"You're so stupid." He licked fluffy orange cream icing from a slice of cake. "Everyone knows babies come when a woman marries a man, and she lies in bed at night, thinking about yellow daffodils and pink lilies. Then God puts a baby in her belly." He used an exaggerated patronizing tone befitting a brilliant, powerful viscount destined for prime ministership—even if "viscount" was only a courtesy title. Meanwhile, Isabella was merely a scary, retired merchant's daughter whom no one would ever want to marry. And, after all, a female's sole purpose in life was to get married and have children.

"No, you cabbage-headed dolt," she retorted. "Cousin Judith told me! She said girls shouldn't be ignorant about the matters of life." Isabella's Irish mother had died, so Cousin Judith was her companion. Randall's mama claimed that Judith was one of those "unnatural sorts" who supported something terrible called "rights of women." He didn't understand the specifics, except that it would destroy the very fabric of civilized society. He would certainly abolish it when he was prime minister.

"Judith said that for a woman to produce children, she, unfortunately, requires a man." Isabella's gray eyes grew into huge round circles behind her spectacles. "That he, being of simple, base nature and mind, becomes excited at the mere glimpse of a woman's naked body."

He was about to interject that she was wrong again—girls were never right—but stopped, intrigued by the *naked* part. Nudity, passing gas, and belching were his favorite subjects.

"Anyway, a man has a penis," she said. "It's a puny, silly-looking thing that dangles between his limbs."

He gazed down at the tiny bulge in his trousers. He had never considered his little friend silly.

"When a man sees the bare flesh of a woman, it

becomes engorged," she said. "And he behaves like a primitive ape and wants to insert it into the woman's sacred vagina. My cousin said that was the passage between a woman's legs that leads to the holy chamber of her womb."

"The what?" Where was this holy chamber? He was suddenly overcome with wild curiosity to see one of these sacred vaginas.

"Judith said the man then moves back and forth in an excited, animalistic fashion for approximately ten seconds, until he reaches an excited state called *orgasm*. Then he ejaculates his seed into the woman's bodily temple, thus making a baby."

His dreams of future political power, the shimmering ocean, fluffy vanilla-orange icing, and a prank on Isabella involving a dead, stinking fish all seemed unimportant. He gazed at his crotch and then her lap—the most brilliant idea he ever conceived lighting up his brain. "I'll show you my penis if you show me your vagina." He flashed his best why-aren't-you-just-an-adorable-little-thing smile, which, when coupled with his blond hair and angelic, bright blue eyes, charmed his nurses into giving him anything he wanted. However, his cherubic looks and charm didn't work on arctic-hearted Isabella.

"You idiot!" She flicked a spoonful of preserves at his face.

"You abnormal, cracked, freakish girl!" he cried. "I only play with you because my father makes me." He smeared her spectacles with icing. In retaliation, she grabbed her jar of lemonade and doused him.

When their fathers and nurses found them, she was atop the young viscount, now slathered in jam, icing, mustard, and sticky lemonade, pummeling him with her little fists.

Mr. St. Vincent yanked his daughter up.

"She just hit me for no reason," Randall wailed, adopting his poor-innocent-me sad eyes. "I didn't do anything to her."

"Young lady, you do not hit boys," her father admonished. "Especially fine young viscounts. You've embarrassed me again."

"I'm sorry, Papa," Isabella cried, distraught under her father's hard gaze. Humiliation wafted from her ungainly body and Randall felt a pang of sympathy, but it didn't diminish the joy of knowing she had gotten in trouble and he hadn't.

The Earl of Hazelwood placed a large hand on the back of Randall's neck and gave his son a shake. "Son, we didn't find any old sea creatures, but Mr. St. Vincent has come up with a brilliant idea to help our tenants and provide a dependable monthly income." He turned to his friend. "We are starting the Bank of Lord Hazelwood. Mr. St. Vincent and I will be the major shareholders and we will add another board member from the village."

Even as a small child, Randall had an uneasy, gnawing feeling in his gut about this business venture that none of Mr. St. Vincent's strange terms, such as *financial stabilization*, *wealth building*, or *reliable means for tenant borrowing and lending*, could dissuade. He was never going to get rid of that rotten Isabella.

Through the years, he and she remained like two hostile countries in an uneasy truce; a lemonade-throwing, cake-splatting war could break out at any moment. Randall would indeed follow his path to political fame, winning a seat in Parliament after receiving a Bachelor of Arts from St. John's College, Cambridge. He basked in the adoration of London society as the Tory golden boy. To support Randall's London lifestyle, the Earl of Hazelwood signed over a large amount of the bank's now quite profitable shares to his son.

He came home from Parliament when he was twenty-three to witness Isabella standing stoic and haunted with no black veil to hide her pale face from the frigid January air as they lowered her father into the frozen earth. Having no husband, she inherited her father's share in the bank and began to help run it. The two enemies' lives would be hopelessly entwined through the institution born that fateful day in Lyme Regis, when Randall learned how babies were made.

For the next five years, bank matters rolled along smoothly. Then the board secretary passed away unexpectedly, leaving his portion to his young bachelor nephew, Mr. Anthony Powers.

That's when all manner of hell broke loose.

One

1847
Stuke Buzzard, England

ISABELLA LIFTED A DELICATE, PERFECTLY COILED TENDRIL of hair in the "luxurious shade of raven's wing" from the Madam O'Amor's House of Beauty package that she had secreted into her bedchamber.

Her black cat, Milton, who had been bathing his male feline parts on her pillow, stopped and stared at the creation, his green eyes glittery.

"This is not a rat," Isabella told him. "You may not eat it."

Unconvinced, the cat rolled onto his paws, hunched, and flicked his tail, ready to pounce.

The advertisement in last month's *Miroir de Dames* had read *"Losing your petals? Withering on the vine? Return to your full, fresh, feminine bloom with Madam O'Amor's famous youth-restoring lotion compounded of the finest secret ingredients, and flowing tendrils, puffs, and braids made from the softest hair."*

Isabella typically didn't believe such flapdoodle.

But at twenty-nine, she was dangling off the marital cliff and gazing down into the deep abyss of childless spinsterhood. Now she finally had a live, respectable fish by the name of Mr. Powers, her bank partner, swimming around the hook. After he walked her home from church on Sunday, she had decided not to take any chances and had broken down and ordered Madam's concoctions. Even then, a little voice inside her warned, "Don't lie to yourself. Who would want to marry an abnormal, cracked, freakish girl?" All those things Randall had called her years ago. Strange that words uttered so long ago still had the power to sting.

After making excuses to loiter about the village post office for almost a week, Isabella had been relieved when her order had finally arrived on the train that morning, just in time to restore her full, fresh, feminine bloom before Mr. Powers called on bank business. Little did the poor gentleman know that for once she couldn't care less about stocks and consuls. She was hoping for a more personal investment with a high rate of marital return: a husband.

Standing before her vanity mirror, she opened the drawer, drew out a hairpin, and headed into battle. Her overgrown, irrepressible mane refused to curl tamely, held a fierce vendetta against pins, and rebelled against any empire, Neapolitan, or shepherdess coiffure enforced on it. She secured the first tendril and studied the result. It didn't fall in the same easy, elegant spiral as in the advertisement, but shot out from behind her ear like a coiled, bouncy spring.

"Oh no, this looks terrible." She tugged at it, trying

to loosen the curl. "I'll just secure the other. You can't tell from just one; it's not balanced."

Meanwhile, her cat eyed her, scheming to get at those strange yet oddly luxurious rats on her head.

The second tendril was no better than the first. "I look even more abnormal, cracked, and freakish, if that were possible. I knew this was a stupid idea. Why did I even try when I knew it was stupid?" She sank into her chair and buried her face in her hands. She just wanted a husband and children. Why was it so difficult for her? Why couldn't she be like her mother—graceful and gentle?

Tap, tap.

"Darling, I hate to nag," Judith called through the door. "But the Wollstonecraft Society meeting is in less than two weeks. You really must practice your speech."

Oh fudge! Isabella didn't have time to remove the offending curls. She grabbed Madam O'Amor's box and shoved it under the bed. Milton, who was teetering on the edge of the mattress, saw his moment and took a nasty swipe at her head.

Judith, founding member of the Mary Wollstonecraft Society Against the Injurious Treatment of Women Whose Rights Have Been Unjustly Usurped by the Tyrannical and Ignorant Regime of the Male Kind, strolled in. Her auburn hair was pulled into a sloppy bun and secured by crossed pencils, her reading glasses sitting low on her Roman nose. Before her face, she held Isabella's draft of her acceptance speech for this year's Wollstonecraft award.

"My dear, this is interesting information, but it's

rather, well…boring," she said. "Unlike you, most people don't remember numbers and—my goodness, what torture have you inflicted on your poor hair?"

Isabella extricated Milton's claw from her head and drew herself tall. "I've styled my hair into tendrils," she said firmly. Her companion was bossy and a relentless nagger. Isabella had to put up a strong front.

"Tentacles?"

"I said *tendrils*."

A tiny pleat formed between Judith's eyebrows. "I hope you aren't doing all this for a *man*?" Her face screwed up tight, as if the word *man* emitted a foul stench.

"No, no, of course not." Isabella had been careful to hide her little infatuation with Mr. Powers. If she didn't, Judith would launch into her standard marital lecture, that Isabella shouldn't give over her freedom and money to a simple-minded, barbaric man who would just gamble away her wealth. "W-what would I do with a man?" Isabella laughed nervously, trying to sound innocent. Her gaze wandered to the bed, and her mind lit up with all manner of things she would do with him.

Thankfully, Judith didn't pursue the subject, but reverted back to her usual obsession: the Wollstonecraft Society. "Now, darling, you need to make an emotional connection with the society members in your speech. You must speak to their desires and pains. Remember how we discussed showing our emotions when writing your book."

Isabella groaned. "We agreed never to talk about the book again."

A fellow member of the Wollstonecraft Society had recently bought a printing press in London. Judith had thought it a wonderful idea for Isabella to write a volume educating women about investing and the stock exchange. She'd pestered Isabella for months. Finally, when the weather turned brutal in the winter, Isabella produced a work she titled *A Guide to the Funds and Sound Business Practices for Gentle Spinsters and Widows* by "A Lady." She gave the pages to Judith to edit and happily forgot about it. Three months later, her companion returned a bound book retitled *From Poor to Prosperous, How Intelligent, Resourceful Spinsters, Widows, and Female Victims of Ill-fated Marital Circumstances Can Procure Wealth, Independence, and Dignity* by Isabella St. Vincent, majority partner in the Bank of Lord Hazelwood.

The entire village must have heard Isabella's mortified scream. To make it all the worse, Judith had taken her modest examples, such as "Hannah was a plain spinster with only the limited means left to her by her late father," and added such Gothic claptrap as Hannah having been used and abandoned by some arrogant lord of a manor.

She had hoped the book would languish unread on some library bookshelf until it disintegrated into dust, but it was now in its fourth printing. And Isabella, who was only a member of the society because Judith sent in her membership letter each year, was to be awarded the society's highest honor: the Wollstonecraft—a large gold-painted plaster bust of the famous advocate of rights for women.

Judith pointed to a paragraph on page two of

Isabella's scribbled speech. "Now, where you say consuls return three percent, you should perhaps say, 'an infirm widow whose husband, a typical subjugating, evil man, had gambled away their savings before drinking himself to—'"

"I can't say those things." Isabella flung up her arms. "You know I'm a horrid lecturer. I just stand there mute or start babbling nonsense. Please go to the London meeting and accept the award. You had as much to do with the book as I. And you know Milton gets mad when I go away, and wets my bed out of spite."

"Isabella!" Judith gasped. "It's the Wollstonecraft! Do you know how many ladies dream of being in your shoes?"

Isabella couldn't think of more than six. "But... but..." *I've almost got one of those subjugating, evil men hooked and squirming on my marital line. I can't leave now. To Hades with the gold bust of Mary Wollstonecraft! If I don't know a man soon, I'm going to spontaneously combust.*

"No *buts*," her companion said, handing Isabella back her pages. Surrounding her neat, efficient words and tables were arrows pointing to her cousin's scrawled notes that read "Young widow must support ailing child," or "Honorable, aging spinster turned away from her home."

"This is wrong. Investing is about numbers, not whether you are abandoned or caring for your dead sister's husband's cousin's eleven blind and crippled orphaned children or such nonsense."

"Now you sound like a *man*." Judith scrunched her nose again at the terrible *M* word. "The women of Britain need your help. They have no rights, no vote, no control over their lives. Money is their only freedom." She placed her palm on Isabella's cheek. "I know what a brave, kind soul you are. Inside of you remains the grave child who didn't cry by her mother's casket and the young woman who waited stoically every day by her dying father's bedside. Don't be afraid of your vulnerability and pain. Use it to talk to your sisters in need."

Isabella's throat turned dry. Judith didn't know what she was talking about. Emotions were wild and confusing variables. Their unpredictability scared Isabella, making her feel like that helpless child unable to stop her mama from dying. Logic was, well, logical. It had numbers, lines, formulas, and probabilities. If she could teach those ladies anything, it would be that the key to good investments was to discard those useless, confounding emotions that only muddied the issues and look at the cold, hard patterns in the numbers.

"I knew from the earliest moments of our acquaintance that you would grow into a brilliant leader of women," Judith continued. "Now you must go to London and accept your calling." She turned and sat in the chair by the grate. "Let's rehearse. So chin up, shoulders straight, and begin."

Isabella stared down at the pages and began to drone, "Thank you, ladies of the—"

Mary, one of the servants, slipped through the door. *Mr. Powers is here!* "Pardon me," Mary said with a bob of a curtsy. "Lord Randall has called."

"Lord Randall," Isabella said, disappointed. "What is he doing here? Isn't his parents' annual house party

starting today? Oh bother. Put him in the library." At
least she could use the loathsome viscount as an excuse
to escape this oratorical torture. "I'm sure this is about
extremely urgent bank business that needs attending to
immediately," she told Judith.

❧

After the last session of Parliament, what Lord Randall,
the House of Commons' famed Tory orator, needed
to fortify himself was twelve uninterrupted hours in
bed with a lovely lady before heading home to his
parents' annual house party and shackling himself to a
powerful Tory daughter, living unhappily, but politi-
cally connected, ever after.

If things had gone as planned, at this very moment
he might have been leisurely arriving on the train after
one last good morning tumble.

Of course, things hadn't gone as planned, as they
hadn't for the last six months. Instead of feeling the
soft curves of a stunning little ballet dancer or actress,
he had felt the bump and rumble of a train as he traveled alone through the night, staring at the blackness
beyond the window, his mind swirling with scenarios
of political ruin. Now he stood in the library of a
woman he was desperate to see. But hell and damnation, he would rather gnaw off his own leg than share
twelve uninterrupted hours of frolicking with Isabella.

He raked his hands through his hair, feeling little
strands come loose. *Great.* On top of everything, he
was losing his hair. *Could something else go wrong?*

And where is she?

He paced up and down the Aubusson rug adorning

her somber, paneled library. Some books lined the shelves, but mostly financial journals in leather boxes labeled by date and volume. A large oak desk was situated between two massive arched windows, its surface clean except for a lamp and inkwell. He tugged at his cravat as if he were choking. How could Isabella live in such oppressive, silent order? It stifled his soul.

He strode to one of the windows and watched the line of carriages and flies from the railroad station heading up the hill to his father's estate. Inside them rode Tories of the "right kind" as his mother had phrased it, along with their daughters, all vying for Randall's hand in marriage. He leaned his head against the glass. "You've got to save me, Isabella," he whispered.

"I'm surprised to see you," he heard that familiar soprano voice say behind him.

An odd, warm comfort washed over him at the sound. He turned and found himself gazing at the fashion tragedy that was Isabella. She wore a dull blue dress or robe or something that made a slight indentation around the waist area and concealed everything else from her chin to the floor. Her glasses magnified her gray eyes, and she had styled her wild hair in some new, odd, dangly arrangement. Still, a peace bloomed in his chest at the sight of her frumpy dishevelment, like that nostalgic, grounding feeling of coming home. Well, not his real home, where, despite all British rules to the contrary, his strident mother ruled. As the rest of his world was coming undone, Isabella remained the same old ungainly girl of his memory—his faithful adversary.

"Just 'I'm surprised to see you'?" he repeated

in feigned offense. "Perhaps 'Good morning, Lord Randall. I've missed you terribly. You haunt my dreams. I'm enamored of your dazzling intellectual and manly powers. There is a void in my tiny, black heart that only you can fill.'" His anxiety started to ease as he settled into the thrust, glissade, and parry of their typical conversation.

For a beat, she just stared at him. The old girl took everything at face value. Then the realization dawned in her eyes that he was ribbing her. "Oh, I was about to say that, if you had waited...for several thousand years," she retorted. "What I meant was that I thought you would be busy at your house party, choosing a wife. At least, that is what the papers claim."

"As you often say when avoiding something messy and emotionally taxing, 'I don't want to talk about it,'" he quoted her back to herself. "Except to say it's a shame that Napoleon could not have enlisted Mama; I believe the war might have turned out differently. The Duke of Halsington sent a late reply, upsetting Mama's meticulous arrangements. He will be joined by his wife, who requires a room conveniently adjoining the Earl of Worthsam's, while his grace much prefers comfortable quarters beside Mrs. Kettlemore's. That little farce resulted in ousting me from my chambers to the Fauna chamber, named for housing my late uncle's stuffed avian collection. I spent the early hours of the morning being stared at by dead birds. But enough about nightmares of being eaten by African lappet-faced vultures." He gestured to a chair. "Would you care to sit down? Oh, wait. It's your home. You were supposed to politely suggest that."

"Would you care to sit down, Lord Randall?" she said, with mock sweetness.

"I don't mind if I do; how thoughtful of you to ask." He pulled up a chair before her desk. "Ah, I have something to tempt you with." He withdrew some folded pages from his pocket and wagged them before her. "I did retrieve the list of new clients for the London bank as you ordered—pardon, I meant *requested* in your last letter."

She snatched up the papers, her face glowing with the same delight he had seen in his mistress's—ex-mistress's—when he had given her a ruby necklace. Isabella was an odd bird. Any man who dared to romance the shrew would have to forgo the floral tributes—and not because of her adverse reactions to certain flowers, grasses, and hay—and arrive with bouquets of financial reports instead.

She took a seat in her late father's massive leather chair on the other side of the desk and scanned the lines of patrons. "This is much better than expected," she said, a small smile playing on her lips—soft and cushy lips, he noted. Rather kissable, not that he would ever consider kissing her. It was merely an empirical observation: the sky was blue; the sun was yellow; Isabella had the kind of lips that should be ravished.

"And by the way," he continued, drawing her attention back to him, "I wouldn't write to someone, calling him a flaming ignoramus of the grandest magnitude for his vote on the Scottish banking bill, and then ask him to spend the afternoon at the new bank building kissing babies and welcoming new customers." Despite the panicky economy, when nervous customers were putting runs on another bank every day and sinking their savings, the Bank of Lord Hazelwood was rapidly expanding, "discovering new markets," as Isabella would say, taking offices in London and Manchester. He and his father's profiles and the family's coat of arms appeared in journals all over England above a caption that read "For four hundred years the name Hazelwood has inspired trust. Place your monies where you place your trust."

"It must have been such a hardship being adored and fawned over," she mocked. "I'm sure every unmarried lady in London was beating down the bank door." She waved the documents. "Incredible. There must be five hundred and fifteen names on this list and about three-fifths of them are women."

"I seduced the Hades out of those stodgy old ladies and spinsters for their pennies. I still have bruises in the sensitive areas where they pinched me."

She paused, then a spark lit in her eyes as she realized that he was jesting again. She laughed, a beautiful, silvery sound. Again, he felt that flood of peace. He had an urge to hide in her library, behind that unfashionable skirt of hers and away from his political woes and his parents' damned house party. But alas, the world marched on. Or marched *over* him, as it seemed these last weeks.

He drummed the great oak desk with his fingers, suddenly feeling vulnerable. He had never let his guard down around her before, always keeping a protective wall of lithe, barbed words between them.

"Speaking of being pinched, perhaps you read about my little set-to with George Harding in the parliamentary railroad committee meeting." He tried to sound casual, even as his heart sped up.

"Little!" She raised a single brow, comically screwing her features. "It's an epic scandal! The financial columns criticize you for standing in the way of England's progress, the political columns believe you have committed electoral suicide with the election coming, and the society columns wonder whose powerful Tory daughter you'll marry to patch up the mess." He couldn't miss that little hint of glee under her words.

He found that he was too restless to sit after all, and rose to his feet. "The railroad committee voted Harding's line down. I merely asked if he was spread too thin. The very words you used at the bank board meeting last winter when we decided against investing in his other lines."

She blinked. "You actually listened to something I said?"

"I didn't mean to. I was just about to drift off when your words hit my ears. Splat! Then they wouldn't come out, just rolling around in there. Anyway, I thought you might be right and—"

"Stop right there!" She held up her palm. "Say those words again."

Despite his worry, his lips cracked into a smirk. "I said I *thought* you might be right."

"Oh God." She flipped open a ledger and reached for her pen. "I must make a note: On this day of our Lord, May 17, 1847, Lord Randall has finally admitted that I was right."

"No, you weren't," he barked. "And I'm glad my

troubles amuse you." His words came out harsher than
he intended.

Her head jerked back. "I'm…I'm sorry."

He pinched the bridge of his nose, cursed under his
breath, and crossed to one of the windows.

She joined him there. Her eyes were tense, con-
flicted between fear and concern. She reached out,
letting her hand hover an inch from his before pulling
back. He knew she struggled to connect with others
and messy emotions scared her. He remembered the
days surrounding her father's funeral, when she'd tried
so hard to hide her sorrow, but he still felt her deep
grief ripping her apart.

"You'll sail through this tiny setback with no
trouble," she whispered, her voice shaky and unsure.
"You'll win your seat. You lead a charmed life." He
discerned a hint of bitterness under her last words.

"Well, it's been quite difficult lately, for all its
charm," he quipped. In the distance, a fly rambled
down the long drive to the Hazelwood estate. "I think
Harding is plotting against me," he confessed.

"Why?"

He ran his hand over the cleft in his chin, pondering what he could politely repeat about the previous
night's bad turn. He probably shouldn't mention to
Isabella the desire for twelve uninterrupted hours in
bed with a beautiful woman, which had made him
stick a red rosebud in his lapel and stroll into a gaming
hell off St. James's early last evening. How he had
drained a couple of brandies, trying to wash away the
anxiety of the last weeks, until he felt the shine of his
old, cocky charm return. That he had been about to

amble over to the perfect quarry—curly, raven hair;
large, luxurious dark eyes—when he heard a sweet,
breathy voice say his name.

He had spun to find Cecelia, his ex-mistress,
standing there, ravishing in pale blue. His throat had
gone dry. The entire room stopped mid-roll, play,
bet, or conversation and watched her, as though the
famed actress were onstage in her own production.
Before he could manage a "good evening" to her,
George Harding had stepped forward, flanked by
three personal flash men, and placed a possessive hand
on her shoulder.

Randall didn't think that Harding stealing his mistress was relevant to Isabella and the business at hand.
Nor did he want to admit to Isabella that Harding was
damned handsome, in an exotic way. While Randall
was tall, the railroad baron towered over him. The
man had bronze skin, a muscular build, a flint-like
jaw, and a shiny, bald head. His black brows were
slashes above eerie, unblinking eyes. So, essentially his
version of the story for Isabella's ears began with, "I
went to a club and saw Harding. He asked me to sit
down for a drink, something about clearing the bad
blood between us."

"Why did you take my railroad, my lord?" Harding
had asked, setting his glass of cognac on the table and
opening his palms. "I try to be a good Tory. I back
your candidates."

Harding's flash men rushed to agree. "That's right,
Mr. Harding. You're a Tory's best supporter," and
"You've always done right by the Tories."

"Do you pay for this personal audience of

yahoos?" Randall had asked. "Or do these cullies follow you around because they don't have any bollocks of their own?"

Harding's flash men had glanced at each other, as though deciding how to react. The consensus was menacing until Harding broke into deep belly laughter. "Oh, you're a funny, funny man." The railroad baron leaned over, plucked the rosebud from Randall's lapel, and twirled it under his nose. "Smells nice. With your title, pretty words, and face, you could have gone far, maybe prime minister. But you supported child labor laws and the repeal of the Corn Laws, instead of building railroads and prosperity. What will become of our golden boy with his empty head and glorious ambitions if he isn't reelected?"

Randall had let a slow smile crawl across his lips. "Careful there, old chap. One word from me and you might lose another railroad."

Harding replaced the viscount's rose. "With your title, you think I can't touch you. The world is about to change; you need to choose which side you're on before the election. Enjoy your house party. I hope you find a lovely, connected wife. I understand you've been a bit lonely of late."

Randall decided it wasn't important to tell Isabella how everyone in the gaming hell had watched the railroad baron leave with Randall's beautiful mistress—ex-mistress—or the stream of colorful curses he'd released under his breath.

Now he gazed out the window in Isabella's library. In the distance, at the entrance of his home, he could make out ladies in expansive skirts stepping from the carriages. His mother must be cursing him for not being there to greet them.

"I know you make fun of me," he said quietly. "I know you, like my critics, think I'm shallow and overly ambitious and you disagree with my views." He turned to Isabella, latching his gaze on her face. "But dammit, I'm a good politician. I've all but given my life to this country. I try—"

"You need something solid to hold against Harding."

"No." The motivation for his visit sounded so conniving, almost dishonorable when echoed back to him. He sank into his chair, rubbed his forehead, and conceded. "Yes."

❧

Isabella studied him—his strong shoulders slumped, head bowed, stray strands of blond hair falling over his brow. In that moment, he reminded her so much of Papa in those months after her mother had died. Again she reached out, desiring to touch him, comfort him, but she didn't know how. Upset people made her feel awkward, because she desperately wanted to make their pain go away. Somehow, though, she always said or did the wrong thing, and just made them feel worse.

What are you doing? It's not your father; it's Randall. Stop feeling sorry for him. This is probably the only adversity he has faced in his life, other than losing a cricket match or two at Cambridge.

"You're being too emotional," she told him.

"Of course you would say that. Tell me your cold and detached solution to my problems."

She crossed to the opposite side of the room, giving herself some space to turn over the problem in her head. Tangible things involving numbers she could handle. After several long seconds, she began to speak.

"I would wager he had several backers lined up, telling them the railroad was a sure thing, until you caused him problems. Now he's in trouble. You see, Harding pays higher dividends than anyone else—five percent—yet there are other people who have just as many or more lines. He's probably working out of his capital or using his four obscure companies to conceal or manufacture money."

He crossed to her and seized her hand. A heated tingle ran up her arm. "Have you considered turning into a man and running for Parliament?"

"As Judith's cousin, I have to ask, is that a compliment or an insult?"

"Why, wanting a woman to be a man is the highest praise he can give her," he said in what she thought was a serious tone, but his eyes twinkled. She wasn't skilled at reading twinkles, glows, or sparks in people's eyes, and the viscount's dazzling orbs especially confused her.

"At least it's better than those usual compliments you insult ladies with." She extracted her hand, which still tingled from his touch, and walked away a few paces, putting a safe distance between them. "You know, 'vision of luscious splendor,' 'ethereal loveliness,' and my all-time favorite, 'dream of transcendent beauty.'"

"And I was just about to say you were looking rather transcendent…well, for you."

She paused and fiddled with her tendrils. "Do you think I'm...j-just a little pretty?" She smacked her forehead. "I can't believe I asked you that. Just forget I said anything."

"No, no, I want to answer." Randall clasped her shoulders, eliciting another unwanted tingle, this time in the vicinity of her sacred feminine regions.

He studied her, lips pursed in a serious line, his eyes scrunched. Something about his gaze heated her skin, turning that bothersome tingle into a throb.

Stop that throb, tingle, whatever, this instant, she ordered her body. *This is Randall.* Even if he weren't wildly attracted to ladies who had difficulty understanding any pesky words with three or more syllables, he was still, unfortunately, a ravishingly handsome viscount. And that was an entirely different genus of miscreation that never cross-bred with awkward spinsters possessing a rather unnatural ability with numbers. All that withstanding, she stood still for his perusal of her face...and lower.

Tingle. Tingle. Throb.

"Hmmm," he considered, stroking his chin with his index finger and thumb. "I would say above vision of luscious splendor but not quite ethereal loveliness. It's your hair."

Her cheeks burned. "W-what's wrong with it?"

"Why is it being attacked by two jellyfish?"

"Judith was right!" She dashed to the mirror over the mantel. "They're tentacles. I have to get these off. He's going to be here any minute."

"He?"

"Oh, never mind." She began to tug at the coils

but the two-dozen pins she used to keep them captive refused to budge.

"Let me help."

She felt his fingers digging into her scalp. "Ouch! That's my real hair."

"Your real hair?"

"Just let go!" she ordered.

"Wait. Don't move. My cuff link is stuck in what may or may not be your real hair!"

"Pardon me," a servant said. "Mr. Powers has arrived."

Isabella whipped around. Pain flared on the left side of her head. In Randall's hand dangled a black coil and hairpins were scattered on the carpet. He stared at the creation, his bright eyes wide. A snort of laughter erupted from his lips and then he quickly shoved the thing behind his back.

Mary stood by the door. Beside her, holding a small box wrapped in a loopy, intricate pink bow, was Mr. Anthony Powers.

Isabella opened her mouth but all that came out was a squeak. Randall, that ever-smooth devil, performed a sweeping bow, the tendril behind his back hanging down like a tail. "Good morning, Mr. Powers."

Two

ISABELLA WASN'T TALENTED AT READING PEOPLE THE way Randall was, but even she could discern the anger in Mr. Powers's pursed lips and lowered brows. The man's gaze shifted from her to Randall and back.

"Good morning, Mr. Powers," she cried, her voice finally deciding to cooperate. "I'm so glad to see you. I've…I've been waiting for you."

A smile broke across Powers's face, and she relaxed.

"I say, I adore your new coiffure," Powers said, performing a low, graceful bow. "So unique and delightful, like you."

Her face heated and she squirmed as she always did when receiving a compliment. Well, a true compliment. Randall's didn't count because he always said one thing and meant another. She was terrible at figuring out his other meanings, but she felt sure they were veiled insults.

She was struck by the difference between the two men when they stood almost side by side. Of course, Randall was nauseatingly perfect: strong, lean shoulders; strong, lean legs; strong, lean almost everything with a hard, chiseled faced softened by vivid blue eyes. Meanwhile, Powers wasn't as handsome or tall, but nonetheless his tousled brown curls falling over his warm, chocolate eyes reminded her of snuggly puppies and nights by a warm fire. His face was rather thin and discolored on the left side of the jawline—darkened skin with a cluster of tiny moles like the constellation Charioteer. But his imperfections made him all the more endearing.

"And I have a present for you." Powers winked and offered up his gift.

She thought her heart would burst. "Oh, thank you!" She accepted the box. "No gentleman has given me a present before."

"That's not true!" Randall protested. "I gave you a locket with a hairy spider inside. Don't forget the melodious rooster, or those sweet mice which nibbled on your pillow, and of course my favorite, the drink I told you was punch." She flashed him a hot, will-you-just-be-quiet glower. It didn't work. "Oh, and the sheep. I forgot about those."

"Don't you have a house party to attend?" she said pleasantly through gritted teeth.

Mr. Powers chortled into his hand.

"Bank business takes precedence over mere diversion. And isn't this little call about bank business? Let us all sit down, then. Here, I shall pull up a chair so we can get cozy."

Many times in the past, Isabella had contemplated killing Randall. But on this occasion she went a step further and chose a murder weapon: the penknife. As she set the present on the desk, she thought how easy it would be to grab the knife from the drawer and lodge it in his handsome throat. Certain political factions might secretly thank her.

Randall took a chair and continued yammering, unaware of his imminent, bloody demise at Isabella's hand. "And speaking of diversion and house parties," he said, "I hope you both plan to attend our dance on Tuesday."

Powers looked at Isabella, his head slightly bowed and brows low, a glow in his eyes that sent a giddy quake through her body. "I wouldn't miss it for the world. And if Miss St. Vincent desires to attend, I hope I am not too forward in asking if I may secure a dance in advance."

"Of course you can…you can have them all." She laughed nervously, wringing her hands in her lap. "Well, except the quadrille. I can't do that one. And certain cotillions give me problems. But I can waltz, even though once I accidently knocked over that elderly couple and the dance leader asked me to leave the floor."

Powers clapped his hands together. "Perhaps all you need is proper guidance. Shall I give you a lesson after church?"

"I would like that above all—"

"Sorry, old chap, you'll have to wait," Randall cut in. "I believe Miss St. Vincent agreed to join my house guests and me for shuttlecocks on the lawn Sunday."

What? She would never agree to visit Randall unless her very life depended on it, and she could hardly walk without tripping over herself, much less play shuttlecocks. She turned to tell him as much only to find him wearing her tendril atop his blond head! "What are you—"

"I do say," Randall said, patting his tendril, "I desire some tea. Where is that servants' bell, Isabella? I can never find the thing no matter the dozens of times I've been in your library."

"Here, let me show you," she said in sugary tones, taking his offered arm and driving her nails into it. She escorted him across the room. "What are you doing?" she hissed, and snatched her tendril from his head. "Leave now before I kill you."

"I'm just giving him a little competition," he whispered. "Be coy. Flirt. You're being too eager."

"Well, you're being... I don't know what you're being, but whatever it is, stop it this instant." She jammed the detached tendril back into her hair, pricking her scalp with pins, and forgetting to ring the servants' bell.

Flirt, she said to herself, smoothing her skirt. *Be coy.* But she didn't know how to flirt or tease or be coy or coquettish, or any of those things other ladies seemed born knowing.

Powers wore a crooked smile as he gazed at her. She couldn't tell if he was bemused, annoyed, or just feeling sorry for her.

"So, did you bring the stock certificates from our Merckler Metalworks purchase?" she asked. *No, no, that's not flirting; that's bank business. You're hopeless.*

"Why don't you open the present?" Powers winked again, making her tingle around the heart region. *Did you just tingle for two men in the space of fifteen minutes?*

She retrieved the gift and took a seat. Meanwhile,

Randall remained standing, lurking about like some vulture over the conversation. She ignored him—her usual policy—and removed the ribbons, savoring her first present from a man that wasn't a nasty prank involving rodents, reptiles, or farm animals. Nestled deep in the box was a stack of lovely illustrated stock certificates featuring a woman standing amid many curling lines, clad in revealing Greek clothes and raising a fork. Below her bare feet were printed the words "Merckler Metalworks." Isabella gasped and lifted the stocks from the box. "They are so lovely. Have you ever seen such lovely stock certificates?"

"But there's more," Powers prompted, leaning forward in his seat, his grin widening.

She drew out the financial report. "Oh my!" She flipped through the pages and gushed. "Just look at that lovely chart of returns." She turned the pages so the other two could see the chart and the steady line moving upward across a span of twenty years. "Such a staid company. A great investment for our bank."

"We were wise to buy deep in Merckler now." Powers sat and draped his arm over the chair back. "Given that they just modernized their factory, the stock is going to take off with the railroads' current demand for metal. At least, that's what George Harding thinks."

"George Harding," both she and Randall echoed in unison.

"What the hell does that rogue have to do with this?" Randall barked.

"What?" Powers blinked, his lips twitched. Then he banged the heel of his palm on his forehead.

"That's right, Lord Randall's railroad committee problem." He gave a short, fast chuckle. "Sorry, old chap. I just happened to overhear Harding in a club, discussing the matter. Of course, I had already bought the stocks then."

"Ah, well, if he endorsed the stocks, that can only be a good thing for us," Isabella said. "His approval will drive up the price, regardless of any political differences he and Lord Randall may have."

The viscount muttered something under his breath that sounded rather impolite as she began to put the stocks back in the box. Then she saw *it*. "Oh."

She held the certificates in question end to end to end. "Oh," she said again.

"What do you mean 'oh'?" Randall asked. "What is this 'oh'?"

Her heart was pounding in her rib cage. *Calm down. Just because stock fraud happens every day doesn't mean it will happen to you.* Nevertheless, she hurried to the desk, yanked opened the drawer, pushed away the penknife she was going to use to murder Randall, and found her magnifying glass. *It's probably nothing. You saw it wrong. You can barely see, after all.*

"Is–is there a problem?" Powers asked.

She didn't respond but leaned over the certificates until her glasses were almost touching the magnifying lens.

"Isabella, say something," Randall demanded. "What do you see?"

"I think…I think the stock issue numbers are overlapping on three of the certificates."

"What!" Randall snapped. "Let me see them."

Before she could slide them away, he had slammed his palm down on the certificates. His perfect eyes darted between the stock issue ranges as his breath rushed through his nostrils.

"By God, she's right. You've bought false stock," Randall thundered at Powers.

"Now see here." The man shot to his feet. He jutted his chin, putting his face just inches from Randall's.

"If you've brought one whiff of scandal to my bank, family name, and political career, you will breakfast on dewy grass in a field at dawn, sir." Randall stepped forward, bumping Powers's shoulder with his strong, lean chest. Powers shoved back. For several long seconds, the two men engaged in a ridiculous dance of circling and bumping, their chests puffed out.

"Just stop it!" Isabella shouted. The men jumped. "It's probably nothing," she reasoned. "A printer's error. Stop your strange dancing and sit down. You are overreacting."

"One of us is overreacting," Powers said, stepping back. "I'll...I'll write Merckler myself and see what I find. That's right. In fact, I'll do that now, and you'll see I'm right." He twisted his hat in his hand. "And I'll expect an apology, or you'll be the one dining on grass," he spat. "Good day, Lord Randall." He stalked to the door.

"Wait!" Isabella cried.

Powers spun on his heel.

She clasped her hand to her chest. "I'm sure it's just a mistake. Are you...you...coming on Sunday to help me dance?"

Powers glanced at Randall and then the side of his

mouth slid into a smile. "I wouldn't miss it for the whole wide world, my lovely dear." He slipped out the door.

He called me lovely.

The viscount seized her elbow. "Do not fall for that lying cur."

"What? He's not lying. He's our bank partner."

"That doesn't mean anything. We inherited him. Did you see the small twitching of his mouth when he spoke and how he never looked directly in your eyes? How he tried to appear casual for the entire visit, but his fingers were never still and his feet kept shuffling about?"

"You saw all that?" Randall could read people by their faces. He could uncover their deepest secrets by merely asking them about the weather. "I'll…I'll have my stockbroker look into it. He's in London and can ask around the exchange."

"My family name is on the bank." Randall began to pace in a tight oval, running his hands through his hair. "I advertise it in journals all over England. If there is one hint of scandal before the election… And what the hell did he mean about Harding?"

"Look, you're getting upset for nothing. It's probably just a mistake. You're being too emotional."

"Don't serve me the 'too emotional' twiddle-twaddle. You know that deep down inside, you're a swirling, scared, emotional mess."

She gasped. Could she hide nothing from him? It felt as if he were gazing into the bedchamber of her heart, opening all the drawers, pulling out the intimate garments or reading all the love letters and diaries—never mind that she had never received a single love letter, and she was terrible at keeping a journal for more than a week.

"Banks are failing every day," he continued. "People are nervous at the slightest whiff of scandal. Hypothetically, if there were to be a run on the bank, do we have enough capital to cover it?"

She swallowed. "Well, since we expanded into London and Manchester, our capital…it…um…"

"Please answer me."

"M-maybe thirty-six point three percent of our customers."

"Oh, hell." He ran to the door. She chased after him, latching on to the bottom of his coat.

"Calm down. I said I would write to my stockbroker in London. He will look into the matter. You just… just go back to the party and find a nice Tory girl to marry. Leave everything to me. You're overreacting."

"The bank has full liability. If it fails, my career is in the cesspool. And you would stand to lose everything—your home and savings." He pressed his hand to his head. "This is that bugger Harding at work. I can feel it," he hissed, and then dashed out of the room.

"You're overreacting," she called after him. "It's a clerical error! Not a scandal! You should be calm like me," she shouted. "I'm extremely calm!"

Three

On Friday, Isabella stood in the parlor on a makeshift stage made of two ottomans shoved together, and rehearsed her Wollstonecraft Society acceptance speech. The early afternoon sunlight fell in slants through the windows onto the green wallpaper. She glanced at the mantel clock to find that only a minute had elapsed since she had last checked. The train carrying the day's mail had rumbled in three hours ago, but still no letter from her stockbroker.

It's too soon for him to reply. Calm down.

But she couldn't. Despite having told Randall not to overreact, she'd spent the next forty-eight hours doing just that. She'd vacillated between telling herself that it was all an itsy-bitsy, tiny, minuscule clerical error, and imagining a violent medieval-like mob, replete with torches and pointy sticks, invading the bank's buildings, demanding their money. Then she saw herself, huddled by the grate at the poorhouse, asking in a consumption-choked voice if another spinster was going to eat the rat crawling across the floor.

"Isabella, you seem distracted today," Cousin Judith

called from where she sat along the back wall. "Is something wrong?"

I'm afraid I'm going to die in the poorhouse, childless and without ever having known a man. Luckily, I won't be alone, as many of my bank's customers will be joining me.

"I'm just nervous about giving speeches," she told her cousin. "Please, please consider going to London for me and accepting the Wollstonecraft. I can't speak before crowds. I start babbling incoherently or turn mute."

"I'll have none of that. Start again where it says 'Mrs. Wilkinson was a penniless, desperate widow, raising her own eleven children, as well as six younger sisters and four nieces.' But don't look at your page the entire time and try not to mumble." Judith sat taller in her seat, her spine erect. "Be confident."

"Confident," Isabella echoed weakly. She wasn't confident on days when the skies were bright blue and the robins were chirping, much less on ones when her entire world felt like a brittle layer of ice covering a deep, barren sea of financial ruin and marital doom.

Tap, tap, tap.

The mail!

Mary slipped into the room and curtsied. "Pardon me, Miss St. Vincent, this letter just arrived for you."

Isabella leaped down, sending the ottomans tumbling and waking Milton from his daylong snooze on the sofa. She rushed across the room, as her heart, stomach, and lungs all rose, vying for a position in her throat, and grabbed the missive. She couldn't wait for a proper letter opener and instead tore at the envelope with her fingernails.

Dearest Unemotional Shrew,

Please tell me that you have heard from your stockbroker?

Sincerely, Kindest Regards, & C,
Lord Extremely Calm

PS: It's a regular Judgment of Paris over here. I've run out of compliments for fair faces, bedecked gowns, insipid singing, and hideous sketches. You can only say "vision of luscious splendor" and "dream of transcendent beauty" two or so dozen times before they become trite. Can you recommend a nearby cliff to leap from to end this misery?

Her heart, stomach, and lungs all sank to their normal places.

"Excuse me, Cousin Judith, but I must respond to this very urgent correspondence," she said. As much as she disliked Randall, this was the second time he had saved her from oratorical torture. That numskull was becoming a regular knight in shining armor.

She hurried to her room and penned:

Dear Suicidal Paris,

I wouldn't expect to hear a reply in less than forty-eight hours. And I'm quite sure the entire matter is a trifling oversight. In fact, I haven't thought about it since I sent the letter.

Sincerely,
Isabella St. Shrewd

PS: Weren't the ladies au naturel for the judgment of Paris?

A mere hour later she received a reply.

Dear Miss St. Fibber,

By God, you are right about Paris. (You may note that in your ledger.) I'll inform the ladies not to wear anything for the ball. Then, to appease my persistent (nagging) mother, I'll make my famed judgment and seal my marital and political fate with the "right kind" of Tories.

Yours Truly,
Lord au naturel

On Saturday afternoon, after another angst-filled, dreams-of-ruin-and-despair night, Isabella headed down to the village. She paced up and down the street containing Mr. Powers's house, hoping to catch him if he happened to leave his home.

Oh, hello, Mr. Powers, she would say in a breezy manner. *Fancy meeting you here. Such a lovely day. Me? Well, I'm just getting some fresh air. By the way, did you ever hear from Merckler Metalworks? I'm positive that you are innocent of stock fraud and theft, and it was all just a small oversight with the stock serial numbers. You would never knowingly endanger the bank, not to mention our upcoming marriage for which you haven't proposed yet, but I'm sure you will. After all, I've already named our unborn children—little Tony, and Aileen, for my mother. You wouldn't want to jeopardize their future, would you?*

She had strolled by his house at least a dozen times or more until, across the lane, the men drinking ale by the tavern window began smirking at her. She gave up trying to casually bump into him and went for a more direct approach: knocking on his door.

Two hours later she composed a letter.

Dear Lord Randall,

Have you seen Mr. Powers lately? I happened to pass by his house when I went strolling this afternoon. Naturally, since he is a partner in the bank, I saw no indiscretion in calling upon him. On the three different times I tried to visit, no one answered, not even a servant.

PS: Of course, I wasn't spying on him, mind you. I was merely curious with regard to the business at hand, which I'm sure is a tiny clerical error.

"Be strong, be strong," she whispered as she sealed the envelope. *There's always tomorrow. Remember, he wouldn't miss your dancing lesson for the world.*

But Mr. Powers didn't attend church. The vicar gave a sermon, and the congregation stood and sang at the correct intervals. Meanwhile, Isabella clutched her prayer book and rocked in her pew, praying in her head, *Dear God, dear God.* She never got past those first two words, repeating them over and over to herself.

That afternoon she was determined not to watch every tick of the minute hand on the clock and distracted herself by going through journals and creating graphs of her stocks. Unfortunately, every other article was about stock fraud or a new bank failure.

Mr. Powers never arrived.

She had to admit the truth: either he had lied to her or had been eaten by a pack of wolves.

How could he do this to me? To our unborn children? To my dreams?

Monday was a blur of going back and forth to the post office, asking if she had received a letter and if the postmaster could double-, then triple-check the bags, and "Do you think it might accidentally have been given to someone else?"

After the fifth such visit, the harried man simply said, "You again? No."

At home, she interrogated all the servants, "Did I receive a letter?"

After the postmaster informed her that he was closing for the day and, no, he wouldn't check the bags again, she trudged home, up to her room, and collapsed on her bed. "Be strong," her father had told her when, as a small child, she'd watched the men carry her mother's body from the house. "Be strong," he had said to her when they first arrived at this home in the maddeningly quiet countryside, so different from the home young Isabella knew, of pounding factory floors and crowded London streets. "Be strong," he had whispered to her on his deathbed.

"Be strong," she ordered herself now, using her bedspread to wipe away the early formation of a tear. She wouldn't cry. She never cried.

Then she saw it waiting on her desk: an unopened letter! Why hadn't anyone told her? She tore open the envelope.

Dearest Besotted Spy of Mr. Powers,

Powers is nowhere to be found. I took the ladies shopping today, secretly ducked away in the millinery shop (they didn't notice), and slipped down to that rascal's domicile. No one was home, no light was lit. I know he was supposed to call on you yesterday. That faithless, lying scoundrel.

Ten trains have arrived from London since our last meeting. Tell me that you have heard from your stockbroker. It's been one hundred and twenty angst-ridden hours of praising embroidery, playing shuttlecocks and archery (ladies are so ruthless to each other in sport), and tossing about at night, suffering nightmares of despair and destruction and being eaten by African lappet-faced vultures. Tell me that our lives are not ruined.

Yours Truly,
Lord Doom and Gloom

She smiled in spite of her fears. For the first time in all the years of wishing Randall to the devil, she was grateful for him. Carrying this secret worry was too hard alone.

Randall's mother must have mowed down all the flower gardens, because the interior of the house was practically blossoming for the ball. The scent of a hundred flowers clogged his nostrils. Candles blazed from all the sconces. Across the chalked dance floor, all the daughters of the right kind of Tories looked at him, some shyly under their lashes, others coyly from above fans, or boldly over their shoulders. The same questions lingered in all their eyes. *Will you pick me for the first dance? Do I get to tell my papa that you spirited me away to the conservatory, dropped on one knee, and then pledged your undying devotion and servitude to me and the Tory party?*

Meanwhile, an edict burned in his mother's strident glare: *Pick one, damn you.*

He reached into his coat, fished out a tiny flask, and discreetly poured brandy into his champagne—something stronger to get him through the night. Before returning the flask, he gulped a direct shot for good measure.

His mother was especially distraught after an embarrassing article appeared in that morning's *Examiner*. The writer had delivered a harsh critique of Randall's performance in Parliament, claiming he was a handsome man of little substance and concluding that he was a detriment to the advancement of Britain and her empire. The article then went on to praise Randall's political opponents lavishly.

Normally, Randall could brush aside the newspaper claptrap, but these words had stung because they smacked of his fears. Dammit, he wasn't just a handsome actor reading Tory lines, but a committed politician dedicated to advancing the welfare of his nation over his popularity and selfish ambitions.

Or was he?

The paper had made the rounds among several important guests before his mother found the offensive column. "Get married," she had ordered her son, tossing the paper into the fire.

Randall had always imagined himself shackled to a graceful beauty with a soft, sweet voice and gentle smile. He wanted what any modern man did: a beautiful angel to adorn his side at societal functions, gaze up at him with admiring, awe-filled eyes, and never say a word of reproach but only praise of his person. Maybe if he weren't being crushed between the boulders of financial ruin and political warfare, he could have fallen for one.

Unfortunately, the one woman who had haunted his thoughts all week, evading him like a coquettish lover, driving his desire higher—his desire to know whether to pack his bags and make for a penniless exile on the Continent, of course—was the least graceful or gentle woman he knew. Certainly one whom he would never ask to marry him. He had sent her a letter yesterday, and that infuriating vixen hadn't bothered to reply. He didn't want to dance; he wanted to stomp down to her house and beat on her door. *Why didn't you answer me?*

"Randall, I got your letter."

For a moment, he thought he had responded to his own question and in Isabella's voice. He was really going insane now. Then she said, "Too many flowers," and sneezed. He spun around.

The object of his obsession stood there, her hand pressed to her chest, her glasses misted from her heavy breath as if she had sprinted all the way to his home. She wore a nightmare of blue silk and numerous layers of lace. She sneezed again, and several long strands of hair escaped their pins and hung down her back. Honestly, though, he didn't care about any of that. What worried him were those pleats between her eyebrows.

Oh, damn.

"I–I heard from the stockbroker," she said between gulping breaths. "I ran here as fast as I could…well, except I had to turn around at my gate and rush back inside to put on a different gown because I forgot about your ball."

The orchestra struck up a dance. In his ears, the violin strings roared like a train. He seized her hand. "The stocks are counterfeit, aren't they?"

She opened her mouth, but her words were drowned out as the orchestra leader shouted, "Quadrille."

Dammit! He had been on pins and needles to talk to her, and now he had to lead an opening dance. He glanced at the young ladies, all decked out in silk and lace, breathlessly awaiting Paris's judgment. "Just come with me," he muttered, clamping onto Isabella's wrist and dragging her toward the forming partners.

"Come where?" she cried. "To the poorhouse?"

"We have to dance."

"Dance!" She rocked back on her heels, making little skid marks on the floor as she frantically tried to pry his fingers from their hold. "We could be ruined. How can you think about dancing? Are you mad? Never mind, I know the answer to that one."

"I need to talk to you. Just follow me."

"What? No! The quadrille and I never got on."

"Too late." He kept a lock on her wrist as he made
a curt bow to her and then to the female dancer beside
him. All around, he could hear the buzzing whispers
of shock. He could feel the heat of his mother's glare
on his back, ready to murder her only male offspring.
Isabella didn't return his bow nor the gentleman's to
her right. Instead, she stared straight ahead, her eyes
wide, mouth dropped open as if something large, fast,
and oncoming were hurtling from the heavens and
about to hit her square between the eyes.

"We have to cross over now," he said, nudging her.
She sneezed and stumbled forward, bumping against
the oncoming lady dancer.

"So, so sorry," Isabella cried as the woman tugged,
trying to extract her lovely ruffle from under Isabella's
foot. There was a terrible sound of ripping silk.
Randall quickly reeled Isabella back, turning her in a
half circle.

"What did he say?" Randall whispered.

"Who?" Isabella righted her glasses on her flaming-
red face.

"The stockbroker."

"In his records, he found some of the same stock
numbers sold to a client five years ago," she whispered.
"Oh no, not the crossover again!" She took a breath,
held it, and scurried across the dance floor as if she
were swimming underwater. The lady with Isabella's
footprint stain on her torn silk ruffle sidestepped to
avoid her.

Randall met her on the opposite side and took

her hand. "We turn now," he said, spinning her. She wobbled like a falling top.

"Have you seen Powers today?" he asked.

"N-no." Sneeze.

"Bloody bugger," he hissed below the music as he untangled her arms.

"But I don't remember the bloody bugger step," Isabella cried aloud, causing several people's heads to jerk in their direction. Realizing what she had said, she slapped her hands over her mouth.

"No, not the bloo—promenade." Randall reached for her right hand, but she jabbed her left hand at him and grabbed his left with her other. Her arms were an inelegant tangle as he guided her around the other dancers. He kept a stiff smile on his face to balance his partner's terrified, the-ship's-going-down-we're-all-going-to-die expression. But inside he was a bottle of corked rage. His honor and integrity were at stake. He had to find Powers. Was the man acting alone? Was this malicious stunt aimed only at his bank, or were counterfeit Merckler Metalworks stocks floating across the exchange? Was a tall, bald-headed railroad baron involved?

He spun Isabella and then gently nudged her forward. She stood paralyzed in the middle of the dance formation, her eyes dilated and shiny like a scared animal's. The lady with the torn ruffle glared at her, shaking her gloved hand.

"Lady chain." Randall patted his knuckles, signaling to Isabella to take the woman's hand. Isabella shook her head, confused, and sneezed. "Never mind." He stepped in and clasped the torn-ruffle lady's fingers. He gave Isabella a gentle bump with his hip at the same time, sending her into the arms of the opposite partner, who spun her and sent her reeling back to the center, as if it were a schoolyard game.

Randall drew Isabella back to his side. "You can rest. It's the other partners' turn."

"Why did I come here?" she muttered. "My entire life is about to be ruined. And I'm dancing."

"It's rather poetic," he quipped bitterly.

She sneezed. "I hate poetry."

❧

For Isabella, the remainder of the quadrille was a blur of Randall issuing calls, more falling hair, stepping on toes—including her own—and repeatedly muttering apologies. When the horrid thing was finally over, she made a beeline for a quiet, flower-infested corner. She had passed all her balls and dances in corners and found a degree of comfort in the familiar. A younger, tenderer Isabella would have suffered hours of acute embarrassment after the quadrille, pledging never to step outside her bedchamber again. But now she didn't care. Her last marital hope was missing, and the most valuable thing her father had left her—the bank—was under threat.

She should have known better than to come running to Randall. Their conversation and correspondence over the last days made her think that he had changed. That maybe he wasn't the golden boy who charmed his way through the world with his handsome face and silvery words, never acknowledging clumsy, tongue-tied Isabella looming about the edges of his life, blighting his otherwise glorious existence.

She sneezed and sniffed.

What was the worst that was going to happen to him if the bank went under? He might lose his seat in the House of Commons—perhaps not such a bad outcome for England, in her estimation. Yes, his family would sacrifice their reputation, their beloved integrity, maybe a good bit of their fortune, but they still had their entailment and peerage protected by law. And rich, beautiful ladies, such as the ones littering the dance floor, would still clamor for his title. As always, the charmed lord would sail across the rough waters unscathed, probably noting only an annoying bump or two.

Meanwhile, having forty shares in a full-liability bank, she stood to lose her home and her savings, and still be left with a massive debt to be paid. She was as scared as she had been in those last moments of her father's life, when the rattle of his breath ceased and his eyes turned empty. She had held his hand then, for the first time. "What do I do?" she whispered now.

If she let the bank go down, she would lose him all over again. She would disappoint him in death as she had during his lifetime—never even marrying or giving him grandchildren or being as beautiful and graceful as her mother. He had been in tight spots his whole life and through his intellect managed to set himself free and turn the situations to his advantage. But he was much smarter than she was. Had he been alive, he would have thought of a way to stop Powers. He would have seen the situation before it happened. Instead, she had been pinning silly hairpieces to her head.

Think, Isabella, think! She banged the heel of her

palm against her forehead, trying to shake loose some stuck thoughts. What would her father do in this situation? The answer tumbled down:

Break into Powers's home and see if you can find any clues to his whereabouts.

Her blood racing, eager to commit a crime, she turned on her heel and came face-to-face with Randall's formidable mother.

A smile stretched across the countess's dainty, thin-skinned face. Her teeth were as white and shiny as pearls. The smile, however, stopped at her eyes. They were hot, blue flames decorated around the edges with long lashes and tight, angry lines.

"Miss St. Vincent, it's so lovely to see you," she said, all sugary and pleasant as she planted a kiss on Isabella's cheek. "You know I think the world of you. I just adore you."

Somehow these words didn't reassure Isabella. The little quadrille escapade could not have gone unnoticed. Hidden under this buttery admiration was an unspoken *but*.

Lady Hazelwood lowered her voice as she linked her arm through Isabella's. "But—"

Ah, there it was.

"—I'm telling you this as a mother would to her beloved daughter." The countess leaned in. "You must get over your little infatuation with my son."

Isabella blinked. "My what?"

"Come now." The woman waved her hand, jingling her bracelets. "Ever since you were a little girl, you've been running to him. It breaks my heart to say this to you after all you've been through with your papa, but, my dear, Randall lives a very different life from you. He needs a wife who will be a credit to his station, his family, his honor, his name. A woman who understands the nuances of fashion, engages in charming conversation, and excels in the womanly arts of music, dance, art, and embroidery. Do you sketch or sing or sew, Miss St. Vincent?" she said in a knowing purr and didn't wait for an answer. "Of course, you don't have time. Having to run my husband and son's bank—"

"I'm the majority shareholder."

"—I think it's brave of you to behave like a man. So you should understand that you must let go of these girlish fantasies of Randall and move on before it's too late. Good heavens, most women have three or more children by your age."

Isabella stared, her jaw dropped, unable to speak for a beat. "Wait, you think I'm angling for *Randall*!" Sharp, hysterical laughter burst from her lips.

"What is so funny?"

Isabella couldn't answer for laughing like a Bedlamite. *What is the matter with you? Get ahold of yourself.* But the strain of the previous days had frayed her nerves to nothing.

"And just what do you find wrong with my son, Miss St. Vincent?" Lady Hazelwood's previously feigned motherly concern was replaced with indignation.

Isabella took a deep inhale, trying to restrain her mirth. "Most everything." She broke into feverish giggles. "Please, pardon me," she choked. "I hope that your son finds the witless, titled, influential Tory beauty of his dreams. But I really must go." *My life is about to fall apart, and I can't marry anyone to save it.*

Isabella hurried away, muttering "stupid, stupid mistake" under her breath. Let the useless viscount dance. She had a burglary to attend.

Four

ISABELLA USED THE LIGHT FROM THE FLAMING TORCHES lining Lord Hazelwood's estate gate to guide her to the Roman perimeter road around the village. The old timber-and-stone buildings in the heart of the village were cast in the deep blue light of the moon, which sat on the rooftops swollen but not quite full, like a fat potato with one side peeled. No one ambled along the walks, and all the house windows were darkened, because at night, every villager over fifteen years of age made for the tavern. She made several loops of the village working up her courage, then looked about her, making sure that no one was watching. She assumed the second rule of a good burglary was not to be seen in the area—the first being not to get caught. She veered into a narrow, winding medieval-ish alley that stank of rotting vegetation and urine. Navigating from memory, she tiptoed quietly behind the houses.

Mr. Powers's home was across from the tavern, and loud chatter and raucous laughter mingling with the howls of an enamored cat echoed around her. She gazed up to find Milton, her roving tomcat, perched on Mr. Powers's second-story windowsill.

"Go home, Milton," she hissed. He ignored her, continuing to howl his lusty intentions to a slinky blond bathing her paws, like a feline Bathsheba, on the adjoining roof.

She gave a quiet knock at the kitchen door and waited. No answer. She jiggled the doorknob. Locked. Then she took a deep breath, bracing herself. Time to break the law.

But how?

She could find a way to pick the lock…but then she would be here all night, trying not to swear, and probably without success—at picking the lock, that is. She would be quite successful at swearing. Maybe smash a window, but that would be noisy and draw attention. She could scale the side of the building and come down the chimney…no, that wasn't logical at all. Her numerous stiff petticoats and bustle pad would never make it down. And besides, the people at the tavern across the street would see her tromping about the roof.

She made a mental note in case she would be required to write a volume on burglary for the Wollstonecraft Society to support herself in the poor-house: *When committing burglary, it is best to have a plan. Don't just show up in a ball gown with no tools.*

"Reorrw!"

"Milton, I said—" She stopped mid-mutter. The glass window behind the cat had been left open just the merest bit. She needed to get up there. Squinting in the dim light, she spied a wooden crate by the back door. She dragged it over and climbed atop. But even on her tiptoes, her arms stretched high, she was still a good two feet below Milton, who gazed down at her and yawned.

"I could use some sympathy," she told her cat.

Approaching footsteps crunched on the cobbles. Soft gold light illuminated the alley. *Oh fudge!* She was trapped.

A man came around the corner, silhouetted by the light of his lantern.

"Oh, hello there, I'm…I'm just getting my cat down," she said, trying to sound casual as she balanced on the crate. "I'm not, you know…" *a desperate spinster attempting to break into a bachelor's home.*

"Like hell you are," Randall drawled, lowering his lantern to reveal his face. "Why did you leave me? Did you think you were going to break in here by yourself?"

"Oh, it's you." Her shoulders slumped with relief. "Well, you seemed preoccupied with dancing while our bank might be going under."

"I wasn't dancing," he said, dropping his bag on the ground with a clank. "I was thinking."

"You can think and dance at the same time?"

A nasty smile hiked the corners of his mouth. "I'm talented in more ways than you will ever know, love."

She rolled her eyes. "Just come here. I need you."

"Here? Now?" He obeyed, that nasty smile curving higher as she positioned him under the window. "What are you going to do to me?" His voice was low and husky. "Will I enjoy it?"

"I'm going to climb onto your shoulders and—wait

a minute!" She swatted his shoulder. "You meant something lurid, didn't you? How can you have your mind wallowing in the gutter at this moment? Just go back home and waltz the night away with your pretty Tories while I save our hides. No wonder you're a politician."

Anger sparked in his eyes. His white teeth glinted in the lantern light. "Very well. Just step on my hand and I'll lift you up."

She kicked off her slippers and lifted the hem of her skirt, her cheeks flaming at exposing her ankles, and a bit more, to him.

Which do you care about more: modesty or bankruptcy? she asked herself, as she slipped her foot into his hand.

"Don't you think there might be an easier way?" he wondered as he was being whapped by her stiff horsehair petticoats. She wobbled in his grasp and fell against him, his mouth landing in the valley between her breasts. "Never mind," he said, his words muffled against her bosom. "This works just fine."

No, no, no, Isabella. Don't you dare feel a tingle when you are breaking into the home of the man who may have possibly deserted you and destroyed your life. Stop that tingling this instant.

She pushed off his palm and tentatively stepped onto his shoulders. "I can do this," she said, pulling up her other foot. Milton continued to gaze on, disinterested. "It's just like when we were eleven," she told Randall, "and we tried to sneak into that hot air balloon." She tugged at the blasted window that wouldn't budge more than the inch it was already open.

"Oh, but we aren't eleven anymore," he said, a

curious, almost intimate arch in his voice. She glanced down. Her gown engulfed his head and the lantern at his feet illuminated the skirt like a lamp shade, lighting all the contents within: her stockings, garters, the split in her drawers, and the passage to the sacred chamber of her womb!

"Randall, are—are you looking up my dress?"

"Where the hell else am I supposed to look?"

She jabbed his neck with her big toe, causing her to lose balance. She waved her arms frantically, trying to stabilize herself, but it was no use. She instinctively covered her spectacles as she fell through the air. *Bam!* She slammed the ground with her shoulder and hip.

"My God, Isabella!" His arms were around her. "Are you hurt? I'm damnably sorry. Do you think you can move? Say something. Anything."

The pain of embarrassment was more acute than any physical ache. She flipped over, slid her spectacles into place, and glared at him. "The bank is full liability," she hissed. "We and our customers could be in massive debt, you cotton-brained idiot."

He made a low whistle, raised his hands, palms showing, and began slowly backing away.

She wasn't finished, her humiliation driving her on. "You have your estate entailed. You get to be the impoverished Lord Randall, the ex-MP. But don't worry, you can always marry some rich merchant's daughter and go on living happily ever after. Me, I get to go to the workhouse. A shriveled, raisiny spinster who has to fight for crumbs of stale bread, and dies alone in a cold, slumping, coverless, flea-infested bed." He picked up his bag and began rooting through it, not paying her any heed. "This was my father's bank and—are you even listening to me?"

"I'm entailed, impoverished, ex-MP, marrying a rich merchant; you go to poorhouse, raisiny spinster, die with fleas," he muttered absently, and pulled a long crowbar from his bag. "Ah. See, if you had waited, I wouldn't have had to look up your dress and get my head bitten off just for spying a bunch of lace."

In spite of the tense situation, Isabella giggled.

He jammed the bar into the door, seemingly uncaring for any damage he wrought. He tugged and a tiny explosion of splinters burst into the alley. Dropping the tool, he swiftly kicked the door and sent it flying against the inner wall.

Isabella watched, her eyes wide. She didn't want to admit that there was something very alluring, very throbby in the sacred feminine regions, about Randall's method of breaking and entering.

He bowed and swept his hand in an "after you" gesture. "Lady burglars first."

After she passed, he closed them into Powers's back scullery and dimmed his lantern. He studied the tiny room. Dirty clay bowls were stacked in the sink and crumbs littered the preparation tables. He followed her into the kitchen. A single dented, tarnished pan dangled from one of the numerous hooks along the walls. The drawers of the silver cabinet were pulled out and empty.

"Dammit!" He slammed one shut, shaking the cabinet. "I'll wager he left in a hurry with anything he could pawn, and the servants carried off the rest."

"He was set up," she cried. "He had to be. And when he realized his mistake—"

"He fled. Because that's exactly what innocent people do."

Her dark gray eyes loomed large and hurt behind her lenses in the low light. Despite his desire to rip off Powers's bollocks and shove them down his throat—if he ever found the goddamned lying cove—Randall felt a prick of tender pity for the backward woman. He couldn't recall a man who had ever been sweet on her. Powers had been the old girl's last chance and the heartless cur had broken her heart.

He rested a gentle hand on her shoulder. No matter how many times he touched her, he was always surprised by the daintiness of her bones and the silky warmth of her skin. In his mind, she always loomed taller, larger, and plainer than she was in person.

"I'm sorry," he whispered.

Her voice was brittle when she spoke. "Let's just see if he left some indication of where he went." Straightening her spine, she swept past him.

The downstairs rooms were much like the kitchens. The furniture, lamps, and whatnots were in the customary places, but there were conspicuous holes where silver candlesticks had rested. Picture hooks dangled from strings, the paintings removed. The bureau in the parlor was empty except for a deck of cards, the usual writing instruments, and a broken porcelain figurine of a hound.

Muffled raucous chatter from the tavern and Milton's lovesick howls drifted in as Randall followed Isabella up the stairs. A waft of her scent filled his nostrils, a subtle sweet jasmine mingling with a tang of orange. More of her hair had fallen, and wavy locks swayed back and forth across her back. He had never noticed how luscious it was before now. He had the unexplainable urge to caress the strands, bury his face in her silken tresses to calm his racing heart.

Good Lord, chap, you're desperate. He really needed a woman, and soon, if he was lusting for Isabella.

Of the two bedchambers on the first floor, one was neat and tidy, a light coating of dust on the chair and commode. The other was not. The drawers in the bureau hung open, letters, bills, and receipts spilling out. The covers were bunched at the foot of the bed. The closet door stood open, revealing a single stained shirt hanging on a hook. Randall set the lantern on the desktop, grabbed a handful of papers, and began to read. Powers owed seven pounds and two shillings to a tailor on New Bond Street, five more pounds to a wine merchant, three pounds to a ladies' modiste, thirty pounds and six shillings for back rent and property damage to a man claiming to be Powers's former landlord, and six pounds and two shillings to a gun maker who noted a special fee for engraving "La Diablo" on the handle.

Just bloody capital! An ignorant, indebted cur with a gender-confused devil gun was going to shoot down Randall's political future.

"My sweet beloved," he heard Isabella whisper. His head shot up, unaccustomed to hearing endearments fall from her lips. The surprising warmth blossoming in his heart stopped when he realized that she wasn't talking to him but reading from a letter. He crossed the room and gazed over her shoulder.

"'How I am counting the minutes until I embrace you again,'" she read. "'My hart cherries'—umm, maybe she meant cherishes?—'the memories of sweet kisses and embrases that furst evening we met. I had never knowed how exqesit'—I wager that's exquisite—'a woman could fill until you filled me. Now no other man can do.'"

The missive shook in her hand. She turned her head, her gaze meeting his. The thick spectacles magnified the hurt in her eyes.

"It-it could be his mother," she said. She shifted the letters, reading another. "'It has ben two weeks and three long days since I was under the spel of your manly insrument'—Ah, how sweet," she quipped. "And this could be his sister." She made a tiny cry, dropping the pages, and covered her face with her hands. When he tried to draw her to his chest, she stepped back. "I'm not crying," she declared. "I'm not. I'm-I'm strong." She blinked and took two deep breaths, her shoulders rising and falling. "I'll look in his commode."

He retrieved the pages she had spilled on the floor—more tiny lust-filled murders of the English language. How did that prawn-like fellow get so many women, albeit barely literate ones? His manly instrument must be enormous.

The letter at the bottom of his pile was written by a Mr. Nicholas Busby. All the words were correctly spelled and evenly spaced in neat lines. The man sent his condolences for the passing of Powers's uncle, but hoped that Powers would make a fresh, respectable start in his new home and honorable profession as a partner in a reputable bank. Busby suggested Powers make a detailed budget of expenses so that Powers might slowly pay down his debts. Randall was reading about the recent birth of Busby's ninth child when he heard Isabella call his name, her voice a quiet, shaky whisper.

He glanced up. She knelt by an open drawer, holding what looked to be an extremely lacy and sheer chemise adorned with several yards of pink ribbons.

He sucked in his breath and tucked Busby's letter into his coat. He squatted before her, resting a hand on her shoulder and letting his thumb caress the soft skin on her neck. He started in on the talk his friends had given him when Cecelia left, which included such banal clichés as "he wasn't for you, and in the end, when you meet someone else, you'll be thankful that this little affair hadn't worked out," "Although it hurts now, and you feel as if you will never love again, in time your heart will heal," "when you find someone new, you will love him more deeply," etc., etc. But even as the words flowed from his mouth, he knew in his heart that he was lying. Powers had probably been Isabella's last hope.

She broke his heart the way she stared at him, her eyes large and inky. He couldn't take it any longer and wrapped her in his arms.

"Ah, Isabella, I'm sorry." He ran his hand up and down her back.

"But just look at it!" she wailed, shoving the chemise against his chest.

"I know, I know," he said, trying to soothe the

distraught virgin. "Why don't you wait in the kitchen? I'll finish going through this."

"You don't understand."

"I know the pain—"

"It's got cat whiskers embroidered on it and a long, pink, fluffy tail!"

"What?" He was mistaken; her eyes weren't large and inky with unrequited sorrow but repulsion. He glanced at the large chemise falling from her fingers. "What the hell is that?!"

Aside from the whiskers and tail adorning the garment, little kitten cupids dotted the sheer fabric. Twin hearts with large red ribbons flowing in their centers were embroidered on the bodice, the right size to fit two ample breasts, with streamers dripping from the nipples.

"What kind of man desires a woman in this gaudy thing?" she cried. "I can't believe that I actually wanted to marry him." He heard a thud downstairs, but apparently she hadn't, because she continued, "It's as I always suspected: something is very, very wrong with me. I—"

In a twinkling, his lips were on hers, his hand behind her head. She squirmed underneath his mouth. "Mut arm mou moing? Ahm gomma mill mou!" she said, her hands beating against his chest. But he kept his mouth clamped hard on her lips—supple, cushy creations. *Dammit, Isabella, be quiet!*

She closed her lids, her lips began to tentatively, nervously move against his, as if the poor dear thought he was actually trying to kiss her and not hush her. *Bang!* Someone slammed into a chair or such below them, knocking it over. Her eyes shot open. He held her captive in his kiss a second longer, because, bloody hell, she was exhilarating. Then, keeping her secured to his chest, he reached into his waistband, withdrew his pistol, and aimed it at the open door.

"You brought a gun?" Unmistakable awe imbued her hushed voice.

"What does it look like, love?"

"Tony, it's your favorite naughty pussycat. Are you home?" A loud, slurring female voice called from the bottom of the stairs. Isabella and Randall glanced at each other, slowly rose together, and edged toward the corridor, still locked in their embrace.

"Pussycat has a wicked surprise for her papa. M—Oh, Lord Randall and Miss St. Vincent. It's you."

At the bottom of the stairwell stood Alice Owens. Her face was flushed with inebriation and dark, shiny sausage curls danced about her bright eyes. She was a favorite among the village men for her comely looks of the merry variety, and her refreshing lack of intelligence coupled with a happy-go-lucky attitude and skirts that were easily lifted by buttery words and sugary punch.

She tried to curtsy but fell against the wall. "Oh, I've had a wee too much of the fruity crank." She giggled. "I was thinking me Tony had returned because the back door was open and what." Her eyes squinted in the dim light. "Say, is that my kitty chemise?" A sly smile curled on her lips and she wagged a finger. "Miss St. Vincent, were you playing Who's Papa's Naughty Pussycat with Lord Randall? I always thought you were a bit spoony for him."

Isabella emitted a tight, choking sound, dropping the

shift. Randall didn't know the specifics of the Who's Papa's Naughty Pussycat game, but he had a feeling that if he asked Isabella to play, she would punch him.

"Mr. Powers was supposed to attend my ball this evening," he said. "When he didn't arrive, we were worried that a terrible accident might have occurred or that he might be ill."

Alice drew her brows together. "Is this sumpin' to do with that bank of yours?"

"No!" Isabella cried. "I-it's because I'm madly, desperately, spoony in love with Mr. Powers."

Randall gazed at his business partner, his heart full of admiration in the way that a war-weary soldier might be for his comrade-in-arms. *Good fall on the sword, old girl.*

"And I was terribly worried about him," Isabella continued in a skittery voice. "That is why we are looking for him. No other reason at all. Nothing to do with the bank whatsoever. Oh, no, no, no. If you thought that might be the reason, you would be terribly wrong. I just—"

"Do you know where we might find Mr. Powers?" Randall cut in before Isabella could sound any guiltier.

Alice didn't answer him but gazed at Isabella. "Oh, you poor little thing. You loved him, and all this time you didn't know that he was wild in love with me." Her triumphant smile of having bested another woman belied any sympathy in her words.

"*Or a whole drawer full of other women,*" Randall heard Isabella mutter under her breath. "Do you know where Mr. Powers went?" she asked.

Alice's eyes lifted heavenward. "Do you ever know

where they go?" she waxed. "They just go. I know how you feel, Miss St. Vincent…well, a little. I do try to dress up a bit nicer than you and take a little trouble with me hair. And you are getting a bit long in the tooth, and you never really had a suitor that I can remember, and me Tony was probably your last chance for happiness and—"

"That wasn't a rhetorical question," Isabella sniped.

"Rhetorical?" Alice blinked. "Does that mean like a joke or riddle? I loves a good joke. Have you heard this one about the naughty vicar and the—"

"No, it means do you know exactly where he went?" Isabella said, annoyance seething under her words. "A destination? An address? A name?"

"You don't have to get all snippy," Alice protested. "It's not my fault Tony likes me better. Anyways, he told me that he was visiting a friend. Someone named…Rigsby? Saxby? Danby? Sumpin' with a 'by.'"

"Busby?" Randall asked. "Nicholas Busby?"

Alice's face lit with recognition. "That's it! Me Tony said that kind Mr. Busby always helped him, lending him money and such. A good sort of fellow, he was."

"Did Mr. Powers say when he planned to come back?" Isabella asked.

"No, but I'm sure he will." She began twisting at her ankles, side to side like a three-year-old. "He said he wouldn't miss seeing me for the whole wide world. Ain't that the most romantic thing you ever heard?"

Isabella groaned.

"Thank you, Miss Owens," Randall said, because he feared Isabella was beyond the power of speech. He stepped into the bedchamber to retrieve his lantern. "Now if you will excuse us, I fear Miss St. Vincent has an excruciating headache."

"Maybe when I'm Mrs. Powers, all proper, I can come to one of your fancy balls," Alice said, as Randall escorted Isabella down the stairs.

He flashed a charming smile. "I look forward to it," he told her, knowing full well Powers had left her, the bank, the village, and Isabella for good.

In the scullery, Isabella yanked her elbow from his grasp and tromped out the back door. He jogged to keep up.

"Milton, I told you to go home," she cried, taking out her anger on the furry feline still perched in the window, howling for the lady cats. "Clearly this village doesn't need any more naughty kittens." He watched her clench her hands and stomp her foot. "I'm so embarrassed. How could I have liked him?"

He couldn't help himself. "Well, you weren't the only one."

The glower she gave him could have boiled the Thames.

"Don't feel so bad." He rested his arm on her shoulder and continued without thinking. "I have made some very poor choices in lovers myself lately." Cecelia's beautiful face filled his mind, tears streaming down her cheeks as she told him that she was leaving him for Harding.

"Mr. Powers wasn't my—my lover." Isabella blushed. "Not like your lovers. We never...I mean, I've never...you know."

"Played the Who's Papa's Naughty Pussycat game?"

Her gentle laughter sounded like rain on a windowpane. "No, thank heavens."

Randall winked. "Well, it's my favorite pastime when I'm not trying to track down a Mr. Nicholas Busby"—he drew out the man's letter—"of Itching-by-the-Ditch."

She looked at the letter and then at him, her eyes glowing with admiration. "You are so clever!"

"I need to note that somewhere." He patted his coat, pretending to look for a notebook. "On this day and year of our Lord, Isabella said something nice about me," he quipped, giving her a dose of her own medicine before turning back to the matter at hand. "I guess I'll take the first train out tomorrow."

"No, I will. You need to get married. Your future depends on having the perfect wife of the appropriate political connections and financial soundness."

He was about to protest—*No, my future depends on slowly eviscerating Powers before he can open his damned mouth*—but realized he would be wasting precious time that could be better spent arguing with his mother. She wasn't going to take his early departure from the house party well. He foresaw a fierce clash, Mama deploying her huge arsenal of tears, veiled and outright threats, and spiky guilt traps. He handed Isabella the letter, having already memorized the address. "The first train leaves at eight thirty. I expect you to be on it while I'm huddled on one knee in the orangery, shackling my black heart and soul for life." He reached for his crowbar and bag, drawing them over his shoulders, and began to walk away. "Godspeed."

"Randall," she whispered.

He spun around. The pale moonlight poured over her creamy skin and reflected off her lenses. Her fallen black hair curled around her bosom. He stood, arrested at the sight. Despite the tension wracking his body, a small measure of peace washed over him. He remembered the touch of her lips, the rise of her breasts against his chest. Again he marveled at the paradox that was Isabella—as sensual as she was awkward, as tender as she was hard, as yielding as she was stubborn.

"Thank you," she said quietly.

He nodded. "Just don't miss the train." He gazed at her for a second more, then turned and headed, weary but resigned, for battle.

Five

ISABELLA COULDN'T SLEEP. SHE HAD READ ABOUT AN Oriental phenomenon called a tsunami, a huge tidal upsurge formed after a volcanic explosion or earthquake. In the early hours of the morning, as she tossed and turned in her bed, she imagined an enormous wave rolling across the ocean, growing bigger and bigger, its rippling foam spelling out her name.

Milton strolled in a little after four and curled up on her pillow, exhausted after a long night of tomcatting on the town. At five, she woke him up out of spite. "I'm leaving for a few days. Don't you dare wet the bedcovers."

He gave her a nasty flick of his tail, rolled over, and fell back asleep.

She slid out of bed, lit her desk lamp, and opened her wardrobe. She began pulling out her frumpier gowns, which seemed to be most of her wardrobe, and laid them on her bed, talking aloud to her snoozing cat in the barely lucid manner of an anxious woman who hadn't slept in eighteen hours. "I'll tell Judith that I'm leaving for the Wollstonecraft meeting a few days early to speak with my stockbroker and the bank manager. That's a good excuse because it's not exactly a lie, as I do plan to make a beeline to Mr. Harker's as soon as I set foot in London." Milton's ears, notched about the edges from numerous cat brawls, slanted back as he gave her a green-eyed, will-you-just-be-quiet-crazy-woman glare.

She dug beneath her winter petticoats, muffs, and heavy woolen cloaks until she located her bag. "I must travel alone. Our servants have the loosest tongues in England. If they get even a tiny whiff of this scandal, the news will travel to the nether reaches of Russia in a matter of days." For all her love of carefully orchestrated order, in her agitated state, she shoved her clothes willy-nilly into her bag. "On the train, I'll pretend I'm a drab, inconspicuous spinster who is visiting her dear sister and her children in Belgravia."

But you are a drab, inconspicuous spinster, she reminded herself. *You don't have to pretend that no man wants to have a thing to do with you. The only reason Randall kissed you was to keep you quiet.* Her face heated with embarrassment as she remembered thinking that, for one stupid moment, her touch had elicited the same tingling in the baby-making regions as his had done.

"Idiot," she muttered.

Now she could add "ruined my first and probably only kiss" to the long list of wrongs the viscount had committed against her.

By seven, when the sun was up and finches tweeted from the trees outside, she had mentally completed a detailed plan of action with several possible outcomes. The worst case involved sewing stones into her gown and sinking into the reeking waters of the Thames. She composed the first lines of her obituary as she stood on the bed and jammed her foot into the opening of the bag, forcing down the contents. Removing her foot, she quickly latched the dangerously overstuffed bag and wiped her perspiring brow. She rang for the servant to bring up a pot of tea and to help her into her plainest, loosest, leave-me-alone-I'm-a-drab-raisiny-old-spinster gown.

After the servant left, Isabella shoved into her corset a pouch containing two hundred pounds and a few of the fraudulent stock certificates. She sucked in a breath, held it, and swung her painfully overstuffed bag off the bed.

"I mean it, Milton, you wet my covers and you're going to live in the stable. I'm not joking this time." Her cat yawned, unimpressed by the oft-heard threat. Fueled by three cups of black tea, her head was buzzing and her muscles jittery as she lugged her bag downstairs to the dining room.

∽∽

Judith sat at the table, dressed in her customary dark blue, her rich auburn hair swept up. She bent over her breakfast, glasses perched low on her nose, reading a letter while she nibbled a cheese muffin. She looked up when Isabella entered, her face as cheerful and chipper as the painfully bright morning light streaming through the windows into Isabella's burning, sleep-deprived eyes.

"The current president of the Wollstonecraft Society writes that they have received numerous inquiries about your appearance at their annual meeting." Judith set down her linen, pushed back her chair, and rose. "So many nonmembers have expressed their intention to attend that the society has had to request a larger venue for your speech. Think how wonderful that will be for the society. We can spread the message of female liberation to the masses. And all because of you." She waved her missive before Isabella's face. "It will be just as I foresaw. You're going to be a great leader of the women of England."

A bark of hysterical laughter flew from Isabella's lips before she could purse them into a tight, inescapable line. The only place she would be leading England's women would be to the poorhouse.

"Isn't that interesting," she muttered, her brain whirling with the drunken sensation of too much tea and not enough sleep. She inhaled and launched into the intricate lie that she had formulated while packing her toiletries. Her words fell out in one big, caffeine-infused splat. "I need to leave early for London on business about some stocks—my own personal stocks, that is. No one else's. Certainly not the bank's, if that's what you're thinking." *Stop rambling. She'll know you're lying.* "I'm taking the eight thirty. Must be off. Have a pleasant morning. Cheerio, then."

"What!" Judith cried, removing her reading glasses. "Why didn't you tell me?"

The hurt in her companion's voice made Isabella feel like the lowest lying cur. She wished she could tell Judith everything, but the truth was so horrid she couldn't let anyone know. Not until she had done her best to hold back the financial tsunami. "I-I just decided last evening."

Judith tilted her head and studied Isabella with hard eyes. "Last evening?" she asked slowly, her voice thick like syrup. "During Lord Randall's ball? The one you went rushing to attend? And you despise dancing."

Isabella's face flamed hot, and her eyes darted around the room—anywhere but Judith's face. *Can you look any guiltier?* "That's correct. R-right in the middle of the quadrille." She turned on her heel, making her break. "So, good-bye then."

"Wait!" Judith grabbed her companion's elbow, wheeling her around. "I still have time to pack. But you really should have told me sooner."

"Oh, but…but…I'll be busy running about the exchange and taking care of boring bank business." Isabella waved her hand in a casual, don't-trouble-yourself manner and struck her own chin. *Ouch!* "I wouldn't be good company. Why don't you just leisurely make your way down a day before the meeting?"

"I would love to spend time visiting old friends. How I miss London. I feel my heart never left the city."

Isabella swallowed and braced herself. "I-I want to go to London alone," she said, trying to emulate her father's firm tone, the one that arrested further discussion on any given topic.

Her companion blinked, pressing her hand to her chest. "What do you think—" Something changed in Judith's eyes. "Isabella," she said in a hushed voice. "Have you taken a *lover*?"

Isabella's jaw dropped. Before she denied the question, the tiniest root of a bad idea took hold in her overwrought mind. "Err, yes. You've guessed it. I've taken a l-lover, and we are rendezvousing in London for a romantic holiday. Just the two of us."

Judith stepped closer and lowered her head until they were eye to eye. "It's Lord Randall, isn't it? I've seen how you've chased after him all these years."

"What? No! Why does everyone think I love Lord Randall?"

"Oh, thank heavens." Judith released a long breath. "In that case, I applaud you."

"You-you do?"

She placed her hands on Isabella's cheeks. "Now, my dear, I understand that a young woman has *desires*. I think one in your position—intelligent, financially independent, and educated—shouldn't have to sacrifice her freedom to some ape-ish, ignorant man to satisfy those *desires*."

"That was m-my thinking entirely," Isabella stammered, her face still sandwiched between Judith's warm palms.

"Such a wise woman." Judith's severe brows lowered with her voice. "You just make him promise to pull out his silly male fertilizer before he violates your sacred chamber with his seed. Don't let him reach his animalistic climax inside your pristine vessel."

Isabella's cheeks, neck, chest, stomach, and feminine region all burned with achy embarrassment. She backed up, colliding with the cupboard. "I-I really have to get along now. I d–don't want to be late for my climax. I mean, train!"

"Now don't forget to practice your speech." Judith straightened Isabella's hat. "The Mary Wollstonecraft award is far more important than any brief, and ultimately unsatisfying, moment of passion with a mindless, barbaric man. You must speak in a clear, confident voice as we have practiced. Do not mumble or stare at the floor." She tapped her index finger on Isabella's collarbone. "And remember, women respond to stories that they can emotionally connect with, not boring, mannish numbers. Understand?"

"No boring numbers, don't emotionally connect with the floor, brief barbaric passion," Isabella muttered absently through her tight, forced smile. "Sorry, but I really must be off now. Can't keep my l-lover waiting."

⁂

"You are not leaving this house to visit some supposed dear old Cambridge friend on his deathbed." The countess whopped Randall's shoulder with a stuffed lappet vulture, sending black feathers flying. "If he were such a dear friend, he would have the courtesy not to die during our annual house party."

Backed against the glass cabinets of the Fauna chamber, Randall shielded his face. "Mama, put the bird down! I'm your only son."

The irate countess whopped him again and then threatened the bird's sharp beak under his nose. "You will go downstairs, eat breakfast, marry a Tory, and have Tory children."

"I can't let Dunbury die without saying good-bye."

"I've never heard of this Dunbury. You've made

him up. I wager this has something to do with that dreadful Isabella St. Vincent. That's why she was here last night, wasn't it?"

"No, of course not," he said in his most soothing voice, disarming his mother long enough to snatch away her bird weapon. *Hah!*

Undeterred, she seized a yellow-nosed albatross by the neck. "Isabella has been trying to sink her marital claws into you since she could think of such things."

"This has nothing to do with her. And stop saying mean things about her. You just don't like her because she's intelligent and isn't afraid to stand up to you."

His mother tilted her head, considering him. She flashed a tight smile and marched across the room. With her albatross clutched to her chest, deadly beak pointed out, she took position in front of the door. "Well then," she said in a bell-like voice. "You get to choose between your dying friend or your dying mother. Because the only way you are leaving this house is over my dead body."

He flung up his arms, raining black feathers down on himself. The hands on the clock over the mantel pointed to ten after eight. He couldn't let Isabella go alone. That was like sending an ungainly giraffe to do a stealthy panther's job. "Very well, I'm going to tell you the truth," he conceded. "Let's just put the birds down."

He set his vulture on his cot and approached his mother, hands up, like a surrendering soldier. He whispered the events of the last days in her ear in case a servant might be lurking about. Their household staff did an inordinate amount of lurking.

His mother's eyes grew wide. The albatross slipped from her fingers. "That-that poor, poor Mr. Dunbury," she said slowly. "What he must be suffering in your absence. You should hurry along. I'll just keep everyone here distracted. Err…*entertained*."

～

From the platform, Isabella watched the Northwest to London Railroad train chug in at eight fifteen. A tired-looking couple and three bickering children disembarked from one of the first-class carriages. As the father passed Isabella, he bellowed to his offspring, "For God's sake, we're on holiday. If you brats can't behave, we'll just take this train straight home to London."

Isabella shoved her bag into the vacated cabin and stepped inside, her soles crunching on biscuit crumbs. The ticket master told her that her bulging bag was too big and would have to be transported in the baggage carriage. Now the bag had shrunk enough to be shoved under the seat, but Isabella wore two cloaks, the pockets stuffed with shoes, petticoats, and a rolled copy of *Important Financial Matters Concerning England and Continental Europe*. She disrobed down to her frumpy dress and piled her discarded garments and extra shoes in the corner.

She stationed herself by the window and scowled as if to say to the people looking in her window for vacant seats, *Don't get in this carriage. It's occupied by a dangerous, sleep-deprived, hysterical woman who wants to be left alone. Stay away. Stay away.* When the conductor's whistle blew and the train started to rumble underneath her feet, she released her held breath and rested her head against the back of the seat.

Wham! The carriage door flew open and a brown leather bag went flying past her, hitting the opposite wall. Randall leaped in just as the train lurched forward. "Good morning, love.".

"W-what are you doing?" she cried, the great plan that she'd spent the night weaving suddenly torn to shreds. "You're supposed to be getting your black heart shackled to some beautiful nincompoop."

"You didn't really think I was going to let you go alone?"

"No, of course not," she stammered, feeling stupid. Why was she so terrible at understanding subtle meanings? She took everyone at their literal word. She should have known better from that slippery snake of a man. After all, he *was* a politician, and a good one, in a profession not renowned for its honesty and forthrightness.

He sat himself down beside her, his woodsy scent clogging her nose and setting her nerves alight. She switched to the opposite seat. "And don't sit next to me. I don't want people to think we're lovers."

"We're lovers?" He shot her a sly glance. "Did you get me foxed out of my poor wits, take advantage of me in my defenseless state, and then not have the courtesy to tell me? Did I enjoy it?"

She refused to dignify that bit of lunacy with a direct answer. "Your mother, Judith, everyone thinks that I l-love you. Oh, my throat hurts for uttering such moronic nonsense."

He extended his legs, cupped his hands behind his

head, and let a charming smile laze on his lips. His blue coat molded to his lean, flat belly and the contour of his sex bulged in his brown trousers. "Naturally they think that," he said. "What's not to love?"

She averted her eyes, determined not to look at his male part. However, the generous, manly swell in the fabric was now emblazoned on her brain. "I really don't have the time to discuss all the things that I don't love about you. The list is quite long, and I'm a bit upset. I didn't get any sleep, and now you are here to complicate everything. I just…just want to read." She unfurled her journal and bowed her head, hoping he would take that as a cue to be quiet.

She gently rocked in her seat, as if it were a comforting cradle, trying to keep her curious eyes from roving back to his lap as she read and reread the first paragraph in an article about interest rates in the banks of Holland. She had almost made it to the second paragraph when she felt his shoulder rub against hers, sending an annoying tingle through her sacred feminine vessel.

"Just relax," he said, settling next to her. "We're not lovers. I detest you as much as you detest me."

"I don't *detest* you," she corrected. "I just don't like you some—well, most of the time."

"I certainly despise you, no question about that. Now that we have our mutual dislike for each other clarified, I think we should play a little game."

She looked at him askew. "The *our bank fails, we lose all our money, and our names and reputations are ruined* game? I hear that it's great fun until they cart us off to the poorhouse."

"No, it's the let's-invent-false-identities-so-as-not-to-cast-suspicion game."

"Oh." It made sense. She hated when Randall made sense.

"And I get so tired of being the responsible Lord Randall. People's livelihoods…railroads…hanging on the most casual slip of my tongue. My every move criticized in some paper."

"I can't believe you just called yourself responsible."

"And I help govern a country. Shocking, isn't it?" He gave her a gentle nudge. "Come now, don't you ever get weary of being you?"

She gazed at her hands. Her fingers were bare except for a small ruby ring that once belonged to her beautiful, graceful mother. "All the time," she whispered.

"So, let's say you're Izzy May."

"Izzy May? I'm Izzy May!"

"You look like an Izzy May."

"What? Frumpy and provincial?" When he didn't argue but flashed a knowing smile, she shot back, "Then you can be Mr. Randy—as in Randy the Dandy. We can be siblings. I'm the older, wiser sister, and you're the pesky little brother whom nobody wants around."

"I think we should be husband and wife. We don't look related unless our mama was a bit loose with her favors."

"No one will believe we're married. The repulsion radiates from us."

"In that case, love, everyone will assume we're shackled."

"But I'm terrible at playacting," she protested.

"Remember the annual Christmas play? You got to
be the wise man and say 'I followed a star and brought
the baby Jesus frankincense. For he shall be a great
leader.'" She mimicked younger Randall. "And the
vicar always gave me the nontalking sheep part. Every
year. I sat there baaing and sniffing, my eyes running
because you know I have that reaction to hay."

"Yes, but then your reputation, your wealth, your
everything wasn't on the line in that puny sheep part,
was it?"

He had a salient point. They really couldn't knock
on the door, introduce themselves, and say, "By
chance, have you seen our errant bank partner running about with our operating capital and a passel of
fraudulent stock certificates?"

He took her silence as agreement. "So when we
board the next train, we'll be man and wife until the
recovery of funds, Powers's arrest, or the poorhouse
do part us." He unbuttoned the bottom of his waistcoat and began to tug at his shirt until it hung untidily
over the waist of his trousers. Then he popped off his
cuff links.

"Are-are you removing your clothes?" Did he
think that they were going to consummate their
pretend marriage? She couldn't deny the little throb
between her limbs at the thought.

"Ey, you're just wishin' your man would do that for
ya," he replied in a hard cockney, then added a belch.
"I'm getting meself into me part."

"Oh Lord."

He opened his leather bag and began rooting in it,
pulling out an ugly, worn coat that looked as if it had

spent a great deal of its existence lying in the dusty
street while being trod on by horses. "Ain't you going
to pretty up for yer man?" he asked. "Where did you
put those little jellyfish things?"

"I can't believe this is happening," she thought
aloud, pressing her fingertips to her throbbing temples.
"My bank is going under, and I'm saddled with
a lunatic."

"Don't talk about your 'usband that way, woman."

⁓

When they stepped out of the carriage to switch lines,
Mr. Randy, now clad in the ratty coat, an equally
appalling hat, which he kept pulled low, and boots that
must have spent several years in service as doorstops,
insisted they practice their marital roles. He snatched
her bag from her hand, determined to be "good 'n'
husbandlike" and carried it to the ticket line. There,
he set it down, groaned, and pressed his hand into his
lower back. "What did you put in heres, woman?"
he quipped in a loud voice. "We can't go nowheres
without ya packing up the entire crib."

"Yous just let me carry it," Isabella hissed, her cockney stiff and uncomfortable on her tongue. Why in
Hades did she agree to go along with Randall's madness? Hadn't this gotten her in enough trouble as a girl?

"No, I said was I chivalrous-like, and chivalrous-
like I am, even if me wife wants to break me back."
He turned, nodded to the young couple behind him.
"Good morning to you. You look like a right 'appy
couple. Recently noozed, are ye?"

The well-dressed man drew the petite woman

behind him, as if to protect his delicate flower from the rough miscreants. "We've been married but a week," he said curtly.

"Ay, I used to be like you." Randall winked and rambled on. "All 'appy and 'opeful." He jerked his head at Isabella. "Me and the missus 'ave been shackled for going on nine years now. All the fire's gone. What, after seven little sprouts, not even a tiny flame to warm ourselves. No 'ope, no 'appiness."

"Now you stops bothering the fine folk." Isabella yanked Randall forward to the ticket window.

"Two third-class tickets?" the clerk asked.

"Third class!" Randall huffed, indignant. "Only the best for me Izzy May. Second class, my good man."

"No!" Isabella cried, not playacting. She didn't want to spend the next few hours in a cramped, open carriage.

"See 'ow she henpecks me," her pretend husband bellowed. "Nothings is good enough for the likes of 'er. You gives her the moon and she nags you fer the sun. Always complaining about me, she is. I just provides 'er a roof over 'er 'ead and chow for 'er seven young 'uns." He dropped their tickets in his pocket and lifted her bag with a heaving grunt. "She's tryin' to kill me poor body, I swear it."

They started to walk away. Isabella bit her tongue, biding her time until it was safe to tear into him about the importance of remaining serious and inconspicuous, when she overheard the delicate young wife say to her husband, "My dear, promise me that we'll never be like that when we've been married a long time."

Isabella and Randall exchanged glances, their lips trembling as they tried not to laugh.

❧

The second-class train ride wasn't as horrible as Isabella had anticipated. The seats weren't cramped, and when the summer wind blew on her cheeks, she felt a temporary lift from her worries. She removed her glasses, closed her eyes, and let the breeze caress her face. Randall found her hand and laced his fingers through hers. She almost stopped him, for fear that people would see, but then she remembered that they were unhappily married. All her life, Isabella had preferred her own company, avoiding Randall—partly for the obvious reasons that he was obnoxious, annoying, arrogant, and privileged, but also because his easy manners and charm, which her father had admired and compared her against, made her jealous and bitterly self-loathing. But for once in the entirety of their unbalanced, antagonistic relationship, she was grateful that her enemy sat beside her, holding her hand.

Six

At the train station in the village neighboring Itching-by-the-Ditch, Mr. Randy gave "me last blessed shilling" to a porter to keep their bags safe while he and Isabella ventured to Busby's, who, the porter had assured them, lived an easy afternoon's stroll from the village.

Randall had rarely heard Isabella use questionable language, but she uttered "oh, hang it" about mile two of the so-called "easy afternoon's stroll," when she snagged her homely gown climbing over a broken fence. Around mile three, she wondered "Where in the Hades is this place?" when she stepped into a cow patty. A little after mile four, she complained "Oh fudge, my feet hurt," when they were mucking about a freshly plowed field. Then she finally sank to the truly profane, stating, "Hell's fire, I think I have blisters on every blessed toe," when they finally reached the oak-lined lane of Busby's drive.

He left her to nurse her poor feet by the protruding roots of a massive oak tree and ambled up the lane, approaching the stately white manor house that rose from the lush sheep fields. The dignified prospect of the home was diminished by the baby dolls hanging in nooses from tree limbs and the broken carriage wheels, baby carts, and articles of children's clothes scattered about the lawn.

Two angry girlish voices blared from a broken window on the top floor. "Those are my stockings. Put them back. All yours are torn, you idiot, stupid, puddinghead."

"Nurse said you weren't supposed to call me names anymore." Then there was a scream and "Nurse, she's pulling my hair. Make her stop. Make her stop."

An unsupervised infant boy with angelic blond locks, dressed in a stiffly pressed white frock, squatted by the shrubs. He scooped up a tiny handful of dirt, giggled, and shoved it in his mouth. Randall decided that the dirt-eater was too young to be of much use, and Randall focused his attention instead on the serious, older boy who was absorbed in painting what appeared to be a human study on the side wall of the home.

"Excuse me, there, my happy young lad," he said in his Mr. Randy vernacular.

The child gazed up at Randall with large green eyes and a sweet, girlish mouth, as blue paint dripped from the brush onto his trousers and shoes.

"Is this by chance Mr. Nicholas Busby's fine residence?" Randall asked.

"He's my papa."

"Is he, then? Well, can you tell a good fellow if a Mr. Powers is visiting yer papa?"

He shook his head. "Mama said that lying, low-bred

scoundrel isn't allowed under our roof anymore. That he's a bad influence on us."

"Do you think your papa would know his whereabouts?"

"My papa knows everything," the boy declared in a definitive manner. "He's a scholar." He picked up an expensive leather-bound volume that was cracked open on the soil by his feet and splattered with paint. "I'm painting the picture in his book. It's called"—the boy slowly sounded out the words—"B-b-ir-th of V-venus."

"Very fine there, young man." Randall nodded and began to back away. "Keep up the good work."

By the time he had cleared the third row of great oaks, he heard a young female scream "I hate you! You're the worst sister in the entire world." He turned to find a girl scurrying across the front lawn, stockings flying like flags from her hands, while another girl pursued her, smacking her sister with a pillow.

A stout, broad-shouldered servant, holding a laughing, naked child in the crook of her elbow, stormed out the door after them.

"Now stop your figh—" The sledgehammer of a woman stopped at the sight of the filthy infant boy dining in the dirt and his brother's illicit artistic renderings on the side of the house. "You wash that filthy hogwash off this instant," she cried. "What did I tell you about Italian art?" She snatched the dirt-eating child from the ground with her free hand. "And you! I just bathed you. You're coming inside, right now," she ordered, marching in the house, a squirming child captive under each arm. "Nurse needs a dram before anyone gets hurt."

Randall strolled back to Isabella, rethinking his future family's size and trying to formulate a plan. He found her sitting on a protruding tree root, rubbing her feet through her boots while being studied by two placid brown mares that chomped on hay from a trough on the other side of the fence. Isabella looked up at Randall and cried, "It feels like someone lit my toes on fire."

Gazing upon her tired face, flushed from exertion, and her hair, tumbling about her face, all wind-blown and sticky with perspiration, an idea shot off like a firework in his head. "You were right!"

"Of course I was." She wiped her brow. "About what?" She began to push off from the ground.

He grabbed her elbow and helped her up. "You're my sister, not my wife."

He quickly set to work, brushing aside her fallen locks and undoing the buttons running down her back. *A very nice, graceful back. The kind perfect for cuddling against in bed on a cold night.*

"What—what are you doing?" she hissed.

"I'm impregnating you, my darling. Be still so I can loosen your corset."

She gasped and grabbed the collapsing bodice of her gown, trying to cover herself. Twisting around, she glared at him with her magnified eyes. "Randall, I don't know what you're thinking, but I am not having congress with you behind a tree."

"*Congress?* With you!?" An image of taking her against the trunk filled his imagination—and he possessed a very vivid and detailed imagination. What he conjured wasn't so terrible. At least, his throbbing cock certainly didn't think so. In his mind, he imagined her soft lips parted with pleasure, her bound breasts freed and bouncing with his thrusts. He wondered what her nipples looked like. Were they pert, pink—

Get ahold of yourself.

"I'm your brother. That's just disgusting in so many aspects." He wagged his finger under her nose. "No, no, dear Sister. You've been playing Who's Papa's Naughty Pussycat with Mr. Powers, and now you've got a little kitten in the oven. At least, that's what I'm telling Mr. Busby."

"I'm pregnant with Mr. Powers's child," she repeated, as if Randall had just proposed the most asinine thing in the world. "That's your plan?"

"Brilliant, isn't it?"

"That's it!" She flung up her arms, causing her dress to fall, revealing the tops of her breasts—those lovely, ample things—over her corset. She must have seen him looking—ogling like a moonling might be a better description—because she blushed, yanking up her gown. "I'm doing this by myself. You're cracked."

She stomped away, wobbling on her blistered feet.

He hurried to catch up. "Think about it. He has nine children. When I tell him that my beloved sister Izzy May was impregnated and abandoned by Powers, it's bound to sway him. It gets right to the heart. No beating around the bush, or should I say arteries, lungs, or belly, not to mix metaphors. We get the information we need and catch the next train leaving the station."

Her spectacles amplified her glower as she considered. Finally she said, "I swear I will repay you for this ludicrousness." She turned, letting him complete his "impregnation." "And trust me, it's going to be painful and humiliating and will traumatize you for the remainder of your life."

"Don't get me excited with anticipation," he quipped wryly. However, his jolly Mr. Headsmith, still reeling from the tree fantasy, didn't perceive any irony in his words, and grew hard at the prospect of Isabella-inflicted trauma. He tried to keep his mind on her plain cotton corset, and not the curve of her neck and waist, or the heat of her body warming his fingers.

When he was done, she clutched her dress to her chest, stomped back to the tree, reached over the fence, and grabbed a handful of hay from the horse's trough.

"What are you—" He stopped when she jammed the hay down her corset. "I didn't think of using hay." He had just intended to loosen her gown a bit. "You're going to itch and cry, but you're brilliant."

❧

Randall used the door knocker. "Are you sure you're ready?" he asked Isabella, who sniffed, her eyes watering as she furiously scratched the space just below her breasts and above the round hay-baby in her corset. Something about the straw bump filled him with masculine pride, as if it were a real baby and one he'd put in her.

What the hell is wrong with you? Your career, your

reputation is in the chamber pot, and all you can think about is making babies with Isabella.

Meanwhile, his Mr. Long Johnson just heard the "make babies" part of his inner lecture and came to attention like a soldier called to duty.

"I feel like I want to scratch my skin off," she whimpered, her face resembling a swollen, wet tomato.

"I'll get us out of here as quickly as possible. You just stand there being pregnant and miserable while I do the talking. Remember, Powers likes witless women."

"What is that supposed to mean about me—"

The door opened. Inside stood a naked infant, maybe a little older than three, looking up at them with large, vacuous eyes. He jammed a tiny finger in his nose and plucked out a nice gift for them.

Nurse, clearly unaware of Isabella and Randall standing on the doorstep, lumbered forward with squirming dirt-eater still trapped beneath her arm and a wet, dripping washcloth in her hand. "Close that door. You're… Oh heavens, callers," she exclaimed with the same enthusiasm that one has for tax collectors.

Dirt-eater was more hospitable. He emitted a happy shriek and clapped his hands as his nurse set him down.

Randall yanked off his hat, placed it over his heart, and grabbed Isabella's elbow. "Pardon me, ma'am. I'm Mr. Randy. A respectable, 'ardworking fellow I am. And this is me sister Izzy May. I'm requesting an audience with the 'onorable Mr. Busby." He lowered his voice, leaned in, and raised a brow. "Regarding an extremely serious personal matter."

The way the nurse looked at him, her eyes weary

and battle-hardened, made Randall think that the only matters that swayed her were of the magnitude of houses burning, children falling in wells, and being down to her last drop of elderberry wine. Before the put-upon woman could speak, a loud, high-pitched voice pierced the hall. "Why, she's increasing!"

Around the hefty nurse stepped a pretty brunette just a few years older than Isabella and Randall. She wore an expansive, bell-like skirt layered in ruffles, and her corset was laced so tightly that it pushed up her ample breasts, forming a shelf of flesh below her neck. In her arms she held a fat, gurgling baby, whose chubby red face looked as if it would burst out of its lace cap. "I just love babies. Yes, I dosy-wosy," she told the infant. "I just adore the little-wittle things. Ouch! Don't pull Mama's hair! Stop!" She ripped one of her spiral curls from the baby's grasp. "So how much longer?" She gazed at Isabella with bright, happy eyes, unfettered by intelligence or self-awareness.

"Longer?" Isabella's brows curved in confusion.

"Until you have the baby-waby, dearie."

Isabella's lips quivered. She looked up at Randall, uncertainty in her eyes. He saw the gaping flaw in his brilliant scheme—neither he nor Isabella knew a thing about infants. Well, aside from how they were made. After all, she had explained the process to him years before, and he had done a great deal of practicing since then—that is, in the act of making babies, but never actually creating one.

"Five months?" Isabella ventured as she scratched her gown above the bulge.

"Just five?" the woman in the mountainous skirts

exclaimed. "This must not be your first little darling-warling. I was an absolute house at just the third month of my second dearsy. A house, I tell you. And what an active baby she was. I couldn't sleep for her kicking me. And mind you, that sweet little hunny-bunny decided to turn around just before she was born."

"Turn around?" Isabella echoed.

"Her little broadside first," the woman explained, and turned her bundle of lace and joy to illustrate. "Sixteen hours I labored before the midwife got the forceps and—"

"Mrs. Busby," the nurse cut in, "remember what your husband said about sharing too many unnecessary details."

But it was too late. Isabella's mouth had dropped in horror. She began to edge to the door, but Randall held her tight. *No, love, we are in this folly together.*

"Oh, don't you fret now," Mrs. Busby assured Isabella. "It was nothing compared to the first, as you well know."

The woman waited for a response. Isabella had none to give but a high, nervous squeak as a bead of perspiration rolled down the side of her face.

"Well," Mrs. Busby continued, "*I* remember thinking that I was being hacked apart by an ax."

"My Lord," Isabella cried, and pressed her hand to her mouth, her eyes watering.

"Oh, are you going to be illsy?" Mrs. Busby's eyes crinkled with concern. "I was so illsy with my fifth. Couldn't even look at cabbage without—"

"Mrs. Busby." The nurse cleared her throat. "Unnecessary details."

"Good heavens, but I do get carried away when I talk about baby-wabys," she admitted, and gazed down at her gurgling waby. "Yes, I dosy-wosy."

"As—as I was saying," Randall said, trying to turn the conversation away from the specifics of pregnancy and childbirth so his pretend sister did not faint—and he wasn't feeling so well himself—"I wanted to talk to Mr. Busby regarding a serious personal matter."

"Oh, of course." Mrs. Busby held out her bundle of joy for the nurse. "Do take little-wittle Lionel. You know how Mr. Busby doesn't allow children in his study. Oh and really, must I tell you again to make sure that Reginald keeps his clothes on and stays in the nursery? We have guests. What they must be thinking."

The handed-off infant immediately began wailing, a piercing, eardrum-bursting, nerve-shattering sound. Isabella jumped, her shoulder crashing against Randall's. He clasped her hand to still her. She twined her taut fingers through his, digging her nails into his palm. Her body was rigid, and perspiration was streaming down from her forehead.

Until two minutes ago, Isabella had bemoaned her childless existence. Now the thought of jumping off high cliffs or repeatedly being run over by trains seemed more pleasant than childbirth. She struggled to stifle her sneezes. She kept the fingers of one hand laced between Randall's and the other clenched at her side, refusing to scratch.

But the itching was killing her. It felt as if wasps were building a hive on her skin, and that baby's wails were like little jolts of electricity shooting through her nerves. *Somebody rock the baby!* she wanted to scream. *Get it some milk! Make it stop crying!* Through her watering eyes, she could see Mrs. Busby smiling pleasantly over her shoulder, immune to the bloodcurdling cries of her dear little-wittle baby.

Mrs. Busby lightly knocked on a closed door at the back of the hall. "Mr. Busby, my dearest," she called. "We have guests."

The three waited for several moments. Isabella released two violent sneezes.

"Oh, dear." Mrs. Busby leaned close and spoke in a low, knowing voice. "If you need it, the necessary is on the right," she said for no reason that Isabella could discern.

Don't scratch yourself. Don't scratch yourself. Well, maybe a little under your neck when she's not watching.

Mrs. Busby rapped on the door again. Isabella heard the lock turn, the clink of a chain lock being released and then another. The door opened and a man in blue-and-gray plaid pants and a deep gray coat peered out. His graying hair was brushed forward over his balding forehead, and thick whiskers grew along the sides of his face. Granted, she and Randall had spent the better part of the day stuffed in train carriages, hiked for miles in the heat of the afternoon, and hay now filled her corset, but surely they didn't smell badly enough to warrant the man's pinched nose.

Randall didn't wait for an introduction. He stepped past Busby, pulling Isabella into the inner sanctum of the man's library. Oak shelves neatly lined with leather books and globes towered along the walls. The chamber possessed a drowsy peace, a quiet order that was entirely at odds with the chaos in the remainder of the house. A large, polished oak desk rested in front of a massive arched window that looked out onto a labyrinth of boxwoods trimmed in even ninety-degree angles. Farther on lay a bucolic pasture of lush grass, white sheep, and two girls rolling about, pummeling each other.

"Nice place you 'ave," Randall said, releasing Isabella's hand. "You must be one of them learned men on account of all these books. I always wanted to meet a smart don type."

She marveled at how easily Randall slipped into the Mr. Randy character, but then, Mr. Randy was a bit of a horse's backside, so it couldn't be that much of a stretch. Meanwhile, Isabella stood about awkwardly, keeping her hands clenched for fear of scratching her skin off, her nose and eyes running, while a tiny beetle scrambled up her thigh.

"Mr. Busby was a teacher before he inherited this estate, married, and started a family," Mrs. Busby explained.

"Being fruitful and multiplying, are you?" Randall picked up a book that was cracked over the sofa cushion and made a show of struggling to read the title. "*The Marquis and the Naughty Debutante*. Aye, must be some of that fine literature you Oxford types read. Full of astronomy, Latin, and whatnot."

In spite of the itching, the running eyes, and the roving beetle, Isabella giggled.

"May I ask what business brings you here?" Mr. Busby asked in a dark tone.

"Aye, I was gettin' to that. Me name's Mr. Randy,

and I'm a respectable man. Goes to church every
Sunday, I does. And this is me sister, Miss Izzy May."

"This is her—" Mrs. Busby stopped midsen-
tence, her eyes widening. "D-did you just say *Miss
Izzy May?*"

Despite the sun shining high and bright outside the
window, an ominous cloud passed over the room.
The Busbys stared at her.

Oh God, they wanted her to speak. She opened her
mouth to say something about a baby and bringing it
frankincense. *No! Stop!* That was the Christmas play.
This was a different play. She wasn't a sheep; she had
lines. *Oh, fudge, what are they?* The shelves, books,
globes, the Busbys, and Randall all blurred in her
wet, itchy eyes. Her body felt like it was on fire. *Say
something!* "But I thought Anthony Powers was going
to marry me!" she wailed.

Mrs. Busby shrieked and buried her face against her
husband's arm.

"I swores I'd find 'im for you, Sister," Randall
cried. "And 'ave 'im makes an 'onest woman of you.
I swores I would."

"H-he said he was going to call on Sunday." Isabella
dug her nails into her gown just above the protruding
hay-baby, desperate to stop the burning itching that
was driving her insane.

"I waited and waited and waited. He never came! I
thought I loved him. He had such a beautiful chart."

"Chart?" Mr. Busby repeated. "Did you say chart?"

"Heart," she heard Randall intercede. "She was
always carryin' on about his beautiful *heart* and such.
There, there, Sister. Don't upset yourself." He gently

tried to push her onto the sofa. "You just sit 'ere on this nice sofa and *be quiet*."

But Isabella remained rigid—except for her mouth, which gushed forth. "He was a lying cur! Sweet-talking about rising assets and assured projected growth. I was under his spell. Then he stuck me with his—"

"Now, Sister, I think you might be sharing a bit too many unnecessary details." Randall gave her a gentle shove, landing her on the sofa.

"Oh, but I let him do as he pleased," Isabella yammered on. "So trusting. You see, it was going to be such a good investment. But in the end, he just took what he wanted and left me with the debt."

"Investment?" Mr. Busby said.

At the same time his wife cried, "A darling baby-waby is a debt?"

"Oh!" Isabella's eyes widened. Did she really say "debt" and "investment"? Dear God, she had ruined their ruse. *Quick, think, Isabella! You have to fix what you've done. Think! Think! Why can't I think?* "I meant—"

"Aye, my sister is so peculiar 'cause she's always speaking in those metaphors. That's why I have to do *all the talkin'*." He gave her foot a soft, furtive kick.

"Yes, metaphors!" she cried. "That's it. Engaging in the act of love before marriage is like…like…investing in options. Yes, options! You're assuming that love will grow, building confidence in the market, the market of…of love, that is."

Randall groaned. *What am I saying that is so wrong?*

She kept going, hoping to make it right. "But then the market loses confidence because maybe love's expected growth wasn't as big as you had projected, never achieving the anticipated rise in… in ardor, or the initial gain rises sharply but then sags off prematurely."

"Oh God," she heard Randall mutter.

"So, so the shares in love go down," she explained. "People start sticking their assets in other promising openings in the market…the love exchange, that is. Meanwhile, you're left holding options that you can't sell. You're stuck holding a…a baby." *Wait, that didn't sound right.*

The room went silent. Mrs. and Mr. Busby stared at Isabella, their mouths gaping. She couldn't see Randall's face because he had buried it in his hands, his shoulders shaking. Was that rogue laughing at her?

She scratched her neck. "M-maybe this wasn't the best metaphor," she conceded and then sneezed. "Perhaps I should say—"

"You have said quite enough, miss," Mr. Busby interjected. "I'm sorry to inform you after that entertaining show that I don't know where to find Mr. Powers, nor do I intend to find out."

"He used my husband abominably," Mrs. Busby explained. "Mr. Busby lent him money to help him begin a new life, since he had inherited a position in a bank from his uncle. He promised Mr. Busby that he wouldn't gamble ever again."

Her husband strode to his desk and slid a letter from under a paperweight. "Then, not a month ago, your Mr. Powers visited, asking for money again. Something about investing in his bank." With a flick, he opened the letter. "But another old student of mine had written me earlier, informing me that he had learned Powers had played deep at a disreputable London club called the Golden Tyger." He dropped the missive to his desk. "I have little doubt that the monies I previously gave him and more were lost that fateful night. So I sent him away. I had to." He rubbed his eyelids. "All his education, his integrity, his living, lost. I believe he might have what some say is an addiction."

"Thank you, guv'nor," Randall said, bowing his head several times and turning his hat in his hands. "I'll keep searching for that rascal Powers. You can see me sister needs a 'usband something bad." He wrapped his hand around her elbow, helping her up. "No needs to trouble yerself. We'll just find our ways out. Don't mean to keeps you from that marquis and 'is naughty debutante. Fine, fine literature, that. Come, Sister."

❧

Randall hurried Isabella from the house. He could feel her skin twitching beneath her sleeve; her face, now swollen and deep red, was shiny with perspiration. By the time they reached the ninth oak on the drive, she released a soul-in-pain cry, shoved her hand down her corset, and screamed, "Get this baby out of me!"

Assuming she needed assistance, he tried to jam his hand in her dress.

"Get away," she shouted, and smacked his knuckles. "Don't you ever make me pregnant again." She yanked and yanked hay from her gown, tossing it in the air, letting it stream about her head like falling flakes of gold. "And you laughed at me in there. For

God's sake, Randall, we are inches from ruin. What were you thinking?"

"Well, I was thinking about finding Powers until you started talking about expected growth sagging off prematurely and…and…" He couldn't help himself, letting a few chuckles trickle out before finally giving in to wholehearted laughter. "Sticking assets in other promising openings," he choked out.

She flung up her arms. "I was using basic economic theory as a metaphor for love. But perhaps your minuscule brain couldn't comprehend it."

"Oh, my so-called 'minuscule' brain caught your meaning and much, much more, you dirty-minded minx."

"I am not dirty-minded!" she cried, and then paused to consider. "How am I dirty-minded? What did I say that was so lewd?"

"Never mind, love, let's just get to London and find out about the Golden Tyger."

He reached to clasp her elbow, but she yanked it away.

"I'm never letting you touch me ever again," she hissed.

They walked side by side in silence, except for the rough swishing noise of her nails scratching her skin and gown. Randall felt horrible as he watched her wobble on her sore feet, but she bravely soldiered on, head high, refusing to acknowledge his existence. Whenever he tried to help her over an expansive cow patty or forge a deep puddle, she would flash a frigid glare that could shrivel the bollocks of the most hardened Newgate murderer.

With his companion refusing to speak to him, he lapsed into more anxious thoughts. Every minute that he wasted tromping past sheep and cows, he felt Powers slipping further from their reach, and Randall's own doom barreling toward him at breakneck speed.

After two miles, when they were climbing the rickety fence separating a sheep pasture from a newly plowed field, his partner came to an abrupt stop on the top rung. "Oh, dear Lord!"

"What's wrong?" he asked, alarmed. "Did you hurt yourself climbing? Do you need a physician? Tell me, what is the matter?"

"When I said that part about sticking assets in other promising openings in the market, do you think that they thought that I was talking about…about a man's dangly part and a woman's sacred vessel?"

He kept his chuckle inside. "'A man's dangly part'?" he asked, feigning confusion as if he had no idea what she was talking about. "'A woman's sacred vessel'? No, no, love, of course not."

She released a low breath, relief easing her features.

"No doubt they thought you meant sticking a man's stone-hard penis into a woman's throbbing, love-oiled vagina. At least, that was my interpretation."

Seven

Forty-five minutes later, Isabella arrived at the train station, her feet blistered, her body covered in perspiration and itching from the pregnancy episode, and her fists balled into rocks, ready to give Randall a facer if he said "promising openings" or "sags off prematurely" one more time before breaking into laughter.

She pushed through the small crowd of tired, bedraggled people exiting the station, lugging their bags and greeting waiting loved ones. Despite her raw, hurt feet, she rushed to the ticket window, desperate to get there before Randall could catch up. He would only start into his Mr. Randy routine again and have them shoved into second class. Izzy May wanted a first-class sleeper all to herself. Her "husband" or "brother" or whatever relation Randall decided to call himself could sleep on the roof for all she cared.

The green curtain on the ticket window shut as she approached. How could the ticket master not have seen her? She rang the bell on the counter. "Excuse me. Pardon me. Hello in there. I know you saw me. I need to purchase a first-class ticket to London. I'm

willing to pay a great deal." A hand slid out a wooden
bar with "Closed" painted on it.

That rude— A hand clasped her elbow and a familiar
male voice said, "Miss Izzy May, dearie, wot seems to
be the problem 'ere?"

Not again. "I know you're in there," she cried,
pounding on the bell. "I need a first-class ticket to
London! My life depends on it. You can't leave me
with this man."

"Ey, you just missed the last train," said a ragged
woman, sweeping away dirt from the empty benches.
"Not another one leaving until seven fifteen tomorrow morning."

"What!" Isabella wailed. "W-we have to spend the
night *here?*" She thought she might dissolve into real,
non-hay-induced tears. *Be strong,* her father's words
echoed in her brain.

"Where is the porter with our bags?" Randall
demanded in his normal voice.

"You mean those?" The woman pointed to their
baggage, which was sitting atop a rubbish barrel. "I
was just about to take them home with me, seeing as
nobody wanted them. And such nice bags they are."

Isabella watched Randall stalk across the room and
snatch up their belongings. "Capital," he muttered.
"Just capital."

The woman stopped sweeping. "If you're needing
a place for the night, Mrs. Sutton across the road runs
the only inn in the village—a nice, clean place." She
waggled her broom handle at Isabella. "But, mind
you, she don't approve of any hanky-panky. You'll
have to be quiet about it."

"What? Hanky-panky w-with him? I—I would rather drink from a filthy, worm-filled mud puddle, get sucked under some soggy, swampy moor, or be bitten by a hundred venomous adders."

The woman raked Isabella up and down and then shook her head. "Aye, like me grandmamma always said, there's no accounting for taste." She resumed sweeping.

"I have extremely good taste," Isabella assured Randall as they left the station.

"Hence your attraction to Anthony Powers," he retorted as they stepped onto the road running through the middle of the tiny village. On one end sat a falling manor house; on the other, a church. In between were old, sloping, timbered buildings. "That cur is probably on his way to Calais for a nice holiday. Meanwhile, we're stuck in this bumhole of a place."

They crossed the lane to a rambling establishment that spanned the width of three normal town houses. Bull's-eye windows ran across each of the building's four uneven stories. Six or so dormers jutted out at odd angles from the slate roof. The wooden sign that hung above the torch by the ancient door read "Mrs. Sutton's Arms." Below it hung a smaller one that said "public house" and below that, another with "post office" printed on it, and nailed to that was a sheet of paper with "We sell thread, fabric, jam, bread, and eggs in the back" written in a slanting hand.

Randall stopped at the door, his hand poised on the knob. "Now, Sister, can we agree that I will do the talking?"

"Just as long as your talking includes ordering me a hot bath and a glass of wine."

He opened the door, and they entered a parlor filled with the woody, acrid smell of a drowsy, low-burning fire, mingled with the scents of dried lavender, coffee, tea, and beefy broth. The timber ceiling was low and slanting; the walls were crammed with paintings of various subjects: portraits, horses, dogs, and pastoral scenes. A matronly, thick woman sat at a desk by the left wall. Her black-and-silver hair was twisted into a neat bun, and glasses perched on her short, button-like nose. Her face was dotted with tiny moles. She was so engrossed in the book she was reading that she didn't hear them enter.

"Afternoon to yer, ma'am." Mr. Randy pulled off his hat, clutched it to his chest, and performed two quick bows. "I'm Mr. Randy and this is me sister. We desire two rooms in your fine establishment 'ere."

The woman glanced over the top of her glasses, and her small, stony eyes swept over Isabella. Isabella could just imagine how she must appear: her dress was torn from where she had itched, her loose hair was stuck to her face and neck, and her skin was red from scratching.

"I'm full this evening," the woman said. "Mr. Eggleson who lives in the red farmhouse further down the road rents rooms in his outbuilding for a shilling."

Randall reached into his pocket and withdrew a handful of shiny sovereigns. "I guess I can pays a shilling."

"Well, now." The woman smiled. "I just remembered that we had two guests leave early." She closed her book and propped it against the lamp. The gold-embossed title glinted in the light.

"Pardon me," Isabella piped up, before she remembered her agreement to Randall concerning opening her mouth. "Are you reading *From Poor to Prosperous, How Intelligent Widows, Spinsters, and Female Victims of Ill-fated Marital Circumstances Can Procure Wealth, Independence, and Dignity*?"

The innkeeper's lips parted with an audible inhale. "Oh, yes, my sister. I've read it at least six times. And every time, I always find some new bit of wisdom that I had missed before."

"Six times?" Isabella blinked. "Really?" *How can anyone read that drivel one time, much less six?* "You don't think it's rather overly sentimental, or that the stories are a bit too melodramatic or unrealistic?"

"What!" The innkeeper grabbed the book and cradled it to her bosom as if it were a baby-waby. "Unrealistic? Melodramatic? How dare you!"

Randall gave Isabella a nudge in the ribs. "Sister, now wot did we agree about me doing *all* the talkin'?"

But it was too late; Isabella had stirred up a beehive.

"Now, you listen to me." The innkeeper pointed a wrinkled, reddened finger at her. "Miss St. Vincent saved my life. When my husband ran off with that trollop parlor maid—always waving her round backside at him—taking what little money we had, then dying in that tart's bed, leaving me with three hungry children and my papa's rundown house, it was Miss St. Vincent who taught me how to take care of myself. She may be a spinster, but I tell you she knows the hard life of a woman. She knew better than to marry or fall for some lying, no-good cur."

Isabella swallowed. She felt like a fraud. She fell for lying, no-good curs right and left, and the only reason she wasn't married was because no such cur had asked her.

"Did you say the author was a Miss St. Vincent?" Randall asked, staring at Isabella, his eyes all glittery. "A Miss Isabella St. Vincent?"

Isabella flushed beneath her flush. She didn't want him to know about that book. In fact, she didn't want *anyone* to know about it. Now he would tease her mercilessly. As if the "promising openings in the love market" wasn't bad enough!

"Yes, she is indeed a saint." The innkeeper raised the book as if it were the King James Bible. "She helped me realize that I had an opportunity, seeing how I was across from the new railroad station. Like she wrote, it's all about realistically assessing a need and situation. I'm so successful that now I've expanded, adding that post office and a public room, and I have a little shop with anything the villagers could want." She glowered at Isabella. "How dare you insinuate that—"

"I'm sorry." The heretic held up her palms, backing away. "I didn't mean—"

"My children and I are alive today because of this book," the woman thundered. "Overly sentimental? My foot. I can tell you're a bit dull-witted—"

"Wait a minute! I am rather intel—"

"Aye, we'll just take the two chambers." Randall squeezed Isabella's elbow. "Being it's the *only* inn in the village and me sister desires a bathing room."

"Bathing room? This isn't the Royal Palace. Miss St. Vincent would never approve of such an extravagant use of capital."

"What?" Isabella cried weakly. She didn't recall in her draft or Judith's horrific edits any injunction against bathing rooms. She was going to make a revision specifically addressing the issue.

"I'll send my daughter up with a proper, decent tub." The lady slid two keys to Randall but kept an eye on Isabella. Even as Isabella walked to her room, scratching an annoying itch on her side, she felt the heat of the woman's gaze boring into her.

Randall carried their luggage up a narrow staircase, turned sideways, and edged down an even narrower passage. "Ah, our rooms are across the corridor from each other," he said. "Do you want the lovely view of the stables or the scenic railroad station?"

"I'll take the one with a view of a clean bed and fresh water."

He opened a door and announced, "I think this one will be yours." He let her pass into an excessively floral parlor. The lumpy, slumping walls were covered in pink wallpaper of rose vines and then further layered with framed paintings of periwinkles. The purple violets on the upholstered chairs clashed with the walls and most measures of good taste. The adjacent bedchamber offered little botanical relief, the bedcover fabric being covered with pale yellow daylilies.

On the commode, Isabella slid over three figurines of shepherdesses to make room for her bag. She opened its latch and started to root around. "Where's

my lotion? I could scratch my skin off." Randall didn't
remove to his own chamber but stayed planted on her
floral carpet. He studied her, his head tilted.

"Why—why are you looking at me like that?"
she asked.

"Like how?"

"I don't know. Just stop. It makes me feel
self-conscious."

"Tell me about this book of yours."

"I don't want to talk about it."

"Ah, your standard answer. Well, unless you tell
me, I'm just going to stand here, staring at you." He
widened his eyes and moved closer, until his face was
mere inches from hers, making her feel all the more
uncomfortable, as well as a bit tingly in the sacred
female regions.

"It's nothing." She flicked her hand, trying to dis-
miss the horrible subject. "I just wrote a small volume
about investing in funds and other business matters.
Anyway, Judith edited it, turning it into this dreadful,
gothic claptrap. Before I could stop her, she had one
of the members from her women's society publish
it." She reached for a bottle wrapped in a stocking.
Dr. Bate's Miraculous Blemish Wash? Where was
her lotion? And why was Randall still staring at her,
making her tingle? "There, I told you. Now stop
looking at me and go to your own room."

He didn't. She should have known better than
to trust him. "The Mary Wollstonecraft Society?"
he asked.

"Do you know them?"

"The more ardent members enjoy decorating my

colleagues' and my parliamentary robes with rotting vegetation and eggs."

Despite herself, she laughed. "I think it's best if we just forget about the society, the book, my upcoming speech, and all of today. In fact, it would suit me if the entirety of this week could be forgotten." She shoved aside a petticoat to peer deeper in her bag. "Where is my blessed lotion?"

"Well, you certainly have a devoted follower in the innkeeper, provided she knew your true identity." He patted her shoulder, sending little jolts of tingling all through her nerves. "You should be proud, Isabella. You helped her."

"I didn't help her. I can't help anyone. She doesn't know what she's talking about. She didn't need me." She pulled out a gown and searched beneath. "Don't tell me I didn't pack any lotion!"

"Give yourself some credit. You should be thrilled. Nothing makes me happier than helping people."

She stopped her hunt. "Really?" she asked, incredulity in full bloom. "*You* enjoy helping people?"

"What did you think?"

"I don't know." She shrugged. "I thought you liked being in Parliament for the prestige, power, and everyone admiring you."

Something in his expression changed. Although she wasn't cold, a shiver went down her spine.

"Is that what you think of me?" he barked, causing her to flinch. "You, like the others, really think I'm a self-absorbed, ruthlessly ambitious, empty-headed, handsome boy."

"I didn't m—"

"I work hard for my country. I stay up all night, worrying, reading, thinking, doing all I can to help this nation. I'm not an idiot," he thundered. "My thoughts, my ideas are legitimate."

Her mouth gaped. She didn't recognize the man with all his charming veneer ripped away.

"Just forget it," he cried. "Maybe I'm not my own man. Maybe I should just read from a script. That would make everyone happy." He spun on his heel and began to stalk away.

"No!" she cried, panicked. She grabbed his arm. "I'm sorry, so sorry. You know I never say the correct thing. You always read people well. You see into their hearts and know that they don't mean to upset you. You are so smart that way…in so many ways."

He bowed his head, released a huff of breath, and rubbed his eyelids. For several long seconds, he remained silent, then he said quietly, "I'm sorry." His hand slid down her arm and his fingers interlaced through hers. "Please forgive me. It's a lot—the election, Harding, Powers, the newspapers filled with articles criticizing me, my mother trying to marry me off. I usually control myself better."

She instinctively moved to draw him into an embrace but stopped, feeling awkward and clumsy. For all the years she had spent trying to provoke and upset him, she had never learned how to comfort him. She didn't understand why people didn't just want to be alone when they were upset, but insisted on hugging and holding hands, like all those callers after her father's death.

"People will say anything," she stammered,

retracting her hand. The warmth of his touch lingered
on her skin. "You have to be unemotional and look
at the numbers. Did repealing the Corn Laws help
people? Yes, thousands of starving Irish. Is Harding
overextended? All the numbers point to it. Of course
he's going to lie." She laughed tentatively, trying to
get Randall to join. "He has to build confidence in the
love market. You know, those promising openings.
But underneath the illusions are numbers."

A smile tugged at his lips. An odd combination
of relief and confusion swept through her. Since she
could remember, she had tried to make him irate at
her for weeks at time. Simmering hostility was the
normal state of their relationship. Why did his anger
suddenly affect her after all these years? Why was she
desperate to make him happy again?

"Thank you for *helping* me." He freed a strand
of hair that was stuck in the hinge of her spectacles.
"You're an intelligent woman with an extraordinary
mind. Don't sell yourself short. Be proud of yourself
and your book."

Her cheeks burned. She didn't like how his kind
words made her feel: nervous and fluttery-like. *He
didn't really mean what he said. He butters up everyone.
You're not special, Isabella. Don't think that you are.*

Still, trapped in his vivid gaze, she understood
how women found him irresistible. Her sacred parts
throbbed from his heat. If she were younger, prettier;
used only two-syllable words; if her papa had been an
influential Tory and her family had the tiniest toehold
in Debrett's—all Randall's marital perquisites—she
could fall madly in love with him. Then, out of

nowhere, Judith's words echoed in her brain. *One in your position—intelligent, financially independent, and educated—shouldn't have to sacrifice her freedom to some ape-ish, ignorant man to satisfy those desires.*

Her imagination lit up with images of Randall stripped to his bare skin. The muscles of his chest, belly, and arms, as well as that enigmatic bulge beneath his trousers, were all exposed and pressing against her. His lips—oh, she remembered the sweetness of those lips—trailed little kisses along her jaw to her ear as he whispered promises about filling her and soothing that maddening tingling, the pulsing, hungry ache. Her tongue turned heavy in her mouth as a low, deep groan escaped her throat.

"Isabella, are you well?"

"Yes!" she cried, pressing her hands to her flaming cheeks. "I just…just need some lotion. I'm throbbing…I mean, itching all over." She snatched something knitted and stringy from her belongings. "Milton's toy? How did his toy get packed and yet I have no lotion?"

He continued, saying something about fetching her for dinner, but she had trouble hearing him for the loud vision of his male part rubbing barbarically against her, satisfying that wet, heavy, thick, pulsating, pesky need in her sacred feminine vessel. Then he finally, mercifully, left.

≈❧≈

Randall discovered the floral motif had spilled into his chamber as well. But he paid no attention to the decor, as his mind still turned over his little outburst with Isabella. Had she really thought he was some power-hungry politician? And why did that surprise him? He never sought her good opinion. Yet his heart had flooded with peace when she assured him that he wasn't a beautiful face with little substance, floating by on his power to charm, and he could charm the angels from heaven if he desired. He could caress with his words, tantalize with his eyes, seduce anyone when on the parliamentary floor. But who was underneath the beautiful façade, the illusion he created? Not numbers, as Isabella insisted, but nothing. He was nothing.

He set his bag down, crossed to the pitcher, and poured water into the basin. He splashed some on his face, unbuttoned his shirt, and let the drops cool his skin. He was the man who had angered half his party when he'd sided with the embattled prime minister to vote down the Corn Laws as starving Irish poured into the city; to enact laws against child labor; to dare and question the most powerful railroad baron in London. He wanted to help people; he wanted to do the right thing, and yet he only managed to alienate himself.

Now he was panicking, terrified that his charming world was falling apart. He was ready to recant everything he'd said just to have the party welcome him back with open arms. Even now, he was racing across the countryside to find that damned Powers and shut him up before he could finish off Randall's career in the House once and for all. Did Randall have any substance? Any backbone?

He glanced in the mirror. Droplets of water fell from his hair. His eyes burned in their sockets, and little bluish crescents had formed around the lids. His lips were tight, his cheeks slightly sunken. He was not the smiling, congenial man he showed the world.

He might tell himself that he wanted to do the right things, but perhaps Isabella was right. Did he want power and adoration more? If this scandal hit, if the run on the bank occurred, Isabella stood to lose her home and money—the bare essentials of survival. Meanwhile, Randall would lose his reputation, his integrity, his parliamentary position, and his ambitions for power, which once included prime ministership. He dried his face.

Starving Irish children with swollen bellies and gaunt faces flooded the hospitals. What were his power-hungry ambitions in the face of such suffering? And if he tried to help them, he lost more political ground.

He opened the curtains, lay down on his bed, set his pocket watch on the table beside him, and stared out the window. He tried to clear his mind as he watched the sun set on the train station, casting the horizon in a lush, jeweled orange and the heavens a purplish blue. But still the thought whirled in his mind: *Who are you underneath?*

He wished he hadn't left Isabella. He wished she were still near him, distracting him with her odd ways. He glanced at the watch—six thirty. An hour before he was supposed to fetch her for dinner. He laid his arm across his eyes, all of his anxieties coming back to roost. It was going to be a long hour.

❧

Fifty-three minutes were close enough to an entire hour, Randall decided. Dandied up as Mr. Randy, he crossed the corridor. He knocked on her door, but the second his knuckles struck the wood, the door swung open, as if it hadn't been shut properly. He heard Isabella call from the bedchamber, "Oh, thank you. I can't believe I forgot my lotion."

After impregnating her that afternoon, he assumed that a new intimacy existed between them. He strode to where the bedchamber door was ajar. He expected to find her fiddling with the final details of her toilette, the kind that required a man's keen eye. He knew from Cecelia and other mistresses that those fine, last-minute fashion nuances could be the most torturous—*Do these earrings make my face appear too round? I think this new coiffure hides my cheekbones; don't you think I have nice cheekbones? Do these emeralds clash with the blue-green color of my dress?*

He opened his mouth to say something about not having lotion, but no word left his lips. Isabella was reclined in a tin tub before a roaring, hissing fire. Her long, wet, black hair fell in shiny waves down the back of the tub, while she warmed her long legs by the grate. And her breasts—oh, those luscious, creamy creations—glistened in the water. Her nipples weren't the cute pink buttons that he had imagined, but rosy, succulent tips that caused his tongue to thicken. This was what had been underneath those frumpy clothes all these years?

"Oh God," he whispered. His cock ached from getting so hard so fast. Her head jerked around. Without her spectacles, her enormous eyes were the color of water at night…shiny, inky pools that he could drown in.

"R-Randall?" she asked, suddenly tentative, nervous, crossing her arms over her breasts.

"Oh, don't do that," he murmured. *Don't cover those beautiful things*. He approached, navigated by his cock, a compass pointing to her.

"Randall!" she screamed. She pushed up from the tub, struggling to stand and splashing most of the bathwater over the floor. "Get out!"

He heard her but didn't move. Time seemed to stop, the earth halting in its rotation as he stood, hypnotized by the drops of water dripping from her breasts, falling down to the graceful curve of her waist and thighs. He had a thirst that could only be quenched by licking the beads of water from her areolas, her belly button, from where they glistened on the dark curls near her sex, and perhaps pooled in that sweet place between her legs. If he could open her...

"I said get out," she screamed. She pummeled him with her balled fists, beating him back into the parlor. "Leave me alone. How dare you! Do you think you can just waltz into my chamber?"

He couldn't react. All he could think about was the becoming flush of anger on her body, the way her eyes shined, and how badly he wanted to take her on the floor, feel her writhing in pleasure beneath him, her nails digging into his skin as she whimpered his name. He wanted to show her a little of his own economic theory—a hard, strong, sustained growth that never peaked too soon.

What the hell are you thinking? You're a gentleman. Get out! Now!

Randall heard a scream that wasn't Isabella's and

then a sharp crash of breaking glass. Isabella continued to beat his chest with her fists, calling him every wicked name she must know: dirty scoundrel, rogue, cur, blackguard, b-bad person. He chanced a quick peek over his shoulder to find a young maidservant had slipped into the room. Her eyes were large with shock, her mouth gaping open. At her feet were a broken bottle and lotion splattered across the floor. She fled. *Oh, damn.*

"Hush, love," he whispered to Isabella, and seized the balled hand coming for his face. "Shhh. I'm leaving. I'm sorry." But when he tried to release her hand and step back, she held on.

She grew still, staring at him, her chest rising and falling with her breath. Her lips parted, her tongue resting on the edge of her teeth. She stepped closer, her eyes focusing and taking in his face. She let go of his hand, but he didn't dare move. She let her fingers trail down his face and whimpered—a sad, yearning, and lonely sound.

He could feel the debate raging inside of her. She wanted him, but she was scared. He knew he should walk away. Every moment he remained, he did more damage. But he leaned closer, letting his lips lightly brush hers. Then he pulled back and waited. What would she do? She closed her eyes and released a low *mmmm*. She pressed her mouth to his and remained still. He realized the poor stunning darling had probably never been properly kissed—and last night didn't count. He drew her closer. His cock pressed against her stomach, but there was nothing to be done; he desired her. Despite his urgency, he caressed her with his lips, calming her, coaxing her until she let him into her mouth. Slowly, he swirled his tongue around hers, tasting her, sinking into her softness.

Come on, love, kiss me back.

Tentatively, nervously, she answered his beckon. He felt a change in her, a realization dawning. She pressed her mouth harder against his, her kiss turning hungry, greedy. The tiny, plaintive cry from deep in her throat broke him. He had the sensation of falling. In the back of his mind, he heard a small voice, possibly his conscience, warning *Good God, man, this is Isabella.* But those years and years of bickering were transforming into something hot and urgent. All he knew was that he had to fuck her. He had to move inside her, pleasure her, have her call out his name until he had worn away the years of tension between them.

His hand trailed across her shoulder, down her chest. Her breasts rose in anticipation, meeting his touch. He flicked his thumb over a tip, feeling her body shudder, her nails digging into his scalp. She released his mouth, sighing out a high whimper as she arched her back, pressing her lower belly against his rigid cock, her leg rising and twining around his. He began to rub his pelvis against her belly as his finger circled the hardened tip of her nipple. His cock burned, it was so taut. He reached for the button on his waistband. "I've got to have you. I want to take you here and now."

Stop, Randall! It's Isabella. You can't marry her or take her as a mistress. All you'll do is hurt her. Don't jeopardize her future.

He released a strangled groan. "I want you," he muttered, resting his head on her shoulder. "I want you so desperately. Oh God." He exhaled, long and deep, and slowly pulled away.

"No!" The word came like a reflex from her mouth—unthinking, primitive. She grabbed his hand, returning it to her breast, moving desperately under his fingertips. "Don't stop, Randall. Don't. It feels so amazing."

"Woman," he hissed, kissing her jawline and giving the pert tip of her nipple a tiny squeeze. She tossed her head back and cried out.

Bam!

The door swung open and hit the wall. She jumped away.

Standing in the threshold was the landlady, her hands on her hips, her brows scrunched.

"What's going on?" poor blind Isabella cried.

"It's the innkeeper." He quickly shoved her behind him, shielding her.

"Is this man molesting you?" the woman demanded.

"Molesting?" he scoffed, trying to sound casual even as his heart thundered. He made a quick lean to the side, snatched a blanket from one of the chairs, and passed it to Isabella. "We—we were just playing a little game." He attempted to muster his Mr. Randy voice.

"I'm asking *her*. My daughter said you were being molested."

"Um, that's right, we were playing a game!" He could hear the panic in Isabella's voice as she gripped his shoulder. "You see, he's…he's my b-brother."

"Oh God," he muttered, sliding his hands down his face.

"Brother?" the innkeeper snapped. She began to shake her head and a finger in slow tandem. "I knew there was something wrong with you," she told Isabella. "I knew it when you said you didn't like Miss St. Vincent's book. Overly sentimental? Unrealistic? Well, maybe if you had listened to her wise advice, you wouldn't have to sell your body to any old—"

"What!" Isabella cried. "You think I'm a...a..."

"A trollop who mistakenly believes she can ply her trade in my respectable establishment."

Isabella gasped. "Well, I will have you know that I just happen to be Miss S—"

"Don't you call my s-sister a trollop!" he interceded.

The innkeeper put her fists on her hips and moved her head in a half circle around her neck. "If she's your sister, then I'm the lord mayor of London. I want both of your sad likes out of here in five minutes."

Eight

"LET'S JUST FORGET THE LITTLE BATHING INCIDENT ever happened," Isabella said, slicing her flattened palm through the air. The inside of the train station was dark except for the blue shadows cast from the giant silver moon peeking through the window like a nosy neighbor and a candle that Randall had thought to pack that sat burning on the floor in a tiny pewter holder. The evening air had cooled, and a breeze whistled through the platform.

They were the only people in the building. Isabella wore her cloak backward, like a blanket, and sat at one end of a long wooden bench, as far away from him as she could get. Her hair hung down her back, loose and wet. Beneath her dress, she wore only a chemise and a poorly laced corset. With five minutes to dress, she'd had to forgo petticoats, drawers, and matching stockings.

"And please stop staring at me in that dazed, stupe-fied way," she barked. She covered her flaming face with her hands. "I can't believe you saw me au naturel and I let you…you…kiss me…and that thing you did with your thumb. What is wrong with me?" She cringed even as her nipples grew hard at the memory of his touch.

"We were naked and—"

"No, *I* was naked," she corrected him. "You were fully clothed."

He tugged at his cravat. "Well, dear, if that's the problem, I can remedy it right now."

"Keep your clothes on," she cried, covering her eyes. "I don't want to see your naked body!" Nonetheless, she opened two fingers and snuck a peek at him. He pulled his cravat free, and her sacred female parts were throbbing to press against him again, this time on his bare skin, his hard member exposed, ready to "take her" as he had said, on this bench in the middle of the train station. Oh Lord, she was losing her mind. "And I don't want to talk about it."

"But what if *I* want to talk about it?" He edged closer to her.

"Stay on your side," she snapped. *Or I might explode.* "We despise each other, remember? You shouldn't be attracted to someone you like about as much as a visit to the dentist."

"We were overcome with desire. Lust has nothing to do with how we feel, either about each other or dentist visits. I was upset about the Powers affair and Harding, and you were beautiful, and I was… My God, you were ravishing. And dammit, how could I have not seen it all these years?"

She crossed her arms over her chest. "You mean my parts other than my face were ravishing." *He thinks I'm beautiful! He thinks I'm beautiful!*

"No, your eyes are dark and luscious pools." Despite her injunction, he slid closer, getting perilously near, his sweet, woodsy scent filling her nose and making her nipples crave his attention and strain against the thin fabric of her chemise. "And your lips when you kissed me were—"

"I didn't kiss you!" She shot across the room and hid in a cold, dark shadow in the corner.

"Yes, you did, and you know it," he called after her. "I wasn't the only one doing the kissing."

Releasing a long, uneven breath, she told her brain to be rational, but her body was undermining her best efforts. It throbbed, pulsed, thrummed, dampened, and tingled all over. What had Randall done? "I-I don't want to talk about it."

"Maybe you *need* to talk about it," he said quietly. "Stop holding everything in and admit that you're confused and scared." *And your body is out of control,* she mentally continued. *And if that innkeeper hadn't interrupted, you would have ripped off Randall's clothes and made him do something about that ache that is driving you mad.*

"I just…I just have these feelings all the time." Her voice cracked. She edged deeper into the dark corner, safe from those penetrating eyes of his that glowed in the candlelight.

"Feelings?" he asked. "What kind of feelings?"

She didn't want to talk about it. She should have kept these things to herself, but her words burst out, years of silent desire and repression rushing forth. "This urgency to…to…touch a man. And it's getting worse. It occupies my thoughts. I can't stop thinking about *it*. All day, I just think and think and imagine and…ugh! Even now, when I'm about to be ruined, when my life is in chaos, I can't help wanting to feel, to see, to *know* a man. I'm so desperate in my desire that I actually found *you* attractive. But of course, you are attractive, just not to me. And I shouldn't feel this way about you. It's wrong."

"Oh, love, it's natural. If it makes you feel any better, I understand your desire. It's been…it's been a long time for me as well."

She peeked out from her corner. "Twenty-nine years?"

"Well, not that long."

She approached him, her hands clasped tightly across her cloak, which covered her wayward breasts. "So can we agree that what happened was an egregious accident driven by desperation, never speak of it again, and continue going on as enemies?"

He didn't respond but tilted his head. The candlelight accented the bones of his jaw and cheeks and the crook of his cleft chin.

"No," he said.

"No!?" she wailed. "Why not?"

"I'm going to continue speaking of it. I just can't turn off my emotions and thoughts like you. For one, why are we enemies?"

"Why must you make this difficult?" She flung up her arms, dropping her cloak. "Oh, f-f-fudge! Can't we just go to sleep?" She snatched her mantle up. "Well, I'm going to sleep." She crossed to the bench, curled up, and rested her cheek on her hands. "Good night."

"Now, Isabella, you have never found it difficult to express how much you dislike me before."

She pulled the cloak over her head.

"Stop hiding like an ostrich and tell me why you detest me so. I can almost hear your brain buzzing away under there." He waited. "Not going to tell me? Well, I guess I'll just sit here and sing a little ditty while you try to sleep—

There once was a curate from Dover,
The fair ladies he liked to bend over,
He'd pull out his—"

"Be quiet!" She tossed the cloak off her face and glared. "Because I embarrass myself every day! Satisfied?"

"No, I'm more confused. Why does embarrassing yourself have anything to do with me? Well, except that time in Bath and that other time at Easter, but I swear I didn't know that pig liked plum jam."

"Every day I say or do something peculiar and people stare at me as if I were a moonling dropped on the earth. It's like everyone else has this extra sense, you know, as though on top of seeing, hearing, feeling, and so on, they also know the correct thing to say or do. Well, I'm missing that."

"No, you're not."

"Admit it, I'm awkward and clumsy. I might as well speak an entirely different language—the language of the odd, ungainly people. It contains a hundred different ways to say 'Oops, I'm sorry.'" She studied the swelled moon peering through the window, its surface lined with tiny gray lines and spots. "I remember years ago in Lyme Regis, you called me abnormal, cracked, and freakish, and said that you only played with me because your father made you."

He closed the space between them. "For God's sake, I was a stupid little boy who deserved a whipping. I'm sorry I said those things."

"Why?" She sat up again. "It's true. And you're perfect. You're handsome. You're charming. Everyone loves you. You always say the right things." She gazed at his face; his eyes were tensed, crinkling at the edges. "I've always been jealous of you. I guess that's small of me."

"You're not small, and I'm not perfect." He clasped her hand, setting off tiny sparks under her skin.

"My father thought you were. He was always saying that I should be more like you." Her throat tightened. She was dancing too close to something painful. She drew her fingers away. "I don't…I don't want to talk anymore. I really just want to go to sleep." She gave him a nudge, hoping to move him away. He didn't budge but stared at the ceiling.

Outside, an owl hooted. The candle on the floor flickered, about to drown in its own melted wax.

After several long seconds, Randall spoke again. "So you're angry at me because you felt like your father preferred me to you?"

She hated when he used his words like a surgeon, making little incisions in her heart and memories, and peering inside. She followed his gaze to the ceiling. She remembered a large design painted there, but in the dark, she could only make out a tiny portion of it.

"'Isabella, you need to stop your stammering and speak up,'" she mimicked her father's deep voice. "'See how Lord Randall deports himself, with confidence? He's going to be a brilliant young man.' Or 'Isabella, you can't get a husband if you don't learn to be more charming. Just look at how at ease Lord Randall makes people.' I couldn't live up to you. He always wanted a son, and he got me and something is wrong with me."

"He had to be proud of you," he whispered. "He had to be. You nursed him those last months. You ran his businesses and the bank. You were a devoted daughter." He rested a hand on her arm. She debated whether to yank it away, but the touch that had excited her just seconds before now offered comfort.

She shook her head. "His ambitions for me—to be like my mother, the graceful and beautiful wife to a respectable man, have a well-appointed home, and give him beautiful grandchildren—never transpired. And now the one thing that I could do that made my father proud—uphold his bank—is in jeopardy. And I can't stop saying the wrong things and desiring the wrong men." She smacked her forehead with the heel of her palm. "I should have been smarter, better, stronger. My father would have seen through Powers; instead, I wanted to marry him. I even named our unborn children."

He studied her without speaking. Something in his gaze made her feel more vulnerable than when he'd touched her naked body and did those other things that she tried not to think about. She had never opened herself to anyone, and she didn't like the scary, unsettling feeling. She had to make it go away. "I'm sorry, I shouldn't say these things. I—"

"I think perhaps you misunderstood your father. Or he wasn't aware of the lasting pain his words caused. In fact, if anything, I should be like you."

"Me?" She released a burst of laughter. "Don't say that too loudly or someone might hear and cart you away to Bedlam."

"You're right. I'm perfect." His voice turned low and gravelly. Her heart made a tiny, nervous flip. "I say the right things and charm the right people. I was born to the right parents. And on occasion I've been told I'm somewhat handsome."

"You're the most handsome man in society. And that's not just my opinion, but every lady's in the village, and all of London according to the society columns in the papers."

He gave a soft, scoffing snort. "When I first came to Parliament, I was enthralled with my power. My every word ended up in a paper. Balls were successes or disasters based on my attendance. It was like opium to be so admired and adored. I was the man everyone wanted to know. But now, I've realized how I was used." He released a long exhale. "I wasn't supposed to have my own opinions; I was supposed to sell someone else's. And maybe my ideas aren't good. Maybe beneath this 'perfection,' this charming façade, there's nothing." He turned her hand over and began drawing little circles in her palm. "That's why I didn't like you. I couldn't charm you. You've always seen straight into my heart. And…there's nothing there."

All playfulness vanished from his features. He

looked older, weary, and tired. "I have no substance," he whispered.

"That's not true! I say that as your greatest enemy." She wanted to embrace him, tell him not to worry, but she was unsure of how to comfort him.

"You've called me the devil, minuscule-brained, and a lunatic, just in the last three days." The side of his mouth hiked in a smirk-like smile—the old Randall she knew.

"I didn't mean them. I just…I just… I called you those things because…it makes me feel better about myself." *Stupid girl! How could you say that!* She covered her face in her hands. "I'm ashamed. I'm a terrible person."

He drew her against his shoulder, her face still buried in her palms. "You're not." He ran his fingers down her back. "You're unflinchingly honest. I adore that about you."

She pulled back. "You adore something about me? Impossible! I've seen the ladies in your world. You know, those 'visions of luscious splendor.' I don't hold a candle to them."

His gaze drifted to her lap and then returned to her face; a light warmed his eyes that she couldn't decipher. "I think you do," he said. "You're a little awkward, maybe, and yes, you do, at times, spout odd things. But what other woman would hike across a county in the summer, shove hay down her dress to pretend to be pregnant, hilariously compare love to economic theory, and then get mistaken for a bawd and booted from an inn? To top it all, you wrote a book that saved a woman's life, and you didn't even take credit for it." He eased a tangled mass of locks from her face and anchored it behind her glasses. "No, Isabella, your father wasn't always correct. I should be more like you: smart, honest, and fearless."

Her bottom lip quivered, so she bit down on it. Those were the nicest things anyone, outside of Cousin Judith, had ever said to her—and they came from Randall, her historic nemesis. Several awkward, fumbling seconds passed. Outside, the wind picked up, rushing by the windows.

For a lady who adored quiet, she couldn't take the tender, raw silence any longer. He was too dangerously close to the scary, insecure, yearning places in her heart that she liked to shove in a corner and pretend didn't exist.

"I t-think this is the longest we've gone without fighting," she said, trying to make a joke.

"Do you think we might become friends?"

Friends? The word sounded so benign—hardly capable of describing the emotional lightning storm in her heart. She forced a laugh. "Never!"

"Well, that's too bad." He slid to his side of the bench, fetched his bag, and opened it. "I'll have to eat my toffees by myself."

He popped one in his mouth and made a show of eating it. "Oh, delicious. Oh, so good," he rudely, cruelly said, as he chewed that little piece of heaven before her. She hadn't eaten since leaving home, and the scent of butter and sugar was pure torture.

"I've changed my mind. You're my dearest, bosomest friend. W-would you care to share a few with an abnormal, cracked girl?"

"Only if you dare to venture from your side of the bench and bask in my perfection."

She scooted over. She was happy that the serious moment had passed and they were back to their normal shallow interplay. Yet, at the same time, she felt a little pang of sorrow. This bank debacle and Randall not behaving like himself had her so confused, she didn't know what she felt anymore.

She selected a lovely sweet and popped it in her mouth, savoring the caramel melting on her tongue. "Oh, thank you. I'm so famished and exhausted. I think I've had three hours of sleep this entire week."

"I've kept a little secret from you all these years: I can be a *perfect* human pillow."

She laughed, pretending that he was in jest, but in her heart, she desired to lie against his chest and surround herself in his warmth and scent. "My cat usually takes over my pillows, so I'm accustomed to doing without."

"Suit yourself. But you're missing the thrill of a lifetime. I don't offer my pillow talents to everyone." Again she laughed, but inside a little voice said, *No, when you kissed me and fondled my breasts was the thrill of my small life.*

She ate three more toffees while he slumped against the side of the bench and closed his eyes. Soon his breath turned heavy and rhythmic as he drifted into sleep.

She studied him in the faint light. His hair and lashes cast shadows on his cheeks, and his lips were parted, all his silvery words, charm, and defenses quieted in slumber. Atop all the other guilt she was carrying, she felt horrible for the mountains of mean things she had uttered about him over the years. He had stood up to Harding and, from everything she had studied about the railroad baron, he was an intimidating business-man. Aside from arguing for several more atrocious Tory economic reforms, Randall had supported Peel in the Corn Laws repeal and factory reform, neither of which were popular, but necessary. Did he really think he had no substance? She was pondering how someone's perception of himself could be completely wrong when his arm swooped up, caught her shoulders, and pressed her onto his chest.

"Stop staring at me and go to sleep, Isabella," he murmured.

She shouldn't sleep *on* him. It was bad enough that they were sleeping together, albeit in an empty train station. It was against all societal rules and moral codes, and downright dangerous after their little kissing inci-dent. But he had captured her, she rationalized. She couldn't escape his powerful, warm, comforting arms. And he did indeed make a perfect pillow. The rise and fall of his breath was like a gentle tide rocking her. Under his coat, she could hear the steady, reassuring rhythm of his heart. For the first time in days, she felt some semblance of safety and peace. She curled against him, clutching his body. She yawned as a merciful drowsiness came over her. Soon, all society's mores and injunctions gave way to sweet, dreamless sleep.

Nine

THE PREVIOUS NIGHT'S SOFT SPELL WAS RUINED BY bells ringing around them before dawn had even broken. Men shouted train arrivals, babies cried, feet shuffled, and trains roared into the station. Isabella would remember the surrounding twelve hours like captioned illustrations in a book: *Lord Randall kisses the naked Miss St. Vincent. Miss St. Vincent and Lord Randall divulge their innermost feelings in a darkened train station. Miss St. Vincent thinks four and a half hours of sleep isn't enough. Mr. Randy finds forgotten money in the lining of his coat and buys first-class tickets. Alas, Izzy May can't fall back asleep because of their fellow passenger's cigar smoke and endless talk of horse racing. Izzy May hates everyone and everything as she arrives in London.*

"I think your days as Mr. Randy are over," she said as they fought their way out of the swift current of people streaming from Euston Station. "You will be recognized."

She looked about the street, and her heart sank. Soot-stained homes sat all the way to a horizon made up of jutting roofs and chimney stacks. Reeking animal manure steamed in the street. People crowded the walks, their hats low, shielding their faces from a sun that rarely broke through the haze of coal smoke. She ventured to London several times a year, and every time, she felt as though she were visiting a strange and very ugly foreign country.

She and her father had fled the city while in mourning for her mother. He told her stories of how Mother would put baby Isabella on a blanket on his factory floor, and the pounding of machines would put her to sleep. She didn't attend school, but stayed in her father's factory office, learning math from ledgers and reading from filing customer orders. Until she moved, she had thought all of England was covered with densely packed town houses, dim skies, crowded walks, and was bombarded with constant noise. Now already five minutes in London, and she wanted to go home to the beautiful, spacious, and clean country. But she had a bank to save or else she might not have a home at all.

"I'm going to miss Mr. Randy," her companion mourned as they rounded the corner. "He was a nice, regular old chap, but his sister, well, she was a bit wild."

She glanced over her shoulder, giving him a roll of her eyes. "Well, I'm going to visit my stockbroker. You can—" She jumped back, letting out a wild, high-pitched cry. "Oh Lord, this is terrible!" She dropped her bag and pressed her hands to her mouth. "How could this happen? No, no, no!"

"What's wrong?" Randall grabbed her elbow.

"I'm going to die! I'm going to die!"

"I'll get you to a physician!" he said. "A hospital! Someplace that can help you!" He stepped out, frantically waving his arms up and down, trying to hail a passing hackney.

"No!" she shouted and pointed. "Look."

He followed the line of her finger, across the street, to a massive stone building constructed in the somber symmetry of the George III era. Across its four massive columns, a banner was strung. Huge letters read: "Miss Isabella St. Vincent, the distinguished author and financial advisor, will be speaking about her book and other investment and business opportunities for gentle ladies." The next to last line gave the speech date and time, and below that, in very small print, was "The Wollstonecraft Society." Attached to the bottom of the banner was another sign: "Few seats remaining," except "few" had been crossed through and the word "no" inserted above.

The first emotion to grab Randall was jealousy. He wanted his name so prominently displayed. Then shame followed for desiring to steal Isabella's fame. *Why do I always crave attention? Why must everyone adore me?* However, he gathered from her red face and the sucking noises she made as her chest fluttered with her rapid breath, the only thing she felt was sheer panic. How could two people be so different? "What's the matter, love?" he asked. "This is wonderful."

"Wonderful!?" she wailed, uncaring about the heads she was turning. "I was supposed to mutter a few words and accept a stupid award. There weren't going to be more than a dozen women there. Who cared what I said? Now! Oh God, I can't speak to—to *people*! Who knows what I'll say." She seized his coat lapels. "You've got to help me! I wrote a speech, but Judith changed it, because it was awful, because she thinks I keep all my sad emotions buried deep, not feeling them or acknowledging them. So she made me write stories and then embellished them, but I can't say them. They're hideous. Like my book. Like the Wollstonecraft. Where am I going to put a big gold-painted head of Mary Wollstonecraft in my house? I should never have agreed to write that volume. I'm going to humiliate myself."

"Now calm down," he said, his voice low and soothing. He had pacified many a hysterical young lady in his years. "Hush now. I will help you. Together, we will come up with something that will amaze the ladies."

"The speech is in my b— My bag! Where's my bag? It was just here!"

"What the devil?" He pivoted, scanning the streets for her gray bag, but it was useless. If the scene were a painting, it could be called *A Study in Gray*—gray hats, coats, shoes, skies, buildings. He dashed down the crowded street, but it was futile. The bag was gone. He retraced his steps to where he had left Isabella in front of the large banner bearing her name. She had taken off down the opposite street, and now stomped back to meet him, empty-handed, her wrinkled skirts brushing the dirt.

"Capital, just capital." She flung up her arms. "I've got to address a huge crowd, and I don't have a hair-brush, a toothbrush, any tooth powder, hairpins, or clothes besides the ones I'm wearing, and I assure you there isn't much under this for having gotten dressed in five minutes."

A foolish passing chap, who had never experienced the wrath of a peeved Isabella, dared to rake her up and down. Before Randall could step in to defend her honor, she shot the man a scorching glower, magnified by her lenses. "And just what are you staring at?" she barked.

He cowered under his hat and hurried on.

"What about your money?" Randall asked, immune to her anger from years of exposure.

She edged closer, and said in a low, sharp voice, "I would never carry my…*you know* in a separate bag or reticule while traveling in London. That's stupid." She scanned the street and released a long breath that sank her shoulders and chest. "Well, I haven't the time to worry about this now. I'm going to my stockbroker and see if he has any further information about Merckler Metalworks. That's the most important thing."

"Wait, we're in this together," he cried, panicked at the thought that she would leave him alone in the city, as if she didn't need him. He seized her arm, removing her from the flow of pedestrian traffic. "Besides, I know someone who can help you with your missing feminine items." He couldn't believe what he was saying. Was he really taking Isabella to the apartment where he'd kept his mistress—that is, before Harding stole her? But he couldn't very well take her to his father's home in St. James's—too many eyes and indiscrete mouths about the corridors. He knew he could trust Mrs. Perdita to keep mum about matters. "She lives very near here."

"Who is 'she'?" A suspicious brow arched over her glasses rim.

"A housekeeper. Just trust me."

She considered as she tried to cram a strand of fallen hair under her misshaped bonnet, only causing more locks to tumble down. She blew them from her face. "First, I have never trusted you and never will, but second, does she have a mirror and a spare hairpin or two or three or a dozen?"

❧

With her bonnet pulled low, concealing her face, Isabella stood outside a black door that, except for the painted number seventeen, matched every door on the street of identical brick row domiciles. How could people live here? She would be forever trying to come home to her neighbor's house.

"I thought you lived in your father's house in St. James's when you were in London."

He shrugged and pulled the doorbell. "This is a place I keep when I want to get away."

The door opened, and a short woman in her mid-fifties appeared. She had unnatural bluish auburn hair that dangled in curls about her wide, lovely face. She was clad in a plain gray servant's gown, which she had accessorized with a rich red shawl, bracelets, necklaces, and earrings. Little biscuit crumbs were sprinkled over her more than ample bosom.

"Lord Randall!" She clapped her hands together. Despite being a rather large woman, her voice was surprisingly high and light, like a small girl's. "I was just reading and nibbling biscuits, happy as you please, no idea that you were in London! Come in. Come in. Oh, and who is *this* young lady?"

Stepping inside the tiny hall, Isabella held out her hand. "Hello, I'm Miss—"

"Izzy May," Randall supplied. "She's an *acquaintance*. Miss Izzy, this is Mrs. Perdita, my housekeeper."

"Perdita, like the famed courtesan of George IV." The housekeeper bobbed her head as she spoke, her curls bouncing.

"Oh." Isabella blinked, not expecting that saucy tidbit in polite conversation. "How, um, interesting."

"I took Perdita as my own name when I entered the theater as a mere baby. Everyone said I resembled the grand lady. You wouldn't know to look at me now, but I was a darling little thing. A regular pocket Venus. All the gentlemen desired me." She waved her hand, clanging the bracelets on her wrists. "Ah, that was years and years ago. Now I just take care of this gentleman here." She inclined her head toward Isabella. "Mind you, he is the best one of the lot, and I've known quite a few men in my day, I tell you. Quite a few." She wagged her finger at the viscount. "But he's a naughty little boy sometimes, sneaking away from his mother's house party. Do come, do come." She hurried through the first door on the right.

Randall clasped Isabella's elbow, trying to escort her, but she dug in her heels. "Just what do you use this flat for when you're in town?" she said through her tight smile.

"As I said, I come here to get away."

She spun. "I'll just wager you do. I can't believe you brought me to...to your pied-à-terre!" she hissed.

"You have gone too far. Don't you dare think that because I let you kiss me that—"

"Do come in," Mrs. Perdita called from the parlor. "Pardon my crumbs. I was reading a most wonderful book—the author is a partner in your bank, Lord Randall. You should have told me about it sooner. Everyone's reading it."

"No!" Isabella squeaked and tried to make a break, but he held her tight.

"She's just going to help you with your toilette," he said, dragging her across the corridor, her bootheels sliding on the floor. "Lend you a few items."

"I doubt we are the same size." She slid across the threshold into the parlor. She sucked in her breath.

She had never been in a man's pied-à-terre, and she expected some garish Ottoman harem–theme with draped fabrics, pillows, and suggestive art and statuettes, not a comfortable room with an inviting leather sofa, draped in blankets, and matching chairs. On the round tables in the corners were small stacks of leather books with little figures on top. A bureau desk stood beside the fireplace. On the shelves were more books. Several newspapers were folded on a side table by the door, and a small fire burned in the ceramic grate.

She was supposed to be outraged, offended, affronted; instead, the low hiss of the fire made her want to curl up on the sofa under the soft blankets and catch up on those hours of sleep she had missed.

The housekeeper stacked several lacy handkerchiefs and a plate of biscuits atop Isabella's volume. "'Twas such a lovely book your partner wrote." She sniffed. "Why didn't you tell me about her?"

"Oh, she's an odd bird." He winked at Isabella. "A rickety, withered old spinster who frightens me." For that, he got a quick jab in the ribs.

"Well, I never thought a book about something as boring as the funds and business would make me emotional. But when she started in about little Hannah being used and abandoned by that wicked baron…" She patted her huge bosom and dabbed her eyes with one of the handkerchiefs. "It was like she knew my own heart."

"My *acquaintance* had to spend the night in a train station and then had her bag stolen by some vagrant," he explained. "I thought you might be so kind as to assist her toilette, perhaps give her any necessary items that might have been left behind."

What? Left behind? By whom? Before Isabella could say "I would rather wear the same grimy, stinking, wrinkled, clingy chemise and gown for a month than dress in your lover's clean, perfect clothes," Mrs. Perdita clapped her hands and exclaimed, "Why, I hid all of those lovely things you gave Cecelia. I wouldn't let that evil devil woman take those clothes and jewelry after what she did to you." She glanced at Isabella. "Broke my poor boy's heart, she did."

All Isabella's outrage was temporarily suspended as she reeled from the amazing discovery that some woman actually hurt Randall. What woman, well, besides her, would not madly desire him? Surely, she must not have heard Mrs. Perdita correctly. "A lady broke your heart?" she asked him.

He kept his gaze down, not answering.

"That horrid Mr. Harding stole her. No doubt out

of vengeance. But you know what I say, good rid-
dance. A selfish, feeling-less girl she was, but my lord
never saw it—too much in love. Oh, but she'll come
back begging. Mark my words."

So, there was more to his dislike of Harding than
the railroad issue. A woman stood between them. The
viscount kept his eyes safe from Isabella's, his head
slightly bowed. She felt a weakening in her heart for
him, an odd protectiveness for her old enemy. No one
could hurt Randall but her. Everyone else had to love
him. That was the natural order of things.

"But this one…" The housekeeper began circling
Isabella. "She needs some help, I agree, but—" The
woman's hand shot out and patted Isabella's waist.

She jumped back. "Don't touch me!"

"—I'll wager she has a lovely figure underneath
this mess."

Randall winked. "Oh, she does." He picked up his
housekeeper's copy of *Poor to Prosperity*.

"How dare you!" Isabella snatched a newspaper
from the table and threw it at him. He held up her
book, shielding himself from the oncoming paper.
"I'm leaving," she announced. "I would rather buy
clothes from a ragman. And…and…stop reading
that book."

"Why, she's a regular lioness," the housekeeper
cried, unfazed. "Rrwwoer." She giggled. "Just let me
get rid of this unfortunate bonnet and see what can be
done with her mane."

The woman snatched one of Isabella's ribbons and,
in an easy move, untied her hat and pulled it free.
Isabella's rebellious hair, seeing its chance to escape,

leaped from its remaining pins and tumbled around her shoulders.

The housekeeper caught her breath. "Look at those tresses."

"Hand me my hat back, please." Isabella yanked it from Mrs. Perdita and shoved it on her head. "I'm really leaving now!" She stomped to the hall.

"Wait!" Mrs. Perdita chased after her. "I've never seen such lovely, luscious locks. I know *exactly* what to do with them."

Isabella's hand gripped the doorknob. She hesitated. "Y-you do?"

Could the woman really do something with the tangled weeds growing from her head?

"You should wear it high," Mrs. Perdita suggested, letting her hand flow from the top of her head and down her neck. "And let it fall in long tendrils to accent your graceful cheekbones and beautiful lips."

Graceful cheekbones? Beautiful lips? *Is Mrs. Perdita nearly blind too?* "My—my hair doesn't do tendrils or spirals or curls or anything except what you see."

The woman's eyes narrowed. Her high, sweet voice dropped an octave. "It will," she growled, like a general commanding his troops.

Again, Isabella hesitated. If she had any sense, she would shout her outrage at Randall, making a huge scene, reminding him that she was a gently bred woman and he had no right tricking her into his den of *amour*.

But could Mrs. Perdita really make her hair fall in lovely tendrils?

"Very well," she heard herself say. Inside her,

another voice waged war. *I can't believe what you just said. How many servants have tried and failed to subdue your hair?*

"I have a wonderful feeling about this one," the housekeeper called to Lord Randall as she clasped Isabella's hand. "So much better than that dreadful Cecelia. I just need to educate her a bit, and she will suit quite nicely."

"A little taming of the shrew," he replied from the parlor.

"I am not a shrew," Isabella protested, stepping forward so she could get a view of Randall, who was now reclined on the sofa, legs crossed, one hand behind his head, the other holding her book. "And I told you not to read that. Put it down this instant. It's for women."

"But poor Georgina's wayward husband's ship just went down, and she has seven children to feed, including little blind Nellie," he cried. "I must find out how Miss St. Vincent would wisely invest the meager bit of the Lloyds' money. So brilliant and wise, that Miss St. Vincent. You should be more like her! Well, except not rickety and withered."

"Pfff," Mrs. Perdita whispered to Isabella. "Don't listen to his teasing. When I'm done with you, he will do anything you ask, dearie. *Anything.* Just leave your gloves and bonnet down here."

Ten

MRS. PERDITA LED HER TO A CHAMBER ON THE second floor. Still no exotic Arabian drapes or beaded pillows in sight, but there was a large canopy bed covered in a deep burgundy spread. *Is this where Randall "takes" his mistresses?* Involuntarily, the memory of his tongue swirling against hers, his thumb flicking across her wet breast, flared in her imagination. Except this time she was under him, reclining on that bed.

"I just want to remind you that I don't care to be Lord Randall's mistress," she said, more for her own benefit than Mrs. Perdita's.

"Well, you should," the housekeeper replied. "He needs one. Cecelia treated him atrociously. My poor boy is always working late and worried about this country. He is far too serious."

"Serious? Lord Randall?"

Mrs. Perdita flicked her wrist. "Oh, pooh, he will tease like all men, but behind the laughter, he is quite serious, sensitive, and vulnerable. All men are vulnerable creatures, more than women. We are resilient, doing what we must to survive. Read that Miss St. Vincent's book. She understands."

Isabella made a strangled, humming noise. *I can assure you that Miss St. Vincent doesn't understand people at all. And men baffle her, especially your employer. He is the most confusing one of them all.*

"My dear, will you help me?" Mrs. Perdita asked. "My knees are doing so poorly these days. Under the bed is a trunk. If you pull it out, open it, and kindly remove the books on the top—I put them there to trick Cecelia because she was always complaining about Lord Randall reading late into the night. Below them are clothes that you may use. You and Cecelia are almost the same size, but you have more curves. He will like that—something to hold on to in bed." She released a few bubbling giggles as she crossed to the vanity table. She opened the drawer and started pulling out hairpins, brushes, and bottles.

Meanwhile, Isabella was frozen by the bed. She couldn't wear clothes from Randall's former mistress, but she was aching to see how he adorned his lady.

"Well, go ahead, my dear," the housekeeper said.

Isabella obeyed, sliding out the trunk, opening it, and removing books of speeches and old parliamentary sessions. Below the literature lay a silk petticoat trimmed in fine lace. And beneath that, even more silk—exquisitely made gowns in luminous shades of blue and red. She couldn't wear these clothes; aside from the taint of having been worn by an ex-mistress, they were for beautiful ladies, not her. Still, she couldn't contain her curiosity and dug even further, pulling out a lace chemise so fragile and beautiful it looked like it had been created by aesthetically sensitive spiders.

"That's from Brussels," the housekeeper said. "Cecelia never wore it. Complained that it didn't flatter her. But it would look lovely on your curves and ample bosom. Imagine how you could tease and torture him if you tied him to the bedposts and danced before him in that." She emitted a few more giggles.

Isabella didn't understand. Why would she want to tie Randall to a bedpost? Wouldn't that defeat the purpose? How could he possibly kiss her body beneath the lace and do things with his manly part if he were bound?

"Now, come sit and let's style your lovely hair."

Isabella dropped the gown and rushed over, desperate for diversion from the visions of lace and lust. She sat and studied her reflection in the vanity mirror, but didn't see any lovely hair—just her usual recalcitrant mop. Mrs. Perdita splashed something from a blue bottle onto the bristles of a silver brush. "Why don't you remove your glasses and rest your eyes. How they must burn under those heavy lenses."

"I can't see without them."

"Oh, but you don't need to see right now. As you might say to milord in bed, 'just close your eyes, relax, and let me do all the work.'" More giggles. The housekeeper pulled out a long strand of Isabella's hair and brushed it. "Of course, I'm not being wicked when I say it."

Isabella cautiously removed her spectacles, folded them, and set them in her lap. With her outer world a blur, she sank into her mind. What was she doing in a man's pied-à-terre, ogling his ex-mistress's undergarments? She needed to leave immediately. But a lurid desire to know more about this other Randall held her rapt.

"We don't have time to put your hair in papers or heat up the irons, so I'll style it in a nice, easy coiffure that we can use when he has stayed the night, and you must go out the next morning. Just look at your hair now. Even though you two wildly frolicked all night, you don't need to advertise your abandoned lovemaking. You must be more discreet."

"You mean my hair made people think that he and I…that we…you know?"

"Come now, don't be shy. We both know how this works."

One of us doesn't. Nonetheless, Isabella kept her mouth shut, paralyzed in her seat with dark curiosity.

"I don't know what men you've experienced before my boy, but he's not like others. He treats his ladies with respect and tenderness, draping them in jewels and finery." Isabella felt a pin slide along her scalp. "You have to understand his work in Parliament is the most important thing to him. It will keep him away many nights and out the door early in the mornings when you just want another cuddle. He has obligations that you must respect."

Mrs. Perdita was describing a man she didn't know. She made Randall sound responsible and dedicated. Almost attractive—*very attractive*—to her. "I don't…I don't want to be Lord Randall's mistress," she managed weakly.

"Oh, but he likes you. He is just wild for you."

He isn't. He couldn't be. He liked those other women, the lovely, shiny, perfect, younger kind. Again, Isabella's gaze roved to the blurry bed. She remembered listening to his heart under her ear, his comforting rhythm and his strong, warm arm holding her snug in the train station. How easy it would have been to raise her head and kiss his lips, let her fingers undo his shirt. "No!" she cried, trying to hold back the tide of her lurid thoughts.

"Oh, yes," Mrs. Perdita countered. "He doesn't know the extent of his feelings yet. He just has an inkling. All it would take is a little sign from you."

"W-what kind of sign?" *Stop! Stop asking questions. Stop imagining you and Randall and that lacy chemise. Why are you torturing yourself?*

"Well, I'll put out candles tonight and you must don that dear little lace chemise. Then, when you're alone, you can slowly undress him, whispering to him how much you desire him, how wonderful he makes you feel when he holds you. Cecelia never understood that these little things are the most important ones."

"Just talking to him?" Isabella asked in a tight voice, because at this moment she didn't want to talk anymore, but rip off his clothes and "take him." Now.

"Oh, yes, my lord is an emotional, sensitive, and intelligent man. To captivate him, you must seduce his mind and body. Whisper in his ear your wildest fantasies of him as you undo his collar. Remark how powerful he is as you caress his nipples—they are almost as sensitive as yours, my dear."

Isabella released a high squeaking sound, shaking the chair, remembering just how sensitive they felt under his thumb.

The housekeeper gently separated another lock and slid her brush down its length. "Tell him how you imagine pleasuring him every minute of the day just before you unbutton his trousers and take him into your mouth."

Isabella gasped. Did Mrs. Perdita just tell her to put Randall's manly dangling part in her mouth? Judith left out *that* significant part in her lecture.

"And, if you are a good girl, he might just give you a little wiggle back."

"A wiggle?" Judith didn't say anything about a wiggle either. Isabella should have known her companion would get the details wrong.

"You poor dear. Have you never had a proper wiggle?"

Isabella wanted to lie, a breezy "Yes, of course. Proper wiggles every day." Instead, she stammered the sad truth. "No."

Mrs. Perdita sighed a knowing "ohhh," that ran on for several uncomfortable seconds. "Well then," she said. "I shall leave that for Lord Randall to remedy. But mind you, don't wake the neighbors in the height of your wanton climaxes." She broke into her giggles again.

No! Isabella wanted to scream. *Tell me! Enough with this mystery. Can't you see I'm about to come undone? I need to have one of those blessed climaxes.*

"There now, put on your glasses and tell me what you think of your new coiffure."

Isabella cautiously obeyed, suddenly nervous. *You're just going to be disappointed*, she told herself. *You were stupid to agree to this.* But her mane, which just minutes before had resembled a wiry, tangled bush, had been styled into shiny, tame puffs with tiny braids running between. One long lock flowed from the top of her head and curled about on the side of her neck. "That's—that's my hair! My hair did that?"

"Do you like it?"

Never mind the woman's scandalous job in Randall's pied-à-terre, her history, or her shocking conversation; Isabella adored her. "It's gorgeous," she burst. "You have such a talent. Women would pay a great deal for...for your help." Isabella saw the entire plan in her head. "You could be an advisor to ladies on their appearance and other relevant, um, love things."

The woman's face lit up. "Such as I could give them practical advice on how to please and tempt their man." She nudged Isabella and winked. "Or how their man should please them."

"All confidential, of course. While Lord Randall is busy or hasn't a mistress, you could create a nice little nest egg that you could invest in Argus Gas Light at four percent."

Mrs. Perdita clapped and bounced on her feet. "It's just like in that book *Poor to Prosperous*. You must have read it too?"

"I'm—I'm a little familiar with it."

"Hmmm," the woman said, as she put away a hairbrush. "I should do as Miss St. Vincent says and write a plan for my little business; think of my potential customers. Not just mistresses, but married people because they want the most help but are afraid to ask. Many men think the pleasure is all theirs and that their wives should just lie there. Then they wonder why their spouses are angry and frustrated with them all the time. I tell you, you want one of those sweet, angelic wives who adores you? Well, sir, you have to keep her pleasured." She wagged her finger at Isabella. "But you needn't worry about that with Lord Randall. I understand that he knows exactly what to do. Such a thoughtful man."

Isabella's gaze roved over to the bed again, her skin heating at the shocking scenes playing out in her mind—slowly undressing, tying to bedposts for some mysterious reason, and wiggles, whatever they were. Her frustrated body ached. And just a floor below waited a man who knew *exactly what to do* about it.

"Now let's find you something nice to wear," Mrs. Perdita said, but the only thing Isabella wanted to don was that lacy chemise and then tiptoe downstairs. "My dear, root about in that trunk until you find a gown the color of twilight. I shall turn you into a regular moonlight seductress."

Thirty minutes later, the regular moonlight seductress clutched the banister. Her sleeves sat slightly off her shoulders and formed a line that made a dramatic, breath-catching plunge about the bodice. The hard bones of the tiny corset were rigid, holding her waist in tight and pushing her breasts high. A cough or a bit of laughter and her nipples might pop out. Even so, she never felt lovelier in her life. She shivered at what Randall might think or where he might look.

"I'm a moonlight seductress," she reminded herself. Inside, another little voice whispered back, *No, you're*

an idiot. What woman visits a stockbroker in this silly dress?
He will think, "No wonder the addle-brained moonlight
seductress bought fraudulent stock."

∽

Randall lay on the sofa reading Isabella's book. Her
volume wasn't weighed down with the usual moral
preaching that accompanied ladies' writings. After
wading through the bombastic stories, he concluded
that the solutions were as straightforward and analyti-
cal as Isabella herself. He enjoyed basking in the landscape of her mind, so different from his. His brain was
like a cluttered attic, everything shoved together with
no rhyme or reason, from which he could pull out
dazzling words and shiny objects as needed to persuade
an audience. She used cool, thoughtful logic, taking in
a situation, stripping it to essentials, and applying that
thing he feared most at Cambridge: math. What he
called "how things were," she called "normal distribu-
tion." What he called "people's choices," she called
"the unknown factors." How different they were. She
needed time and distance to shear off all the pesky
human sentiment and nuances that confounded her
in order to find the numbers and patterns underneath.
Meanwhile, he loved swimming in the swirling,
irrational seas of emotion and passion, seeing no order
or meaning beneath anything. When things got too
quiet or unsure, he needed those pesky, unpredictable
people around him and to make a huge wave.

Like now.

And unlike Isabella, he hated to be alone, so he took
advantage of her weaknesses: her inability to think on

her feet and decipher people's emotions. What he was doing was selfish. He couldn't take her as a mistress, and he surely couldn't marry her, so why had he kissed her? Why did he want her to sleep against him? Why did he bring her to his flat where he kept his mistresses? Was he addled with unacknowledged passion and desire for her? Or desperate for female contact? Or just scared and wanting comfort—any comfort? For a man with a reputation for reading people, he didn't understand his own mind. All he knew was that she had been gone for over forty-five minutes and he was feeling restless.

He turned the page and tried to settle back into the book, but his thoughts kept drifting to the feel of her breast under his hand, her shuddering breath, and how she pressed her pelvis against his. He was growing hard just thinking about her. Dammit! *Look at the boring numbers in the book!*

"Randall," he heard her whisper. His head jerked up, but all he saw was an empty threshold. His heart pounded. In a swish of blue, the woman whom he had known for a good majority of his life now appeared like a stunning, beautiful stranger before him. Only her spectacles were reminders of his old enemy.

She clasped and unclasped her hands, smoothed her skirt which didn't need it, fingered the lock of hair curling along the side of her neck, then clasped her hands again. She blushed all the while, her face, with its majestic cheekbones and generous lips, turning a lovely rose color. His Mr. Headsmith grew so hard that it burned. He yanked the blanket from the back of the sofa to cover himself.

For several awkward and painful seconds, they didn't talk. Her flush deepened, spreading down her neck and spilling onto her chest. "W-well, how do I look?" she finally stammered.

"Well enough." Anger seeped in as he studied her lovely breasts. "You look well." He remembered that blue dress from before—something about Cecelia calling the gown plain—except on Isabella it was almost indecent. The color highlighted her alabaster skin and the cut draped on the curves of her body. *Damn Mrs. Perdita!*

She blinked. "Well enough? That's the best you can say?" Anger tightened her lovely features. "Not transcendent or…or…sublime, ravishing, unparalleled beauty, or your usual drivel?"

"You don't look like yourself," he accused. "You've changed." He wanted back the old Isabella of the flying-loose hair, the tumbling glasses, and the frumpy clothes. After last night, he knew she was a ravishing, sublime, unparalleled beauty, but he didn't want everyone else in the world to know it. She was his secret. A voice inside him, probably emitting from the general region of his rock-hard cock, growled, *You are mine.*

"But that's how I want to look, not like me."

"Why not? You're…" He paused. What was he going to say? *You're awkward, your hair is a rat's nest, your dresses would make a Parisian lady die from horror… and that's what I adore about you?*

So they both waited in that unrelenting, raw silence, until she caved. "I'm going to see my stockbroker," she said, and spun on her heel.

He bolted up from the sofa, erection and all. "You may not visit a man alone." He thundered like some angry father.

She pivoted and stared at him, eyes hot, her mouth forming an outraged *O*.

"It will damage your reputation," he choked. And wasn't he the one who was excellent at thinking on his feet?

"It would be rather shocking, wouldn't it?" she replied in a low, smooth voice that oozed of sarcasm. "Visiting a gentleman's place of business is almost as bad as visiting his pied-à-terre alone and wearing his ex-mistress's clothes."

"This is different! We are in a crisis. And you—you can't leave me."

She threw up her arms. The sound of a ripping seam echoed in the hall. "I can't exactly bring Lord Randall in tow either. I must think of my reputation."

"Well, then I'm your long-lost Irish cousin, Mr. O'Randy," he said, affecting an Irish brogue through his clenched teeth. "Fresh from Dublin."

"Don't you dare!" She reached for her gloves, which were resting on the table by the door. She jammed them on her hands, and flexed and then balled her fingers. "You are staying here."

He snatched his gloves and shoved them on before her face. "You are not going out alone."

She bumped him with her hip, pushing him out of the way of the mirror, and arranged the ribbons of the tiny bonnet on her head. "I won't be alone. I have an appointment with my stockbroker. He's a sensible young man."

Young man! Randall grabbed his hat, stepped in front of her, and watched her angry, pinched features in the mirror as he donned his hat, cocking the brim at an angle and then thumping it.

"You are behaving like a spoiled child," she hissed. "What is wrong with you?"

"My future is at stake, and you think I'm just going to lie about here doing nothing." *And I'm not letting you see a young man alone in that dress.*

She stepped around him, putting her face just mere inches from the mirror, and patted the netting of her bonnet. "Well, it's too bad that your mistress left you. Then you could lie about doing…doing whatever you *do* with your mistress." She hiked the edge of her mouth, half flirting, half challenging. When did she learn that seasoned move? "W-which obviously wasn't that good, else she might still be here."

That did it! This inexperienced spinster didn't question his manhood. He seized her by the shoulders, lowered his head until his hot eyes were level with her flaming dagger ones. "I assure you that whatever I do, I do better than any man in London," he growled. "It's just too bad that no man liked you enough to do it to you."

She pressed her palms to his chest and shoved. "You certainly liked me enough yesterday when you did…that…that *thing*!"

"'Thing'? You mean when I was fondling your breasts and you cried, 'Don't stop, Randall. It feels so amazing'? Because obviously *that thing* I did was good enough for you." He leaned closer, his lips almost on hers, her intoxicating jasmine and orange scent engulfing him. "And, love, that was just the very beginning. You only think you were begging then. I can show you pleasure that your virgin body never knew existed." His anger rose as did his hard cock. Was it anger? Or frustration because, forget railroads, Parliament, lying bank partners, and political careers, he wanted to do nothing more in his life than to take her on the floor in a frenzy of lovemaking? And he couldn't. He wouldn't. "But you will never know that thing I do," he hissed. "You will never be my mistress and certainly you will never ever be my wife!" The words cut like a sword blade he had thrust in his own heart.

"Your wife? Your mistress?" she echoed, her features contorted with horror at the thought of sharing her life with him. "Not while there are perfectly good trains to throw myself in front of! Fine India teas to be doused with hemlock! Or…or…" Her face softened as a slow, devilish smile curved her angelic lips—one worthy of, well, him. "You know, Mr. O'Randy, I think this could be a grand idea," she said coolly. "But why don't you put on your shabby brown coat. The stockbroker knows that my Irish mother, and my father, for that matter, came from very modest means."

Eleven

IN THE HACKNEY DRIVE TO THE STOCKBROKER, Randall watched Isabella as she stared out the window, refusing to acknowledge his presence. The sunlight brightened the lenses of her spectacles; beneath them, her eyes were large and hurt, but her jaw was clenched and determined. He felt ashamed of his little tantrum in the hall. Why didn't he just tell her the truth, that she was beautiful? He didn't want her to be ravishing or a resplendent vision of paradise. He didn't want everyone to know her secret. Because if they did…

The truth hit him hard in the belly: Someone might take her away just as he needed his comfortable, familiar Isabella.

"Aye, you're a pretty lass," he said in an obnoxious Irish accent, trying to melt her icy expression. *Look at me! Just look at me! My world is falling apart, and if you look at me, you will make it all better.*

She didn't respond.

"Mother Mary, it's good that your faithful, devoted cousin Mr. O'Randy is watchin' out fer ya."

Nothing.

"Are you ever going to talk to your old cousin O'Randy again?"

She closed her eyes and then opened them.

He could always get a rise out of her. Her silence was driving him wild—that and the little piece of blue thread resting on her left breast, the fallen wisp of hair curling along the line of her cheekbone, and her subtle scent of jasmine and orange. What had he done, putting her in Mrs. Perdita's powers?

When the carriage stopped and the driver opened the door, she jumped down without his assistance. She reached into a beaded reticule and gave the driver some coins, ignoring Randall's pleas that he pay the man. By the time Randall's feet hit the street, she was already across the walk by a large, carved-wood door with a brass plaque that read "Harker and Son."

The driver flipped his shillings in the air, shaking his head as he watched the ruffles on the back of her dress swish with her motion. He released a soft, admiring whistle and winked at Randall. "Pretty little bit of frock, that one."

"Keep your damn eyes to yourself." Randall's hands balled into fists. "Or I'll permanently close them." He hurried to catch up with Isabella before she could reach her young stockbroker and have him fall madly in love with her.

She pulled the doorbell and then turned to Randall. "Just remember, dear cousin O'Randy, the Harkers are like my family. So *I* do the talking this time."

"Just don't mention your promising openings."

Scientists had yet to measure something as hot as the glare she gave him.

The door opened, revealing a young man in a neat dark suit with hair that spiked about his part. He emitted a jittery energy as of a nervous rabbit that had just downed four pots of black tea.

Isabella smiled. "Hello, I'm Miss St. Vincent."

"Miss St. Vincent!" The clerk bowed three times in rapid succession, accidently hitting Isabella's hand. "I'm so sorry!" Terror tightened his features as if he had struck Queen Victoria herself. "I didn't mean... I'm terribly sorry. Terribly sorry."

"It is well," she said calmly. "May I come in?"

"Come in? Yes, of course, of course." The man leaped from the door. "Please, sit down. Shall I produce some tea? No, wine! Our finest red, of course. Will you take biscuits or sandwiches? Do make yourself comfortable on the sofa. Do you require extra pillows? Shall I stoke the fire? Are you cold? Are you warm?"

She blinked, flustered by the attention. "I'm well. I need nothing but to speak with Mr. Harker. I hope I'm not disturbing him."

"Oh no, you can never disturb him. Never!" The clerk bolted from the room, sprinting down a corridor.

"Aye, they certainly admire you here, dearie," Mr. Randy said in his Irish brogue. "Regular royalty, you are."

She didn't respond but picked up the journal *Funds and Figures Relating to the Commerce of Great Britain* from a side table, sat down on one of the hard chairs, and began studying the pages filled with numbers.

Randall scratched beneath his cravat, feeling edgy in the stockbroker's parlor. There were no books, no knickknacks, just neatly spaced, plain blue chairs. Charts with stock numbers and lines sloping upward, maps of rail lines, and decorative stock certificates hung on the walls, all evenly distributed and aligned. He glanced at Isabella. She thumbed through the journal pages, obviously at ease in the room of ninety-degree angles and hard lines.

"I am profoundly sorry that I must attend to this urgent family matter," a rich, male voice boomed down the corridor. "A very serious family matter, indeed. May I call tomorrow to finish our discussion of foreign mortgage bonds?"

Two men strode into the room.

Randall snatched up a neatly folded newspaper and concealed his face from a Whig leader who was being escorted by a serious, honey-haired gentleman.

He listened to exchanges of pleasantries, including the opposition leader's praise of the stockbroker's financial prowess. "Good day then, Mr. Harker." The door closed. Randall tentatively lowered his paper and studied the man who was like family to Isabella.

He was medium height, maybe a year or two older than Isabella. He possessed the soft face of one who enjoyed too much butter and bread, but his jaw was hard. His receding hair was neatly barbered and brushed. His sharp eyes were well lashed and his lips a little on the thin side. Had Randall met the man in a club or boxing match, Randall would have described him as a "fine old chap." But under the circumstances, he hated him on a primitive, tribal, gut level, especially the way his gaze traveled from Isabella's face to her breasts—those skinny lips of his parting and an awe-like light infusing his face, as if he were gazing upon a Michelangelo or a Da Vinci.

"Miss St. Vincent, you've changed," he stammered. "Y-you are beautiful." He inflected the last word like a question. For a moment, he stood, fixed to the spot, staring like a slack-jawed moonling. Then he shook his head as though awakening from a dream—a dream of Isabella's lush bosom. "I meant to say you've always been beautiful, but today you are gorgeous, lovely, ravishing. I grapple with words to express your radiance."

Isabella blushed, heightening that radiance.

Gorgeous, lovely, ravishing—the trite compliments Randall should have said at his apartment when all he could muster was a "well enough." Randall despised the man even more. It was easier than despising himself.

"Aye, she's a vision of luscious heaven, she is," he said in his Irish brogue, trying to turn her smile in his direction. He received a frown for his efforts. He tried again. "A beauty unrivaled by angels."

"I'm sorry," Mr. Harker said, offering up his hand for shaking. "I don't think we are acquainted."

Randall opened his mouth, ready to elevate his status from watchful Irish cousin to violently protective Irish suitor when Isabella cut in. "Oh, this is my footman, O'Randy." Her voice was all honey as she lifted an eyebrow over the rim of her glasses. "Remember what I said about not talking." She plucked off her gloves and slapped him on the chest with them. "And do hold these."

So, I'm the footman, he thought, taking the gloves.

That's our game. He gazed at Harker, who was sneaking furtive glances at Isabella's breasts, and a slow, unamused smile spread over Randall's lips. *Very well, then.*

"Ey, sorry, miss," he said. "I keep forgetting how you tell me not to ruin the mood by a-talkin." He nodded at the stockbroker. "I'm just supposed to stay silent and handle her. I'm good at that. That's why she hired me."

Isabella's hot eyes could have melted huge swaths of Greenland.

The stockbroker wrapped Isabella's hand in the crook of his elbow, steering her toward the corridor.

"I do hope I haven't interrupted you," she stammered. "If you need to see to a family matter—"

"My dear, you *are* my serious family matter," Harker replied in a dusky tone better suited for a bedchamber than a place of business. "In fact, my last client can hardly be upset. I made him a great deal of money after you tipped me off about the Wilson Insurance futures. Just brilliant. Have…have you had any other insights?"

Get your own ideas, Randall wanted to spit as he trailed behind them. *Stop using Isabella's.*

Harker led them to a paneled office that shared the obsessive symmetrical motif of the front parlor. More rail maps, charts, and stock certificates adorned the walls. On the left, old-fashioned pane windows gave a fine view of the building across the street. Unlike the parlor, this room contained books—all the same height and color, of course—neatly placed in twin bookshelves. A massive oak desk jutted out into the room, decorated by a lonely inkwell. Before the desk stood two parallel leather chairs, both with folded blue blankets draped on the backs. Only the tiny flames, dancing in the grate, escaped the repressive precision of the room. Randall tugged at his cravat; the stark order seemed to be sucking up all the air.

"Ah, you've moved into your father's office." A sad smile curved Isabella's lips. "I remember this chamber so well," she said in a soft, faraway voice. "I used to play with my dolls under the chairs while our fathers talked."

"I think it's precious how little girls take care of dolls, one day replacing them with their own adorable babies," Harker said. But if Randall were translating the true meaning it would be: *Let's make our own adorable babies on the desk. I'll just move that inkwell twelve exact inches to the left.*

"Oh no," she replied, his darling, ravishing lady ever oblivious to subtext. "My favorite doll would own the mill, and all the other dolls would work for her."

Randall laughed into his balled fist.

Harker shot him a nasty glance. "I think you were supposed to remain silent." Then he clasped her hands and squeezed. "I know you miss your father terribly." His eyes grew large and puppylike. "I certainly do. What a brilliant man."

"I wish he were here," she whispered, gently trying to extract herself from his grasp. Randall knew both her emotions and the stockbroker were too close for comfort.

"Well, I'm here for you now." The stockbroker released her hands only to wrap his arm around her, taking a little peek at her chest in the process. *Dammit!* Randall didn't miss the rogue's attempts at ye old seduce-her-with-compassion ploy, mentioning her deceased father to break her down and then moving in for the romantic kill. Randall acted quickly.

"Just let me pull up this nice chair fer ya, Miss St. Vincent." He yanked a chair over and shoved it under her knees. She fell onto the cushion and out of Harker's captivity.

"What are you doing?" she demanded.

"Aye, it's a bit drafty in here," Randall said. "Why don't I just put this blanket around your shoulders, all snug-like. You know how *we*, er, *you* like to cuddle in a warm blanket." In a flamboyant motion, he flung the blanket in the air above her, letting it fall over her shoulders. He patted it in place, making sure to hide her bosom from Harker's further perusal. For his efforts, he received a hard, discreet swat.

"Well, I'll just go and a-stoke the fire for you." Randall swaggered over to the grate and hefted the poker. "Oh, what a nice poker you have here." He jabbed it in the air, as if he were fencing. "You could really hurt someone with it if you weren't careful."

"I recall that the lady asked you not to talk." Harker's voice was hard as flint and deep with authority to intimidate a brazen servant.

What the hell are you doing, Randall? Have you lost all reason? This man is not your enemy. Don't you have bigger issues to be concerned about? Such as your career? Your integrity and honor and family name? Just keep quiet.

He hadn't had a drop of alcohol since leaving the house party, but Randall felt drunk. His logical mind was a blurry haze. The only thing he knew with certainty was if Harker snuck another glance at Isabella's body, this red-hot poker was going up the man's arse. And Randall would remember not to say a word in the process.

"What brings you to my office, my dear?" The stockbroker pulled up the chair beside hers, letting his fingers dangle on her knuckles. "You know you can trust me with anything that is worrying you." The man lowered his voice. "Anything."

She gazed down, silent for several long seconds, before whispering, "I'm afraid."

Just great. Randall stirred the coals, sending the sparks flying. *Now she's submissive and shy, so the stockbroker bumhole can be manly and protective.* And why couldn't she ever be submissive and shy around him or tell him when she's afraid?

"I'm afraid that my bank may have purchased fraudulent stock in Merckler Metalworks." She shifted, causing the blanket to slip off a creamy shoulder. "Can you please tell me more about the duplicate stock numbers that you found?"

Harker shrugged. "My father had recorded the same certificate numbers for a client who bought his shares years ago and has since held them."

She pressed her fingers into the bridge of her nose and squeezed her eyes shut.

"Oh, my darling, don't cry." The stockbroker moved to take her into his arms. Randall poised his poker.

"For heaven's sake, I'm not crying," she said. "Why would I cry?" She rose, slipped from Harker's hold, and set herself away from the men. Head slightly bowed and hands clasped behind her back, she began to pace. "Do you know anything else?"

"I spoke to some jobbers—discreetly, as you requested," Harker answered. "No one had received such a report as the one you had sent me. The only thing I can tell you is that Mr. Merckler, the company founder and majority shareholder, had passed several months shortly after modernizing his factory. His wife inherited his share of the stock and a new manager was appointed."

She shook her head. "I knew about Mr. Merckler's death. I researched the company behind my new bank partner's back. I shouldn't admit that, but I would never have allowed my bank to make such a large purchase had I not." She gazed at a small spot on the far wall. "Merckler had been around for years giving staid, steady payouts. With the recent modernization, it seemed like a wonderful opportunity. I should have seen something amiss, some tiny detail. My father would have caught it."

"Miss Isabella, you're just a woman," Harker said soothingly. "Don't distress yourself."

"Yes, I'm just a woman—a spinster. I was blinded by my affections for this bank partner. And now, having saddled my father's bank with false stock, he has fled the village." She covered her face with her hands.

"Some rascal hurt you!" The stockbroker rushed to her side. "I shall not stand for it." He wrapped her in his embrace.

Randall swiped his poker, knocking off the clock on the mantel, sending it shattering to the floor. "Oh,

Mary, mother of God, look what a mess I made with this hot, hard poker."

"Just put it down, stand in the corner, and don't touch anything," Harker thundered.

"Don't be so harsh." Isabella escaped the man's grasp, leaping in front of Randall. "He's–he's rather dull-witted."

"You should not stand for such incompetence," the stockbroker said, now using his commanding tone on her. "You let him go immediately."

Her jaw dropped. "He is my affair, not yours!"

"That's right, sir," Randall affirmed. "I'm her affair."

She paused for a moment, then slapped her fore-head. "I didn't mean an *affaire* like he's my…my French love pet."

Harker blinked. "French love pet?"

"I personally prefer *footman d'amour*," Randall said.

"I told you to be quiet!" She jammed her index finger at him. "You'll be lucky to be footman d'rubbish heap if there is a run on the bank." She closed her eyes and breathed in and out several times before turning back to Harker. "I understand that my bank partner was in debt. He had lost heavily in cards at a place called the Golden Tyger. Do you know of this club?"

"That is a den of serious, high-stakes gamblers. In fact, several former jobbers haunt the tables. It's a deadly place for a novice player."

"I'll wager there are more people involved than just our bank partner," she said. "There had to be a printing press, a fabricated report. After all, why would any metalwork factory need to sell false stocks when people are building railroads all over the world?" She paused. "Something larger is at work here."

Perhaps a towering, bald railroad baron with a vendetta?

"What fine mess have I gotten my father's bank in?"

"What you need is a man to guide you," Harker assured her. The look in his eye, if translated, would be, "I am that man, just let me guide you to my bedchamber." Harker wrapped his paws around her again. Randall reached for his trusty poker. A bloody, one-sided altercation was about to commence when the door swung open and a kindly faced lady with a headful of upswept gray hair popped in.

She waved a Wollstonecraft Society pendant. "Miss St. Vincent, you'll never guess! I've bought tickets to your speech."

"Mama!" The stockbroker leaped away from Isabella.

"My, you have changed," the woman told Isabella. "Very elegant. I simply love what you're doing with your coiffure." She leaned in to whisper behind her hand. "You must tell me who you are using." Before Isabella could answer, the woman continued. "May I steal you away for just a few minutes? I have a dozen copies of your book, and I would adore if you could sign them. You know, I'm the envy of my friends because I know you."

"Of course." Isabella's lips lifted into a pained, stiff smile. Randall had never known a woman who shied away from attention as much as she did. As she followed Mrs. Harker out, she flashed Randall a pointed glare that said "If you say one word, I will kill you in a most torturous and barbaric manner. Don't think I won't."

So he and that scoundrel stockbroker were left alone. Randall hung about the corner, trying to be the proper servant and not act on his urge to taunt Harker. He would hate for Isabella to return and find her trusted stockbroker sporting a poker up his broadside.

But Harker started it. "Footman *d'amour*." He gave a patronizing chuckle.

"I'm very skilled at my job, sir."

"No, you're a pathetic, empty-headed, pretty chap. I find your jealousy of me amusing." Harker sat behind his desk, leaned back in his chair, and rested his hands on his soft belly. "Do you know what I am?"

A foolish cove who is about to eat his own bollocks for dinner?

"A successful gentleman. You're just a toy. When she's done playing with you, she'll push you aside. She is not like other ladies. You know nothing of her mind."

"Aye, you certainly do, sir. I'll wager you can finance this fine office because Miss St. Vincent tips you off about the market."

The man's teeth glinted below his tight upper lip. "Don't get too comfortable, O'Randy. A certain future event is going to change your employment."

"Love her, do you?"

The man gazed out the window in a romantic, yearning fashion. "Yes," he said quietly.

"Odd, that, seeing how you had all these years to ask her for her hand." Randall shrugged. "Maybe it was because she came waltzing in today in a low-cut gown. Now you love her for more than her money but her body as well. I'm rather romantic. I love her for her brilliant mind and kind heart." His words were meant to be a nasty joke, something to belittle Harker's shallow marital ambitions. But when "love" and "heart" and "mind" flowed from his mouth, their sound echoing back in his ears, his fears put into words, a deep, a knowing peace washed over his own heart.

Oh God!

Randall turned stark silent as Harker rambled on with his insults. The man's jabs didn't make a dent in Randall's anxious thoughts. Had he really done it? Had he fallen in love with Isabella? No, no, it was because of their tense situation. That was all. He could never truly love Isabella. He just wanted her luscious body in the most obsessive, desperate way. It was only lust, simply lust that he would never act upon. It was against all that was right. She was like a sister—one that he never liked. It felt incestuous or just very, very wrong, like mating exotic zebras and dull stock horses—possible but horrible.

At that moment, the object of his obsessive lust reentered. The air crackled with tension, and even typically oblivious Isabella perceived it. She looked from Randall to Harker and back to Randall. "What have you done?"

"Nothing," Harker answered for him. "I'm just teaching O'Randy how to behave around his betters."

Then she did something that warmed Randall's heart and jeopardized his entire it-was-only-lust theory: she giggled.

Twelve

THIRTY MINUTES LATER, ISABELLA STRUGGLED TO disentangle herself from Harker. She just wanted to be alone to digest all that she had learned, but the stockbroker kept her hand captured, asking her opinion about different funds. Meanwhile, Randall continued his stupid act, stomping about the room with a poker, ignoring her injunction not to speak and uttering embarrassing things such as "Isn't it time for your afternoon tea and foot rub?" She pretended to ignore him, keeping her lips curled in some semblance of a smile, patiently answering Harker's numerous questions, all the while stifling her desire to grab Randall's poker and beat him with it, screaming, "For God's sake, can you behave for once!" Making him her footman was to have been such sweet revenge for the pregnancy episode and saying she only looked "well enough," but that slippery snake had turned it against her. No telling what her stockbroker was thinking.

Finally, when she managed to free herself, she stomped from the office, leaving her "footman" behind. Despite her desire for him just hours before and the night she had passed cuddled in his embrace, at that moment she wouldn't have cared if he fell off the earth. She was too agitated to hail a hackney, so she chose to walk and think about this Merckler Metalworks problem. She didn't get too far before Randall caught up with her like an unwanted, noisy fly that eluded a swatter.

"Footman *d'amour!*" she thundered. "I'm trying to determine why we are being ruined and you're the footman *d'amour*. How very helpful of you. You know what? I'll save the bank, and you can just continue diddling about as you usually do."

"I had to do something or else Harker would have devoured you."

"Devoured me? No doubt he is angry that I've gotten him involved in our problems."

"Angry? You think that was anger?"

She stopped. Randall was giving her a look. What did it mean? Was he making fun of her or being serious? "I guess," she ventured.

"Love, Harker was ready to get on his knee, propose, and then go straight to the honeymoon right there on the desk without the necessary paperwork."

"You think Mr. Harker was attracted to—to *me*?" A respectable man liked her! What was she doing wasting time arguing with Randall the footman? She spun on her heel, ready to beeline across the muddy street back to her stockbroker's office.

Randal seized her wrist. "Where are you going?"

"A man who possesses his wits, is somewhat attractive, and under the age of forty likes me. Me!"

He held tight, letting her dangle off the edge of the walk. "Are you that desperate?"

"Yes, Randall, I am." She writhed in his grasp, trying to free herself. "I figure if you can marry for money to get out of this little financial mess, then so can I!"

He tugged her arm, sending her careening into him. Despite the people passing, he held her shoulders, peering into her face. "He doesn't want you for you. He spent the entire time sneaking peeks at your brea— bosom and stealing all your good investment ideas."

"I perceive no problem if there is a wedding ring in the offering."

"Please don't bite my head off if I dare point out that you really don't make the best decisions with regard to men. For example, your last light o' love may just land you and your customers in the poorhouse. All the while, he's playing Who's Papa's Naughty Pussycat on some beach in France."

Touché. She blew out her breath and hung her head. "You're right."

"I'm glad that you can finally admit it so freely."

Oh, he has to get in every last little jab. She was about to fire back a nasty retort when she saw two small girls, no more than four and six, huddled together in a torn gray blanket under a tea shop window. Their eyes were large in their bony, dirt-smeared faces. Her heart hurt for them. Suddenly, her problems came into focus. Soon her situation wouldn't be about banter and besting Randall, but about true poverty and desperation. She reached into her reticule and fished out two sovereigns.

Randall squatted on the pavement, talking kindly to the children.

"Do you have any parents?" he asked.

The older one shook her head.

"There is a kindly orphanage on Tottenham Court Road," he said. "It's beside a shop with large yellow-and-red parasols open in the window. You can eat there, get medicine, and learn a trade." He drew a card from his pocket. "Give them this and tell them to take you in. I'm a patron."

The older girl took the card, turning it over and over, clearly unable to read the gold writing. "Thank you, sir," she said in a thick Irish accent, and then nodded to Isabella, accepting her offered coins. "Thank you, miss. God bless you." The older girl helped the younger one up and they hurried down the street, their shoes splitting from where they had outgrown them. Isabella said a small, silent prayer for them.

She studied the viscount. His jaw was set, all the light gone from his beautiful eyes. She regretted every mean thought of wanting to beat him with a poker and then having him drop off the earth. All she could think was that this Cecelia lady was touched in the head. "I—I didn't know you were a patron of an orphanage." She was learning about so many hidden aspects to a man she thought she knew.

He shrugged. "Too many poor Irish orphans. Innocent children shouldn't suffer. It's heartbreaking."

Her throat burned. She didn't know what to say. As embarrassing as it was, she'd felt more comfortable having him walk into her bath than she did at this moment, with his compassionate heart exposed. He remained still, staring after the children. She could see the muscles around his Adam's apple contract as he swallowed. What was he thinking? She wished she knew his mind…his heart.

Then he jammed his hands into his pockets and started walking again.

She hurried to catch up. She wanted to say something comforting, but she didn't know the right words. In the end, all that popped out was the stupidly mundane "I'm going to check into my hotel, and then we can go to the Golden Tyger tonight."

He whistled and shook his head. "Oh, no, no, *me*. You're not going near the Golden Tyger. It's full of high-flying gamblers and cardsharps."

"But—but you said that we were in this together, that I couldn't leave you. Well, you can't leave me either. I have more at stake than you anyway. And I'm great at cards."

"It's not a place for ladies…just courtesans and mistresses."

"Then I can be your mistress," she said without thinking.

He halted and stared at her, one disbelieving brow raised. Did she really just offer to be his mistress?

"I m-meant for an evening. J-just pretend. As Izzy May."

"I don't think so," he said quietly. "I have to be Lord Randall tonight."

Her heart felt as if he had kicked it. He didn't want her? He had rejected her? Then slowly, the painful truth dawned. "Oh, I see," she began slowly. "I can be your odd pregnant sister, your haggard wife, and your promiscuous employer, but I can't be your mistress. When you're Lord Randall, you're embarrassed to be seen with me. That's it, isn't it?"

"What! Of course not."

"You're worried that I'll humiliate you because I'm clumsy and homely and old, and I'll say something odd."

"That has nothing to do with it."

"I'm too ugly to be your mistress. Admit it!"

"Goddammit, woman." He seized her arm and yanked her down a narrow walking path leading to a stone churchyard. An elderly vicar, dressed in black, was stooped over, watering puny shrubs that appeared to be growing from the pavement.

"Why are you doing this to me?" Randall demanded of her, shaking his hands before his face. "Why do you want to drive me insane?"

Because you don't want me, she almost blurted. Never mind that *she* didn't want *him*…or did she? "You know I play cards better than you," she stammered. "Harker said the Golden Tyger was a den of serious, high-stakes gamblers. And remember when we were children? You always gambled away your Christmas money to me."

The vicar's head shot up.

"I'll just be a random courtesan," she concluded. "My father's bank is on the line. I can't let you go alone. You'll get fleeced. You can pretend not to know me. We won't even look at each other."

"No! I want you to be my mistress but…" He growled. "I want you… Dammit!" He released a

deep, guttural groan that echoed off the brick buildings. "But it's not safe. Will you listen to me? For once
in your stubborn life?"

"But you will be there. I may be confused in these
matters but…" She paused, eyeing the curious vicar.
She leaned in and lowered her voice. "As your mistress, aren't I under your protection? Or maybe you
can't protect me?"

"Oh, that's it!" he shouted. "Enough. You want
to be my mistress? Just capital! You're my mistress."
He turned to the clergyman. "Do you see this addled,
hardheaded, beautiful woman?" he said, pointing to
her. "Well, she's my mistress." The shocked vicar cradled his watering pot to this chest and hurried inside.

"Are you happy?" Randall asked her. The well-
shaped finger that he had used to point now wagged
before her nose. "And as my mistress, I expect you to
do what I say. Now I'll take you to your hotel room."

She gasped. "I—I said it was for pretend! I'm not
really your mistress in that way!" But she couldn't
deny the tingle the thought elicited.

He stepped closer, putting his chest a hairsbreadth
from her breasts. Her rebellious nipples hardened and
strained against her corset, wanting to feel his touch
again. With the backs of his fingers, he caressed her
jaw. "Come," he said in a low voice that was rough
around the edges. "Don't you think we ought to
practice for realism?"

She swallowed, lost in the power of his vivid,
piercing eyes. In her mind, she returned to the bathing episode, his thumb flicking across her nipple, his
dangly part hard and pressing against her bare thighs.

She wondered what he looked like beneath his clothes. Was his body as handsome and mesmerizing as his face? It wasn't fair that he should get to see her au naturel and not give her a tiny peek at what was beneath that bulge in his trousers. "Well, p-perhaps a little…you know, like last night m-maybe."

"Oh, Isabella, Isabella, Isabella." He leaned his head on her shoulder. "You can't comprehend when I'm joking, can you, love? I'm sorry. I was just going to escort you to your hotel. But if you want me to—"

"You were joking!" She jumped. "You…you trapped me into saying that." She pressed her hand to her mouth, feeling like she would burn to death from the inside out. "I'm so embarrassed."

She sprinted through the narrow lane and into the jostling street. As much as she adored the gown Mrs. Perdita had lent her, it was not ideal for running. Her breasts threatened to bounce out of the top at the same time her lungs were being squeezed. Randall caught up in a matter of seconds and grabbed her arm.

"Just leave me alone," she yelled, yanking free.

"Where are you going?"

"Away from you!"

She frantically waved her hand at an empty hackney, but it just drove by. "I'm right here!" she shouted after the driver. "How could you not see me? Ugh! Never mind."

She gazed up at the rooftops to determine her location from the skyline. She was just a few blocks from the hotel she used when she came to London. "I'm going to the Copenhagen," she told Randall.

"Without your escort. I'll meet you at the Golden Tyger tonight."

"The Copenhagen is too far from me. We might need to exchange information. There is a pleasant, *respectable* inn near my flat. Then I can come and escort you to the Golden Tyger. After all, you are my pretend mistress. It would look odd if I let you arrive alone."

She considered. He had valid points. She hated when he had valid points. "This had better not be some horrible hotel of ill repute where you put your extra mistresses," she finally conceded.

"Extra mistresses? Oh no, I keep them at the Copenhagen."

❧

Isabella watched Randall stand on the edge of the walk, casually flick his hand, and a hackney came to a dead halt in the middle of the street. Once in the carriage, they sat beside each other, quiet. Despite her self-admonishment of the seriousness of their desperate situation and the lingering embarrassment of agreeing to practice being his mistress, her body tingled away and her mind lit up with enticing images of what being Randall's real paramour might have entailed. And just exactly what was a "proper wiggle"? *Do you think this might be why your bank could fail? You're in the struggle of your life and all you can think about is naked men and wiggles.*

The inn was around the corner and down the block from Randall's flat. She asked him to wait outside while she registered as Izzy May for fear of her real name being recognized, and requested that a maid be sent to her room in fifteen minutes to help her out of her clothes. Then she walked outside to meet Randall. He was leaning against the black railing, hat low, arms crossed, his muscles bulging through the sleeves of his ugly brown coat. He appeared to be lost in thought, gazing, unfocused, at a spot on the pavement. She paused and just observed him. What was he thinking about? Who occupied his thoughts? How did he spend his days? Who was this man she had known most of her life?

He cocked his head. "Well, was it a sordid den of deprivation?" he asked her.

"It's quite nice."

"And you told me that you didn't trust me." He made a clicking sound with his tongue as he retied her bonnet, securing it tightly under her chin. "Why don't I fetch you around seven o'clock?"

"Shouldn't I see Mrs. Perdita first, perhaps put on something different?"

He waved his hand. "But I adore what you're wearing."

"That's *not* what you said earlier," she reminded him. "You said it was merely 'well enough.'"

"Well enough for my mistress. Perhaps I was taken aback at seeing my old enemy dressed in my ex-lover's clothes."

"I know they looked better on her." She smoothed the skirt. "No doubt your mistresses are the most beautiful ladies in London."

He didn't respond but studied her with a dark, undecipherable light in his eyes that elicited another cursed tingle.

"It's only for one evening," she stammered. "Then you can say that you left me and that I pleaded for you not to go in some melodramatic fashion."

"Very well, you're my mistress for an evening, and then I'll break your heart in a bombastic Gothic manner." He bowed. "We have a plan. Until seven, then. Try to relax." He took her hand and kissed it, his lips tickling her skin. If he could just trail that kiss up her arm, maybe detour across her breasts, up her chin, and to her lips.

"Mmmm, good-bye," she whispered.

He nodded and started to stride away. After a few yards, he turned and walked backward, keeping his gaze fixed on hers. When he reached the corner, he waved and disappeared behind the brown town houses.

She remained, staring at the space he'd vacated. A lonely, overwhelming feeling engulfed her, as if she could feel the financial tsunami rolling across the ocean, ready to wash her away. She wanted to run after him, let his presence chase away her fears.

Be strong, her father's voice echoed.

She took several long, measured breaths as she walked back to the hotel. In her small room, a young, pale-faced, expressionless servant eased Isabella out of her tight dress and corset. She released a sigh as all her internal and external body parts returned to their normal positions. The servant left, promising to return at six. Isabella curled under the covers. The sheets were cool and clean, the mattress was soft and firm—but the bed didn't have the safety and warmth of Randall's chest. She stared at a Y-shaped crack in the ceiling. Outside the window, she could hear muffled chatter and the rattle of passing omnibuses.

She closed her eyes but couldn't rest. She tossed and turned, unable to get comfortable. Odd that she could snooze next to Randall on a hard bench in a drafty train station, but not fall asleep in this snug bed. She had always enjoyed being alone, when her mind could unfurl in the quiet. She could turn her problems over, analyze them, rearrange them. Even when her parents had died, when she'd stiffly accepted acquaintances' embraces and words of sympathy, she'd wanted to run away to the solitude of her bedchamber.

But now she didn't want to be alone. She was scared.

She remembered Randall's eyes catching hers one last time before he disappeared around the block. The press of his lips when he kissed her hand. His kindly voice when he squatted before the suffering children. *Do you have any parents?* he had asked.

Her throat burned, and tears threatened her eyes.

Be strong.

She wiped her eyes on the pillow and then slid the hand he had kissed beneath her cheek. After some minutes, her anxious thoughts transformed into an anxious nightmare: Her belly was swollen, filled with a baby ready to be born. She stood at an altar, sneezing, holding some limp daisies, her huge body sheathed in a dingy white wedding gown. Powers and Harker were in the back of the church, fists flying, slamming each other against the choir lofts, both claiming to have fathered her child. Meanwhile, Randall was asleep in the front pew. He was clad in his ugly brown coat over the black formal clothes he'd worn

at the ball. The vicar held a watering pot and glared at
Isabella. "Have you fornicated with these men? You
wicked, wicked courtesan. No wonder your bank is
going to fail."

Randall bolted from his seat. "I didn't fornicate
with her. We pretended to fornicate. I could never
love her. Just look at her."

Meanwhile, Judith was in the front row, wailing
"They defiled her sacred, pristine vessel."

Beside her, Mrs. Busby was saying "Don't share
unnecessary details."

And all Isabella could think was that she'd had
relations with two men and pretended with another
and couldn't even remember it. "I have to check my
ledgers," she told the vicar. "I know I recorded the
stock series numbers and price when I fornicated with
them. I'm usually very careful about that." She was
mercifully awakened by the returning servant knocking at the door.

Isabella blinked, disoriented. She patted her stomach—it was flat. She wasn't going to have a baby. A
strange, empty despair filled her.

She beckoned the maid to enter, slid from the bed,
and checked herself in the mirror over the oak commode. *Oh, hang it.* That miserable nap had wreaked
havoc on her hair. A tiny braid was loose and flopping
on her forehead, and hair shot out from the nice puffs
Mrs. Perdita had created. Between the servant and
Isabella, they only succeeded in doing more damage
when they tried to repair the coiffure.

*I will insist that Randall let me visit Mrs. Perdita for
a few minutes*, Isabella thought as she headed to the

lobby, her body once again held in check by tight
seams and laced-up stays. If she managed to pull off
a financial miracle and save her bank and her own
savings, she would steal away Lord Randall's pied-
à-terre housekeeper.

⚜

Her heart sank when she found the lobby empty
except for a clerk sitting behind a desk, snickering over
the contents of a book he was reading. She didn't realize she had been anticipating Randall's smile to ease
her worries until he wasn't there.

She nodded to the clerk, sat on the edge of the
sofa, and picked up one of the ladies' journals that
were fanned on the round marble table. She thumbed
through pages of poems and sordid short stories. How
could other ladies read this useless, numberless rubbish?
With her foot tapping, she perused *A Ladies' Journal of
Belle-Lettres*, lifting her eyes at every pedestrian passing
the window and then checking the large clock over
the fireplace. Where was he? Twice the clerk asked if
she required tea or biscuits.

Had she heard Randall incorrectly? Was she supposed to meet him at his flat? At twenty-five past
seven, she decided that was the case and rose to go
just as a young courier, dressed in old-fashioned
green livery, entered, hefting a large box wrapped
in white paper tied up in a looping yellow bow.
"Miss Izzy May," he called out. "A package for Miss
Izzy May."

She raised her hand. "That is me."

The young man set the package on the table and

bowed. "Good evening, miss." He hurried from the room.

What is this?

She opened the box. Nestled in tissue was a bottle of wine, two canisters of chocolate, a box of marzipan, vanilla soap, Madame Olavera's Secret Turkish Lotion, a toothbrush, tooth powder, a hairbrush, and a copy of *Monthly Financial Matters of Britain and her Spheres of Influence.*

Below all of these was a letter with a gold *R* stamped in wax and the name "Izzy May" written in Randall's elegant hand. She opened the envelope, drew out the folded stationery, and read.

> *Dearest Beautiful, Brilliant, Pretend Mistress,*
>
> *Please consider yourself under my protection. I ask that you enjoy the chocolate and an undisturbed bath. I shall tell you what I learn about Powers.*

"That…that…scoundrel!" she cried. "He lied to me!" She stomped across the room. "Do you know where I might find the Golden Tyger?" she inquired of the clerk.

His face pinched, as if she emitted a foul odor. "I'm afraid I do not know the location of such a disreputable gaming h…" He paused, staring down at the half-crown that Isabella had placed on his desk. The coin gleamed in the lamplight. The haughty look melted. "It's in Soho Square."

"Thank you." She rushed for the door and then stopped. "Oh, and please take that box up to my room."

Outside, the night was a deep blue, lit by a swollen full moon sitting on the rooftops and the gold light glowing from windows where families were gathered around tables or in their parlors. Except for the usual coal smoke clogging the skies, the night was clear, the heavy clouds and fog at bay. She reached to hail a hackney and then stopped midwave. Instead, she turned on her heel and hurried down the street, around the corner, passing the identical town houses until she came to number seventeen.

She knocked on the door. Mrs. Perdita opened it. She was in servant gray but had donned a flowery, silken, kimono-like robe over her dull gown. Tiny biscuit crumbs lingered about her unnaturally bright lips.

"Hello, I need to meet Lord Randall at a club tonight." Isabella leaned in. "I want to give him that special sign you talked about—you know, the one to show just how much I adore him." She tried not to choke on her words. "But, you see, my hair has fallen—"

"Stop!" The woman's eyes grew large. "Don't say another word."

Isabella caught her breath. Had the viscount told his housekeeper the truth? Was her ruse over?

Mrs. Perdita clapped her chubby hands. "I have just the thing that will drive him wild."

Thirteen

RANDALL PAUSED ON THE PLATFORM WHERE TWIN staircases met. He gazed through the haze of smoke to a huge painting of a golden-eyed tiger resting beside a nude woman who stroked his fur. On the walls, the tiger's stuffed brethren were affixed beside decorative maps of India and Africa. Randall's hope faded as he took in the hundreds of men clad in dark clothes, standing about the bars or sitting around tables, cards fanned in their hands, cigars sticking from the sides of their mouths, and lovely ladies in bright silk dangling on their arms.

How was he going to find out anything about Powers here? The man was just another loser, chewed up, spat out, and washed away in the tide of faceless men just like him. Randall was wasting time and energy trying to hold back the inevitable. He wished Isabella were beside him. He closed his eyes and remembered her as he had left her on the street that afternoon, the sunlight shining on her dark hair, reflecting off her thick lenses, and glowing on her soft lips. He couldn't let her down.

By God, he wouldn't give up without a fight.

"I'm looking for an ugly cove who lost a vast amount of money here a couple of months ago," Randall informed a male servant holding a silver cigar box. "He's shorter than I am, greasy brown hair, vacant brown eyes." The servant raised a brow, as if to say *You've just described half the guests*.

This is useless, Randall thought, but still he trudged on. "The only thing of distinction about the vile bugger is a strange constellation of moles on his jaw."

The man's eyes lit. "Ah, like the Little Dipper, sir?"

"Exactly. Have you seen such a cur this evening?"

A cloud passed over the young man's features. "No, not tonight."

Randall drew a crown from his pocket and pressed it into the man's free hand. "When did you last see him?"

The servant stared at the money, gave it a tiny toss, and then jammed the coin into his pocket. "I would say a few months ago, when he was lushy, losing his shirt at the vingt-et-un table, and making eyes at my best gel, carrying on about some pussycat game. An odd type, that one."

"Which dealer?"

"Harvey Spinkell." He nodded to the right. "In the corner. With the long nose and hair over his eyes." Randall identified such a man; his table was full. That wasn't a concern; he wanted to wait, appear to be a bit foxed when he ambled over to play.

"For you and your best gel, my good man." Randall tossed another crown to the helpful servant.

He strode down the stairs toward one of the bars.

As he folded into the crowd, men began slapping his back and asking why he wasn't at his house party. He winked and replied that he needed a quick bit of London sport and then shared in the men's dark, conspiratorial laughter.

He ordered a brandy, drank it by the edge of the bar, and wondered what Isabella was doing. Probably cursing his name, wishing financial and political poxes on his future. But he couldn't in good gentlemanly conscience have brought her here. Some of the most debauched men and· ladies in London infested these waters. But dear Lord, he was going to get an earful later. How should he calm her? He remembered the feel of his mouth on hers, her nipple wet and slippery under his thumb, and her body rubbing against his. He ordered another brandy and slowly sipped it. A smile played on his mouth as he fantasized about making love to her: the slow, teasing foreplay, the act in various positions, the wild, crying out climax, and then holding each other, their bodies drained and sated. Her imagined touch gave him the strength he needed. He set down the empty glass and began to wander toward Spinkell's table.

"Randall," a fragile female cried.

He had the sensation of ice sliding down his back. *Oh God, not tonight.* He recognized the timbre and softness in the woman's voice from the times she had whispered her love and devotion as they rolled together under the sheets.

Damnation. Heaven forbid Randall should come to London for one night and not run into his ex-mistress. He turned. The crowd had formed a semicircle around Cecelia, giving her a stage. She was breathtaking in a shimmering ice-blue gown that matched her large, delicate eyes, which always appeared seconds away from tearing up. Her white-blond hair fell in glossy, perfect rings. He stood staring, waiting for that sinking, melting feeling to engulf his heart as it did whenever she was near—that or the bitter sting of hurt and humiliation as he remembered how she had left him. Nothing came but an odd emptiness.

"Oh, hello," he said.

She didn't respond but continued to gaze expectantly at him from under her long lashes.

When it was apparent that he had forgotten his lines as the jilted, heartbroken lover, she prompted, "How do I look? Isn't this dress beautiful? I just had it made." She leaned in, lowering her voice. "Do you think it makes my waist look huge? I told the modiste that I thought it did. She assured me that it didn't. But how can I trust her?"

"It looks…*well enough*," he replied, laughing inside. Plus, he knew better than to get involved in her "do you like this on me" game. Once ensnared, he would have to compliment every tiny detail of her appearance.

"Well enough!" Cecelia puckered her lips in a sweet pout and flipped a curl. "Harding says it looks wonderful."

"I believe you've established your preference for Harding and his opinion." Across the room, a man was leaving the vingt-et-un table where Spinkell dealt. "Good evening, then." He started to stroll to the vacated space, but Cecelia seized his elbow.

"W-where are you going?" she demanded. Randall blinked. He hadn't heard that tone from her offstage.

"To play cards." He shrugged. "It's a gaming hell. What else am I going to do?"

She edged closer, looking at him from under her lashes, letting her finger draw little circles on the back of his hand. "I—I miss you, Randall. I think of you all the time." She reached up and smoothed a fold in his cravat. "I think I made a mistake."

Oh hell, a man had beaten Randall to the empty chair at Spinkell's table.

"What!" He removed her roving fingers from his person. Strange how the touch that once excited him now turned him cold.

"I said I made a mistake," she repeated, her eyes moistening with tears. "A terrible mistake. George has friends at *The Examiner* and the other papers. You know *The Examiner* never reviewed me. Not once. He said he would talk to them, but he didn't."

Her lips lifted in a sweet, quivering smile that not so long ago would have had him leading her to the door and making love in his carriage on the way back to his flat. He realized in the play that constantly ran in her head, this was the climactic moment when he was supposed to fall on his knees and admit how much he missed her and couldn't live without her. And maybe a few weeks ago he might have performed an abridged version of the scene.

"You left me—you betrayed me—when I needed you the most," he said, in a low serious voice. "I want something more than you can give."

"You found another lady!" Cecelia cried. The

entire club turned in their direction, the conversations hushing. "She can't be as pretty as I am. She can't. I am pretty, aren't I? All the reviews say I'm lovely, even the bad ones." She began to quote, "'Her arresting beauty overshadowed her melodramatic, hammering performance, which lacked the needed nuance and subtlety required of the intellectually demanding role.'"

What had he ever seen in this woman?

"Actually, I have met someone," he retorted. "Or should I say, I've come to know someone better. She is brilliant, funny, and unaffected. I can't stop thinking about her—and trust me, I try hard not to." Maybe he wanted to hurt Cecelia as she had hurt him—or maybe he just needed to say the words. He desired a woman he could never have unless he planned to commit social and political suicide.

"Who is she?" Cecelia screamed.

"I'm sorry, but I no longer—oh, hell!" Another man was leaving Spinkell's table. Randall shot across the room with the tenacious Cecelia at his heels.

"You still want me. You know you do!"

"Mind if I join you fine gentlemen for a congenial game of cards?" Randall asked, trying to appear as if he had casually ambled over despite the hysterical actress clinging to him.

"I want you back," she cried. "I'm throwing myself at you."

"No, you're attaching yourself to me. Please let go." To his dismay, Cecelia lingered on, her tiny fingers wound around his elbow as if she had claimed him.

Spinkell bowed and gestured to the vacant chair.

Up close, Randall could see sharp, watchful eyes below the dealer's floppy hair. Their coldness was mitigated by a sullen, boyish mouth and soft chin. He looked over Randall's shoulder, and his face made a subtle change, a tightening around the lips and eyes. The crowd took a collective intake of breath and turned silent.

"Trying to take Cecelia back from me?" a familiar baritone asked, and then broke into a low, easy laugh.

Randall pivoted. Harding, flanked by his three flash men, waited in dark evening clothes. Across his silk scarlet waistcoat, he wore a gold poppy watch chain—a remembrance of the man's younger years spent running opium between India and China. The chandelier light overhead glowed on his bald head, and accentuated his chiseled face and intense eyes. "Are you not content with any of those sweet flowers your parents invited to their house party? Come here, Cecelia."

"I prefer to remain." She drew up, her body and face assuming the dramatic role of wronged but defiant lover.

A low whistle ran through the club.

Dammit. This evening was supposed to be Randall talking to Spinkell and then going back to Isabella, getting slapped, telling her what the dealer had said, and then fighting the urge to seduce her enough to glimpse those stunning breasts again. That was all. Now Randall found himself taking Cecelia's hand and slowly kissing it, while keeping his eyes trained on Harding.

"Seems she wants to stay with me, old boy,"

Randall purred. "Something about satisfaction in the bedchamber. Sorry, but you should know by now that you don't always get what you want."

"I love him, George," Cecelia cried, then broke into dramatic sobs on Randall's chest, but taking a small peek to see how her performance was affecting her audience.

"What can I do, old boy?" Randall opened his palms. "She loves me."

Harding's slash-like brows slanted, the side of his mouth slightly hitched. While every other man in the club might be intimidated, Randall stood his ground. *Make a move, Harding.* Just a slight motion, a tiny jab, and Randall would relish unleashing the mountain of anger and tension from pent-up desire packed in his muscles.

After a long pause, Harding tossed his head back and laughed again, long, deep, and calculating. "Well, never let it be said that I would stand between true lovers. I'll tell you what. I'm bored tonight, so let's play for her. One hand. Between the two of us, the closest to twenty-one wins the lady."

What? Randall just wanted to give a few nasty jabs to Harding's gut, not truly get Cecelia back.

"You can't bet me like…like…money," the actress wept. "As if I were nothing." She clutched Randall's lapel, tears streaming from her eyes. "Don't let him win, Randall. I would rather die than let him touch me," she cried in her stage voice. She buried her face in his coat and wept.

"Sorry, the table is full," Randall told Harding, trying to get out of the wager on a technicality.

The railroad man put his hands on the shoulders

of the elderly men playing at the end. "Boys, why
don't you take these kind gentlemen over to the bar,
give them as many drinks as they want. On me." The
graying men knew better than to protest, and hur-
riedly scooped up their meager winnings and followed
Harding's minions across the room.

Harding took both the empty seats, draping his arm
over the vacant chair at the end. "I'm feeling rather
lucky this evening."

"I can't watch," Cecelia cried, still buried in
Randall's coat. "I can't bear it."

"That's well and all, darling," Randall said, "but I
need to sit down to see the cards."

The actress sucked in a deep breath, composing
herself, and stepped back. "I shall be strong for you."

"Thank you." Randall released an annoyed exhale
and sat down between Harding and the poor chaps
remaining at the table. If Randall managed to get out
of here tonight, he might just give in to that urge
to seduce Isabella and treat himself to those breasts.
Provided, of course, he didn't have his ex-mistress
in tow.

Harding gestured to the dealer. "Let's begin."

Spinkell slid a card across the table. Randall lifted its
edge: the queen of hearts.

And then it happened again—the collective inhala-
tion and hush. A shiver crawled up his spine, raising
the hair on his neck when he heard Cecelia screech,
"Who is *she*?"

Before he even raised his head, Randall knew
Isabella was near.

She stood on the landing, gazing down at the club,

a ravishing vision in a red silk gown. Her hair was pulled from her face, and cascaded from the top of her head, winding down her neck and falling about her creamy, pushed up bosom. A tiny net of diamond-like gems dotted her hair and fell in a *V* on her forehead. She wasn't wearing those spectacles which concealed her face; instead, the chandelier light poured onto her bare face, accented the contours of her plush lips, stunning cheekbones, and lashed gray eyes that lifted exotically at the edges.

Randall stared, motionless, thoughtless, and breathless. Then deep inside him, a root of raw, primitive anger broke through.

I'm going to throttle her. Randall was supposed to be the only one who knew she was lovely. She was his secret. It was bad enough that her stockbroker knew, but now all of London was in on the secret. *I'm going to put my hands around her lovely white neck and shake her until some sense falls loose in her thick, beautiful skull.*

Fourteen

Isabella withdrew her glasses from an odd pocket in the side of the dress, which Mrs. Perdita had said was perfect for keeping a sponge, in case, *you know*. Isabella had assured her that she wouldn't spill anything on the lovely gown that required a sponge to clean and, instead, used the pocket for her glasses and money. Now, she took a quick peek at the blur-turned-servant, who held a box of cigars and stared at her in a strange, slack-jawed manner.

"Pardon me," she said, returning her spectacles to her pocket. "I'm looking for a particular gentleman. He's quite handsome, a little taller than I am with luscious brown curls and deep-chocolate puppy-like eyes that make you think you can trust him but you shouldn't, because he's a lying scoundrel. Oh, and there's an adorable set of moles on his jaw that look like—"

"The Little Dipper?" the servant finished.

"Actually, I thought it resembled Charioteer."

"Aye, I can see that too. He's not here, but he was playing deep a few months ago at Mr. Spinkell's table there on the far right."

"Oh," she said to the exceptionally, yet oddly, informed servant. "Thank you." She gave him a crown.

Gripping the banister, she carefully eased down the steps, patting each tread with her toe to make sure it was there. She could hear the murmur of hushed conversation and the pinging of glass and bottles set on tables. The sweet, acrid congestion of food, perfumes, alcohol, cigar smoke, and burning coal assailed her nose. She should wear her glasses, but she was the most attractive that she would probably ever be in her life. For once, she was the pretty girl, and she wasn't going to ruin the moment by putting on glasses and turning her eyes into huge moons.

Then a female voice shrieked, "She's wearing my dress!"

What! Isabella's cheeks flamed. *Was Randall's old mistress here?* "Ahh!" She missed a step and swan dived into the air.

Dozens of hands were about her, catching her, lifting her up, telling her to "Watch yourself, pretty lady" and "Are you well, my lovely dove?" She heated all over with embarrassment and stammered her thanks. *Just find out about Powers.* She straightened herself and headed off in the direction of the back right, only to slam into someone carrying what sounded like a tray with a dozen plates. "I'm so sorry!"

A familiar and annoyed male voice rang out. "Izzy May, for God's sake put your glasses on."

Isabella wanted to shrivel. Could she not be clumsy just once in her life? She dug her spectacles from her gown and slid them on her nose. At the table in the far right corner, the one she assumed was Spinkell's, stood Randall. Besides him was another blond. This one was female and ravishing and had her arms wound around his body. Isabella's gut turned as the realization sank in: no wonder Randall wanted her to stay away.

"That's my dress," the vision snapped, and then asked Randall, "It looks better on me, doesn't it?"

She felt like a little girl dressed up in her mother's clothes, but, in this instance, it was Randall's real mistress's clothes.

"Now, Izzy," Randall said, his hands out, palms up. "I told you to—"

"Don't you dare 'now Izzy' me after you left me at the hotel," she hissed.

"Is this her?" the blond demanded. "The one you can't stop thinking about." She turned to Isabella and raked her up and down. "A bit blind, are you?"

"Quiet, Cecelia," Randall growled.

Isabella blinked, hurt. So this was the notorious Cecelia? Mrs. Perdita was right. She was atrocious. What did Randall see in her? Oh, bother that half-witted Randall.

"Izzy is…is my new mistress," Randall said, his lips as tight as if he were in pain.

"I am *not* your mistress," Isabella countered, her words breezy yet cutting like thin razor blades. "You already have one. I am an unattached courtesan." She glanced at the table where cards and money lay—*oh, sweet numbers.* "I would like to speak to Mr. Spinkell, if he is available."

"Pardon me, Miss Izzy May, but Mr. Spinkell is dealing an important game of cards," a smooth, rich baritone said. A warm, strong hand rested on the

bare skin of her shoulder, sending a tingle through
her body. Isabella turned and was left momentarily
stunned at the striking male specimen by her side: a
lean, bronze face with glowing eyes; a bald, shining
head; and a tall, muscular body. She didn't understand
why, but she had a primitive urge to meow like her
lust-inflamed cat Milton.

"Would you care to sit down, my little starling?"
said Mr. Wildly Exotic. She acquiesced, entranced by
those cocoa eyes he kept locked on hers. A heavy gold
ring with rubies clustered in the shape of a poppy sat
on his index finger. He bent the digit just the slightest
and a waiter materialized. "Please bring this stunning
lady and me the house's finest red."

"Goddammit," said the blond man behind them—
Randall somebody. "I told you she was under my
protection. Get your hands off her, Harding."

"Harding?" Isabella echoed. "You're—you're
George Harding of Southern Manchester Railroad
Company and Eastern Kent Railroad Company, and
other sundry companies, as well as being on the boards
of numerous joint stocks?" Why hadn't Randall told
her Harding was attractive as the devil? She'd expected
a dour, older man, not this tall, dark, and alluring pot
full of tingle and throb.

Harding chuckled and turned over the card lying
facedown before him. An ace of diamonds. "I busted.
Lord Randall won."

"What!" the viscount hissed. "No, you didn't bust."

"My love, how I missed you." Cecelia lunged into
his arms. Isabella's heart squeezed. She felt like she
was nine again, the strange girl Randall didn't notice

except when he was making fun of her. "Just wait," he said, gently pushing back the woman. "Look, Harding, both of these ladies are my mistresses."

Whistles of admiration rang out around the room, as well as "Congratulations" and "Well done, old chap."

"I believe Miss Izzy May said she was an unattached courtesan." Harding drew his finger along Isabella's jaw and down her throat. "Of course, that can always change." Tiny eruptions exploded under her skin, as when Randall had kissed her after interrupting her bath. If that wasn't scandalous enough, her mind lit with the image of both Randall *and* Harding touching her wet, slick body at the same time. Randall with his mouth on hers and Harding's hands on her—*What is the matter with you?* She flinched, almost falling out of her seat.

"Is something wrong, my stunning dove?" Harding asked.

Yes, I'm in deep waters, far from the shore, without a boat, and there are fins circling. And I don't know how to swim—metaphorically, that is. "I wish to—to speak to Mr. Spinkell. Then I'll just go home."

"You will have to wait until Mr. Spinkell has a break," Harding answered for the dealer, glancing at Spinkell, who nodded in agreement. "Do you like cards, my sweet canary?"

Cards! Yes, that's what she needed—something she understood. Randall could have his old mistress back and she could have her numbers—her male mistress, her footman *d'amour*. "Very much," she said.

Harding motioned to Spinkell. "Deal in the beautiful

swan." Isabella quivered. Did one of the most powerful men in England really think she was beautiful? Randall was right; Harding couldn't be trusted.

The dealer produced a new deck from under the table and began passing out cards, omitting Randall. "I came to play," Randall said, and tossed three sovereigns on the table.

Spinkell's face paled. He muttered his apologies and gave Randall a card.

Isabella reached into her pocket and drew out her money pouch. From it, she removed ten sovereigns for her bet.

Spinkell blinked. "Pardon me, ma'am…"

Isabella looked at him, brows lowered, waiting for him to finish. When he didn't, she slowly said, "I thought we were playing cards." Had she made a mistake?

"But ten pounds is rather—"

"The lady bets high out of the gate," Harding said. "I can respect that." He placed ten pounds on the table as well. Randall added to his initial bet.

Isabella picked up the card that had been dealt facedown. It felt good to hold it, letting her world shrink to two numbers: a seven in the hand and an eight showing, no nuance, undertone, or subtlety to their finite meaning. With a fresh deck started, it would be unwise to ask for another card. She might lose a few hands before she could have a better idea of the numerical landscape. Meanwhile, Randall asked for another and then threw it down and cursed. He never learned, even after all those years she had taken his Christmas money. He had no strategy, no sense of numbers. But then, he had Cecelia practically sitting on his lap to comfort him, so let him lose.

The dealer had seventeen. Only Harding won with nineteen.

"You lost a great deal," Harding told her, taking a glass of wine from the waiter's tray and setting it on the table before her.

She jerked her head back. "I haven't lost."

Harding leaned closer, bathing her in his dark musky and floral scent. "We are playing vingt-et-un." He spoke slowly, as if she were a dull child. "The idea is to get closer—"

"I know the rules," she sniped, annoyed that he would dare to question her prowess. "If I leave this table with more money than I came with, then I've won. And really, you shouldn't play if you get upset each time you lose. You won't win every time."

A smile snaked across his lips. His teeth were stark white underneath. "That's a rather defeating attitude. You should be more optimistic, more bold. That's how I am in business."

"I know," she said. "I've read about you." She took a sip of wine, the cherry and oak flavors unfolding on her tongue.

"Did you like what you found?"

She studied Harding's hands. He had smooth, square fingers with powerful knuckles, like her father's. "I don't know," she said. "You don't put everything on the surface."

"It's true," Harding replied. "I like to keep some things hidden. Would you like me to show them to you?"

"Dammit, Harding," Randall said. "She doesn't understand subtle meanings. Leave her alone."

"I do understand subtle meanings!" Isabella retorted. "He has companies that he keeps hidden for financial reasons." *And don't talk to me when she's sitting in your lap.*

She watched Randall run his hand down his face and gaze heavenward. "God, I told her to stay at the hotel. Why didn't she listen?" He nudged his mistress. "Cecelia, can you find another chair, please. I need to concentrate." She only cuddled closer.

The dealer slid a card forward. Isabella lifted its edge. A seven of spades.

"Be bold, my chickadee," Harding whispered to her.

"I do not believe in boldness," she said absently, as her mind organized every card that had been played by suit and rank. "Or optimism or even pessimism, for that matter."

"What do you believe in, then?" Harding asked.

Isabella received the second card—a jack of spades. Again, she would stay. "Calculated risk." She took another sip of the lovely wine. "You move according to analysis of numbers. The numbers will predict the correct course. Now look, the dealer has nineteen. I've lost again. Oh, well."

After she lost the third game and the fourth was being dealt, Harding said, "I don't think your method of calculated risk is working. Shall I tutor you in boldness? You might like it." He kissed her on the earlobe, letting his warm tongue touch it ever so lightly. "You see, bold."

Isabella jumped in her seat and cupped her hand over her ear. "Mr. Harding! Are you…*flirting* with me?"

It wasn't Harding, but Randall who answered, "Well, darling, you told him you were an unattached courtesan."

One of the most powerful men in London—no, Europe—was flirting with her? Her! And Randall dared to mock even as he had a stunning mistress dangling off his person. Isabella threw down her cards: a king and queen. She beat the dealer as well as Harding and Randall, who busted anyway.

Maybe it was the swollen moon overhead, or the heady sensation caused by the wine, or how her scarlet dress glowed in the chandelier light, or the way Cecelia twined a lock of Randall's hair around her finger that made Isabella say, "Leave the earnings on the table. I'll bet it again." She glanced at the railroad man from the corner of her eye, and said, with a pouty puckering of her lips, "I want to be bold for Mr. Harding."

You flirted! You really did it! She felt so out of control, scared, powerful, proud, and excited at the same time. Her entire body was jittery. *Just focus on the cards*, she told herself. But, oh, Harding smelled so nice, and he continued to watch her with a strange, dark smile on his face that made her insides goosey. Meanwhile Cecelia nested in Randall's arms, whispering in his ear.

Isabella swallowed a mouthful of wine and then another and another. She had a wild desire to flirt with Harding again and again. Tonight, she wasn't Isabella, but Izzy May, the reckless, exotic, and unattached courtesan.

People had gathered around the table to watch.

After two more hands, she had a three-hundred-pound bet sitting on the table. Her entire body quivered, akin to when Randall played upon her nipple. She held a five to her chest, and a ten was showing. A six of hearts, an ace and a seven of clubs, and a jack of diamonds were still out, as well as several low cards in various suits.

"This is what it's all about," she heard herself say, the wine and excitement loosening her lips. "Do you feel it?" she asked Harding. "The power? The rush?" She took a deep breath through her nose, her breasts straining against the tight, low bodice.

"Oh, sweet God, I do feel a rush," Harding said. Behind him, Randall cursed.

"At this moment"—Isabella gestured about her—"everything is possible. I love this feeling. I love it. There is no playing it safe now. In an instant, all could be realized or lost. Still, you want to stay in this moment, keep this excitement, this energy a little longer." She gazed up at the chandelier and sucked in another deep breath, feeling the tilt of the earth, the pull of the fat moon, and the charge of the air. "I'll take another card," she whispered.

An electric murmur ran through the crowd; then the guests settled into a tense silence. Spinkell slid the card across the green velvet covered table. She kept it down, refusing to look at it, but rubbed it tenderly with her index finger. Spinkell turned his cards: a jack, three, and seven. Twenty. Randall and Harding tossed in their cards.

Isabella slowly set the five of diamonds, which she had kept hidden to her breast, beside the ten showing.

She removed her glasses, blurring her world, and reached for the remaining card. She flipped it. The room went dead silent.

"I think I'm in love," Harding said.

Wild cheering erupted. She felt an arm go around her neck and warm lips found hers. They didn't induce the body-throbbing, world-stopping, thousand-shooting-stars passion that Randall's lips did, but they were cozy and tasted of red wine and made her sigh, wanting to linger in their warmth.

❦

Randall saw Harding put his filthy mouth on Isabella's. Blurry, black spots clouded his vision. He bolted from his chair, sending Cecelia stumbling a few steps. He grabbed the railroad man's shoulder. "I told you not to touch her, you arse." Randall ripped the rogue away from Isabella.

She gazed up at the viscount, her enormous eyes all inky and unfocused, her soft lips parted, the edge of her pink tongue just visible. His heart squeezed. *How could you do this to me?*

In a twinkling, Harding's trio of yahoos was at their employer's side.

"I believe Lord Randall is a little upset." Harding laughed, slicking his hand over the side of his head. "It's not my fault she prefers me, old boy. I'm more her style. Now take Cecelia and leave us alone."

"I don't want…" *Cecelia.* What had Randall's stupid masculine pride driven him to? "Dammit, I told you that they were both my mistresses."

"I'm not sharing you…with…with…*that* hideous

woman." Cecelia lunged at Isabella, sending her tumbling off her chair. She grabbed the net of gems in Isabella's hair and tried to rip it out. "These are mine. He is mine."

Guests began clapping and stomping. "Totty brawl! Totty brawl! Totty brawl!"

Isabella, who wasn't wearing her glasses, hadn't seen the vixen coming in time. "Ouch! She's hurting me," she shrieked, trying to pull away, but the jealous actress held tight to the headpiece.

Isabella shoved Cecelia, sending her reeling into Randall. In her tiny, wiry fingers, the actress gripped a jeweled net hairpiece with tufts of black hair dangling from it. "You get out of my dress, you…you… blind tart!"

"Totty brawl! Totty brawl! Totty brawl!"

"Make her go away," Isabella screamed, fumbling about the floor, her tresses loose. Randall tried to help her, but Cecelia huddled, all weepy, against his chest, blocking him. Harding reached Isabella first, drawing her into a protective embrace.

"Get that banshee out of here," the railroad baron hissed at Randall. "She's all yours. Congratulations."

Spinkell handed Isabella her spectacles.

"Thank you." She sniffed, coming to her feet with Harding's aid.

"This has been a most exciting evening." The dealer bowed. "Good night, gentlemen, ladies."

"Wait, I need to talk to you," Isabella and Randall said in unison.

"No, no, you're not talking to anyone," Randall told her, trying to disentangle himself from Cecelia—dear

SUSANNA IVES

God, it seemed like the crazy woman had a dozen arms. She was a bloody octopus. "You're going home."

"You don't hold that trollop and tell me what to do." Isabella eyes, now magnified, were hot and sharp, and Harding's arm around her was strong and flexed.

Damn Cecelia, damn Harding, and damn Isabella. Especially damn her. How could she hold on to the very man trying to destroy him?

Randall watched Harding take her elbow, an intimate, predatory smile lazing on his mouth, as he led her away. "Love, you've got to tell me where you've been hiding all this time."

For years, she had been Randall's homely, awkward, and clumsy childhood nemesis, but suddenly she was a radiant flower. Harding had discerned in a matter of minutes her creamy breasts and stunning figure…and lovely smile…and gambling prowess… and brains…*and bloody hell!*

Isabella tried to reach back for Spinkell. "But I need to talk to—"

"Me," Harding finished her words, drawing her captive to his chest. "You need to talk to me and no one else here."

"I'll just be around the bar if anyone wants to see me," Spinkell announced, and drifted off in the opposite direction.

Randall released a deep, soul-wrenching "Bugger!" He didn't know a thing about Spinkell. Where did he live? What did he do when he wasn't dealing? Meanwhile, he knew where Isabella would be staying tonight…and alone. He was going to make damned sure of it. Until then, she wasn't leaving his sight.

Isabella glanced over Harding's shoulder, flashing Randall a hot look that said "Go ask him about Powers, you idiot," jerked her head toward the retreating Spinkell, and then returned her attention to Harding.

Cecelia wrapped her fingers around Randall's elbow. "I look better in that dress than she does."

It took every bit of Randall's restraint not to say that Isabella looked a thousand times better in and out of that dress and any other dress. "Darling, why don't you order a bottle of wine and find a dark table?" he said, trying to put her someplace while he went after Spinkell.

Cecelia gave a purring laugh, raised onto her tiptoes to whisper in his ear something about the best love he had ever experienced, all night long, oil, licking, beads, climaxing over and over, and... *Would she just be quiet!* Across the room, the railroad baron had drawn a chair next to Isabella's. She laughed, that silvery, head-tossing kind, and then wound a strand of hair around her finger. Was she flirting? No, because Isabella didn't know how to flirt. Then she bit her lower lip and gazed coyly at Harding from under her lashes. Oh, that was definitely flirting. Randall couldn't miss it; her lenses magnified the blatant act.

Just get what you need from Spinkell, then march Isabella back to her hotel and throttle her...or kiss her...or fuck her...

"Are you even listening to me, Randall?" Cecelia demanded.

"Sounds well enough, w-whatever you want," he stammered, not quite sure what love acts he was committing himself to. "Just excuse me." He made a beeline for the bar.

❧

Spinkell stood at a round table by the bar's side, near the entrance to the back stairs. Away from the gaming table, his energy was more frenetic. He ran his hands through his hair and sipped from a glass of ale. He bowed as Randall approached. "I think you can see *both* your mistresses from this vantage," he said. "The one you don't want anymore and the perfect one you just lost."

He chuckled, but Randall didn't think anything was funny. Under normal circumstances, the viscount would have tried to ingratiate himself with Spinkell, shown him what a fun, easygoing, everyday chap he could be. But he didn't have the time, what with Isabella learning to flirt and the devil as her tutor. Her words last evening in the train station echoed in Randall's mind: *I can't help wanting to feel, to see, to know a man. I'm so desperate in my desire*. He put three crowns on the table.

"About two months ago, you dealt to a man named Anthony Powers." Randall described Powers, moles and all. "He lost a great deal that night."

Spinkell looked at the money. His lips protruded where he ran his tongue over his upper teeth. "Many men lose here," he said slowly. "I can't remember them all."

Randall added a coin atop the others.

"I remember him now. He kept flirting with the women, something about some cat game. A bit of a queer bird."

Across the room, Harding was pulling the stray pins from Isabella's hair. She giggled, all flushed and flustered. She had better not be explaining her economic theories or talking about her promising openings with that scoundrel.

"Was Powers supposed to lose?" Randall made the tower of coins a little higher.

Spinkell's lip twitched just the slightest. He rubbed his mouth. "Look, I need this job. My wife just had a baby. I can't…"

Two gold sovereigns were added. "Congratulations on the addition."

The dealer released a long, uneasy breath. "Sometimes the manager has a special request."

Harding had removed Isabella's glasses and was making a game of moving them around the table, just beyond her reach. As she patted about, searching for her spectacles, the railroad bumhole enjoyed the fine view down her bodice.

"Do you have any idea who wanted Powers to lose?" Randall managed to say through a clenched jaw. He was blindly throwing money on the table at this point. *Pop it out, Spinkell. I've got to murder someone.*

The dealer's throat contracted with his swallow. He glanced off in the direction of Harding and Isabella.

Harding ran his finger down one of her locks and then drew tiny circles on her collarbone, dangerously close to Randall's breasts. Technically, the lovely mounds were on Isabella's body. But Randall had been the first man to discover them, so he claimed them like some wilderness explorer.

"You might want to rescue Miss Izzy May." Spinkell looked dead level at Randall and spoke slowly. "I wouldn't trust Harding or his men." He swept the money from the table in an easy motion and slipped behind the door to the back stairs.

"Goddammit, I knew it." Randall stomped across the room. Harding's muscled triplets came forward to stop him. Randall shrugged them off, too scorching angry to be intimidated.

"Get your bloody hands off her," he growled at Harding. "She's my mistress, under my protection. And I *will* protect her." He drew his coat back, revealing a pistol peeking above the waist of his trousers. "If you have a problem, we can settle it as gentlemen."

"What's happening?" Isabella cried. "Where are my glasses?" She beat on the wood with her palms, locating them across the table. She jammed them on her face and gasped. "Randall, w-what are you doing? Put your gun away."

"Gun?" several men in the club repeated. Whispers blazed through the room, and then all heads turned, breaths bated.

Harding's easy expression drained from his face, leaving the cold hardness beneath. He slowly rose and put his hands on his hips, his gold poppy chain glinting in the chandelier light. "Son, you should know I'm not going to back down from a fight. Nor am I going to lose. Are you certain you know what you're proposing? I'm giving you thirty seconds to reconsider how you want to end your life."

"Let me talk to him," Isabella pleaded. "Please. Just for a minute." When Harding didn't budge, she slipped onto the floor and under the table. "Come, Randall," she said, crawling out the other side. "I'll just be a moment," she told Harding. "Please, wait for me." She clasped Randall's elbow and tried dragging him toward the stairs. But Randall was ready to fight, with his fists, gun, chairs, wine bottles, utensils, whatever weapon he could make. His body quaked with pent-up violence. The world would be a considerably better place with Harding removed from it. Then a screaming ball of blue silk and blond hair shot from the crowd.

"He's mine," Cecelia screamed. She grabbed Isabella's bodice. "Get out of my dress." She yanked, ripping the fabric, uncovering a white, lacy corset.

"Totty brawl! Totty brawl! Totty brawl!" the crowd began chanting again.

Cecelia held a square of red silk in her fist, her teeth gnashing. "You are not going with him, you blind, ugly bitch."

The last shred of Randall's restraint broke. "You're the ugly—"

Isabella pressed the back of her hand on his chest, halting his words. "Hand me your gun," she said with creamy menace. "We're going to settle this problem like gentle ladies."

Cecelia shrieked and fled. "She's cracked. She's mad. She wants to kill me."

Isabella straightened her back, smoothed her torn gown, and turned on her heel. "Come, Randall." *Totty brawl, indeed.*

Fifteen

RANDALL HELD HER HAND SO TIGHTLY THAT HER fingers were smashed together. He stomped with her to the lobby. There, he jerked his head at a servant. "Hat. Coat," he barked, his body drawn tall, assuming his imposing Lord of the Realm stance. Then he turned to Isabella and, in the same imperious tone, ordered her to stay while he jammed his hands into his gloves. Having none of that, she headed for the door.

The night air was still warm and humid. A fat, silver moon lazed on the rooftops.

"I told you to wait," Randall barked, stepping outside, his greatcoat half on.

"I don't take well to being ordered about."

"You're coming with me." He grabbed her elbow.

She tried to dig her heels into the pavers, but the dratted slippers were useless and she slid along.

"You're my mistress, remember? Therefore, you have to do as I say," he growled, drawing her into a darkened alley.

A yellow-striped cat was atop a black one amid the rotting crates, biting its neck as its hindquarters quivered. The black feline was screeching her excited mating calls to the entire neighborhood. The cats shot out of the lane as Randall pulled Isabella into its shielding darkness. Only the dimmest light escaped the bull's-eye panes of the buildings around them, lighting the contours of their faces and casting the rest into shadows.

"I'm not your mistress. You already have one, and she's stunning, gorgeous, and, I think, perhaps insane." She tried to yank her hand away, but he held tight. A tug-of-war ensued.

"You let go of me this instant!" She tried to pry his strong fingers from her wrist.

He grabbed her other hand and backed her against the wall, pinning her on the brick. "What do you think you were doing with Harding?" His words were a blast of anger.

"Diverting him while you were talking to Spinkell," she fired back. "What do you think, you arrogant cabbagehead?"

He slowly nodded. "Ahh, you were diverting him." He spun a lock of her hair around his finger. "Diverting him like this…a little flirtatious, maybe." He unwound the curl down her neck and onto her breast, circling the exposed skin with his finger. "Or this, yes, that's quite diverting. That might border on bold seduction."

"He—he didn't touch me there." Despite her wrath, she couldn't deny the hot shiver rushing over her skin as her body rose to his touch, so different than Harding's, which was pleasant and heady, but Randall was another matter. His magic was powerful, primal, dark, and resonated deep in her core, quickening her pulse…and raising her anger higher.

"What did Spinkell say?" Her words came out a choked whisper as his finger dallied beneath the edge of her bodice, so close to that heated, hard tip.

"He said that he was told to deal to Powers, to bleed him. Harding may have been behind it. So, my dear vixen, you were flirting, I mean, *diverting* the very man orchestrating your downfall."

"You said 'may.' That's not definite. And I'm shocked you would notice me flirting, diverting, whatever Harding now that you have your luscious, mentally unstable Cecelia back. You should thank me." She jutted her chin, pouting her lips.

He pulled his circling finger away. *No! Don't!*

He moved closer until his lips waited over her ear, his body pressed against hers, his chest on her breasts, his thighs on her belly, his heat engulfing her. "Oh, I see." He kissed her ear, letting his tongue slide along the lobe. He moved his lips down her neck, over her shoulder, lower and lower. "You're jealous." He licked her skin. His low and sultry laugh broke something inside her. He was toying with her because he knew she couldn't resist him, because she was a pathetic spinster who fell for any male attention— including from the man who *might* be orchestrating her downfall.

She pressed her hands against his upper arms—taut with hard muscle—and shoved. "No. It's—it's about trust. You told me that we were in this together and then you left me. You *left* me, Randall, after you said you wouldn't."

"I was protecting you."

"Protecting me?" she cried. "How dare you? I have a bank that I've invested a decade of my life building. It has a thousand customers on the line. I am not a child, and I don't need protecting." Shaking her head, she hiked the top of her dress up and turned to head to the gaming hall. "I should have left you at the railway station."

He seized her elbow. "Where are you going?"

"If you believe Harding *may* have something to do with it, then I'm going to find out."

"Oh, now you're going to sweet-talk Harding? Don't make me laugh. You'll just get flustered and tell him about your promising openings in the love market."

She could hear her breath rushing through her flared nostrils. At that moment, she positively hated him. She wished she were a girl again, when they were the same size. She would give him a hard jab to the gut and then kick his shins. Instead, a strange calm descended as she studied his eyes burning in the darkness, the glint of his teeth beneath his lip and the scowl drawing his features. Suddenly, she read him. For the first time in her life, she could see inside him. He was primed and just needed a lit match to go off. She should be scared, but all she felt was dizzying power. She heard herself chuckle, a strange and alien sound originating from some unexplored region inside of her. The same laugh she had heard Randall give a thousand times—deep in the throat, lazy, and dripping with sarcasm—now came from her.

"Well, I might," she said, her voice smoky and low. "After all, I'm an unattached courtesan." She turned and started for the street, but he snatched her arm again—as she somehow knew he would—and she wheeled around.

"You don't want to be protected?" he growled. "You're not a child anymore? Not that scary, strange girl that once loomed around me? Well, fine, my lovely, unattached courtesan." He pulled her close, until his lips were less than an inch from hers. "I want to buy you for the evening."

"You lost your money. I should buy you!"

"Oh, but you don't want money." He kissed her jaw again, his tongue tasting her. His scent filled her nose. His free hand rose, cupping her breast, running his thumb along the top. Oh Lord, he had trapped her again. Not with bars or ropes—she was just bound by her own desire burning between her limbs. "What did you say that night in the train station?" He began to quote her. "'I can't help wanting to feel, to see, to *know* a man.' That you were desperate in your desire."

"You're not being fair," she choked out.

He raised his head, taking his kisses away, but still his fingers caressed her. She released a high, tight squeak.

"Life's not fair," he said. "I would hate to protect you from that cold fact. I can't coddle you like a child, because you're a woman…a wild, beautiful courtesan." His gaze never left her face, trapping her thoughts. "I don't want to protect you when I say that I dream about your body all day. That I want to feel you again, make you quiver with pleasure." His fingers dipped into her gown, finding a rebellious nipple hard and straining for him. She couldn't stifle her whimper.

"If this is not what you want, lovely courtesan," he told her, "you can walk away right now. Go to Harding."

He gave her tip a gentle squeeze that sent a hot, electric wave straight to her wet sex. Her lips couldn't form consonants. She arched her back, pushing her body against him. He pressed back, his male part rock hard and large against her belly.

"I want you," he said, his teeth clenched. "But I can't have you. I can't marry you, and I can't take you under my wing. Our worlds can't merge." He ran his free hand behind her head, tangling his fingers in her hair, pulling her mouth toward his. He overwhelmed her senses. Everything was him: his tongue, tasting of red wine, swirling against hers; his male part pushing against her belly; his heat, his scent. Her body was surging. She didn't know what she was doing, but she instinctively met his rhythm. Her sacred vessel was slick, ready to take him into her.

He tore his mouth away and hoarsely whispered in her ear, "I was trying to protect you from this simple truth: I want to pull up your skirts and bury myself inside you. I want to thrust and thrust and thrust, filling you up, making you cry out in pleasure. I want to feel your thighs shake around me until your climax contracts around my cock. I want to release deep inside you, spilling all this tension." She raised her head and cried out, soft, high, and yearning. He grabbed her hand and pushed it onto his cock. "I want to fuck you, Isabella. I want to fuck you so badly."

He dropped his forehead on her shoulder. "If you weren't a virgin, I'd take you here. Against this wall. Are you scared? Maybe you don't want to be a courtesan now? Maybe you want me to protect you from this, after all?"

He flung himself back, his palms up, his chest rising and falling fast and hard. Though the night was warm, Isabella's skin turned cold now that she was separated from him. She throbbed with want. All her emotions piled on top of each other. Judith's words rang over and over in her mind, applauding Isabella for taking a lover, for satisfying her desire with no attachments. The man she craved at that moment couldn't give her a future even if she wanted it, even if she foolishly fell in love with him. But her future was so precarious now anyway. This might be her last chance to know a man before ruin—and the most handsome one in London at that. She swiped at the air, trying to draw him back, but he remained out of her reach, his eyes focused on the ground. Then a strange, unspoken knowledge bloomed in her mind. He was scared.

He swallowed, removed his hat, and raked his hand through his hair. "Come, I'll take you back to the inn—"

"No!" she cried. The night was changing; there was a quickening in the air, a charge, much like when the market or cards were turning in her favor. She knew better than to fight the flow of the moment. "No," she said again, this time a whisper. She gently brushed aside the strands of hair falling in his eyes. "I don't want to marry you or be your mistress. But I'll be your courtesan for a night if you do everything to me that you dream about."

"This is a mistake." He tried to look away, but she captured his chin. "I can't… I shouldn't…" She placed a finger over his mouth, hushing him. She rose to her tiptoes and replaced that finger with her lips, giving him a brush of a kiss.

"Don't protect me. Don't make me feel like this and then stop. I'm dying inside. We don't like each other anyway. Why does it matter?" She pressed her mouth against his and ran her fingers down his taut back, coaxing him. He began to respond again, slowly. She never realized how wonderful it felt to touch someone, the softening and warmth inside of her. Even when her father was alive, he never embraced her. Since his death, she had been alone, cold and unconnected. Now it felt like years of isolation were floating away. She weaved her fingers in Randall's, lifting them back to her breast. He released her mouth and gazed down at where her nipple peeked over the edge of her bodice.

"Oh God." His sigh warmed her skin. His body shook. Her hand slowly drifted down his chest and finally to where his sex strained against his trousers. She kissed his forehead. "I want to be your courtesan for the evening. Just an evening." Her fingers slipped inside his waistband. "I want to fuck you, Randall."

"Dear Lord." He seized her wrist. "Come with me before I think better of this."

❧

Hand in hand, they bounded down the street like two reckless children on a wild adventure. He waved down a hackney. Once inside, he kept his fingers laced in hers. The air was crackly, like the moments before an electrical storm, when the winds kicked up.

"Are you sure?" he asked. "Because if-if you're not—"

"I am."

He watched the rise and fall of her chest with her shallow breath, her breasts pushing against the edge of her gown. Her locks fell about her face, and her lips were reddened and swollen from his kisses. His cock threatened again. He tried to think about the price of wheat, Queen Victoria's speeches, and boring trade talks—anything sliding his cock inside her. He just had to get her to the flat. He just had to keep himself in check for ten minutes, six hundred torturous seconds.

Sixteen

His hands trembled as he assisted her from the carriage. He scooped some coins from his pocket, tossed them to the driver, and hurried her to the door. The driver called out something about wanting change.

"Just keep it," Randall said. "Keep it, man." He yanked open the door, guiding her inside. The gold light from a lamp burning in the parlor drifted into the dim hall.

"Randall," she whispered. Her voice—the plaintiveness, the yearning—broke his last thread of restraint. He nudged her against the door. His mouth found hers and his tongue delved inside, silencing the doubts that told him he was going to regret his actions. He cupped those generous breasts that had taunted him all evening. Surrendering to the erection he had fought so valiantly, he rubbed his cock against her thighs.

"Dear God, Isabella," he groaned, and repeated her name over and over, the same one that as a boy he had accompanied with an insult: stupid Isabella, scary Isabella, cracked Isabella. Now she was luscious, taunting, and sensual Isabella. His world whirled on its axis, a new day coming and the old, long one dying away.

Her fingers yanked at his cravat. In an easy motion, he removed the knot and pulled the cloth away. Her mouth found his hot pulse beneath his ear, the tip of her tongue circling on his bare skin. He tugged at her bodice and corset, trying to get at her treasures. A loud rip echoed in the hall, and her rosy nipples finally popped over the fabric's edge.

He knelt before the stunning creations. "Sweet, lovely beauty," he whispered, and suckled one. His tongue licked across its tip while his fingers played upon its hard sister, plucking, flicking, massaging.

Her nails dug into his scalp, her cascading curls falling over his head, as she released soft whimpers. The sound of her pleasure resonated in his chest and throat, like listening to beautiful music reverberating in the high domes of cathedrals. She took him to a place no other woman had—to the edge of something unearthly.

"Lord Randall," he heard Mrs. Perdita call from the kitchens, breaking the spell. Isabella stiffened, but he held her tight, covering one breast with his mouth, the other with his hand.

"You are h— Good heavens!" The housekeeper released a bark of laughter, and then she scurried up the stairs, giggling all the way.

He had to relax Isabella again. He resumed the slow licks and kisses of her rosy tips, until she was writhing and catching her breath in short stops. He gave her a little nip. She whined deep in her throat and shoved herself deeper into his mouth. Her fingers interlaced with his, both caressing, pinching her nipple. He chuckled, low and dark, her breast still in his mouth.

"Don't laugh at me." She shoved his shoulders, sending him tumbling onto the floor.

"What are you—"

She fell to her knees, ripped off her glasses, and leaned over, her silken hair feeling like feathers on his face. She sucked his lower lip, then released it. "I want to feel your body."

She yanked back his coat and made quick work of his vest buttons. Then she lifted his shirt. She hummed as her fingers trailed along the taut lines of his muscles and his belly button. He loved how she used her touch to "see" him.

"So strong," she murmured.

He wished he could relax into her caresses, but his cock was burning. He clasped her hand and slid it to his trousers. "Touch me, Isabella. Please."

He swallowed and held his breath as her small hand moved under his waistband, unbuttoning and releasing him. "Oh my." Her fingers slid along his length, exploring his head, down his shaft, to his tight bollocks, and up again. He wrapped her hand in his and guided her along, stroking the head and then down. A few drops of his hot liquid escaped onto their skin.

"I love how you feel," she said quietly. "Hard yet smooth."

Her smile was tender and unguarded. Was this the same woman he had known most of his life? Why only now did her smile penetrate his depths? He slowly spun and unspun a lock of her hair near her cheek, his eyes half-closed, floating on the pleasure she induced.

He released the curl, drew a line with his fingers over her cheek, across her lips, pressing two inside her mouth to moisten them, and then back to a breast, dancing over the nipple, showing her the tempo and pressure that he desired. She emitted a little choked whimper, and her hand moved faster, matching his rhythm. "Like this?"

"Yes." He released the last *s* like a long sigh through his clenched teeth.

She laughed, low and soft.

"Cruel vixen," he murmured, lost in the blissful haze of her touch. "Don't laugh at me either."

"I'm laughing because I'm making you happy, silly boy. Because…" She whimpered as he squeezed her tip, turning her voice high and tight. "I love how your pleasure feels inside of me."

"Kiss me," he whispered. "Kiss me, please." She leaned down. His tongue ravished hers, wild and deep as he shoved his cock against her palm. He wanted more, to bury himself in the snug slickness of her unexplored core.

His mind was turning black, shrinking to a point. He seized her hand, pushing her away before he released. "We have to stop," he rasped. "I'm too aroused. I want to be inside of you. I want to feel your quivering climax around me." He yanked up his trousers and hastily buttoned a single button. He rose, slipped out of his shoes, and then lifted her. She tried to straighten her bodice.

"No, I'll have none of that. Don't you dare cover those lovely darlings." He swooped her into his arms.

"Randall!"

He chuckled. He was too excited to take her up the stairs to the bedchamber, like a civilized lover. He could just make it to the parlor sofa. Laughing, she spilled onto the cushions—a blur of black hair, red silk, and white petticoats. Despite his jutting, burning erection, he had to stop and study her, smiling, vulnerable, and wanton. He wished he could capture this moment and keep her this way forever. The old Isabella, his critic, his enemy, stripped away, just this joyous, abandoned beauty in her stead.

She turned silent under his gaze, her glittery, unfocused eyes tensed. She reached out. He realized that she couldn't see him.

"I'm here." He knelt at her side, taking her hand, kissing it.

They peeled off his coat, vest, and shirt. She found the button to his trousers and he rose, letting them fall. His erection jutted out at her eye level. He let her study him.

She brushed a strand of hair behind her ear and edged forward, slowly taking his head into her mouth, kissing him, her lovely eyes gazing up, unsure. "Yes, my angel," he whispered, assuring her, giving her confidence. He was glad that she couldn't make out his face because she would find something there that wasn't part of their game: raw tenderness and awe. Every little thing she did, every move, every word cut a little closer to his heart.

What game had he agreed to? What would he say

in the morning? Could he undo the damage she would wreak? But daybreak was hours away, he told himself, and he reached for her. "My wonderful love, let me pleasure you for now." Using every ounce of his will, he removed his Percy from her sweet mouth. "I've got to get these clothes off you. I've got to see that beautiful body that haunts my thoughts."

He felt her shiver as he turned her. She lifted her hair so he could undo the buttons of her gown. "Do you really think about me?"

In the last few days, almost every waking minute, he wanted to reply. But he didn't know where their game ended and the truth began. He couldn't respond; it was far too dangerous. He just kissed her neck and licked the shell of her ear. He felt like a sculptor, chipping away button after button, clasp after clasp, knot after knot, discovering the art beneath the surface. In the end, the lamplight illuminated her bare alabaster skin, the rose of her areolas, the taper of her waist, and the glossy curls between her thighs.

"Good God, Isabella. Why didn't you tell me you were stunning years ago?"

She glanced from the lashed corner of her eyes. "Don't you mean an unparalleled paradise of beauty and delight?"

He could josh as well as she could. "I would say a delicious, unspoiled vista of heaven, except for these stockings."

Her giggles turned into a gasp when he grabbed her ankle and slid her down the sofa cushions, anchoring her legs around his waist. He tried to keep up the

flirtatious game as he raised her knee, taking her stocking string between his teeth and pulling, but then he
caught a glimpse of her rosy, wet vulva, and his mind
went blank, except for one thought: *get inside her.*

❧

"Damn," she heard him say. She couldn't see his face,
but she felt the pressure of his fingers on her skin and
cool air between her open legs, the heat of his eyes
studying her intimate details.

She had never been so exposed to anyone. She
hadn't expected this turn in their game. Fear flooded
in, and she instinctively tried to close herself.

"No, Isabella, you are lovely." He kissed her inner
knee. "Don't be afraid."

She hesitated, unsure. All the while, her body lay
open, vulnerable to him, and the world didn't shatter
like glass or stop spinning.

"Don't be afraid," he repeated. "Just relax and let
me do everything."

Relax? Let someone else do everything? How?

He squeezed her hand. "If you want me to stop,
I will."

No! Let him think, let him take care of the world
for a small time; let him shoulder her fears and loneli-
ness. She had held so tight for so long in her stark
existence of numbers and empty, silent rooms, desiring
the husband and children that she was never going to
have. The most handsome man in England—a man
whom she spent years despising—simply wanted to
pleasure her. This was the moment of all possibility.
She could stop, but then that painful, hollow desire

that kept her up at night, fevered with want, would continue unabated, driving her mad.

It's just a game, Isabella. For one night and then it's over.

He would soon find another ravishing mistress or marry a brainless Tory beauty and put babies into her belly. Would Isabella regret playing? And would it matter if she was just going to the poorhouse anyway? At least she would die having known a man.

There were too many variables to calculate the risk.

As his lips brushed the soft skin of her thigh, she realized she couldn't win. What was on the other side of her fears, the mystery that consumed her thoughts? She wanted an answer. Settling her head onto the cushion, she bit the edge of her lip and shut her lids, giving herself to him.

For one night.

Only.

"Relax," he repeated as his finger moved along the wet folds of her sacred feminine place. Terror and excitement mingled together at being intimately known. She clutched the cushion, letting him explore her. He found that tiny mound at the top of her slit and flicked his finger over it. She gasped as spasms of pleasure jolted through her. He chuckled, dusky and knowing. His finger began to swirl in a tight circle, radiating powerful, hot waves through the rest of her body. She moved with his touch as if from some ancient memory. She released humming whines as a white intensity built inside her. The years and years of frustration transformed into heat and pleasure. If he didn't stop, she would combust, burst, or break apart.

"Please." She begged for relief even as her body pressed against him, seeming to know some innate destination. "Please."

He only slowed, worsening the torture. Another finger slid inside her. She cried out, rising up, clawing the air, trying to reach him. The scoundrel muttered a curse. His finger danced faster over her mound as the others pressed further into her. She fell onto the sofa, her back arching, her legs wide and trembling. She opened her mouth in an unvoiced scream.

"Bloody hell," he hissed, and then his hands were gone.

"No!" she begged. "Don't stop. Don't."

He muttered something unintelligible. She was seized by the waist, pulled to the edge of the sofa. He wasn't gentle anymore, nor was he rough. She could feel the pressure of his cock at her opening. *This is it*, she thought. *The mystery is about to be solved.* She wished she could see his face, that he wasn't lost in the blur. He pushed, but her body wouldn't relent. "I'm scared I might hurt you," he cried, fear breaking his voice.

"Hush," she whispered, and pressed against him. She felt the pang of losing her maidenhood and then he slowly slid into her. For a moment, they were both still. She could hear his breath—hard and restrained—as she adjusted to sharing her body with his strength, his energy, his being. She hadn't realized how acutely lonely she had been until he filled her.

"My love, my love, my love," he murmured. "You have undone me."

She knew he didn't mean "my love," that it was

just something he said. But tonight, in this game, she would pretend that the endearment was true.

He began to move, back and forth, slowly and carefully. Her pain receded, surpassed by pleasure, more powerful and primitive than before. Instinctively, her back arched, allowing him further inside. She whimpered as she participated in this lovely dance of advancing and retreating, so easy even she could do the steps. "Oh, sweet Isabella," he muttered, his voice syrupy with desire as he thrust deep into her. An amazing revelation unfurled in her mind: she had the power to delight him. She tightened the muscles of her sacred vessel and listened to his deep, gut-level groan. *I did that! I made him happy!*

Then the tables turned. His finger found her mound again, and her mind turned blank as she cried out. She was tumbling down, down, down to a place of dark pleasure. Her body surrendered to his thrusts, his finger flicking, their skin slapping, her breasts bouncing. His groans mingled with her high, quiet whines as she writhed and pushed and ground against him, desperate for some resolution to this aching, mounting pleasure.

Then he moved his finger just a fraction higher. Her world went silent and a thousand tiny explosions burst beneath her skin, burning up all her tension in hot waves. She opened herself as wide as she could, wanting all of him as she contracted around his cock.

"Fuck," he uttered. She closed her eyes, her muscles going limp as her body drifted into an amazing peace. But all that energy, frustration, and desire now blazed in his body. He grabbed her leg, goosey and languid, and pressed it high against his chest, letting the other dangle free. He penetrated her, deep and fast, rock hard and heavy. Despite her desire to curl into a happy, satisfied ball, she met him thrust for thrust in this beautiful violence, wanting him to know the same pleasure he had given her. Judith's words echoed in her mind, reminders not to let him violate her pristine vessel with his seed. But this wasn't violation; this was adoration, worship, praise. She didn't dare suspend his joy. And in some small place in her mind, the idea of having a child—his lovely child—thrilled her.

Then, in a twinkling he was gone from her body. "Wh—?"

His hard cock pressed against her belly. He grunted as spurts of warm liquid splashed onto her skin. His body heaved with his breathing until, finally, he grew silent. He knelt beside her and kissed her gently on the mouth. She framed his face in her hands, keeping him close enough to see him. "Thank you," she whispered, not looking away, not ashamed or angry or scared. Of all they had done, this was the most intimate act of all. "I never thought it would be you. Never in a million years."

"If you had told me a week ago that we would…" He didn't finish but chuckled and then kissed her again. "Did you enjoy it?"

She smiled, free and unguarded. "What do you think?"

"What do I think?" He drew back, his face becoming blurry as his old teasing tone returned, but she could hear a quiver beneath the words. "I think I've bought you for a night and I've just gotten started."

"There's more?" Could it be any more miraculous?

"This is just the beginning." He intertwined his fingers through hers and lifted her from the sofa. He retrieved her glasses from the hall and slid them onto her face, giving her nose a small kiss. Hand in hand, they scrambled, naked, up the stairs, laughing like wild children who had escaped the nursery. And in a way, they had escaped, just for a few hours, from all the troubles that hounded them. The sun would rise tomorrow, bright and harsh on old, dull Isabella, the spinster, and Lord Randall, the beloved, privileged Adonis, but in the darkness tonight, she was his exotic, beloved courtesan.

❧

In the bedchamber, candles flickered, the flames dancing on the wineglasses that had been set on the bedside table. The lacy chemise Isabella had admired now rested on the bedcovers, red silk ties curled beside it. Randall lifted one, letting the shiny fabric drape down.

"Mrs. Perdita is being naughty," he said, making clicking sounds with his tongue.

"She said I was s-supposed to tie you to the bedposts and dance for you." Isabella laughed, jittery and unsure. She didn't know what she was talking about. Perhaps Mrs. Perdita was joking.

He cocked a brow and flashed a devilish smile. "She did? Well, you better get to it. I want a show, my courtesan." He gave her a tiny, painless spank.

She gasped.

He leaped onto the bed and spread out his arms. "Tie me up, love."

She paused, the ties draping from her hands as she

studied his body in the candlelight—the contours of his chest, his belly striped with muscle, the light curls about his manly part, which was now relaxed. She was transfixed. He was so beautiful, he could be art— Michelangelo's *David*. "I'm waiting," he prompted, something dark and titillating in his dusky tone. She shook her head, waking from her dream to find she wasn't dreaming.

She pulled the lacy chemise over her head with trembling fingers and flipped out her hair, feeling the heat of his gaze on her body the entire time.

She approached the bed, unsure, and carefully crawled atop, wrapped one ribbon around the poster and then about his offered wrist. He stared on with glittering eyes, his lips unsteady, as if he might break into laughter at any moment. Having rarely sailed or done anything that required an intricate knot, all she could manage was a big, looping bonnet bow.

"Am I doing this correctly?" she ventured.

"Perfect," he murmured, pressing his face between her breasts. "Hmm…just perfect." His lips found her nipple, suckling her. She had to stop for a moment, arrested by the waves of pleasure cresting through her. He groaned, releasing her, and let her finish her tying business. Sitting back on her calves, she studied her work. Two large, pretty bows bound him. She giggled.

"You look like a big Christmas gift."

"Oh, I have a big gift—an enormous gift just for you, love. If you want it, you'll have to dance for it."

"I'm not going to dance!"

He jabbed her with his toe. "But you're my courtesan, remember? You're breaking the rules."

"You know I'm not a good dancer."

"I love how you dance. I've never seen another woman dance quite like you."

She put her glasses on the mattress and slowly rose to her feet. "I don't think that is a compliment. And don't you dare make fun of me."

"I would never make fun of you."

"Except all those thousands of times you have in the past."

"But you weren't naked then."

She laughed and began to awkwardly sway before him. Closing her eyes, she let her hair swish about as she hummed softly, her muscles beginning to relax. In her mind, she wasn't Isabella, but an exotic, graceful eastern dancer.

"Stunning," he whispered. "Come here; let me feel those wild, luscious tresses of yours on my body."

She knelt down, letting the wild, unruly mess pool around his face as she kissed him, her tongue swirling with his. And he couldn't do anything to stop her from getting what she wanted. When she pulled away, he tried to follow her lips, but the ribbons constrained him. He released a frustrated, grunt-like groan. "Come back," he beckoned.

Aha! Suddenly she understood this game: she was supposed to torture him. And she excelled at that! To test her hypothesis, she slid closer, putting her nipple just an inch from his mouth. When he rose to taste it, she snatched it away.

"You evil, evil vixen."

"I think I understand this game." She laughed and then kissed his neck, his chest, his belly. She felt the contraction of his muscles as he sucked his breath. She trailed her kisses lower, placing one on his manly part which rose, hard and ready to greet her. She now studied his sex, its contours and shape as she caressed him with her fingers and mouth.

"Oh, dear God," he muttered.

A man's penis wasn't the dirty, ridiculous thing that Judith had claimed, but a stunning, paradoxical creation, hard and fragile at the same time. She loved touching its skin, feeling the heat beneath, the power she had over it.

"Take off the chemise, Isabella," he said, hoarse and quiet.

She wasn't going to comply so easily; it was against the rules. But she crumbled when he uttered, low, teeth-clenched, beseeching, "Please."

She slowly rose to her feet and drew the chemise off, inch by inch, up her thighs, over her curls, her belly, her breasts, her head, until she was standing nude before him again.

"I can't believe I let this body live beside me for so many years unexplored," he said. "I blame you for hiding yourself from me."

Her throat tightened. "Well, up until a few days ago, I thought I had a future that didn't include a poorhouse and desperation."

"No, no, no, Isabella," he admonished. "Don't say that. Not tonight. No anxious thoughts are allowed in this bed. Just pleasure."

"I'm sorry."

"You should be. Now I'm rather low. My cock is downcast. There's nothing to be done but to shake them for me."

"Pardon?"

"Shake those lovely tits, love."

"Randall!" She gave him a tiny kick.

"Ouch!" he cried, overreacting. "I love your breasts. You don't know what torture they've been giving me this last day. Just one tiny shake, please, my courtesan of sublime ravishingment."

"'Ravishingment'? That's not even a word." She giggled, shaking her shoulders, trying to jiggle her bosom. In the process, she stepped onto the edge of the mattress, losing her balance. She gasped and waved her arms frantically, but she couldn't stop the fall. She tumbled over, landing on the carpeted floor beside the bed. She felt no pain except that of embarrassment. So much for being the exotic, dancing courtesan; the old Isabella kept breaking through to spoil everything.

"Darling!" she heard him call. "Love! Are you well? Talk to me. I'm damnably sorry. Say something."

"I'm not a very good courtesan." She pushed off the rug.

He released a long, relieved breath. "No, love, you're not. You better get me out of these ties before you hurt yourself any further."

She climbed onto the bed, replaced her glasses—resigned to being dull, clumsy Isabella again—and began to work on his bows. He waited patiently as she extricated one wrist, all the while watching her face, no doubt wishing she were another woman—a graceful, lithe one, like a ballet dancer. She was pulling the second ribbon free when, in a fast motion, he grabbed her arm and flipped her onto her back. "Randall, what are you…"

With amazing speed and dexterity—as if it were some kind of timed sporting event—he bound her in tight, bowless knots. "Impressive, no?" he asked, sitting back on his haunches to survey his work.

"You tricked me!"

"You of all people should know that I'm wily and sneaky, and not to trust a word I say." He stroked his chin with his index finger and thumb, exaggerating his thinking pose. "What to do with you? How can I revenge all those years of insulting and belittling?"

"You called me names too. You belittled me."

"But I'm not tied up now, am I?" He winked. "You had your chance." His eyes drifted from her face, down her chest, over her sex, and to her toes. "And I know the perfect torture," he said. "Something to shock our innocent Isabella's unsullied mind. You will not want to see what is about to happen." He removed her glasses, letting his tongue lick her ear and then pulling away. She strained against the ropes, wanting to feel him again. He laughed, thick and dark. "Turnabout is fair play and such, darling."

He proceeded to kiss the heated pulse on her neck, trailing kisses down, his breath tickling her skin, until he reached her left nipple. His tongue flicked over the tip as his hand pleasured the other. He kept up this torturous game until she was whimpering. "I hate you," she gasped. "You're cruel."

"Well then, I won't feel any guilt for the pleasure I'm about to inflict." He slid his knees between her legs, spreading her. She was wild with the thought that he was going to enter her again, but instead he moved his lips lower, licking her belly button, down her pelvis to her curls and then… *Oh my!*

Seventeen

Six hours later, Randall stared at the ceiling, not the least bit sleepy despite a night of repeated love-making. He should be spent. Instead he was restless. His head ached as if he had drunk too much, but the only thing intoxicating him the evening before had been Isabella's body. He had excessively overindulged in her. Now her cheek lay on his shoulder, her arm draped possessively across his chest as she slept. The fat, full moon spilled blue light through the crack between the curtains and the last candle was sputtering, about to die. She snuggled closer, a sweet smile curling her mouth. What did she see in her dreams? Was he there?

In his arms, she had laughed, explored, and climaxed over and over. But deep in the night, their courtesan game chafed his nerves. He wanted her to gently touch his face, as she had that moment on the sofa, when she gazed at him, her eyes tender and vulnerable. He wanted to make love to her slowly, tenderly, and release deep in her womb, complicating his life even more. He wanted her to whisper three words that he wouldn't dare tell her.

The sun was coming. He didn't know how many more hours they had until the news of the fraudulent investments broke. But this pending disaster had been looming even before Powers's nasty little trick. Randall had been struggling to keep his world afloat for the last year. Now he wasn't sure who or what he was trying to save. Nothing seemed real anymore, except the pressure of her soft breast pressed against him, her thigh across his leg. She said the game was for a single night. And in those hours, he had managed to break through that cold, hostile wall she always kept between them, discovering a trusting, loving, and playful woman on the other side. Emotions had washed through him more profoundly than he had felt with any other lover, as his body had moved in hers. He pretended along in this courtesan game, but was he truly pretending?

Memories drifted through his mind. When did he learn to be the man everyone wanted? He started as the golden boy sailing through school, taking the don's own words, embellishing them, and retelling them back. In Parliament, he took his party's arguments and spun them into golden, majestic stories. He knew a truth: people just wanted to hear their own thoughts. That was how he charmed them. This was his gift. He could ride this cushiony bubble to prime ministership if he married right, if he mopped up the mess with Harding, if his bank didn't fail, if he didn't have the desire to speak his own mind or be his own man…if he didn't fall in love with the wrong woman.

He glanced at the wrong woman. Her lashes cast shadows on her cheeks, her mouth lay open, and her warm breath rustled the pale hairs on his chest. He closed his eyes and kissed her forehead, lingering there.

Someone was bound to figure out that Izzy May was actually Isabella St. Vincent, the famed author and women's rights advocate. He could laugh it off and say that last night was a small joke between them. He could say he was drunk and confused. He could sweep Isabella under the rug to save his career. Even as a mistress, she was damaging.

What if he let it all fall apart? What if he walked away from his political career and let his bank fail? "Randall," she murmured. Her fingers tensed, then relaxed again. The acute pain in his heart made his eyes water.

Oh God, what madness had he agreed to last night? How could he face her and pretend it was all a game? He nestled his face in her hair, her citrus and sugar scent mingled with the earthy scents of lovemaking. He wished he could make this night last on and on.

But he couldn't keep her. He had responsibilities to his family, his country, and she to her bank and the Mary Wollstonecraft Society. To keep her, he would have to sacrifice his political career and disgrace his family's name. Mere half-Irish, rights-of-women advocating, merchants' daughters were not allowed into the sacred Hazelwood family tree.

Their lives were so different, yet their bodies fit so perfectly.

In his mind, he began to turn over the words he would tell her. They would be sweet, lovely, yet heartless at their core. He would rip her heart apart—that tender, fearful organ he was just beginning to understand.

But how could he go on living beside her and not think about this night?

He drew her closer, remembering what she had said earlier that evening in the gaming hell: "At this moment, everything is possible... There is no playing it safe now. In an instant all could be realized or lost."

"Lost," he murmured, his eyes moistening.

He didn't realize that he had drifted into sleep until he awoke to the gray, drab light of the morning streaming under the curtains. He jolted up, knowing something was wrong before he could name it. He was in bed alone. The lace chemise she had danced in was now neatly folded on a chair. The silken ribbons that she had strained against in orgasm were rolled into little circles and placed atop the shift.

Where did she go?

He slid out of bed, pulled the covers over himself, and padded downstairs, barefoot.

He found her by the front door. She wore another of his ex-mistress's dresses, her hair tidy and hat in place, showing no signs of the previous evening's ravishment.

"Good morning," she said, focusing on sliding her gloves on. "Mrs. Perdita was so kind as to retrieve some of my things from the hotel."

No morning kiss? No "Did you sleep well?" No "By the way, I fell in love with you last night. What are we going to do about this emotional mess?"

He squinted in the slant of the early sun beaming through the half-circle window above the door. "W-what are you doing?" he stammered, his brain confused and still dulled from sleep.

She raised her head, her face pale and expressionless. "I'm going to take the train to Tupping-on-the-Water to visit Merckler Metalworks."

For a moment, he couldn't speak. He stood, draped in his bedcovers, his mouth gaping, his feet cold on the wood planks. Did she not feel anything? Did she not wage some emotional battle in her head that made her question everything she thought she was, as well as her past and her future? Exactly who had been bought and used last night?

"Do you think I might like to go?" he asked, hearing the anger rising in his voice. "Seeing as my future is at stake as well?"

"You were sleeping." She shrugged, as if this were just another day, as if he hadn't taken her maidenhood the night before and then proceeded to make wild, uninhibited love to her into the early hours.

"That's typically what I do at six in the morning."

"Well, I've got to get down to the train station to catch the first train." She spun on her heel.

He seized her elbow. "You are not leaving me! You're going to have to wait until I get dressed. And I'm a little hungry. I don't know about you, but I had a rather physically taxing night. I pleasured an insatiable courtesan who demanded that I take her over and over."

This was going all wrong. He was supposed to deliver his gentle speech about how they could never be together. She was supposed to become upset and beg, while he remained firm but compassionate. She wasn't adhering to her lines in his play.

"That was last night," she said, and yanked away,

flashing him a scorching look that, through her thick lenses, could set fire to forests.

"Yes, last night when I took your virtue—when you knew a man for the first time."

Her chest palpitated with her rapid breath, her nostrils dilated. "I'm going to the train station now. I've got to find out if this Merckler Metalworks knows of its fraudulent stock."

"No." He dashed around her, blocking the door with his body. "First, we are going to talk about what happened last night."

"What is there to talk about?" she cried. "The game was a courtesan for the evening. Now it's done."

"What?" He shook his head in disbelief. "Do you have a heart in there?" He tried to cup her left breast. She slapped his hand away.

"Do you have a brain in there?" She pointed at his head. "We played a game. It had rules. You shouldn't have played if you can't abide by the rules. Why are you so…so emotional? This is why you lose at cards."

"Emotional. No, love, I'm what you call normal. Where is the lady who was here last night? You're—"

"Isabella." She flung up her arms. "I'm Isabella. Your enemy. The strange, scary girl. The lady you could never…never…" She didn't finish her words but rushed to the door. "Ugh! I've got to go."

Again, he blocked her. "You are not leaving this house without me. You will sit down and have some goddamn tea."

"Don't tell me what to do," she shouted.

"Don't make me tie you to the dining room table and force-feed you, because I will," he shouted back.

Her eyes narrowed. "You have five minutes. I'm not missing the train because of you."

He stared at her, all those gentle smiles and tender eyes from the evening before were gone. "What the hell is wrong with you?"

Her mouth dropped. "I'm trying to save our bank. That's what's wrong with me. I'm sorry if financial disaster interferes with your sleep." He tossed up his hands, dropping his covers.

She gasped, pressed her hand to her mouth, and pivoted.

"That's right, don't look at me!" He spread his arms wide, letting his Percy dangle free. "But you certainly couldn't stop looking last night. You couldn't get enough. I had to pry your mouth off my cock."

"Don't you ever talk about last night again!"

"Last night!" He stepped in front of her, trying to force her to see his naked body. She only turned the other way. They continued this little don't-look-at-me game as he yelled, "Last night! Last night! When you climaxed five times, including when you were straddling me." He backed her into the corner. She kept her face to the wall, refusing to look at him. "Last night! When I came on your breasts."

"I said never talk about it again!"

"Of course, we shouldn't talk about it. We might have some *feelings* or, heaven forbid, *emotions*."

"Y-you sound like Judith now," she said, her voice muffled by the wall.

"Oh God, how do I sound like that zealot—pardon me. I mean *wise advocate*."

She slowly turned. "Don't—don't talk about Judith that way. She says…she says…"

"What?" He crossed his arms. "Just say it."

"That I'm afraid of my emotions." Her words burst from her mouth. She squeezed her eyes shut. "Like my father's or mother's death or…" Her voice closed to a tight painful squeak. The tiniest tear tried to roll from the corner of her eye. She quickly brushed it away.

His heart contracted. He had never seen her cry for anything except hay and flowers. It destroyed him. All his rehearsed words about how they couldn't be together flew away. He had seen her fall from trees, scrape her knees, bury a father, be betrayed by a cheating business partner, but never had he seen her truly cry. What the hell was he doing? "Oh, Isabella," he said tenderly, stepping forward to wrap her into his arms. "I'm sorry."

She pushed against his chest. "What do you know about anything?" Her voice cracked as she threw her words like jagged knives. "T-this is the first bad thing that's ever happened to you. It's so terrible. People might not love you. They might not think you are a fine old chap." Her lips trembled.

"Let me hold you, my love." He kept his voice low and soothing, edging closer to her, as if she were a wild, injured animal. Another tear dared to form. She swiped it away as if it were something shameful. "Don't. You can cry." He tentatively caressed her taut shoulder muscles, trying to draw her into his embrace.

But she made a quick move, ducking under his arm. She yanked the door open and slipped away before he could catch her.

"Dammit." He chased after her. He was about to step over the threshold when he remembered that he was naked.

A tiny girl, holding her mama's hand, stopped on the street, pointed at him, and giggled. Her mother shrieked and covered her child's eyes. "You—you wicked reprobate!" she yelled at him.

He leaped inside and snatched his bedcovers from the floor. Holding them bunched over his private parts, he scrambled to the parlor and shoved the window open. He poked his head out and recognized Isabella's slim form and odd, wispy gait heading down the walk toward the train station.

"You wait for me, Isabella!" he shouted. "You can't leave me."

❧

The sun was bright and she turned her face to it, trying to dry her eyes. It had been a game, for God's sake. How dare he talk about her emotions? He, whose life until last week had been like a happy holiday to Brighton. Emotions were useless. They couldn't change the flip of a card, the spread of a cancer or catching of a chill, nor stop an errant bank partner. They just throbbed like a fresh, bleeding wound.

What did he want from her anyway? What did he want her to say? *I think I may be falling in love with you. Your old enemy, clumsy and awkward Isabella. Pathetic, isn't it?* Did he really think she would just stand there and listen to his charming, silvery words, explaining how he could never return her love—if this feeling were indeed love, because love shouldn't feel so gut-wrenchingly terrible. It shouldn't burn in her stomach or slice clean through her heart. It shouldn't feel like a death. If this was love, she hated it.

She hated herself.

This is your fault. Stop acting like a baby. If you can't take the risk, you shouldn't have played.

She raised her head, stiffened her spine, and walked on. *Be strong.*

❧

Isabella waited in a long line that wove around Euston station. Policemen patrolled the building, drumming their batons in their palms. The chatter echoed off the high ceiling above it all, and a man shouted arrival and departure times while another, selling newspapers, sang out rhymes made for the day's headlines.

> "Lord Randall, that golden boy,
> The progress of England he intends to destroy,
> What will become of his family's old glory,
> When challenged by two Whigs, a Chartist, and Tory?"

She listened to the songs, terrified that she might hear Bank of Lord Hazelwood in the stanzas of the nasty little ditties.

By the time she reached the window, the train for Tupping-on-the-Water was departing in thirteen minutes. She could just make it.

She opened her mouth to speak when she heard Randall's voice thunder, "Two first-class round-trip tickets for Tupping-on-the-Water."

She turned to find the viscount sprinting along the line. Her rebellious, stupid heart lifted. Perspiration spiked the hair about his forehead and temples. His coat flapped behind his elbows and his vest was held by a single button. He sidled in beside her, breathing heavily.

"Y-you're breaking in the queue," she cried. "I hate when people do that."

"We're together," he told the ticket master, taking her elbow. A current of hot, crackling electricity shot up her arm and down to her female regions.

"No, we are not," she countered. "I'm tired, and I prefer a car to myself." In truth, she didn't want to be near Randall. She wasn't strong enough yet. Even now, his touch was undoing her.

"Me lady," the annoyed ticket master began, "this line is filled with people trying to get on the train to Tupping—"

"Give us two seats in the same carriage," Randall said in that annoying, commanding, male way of ending discussions.

"Don't listen to him," she cried. "What if he were a murderer intent on strangling me?"

The ticket master released an annoyed huff and slid two tickets across the marble surface. She and Randall raced to collect them. He beat her, his palm slapping down on the slab, covering the tickets. She pried at his fingers.

"My death could be on your hands," she told the ticket master, who didn't appear to be overwrought at the prospect of her homicide, except to signal to an approaching policeman.

"What is the matter here?" the policeman inquired.

"She just wants to be alone," Randall explained, scooping up the tickets and shoving them in his pocket. "So she won't have to confront her feelings."

"Not everybody feels the immature need to spout their every emotion," she retorted, her voice echoing to the ceiling. "Some of us are perfectly content remaining calm and stoic."

"Calm and stoic?" Randall barked a laugh. "Don't you mean repressed and rigid?"

"All right, all right then," the policeman said, his voice weary. He seized both of them by their arms. "Let's have your little lovers' quarrel in a more convenient location."

"We are not lovers!" she shouted at the same time the viscount said, "Unhand me, I am Lord Randall!" All the heads in the line whipped around to stare. The room turned silent. Mortified heat burned her cheeks.

Then the newspaper seller cried, "Aha!" and began to sing:

"Viscount Lord Randall
Caught in a scandal
First class, please, for the fair lady and scoundrel."

Isabella turned and fled for the platform.

Eighteen

Isabella found an empty seat on a carriage containing a severe family consisting of a withered mother, dour husband, sullen grown sister, and bored younger brother, all dressed in mourning. The grimness was broken only by a white lily in a pot on the mother's lap. Isabella sneezed. Could she take an entire train ride of watering eyes and sneezing? She glanced out the window to see Randall running down the platform, calling her name. Yes, she could.

She murmured her greetings and condolences to the family and took the empty seat by the window, furthest from the flower. As the train started to move, the door burst open. "There you are," Randall cried.

Fudge! "This carriage is full," she told him.

"Oh, what a stunning lily," Randall said to the withered woman, removing his hat. "The flower is nice as well." The woman's severe face softened. She scooted over, letting him sit between her and her husband.

Honestly, Randall can romance any woman. I must have been easy prey.

She felt safe with the dour, quiet family separating her and Randall. Unfortunately, they got off two stations down the line.

As soon as the door had closed, Randall shot across the carriage. Why couldn't he be like her and just let what happened last night lie silent, smoldering and festering, in a hidden grave in his heart? But he had to speak. After all, he was the famous orator. He slid beside her and tried to entwine her fingers. "I think we—"

"Can we just save the bank?" she protested, edging away from him until she was jammed against the window. "That's all that really matters. Then you can go back to…to Cecelia or someone else. Or marry some Tory's ravishing daughter and continue your golden path to prime minister and never utter another word about last night."

He stared at her and then flung up his hands. "Very well. I'll play this ridiculous game. So, what about you, Isabella? What if we save the bank? What happens to you?"

"I don't starve. I-I don't ruin my father's memory or lose all he worked for." Isabella's eyes moistened. The essence of that stupid lily obviously still lingered in the carriage. She wiped her eyes with her gloved hand. "For God's sake, it was a game. Just a game."

"One we shouldn't have played. It was a horrible mistake, and I'm damnably sorry."

"You…you are?" She wished he hadn't said those words. He was supposed to say something like, *It was a wonderful game—the best I ever played. It's a shame we will never, ever do it again. And even though I can't stop thinking about how beautiful and amazing I felt in your arms and how I'm going to live the rest of my life knowing I will never experience anything that perfect again— I'm not going to talk about what happened. Silence to the grave.*

But instead, he regretted her. She was his "horrible mistake."

"Aren't you?" His beautiful eyes searched her face, but she couldn't look at him because of those blessed tears threatening again.

She closed her eyes and tried to force a lie about how last night meant nothing to her, just a pleasant diversion from these tense hours. But when she opened her mouth, no words came, just a hurt squeak. *I'm not a mistake.*

"Oh, Isabella." He leaned in to wrap her in his embrace. She didn't have the strength to fight him. Then, in a twinkling, he flew across the carriage, leaving her to hug the cold air.

"Wh—"

The door burst opened and a footman helped a woman into the carriage. Stiff coils of salt-and-pepper hair fell about her face, and she wore a blue fur-lined cloak over her expansive skirts. A tiny, furry dog's head poked out from her green valise.

"Lord Randall!" the woman exclaimed. "What a surprise! I thought you would be at your house party."

He flashed a pleasant, polite smile, as if the previous minutes when he'd broken Isabella's heart hadn't happened, and rose to assist the lady. "I'm afraid I'm taking a sad journey to visit an ill friend," he said, his voice low and mournful.

The woman pressed her palm to her chest, clanking her bracelets. "Oh, I'm so very sorry." She whirled around. "Did you hear, my dearest darlings? Poor Lord Randall has a sick friend." Behind her massive skirt stood two young ladies, waiting their turn to enter. The dearest darlings murmured their sympathies, but their cheeks were flushed and eyes dancing upon hearing the "sad" news that they would be sharing a train carriage with Lord Randall.

They broke into giggles when he clasped their fingers, leading them to a seat.

"I'm dreadfully sorry, monumentally sorry, that I had to decline your family's kind invitation," the mother continued. "Weren't we, dearest darlings? But it is Mama's eightieth birthday. We simply couldn't get away. Ah, but now you are here. We shall have a nice, cozy chat." The little dog began to yip. "Yes, we will, my little poo-poo," she cooed to the hound, tugging its ear. "Oh, good heavens! I didn't see you there," she cried, spying Isabella, who was smashed against the window and was covered in reams of the dearest darlings' overflowing skirts. She must not have assumed any connection between Isabella and Randall because she didn't wait for an introduction. "I'm Lady Rexmore. My husband is the Earl of Rexmore and Mama is the Dowager Duchess of Fenshire, you know."

Maybe Isabella's lack of sleep or anxiety about her future or acute heartache subdued the typical tongue-tied nervousness she felt whenever meeting new people. A tiny devil danced in her eyes when she tartly replied, "I'm Miss St. Vincent, spinster, member of the Wollstonecraft Society for the Rights of Women. Mama was an Irish immigrant, you know."

"Oh," the woman said after a long, shocked pause, and then, "Oh" again and finally, "How nice for you." She tucked her little dog closer, as if it might contract whatever disease Isabella carried. At least Isabella regained valuable seating territory, as the daughters retreated closer to Randall, their protector from the dangerous spinster.

She kept her ear pressed to the glass, hoping the chug of the engine would drown out the giggle-infested, insipid chatter about people she didn't know or teas, balls, and house parties that she wasn't invited to. He rolled along with the ladies' banter, knowing all the names and addresses, and sliding in devious little comments which caused the misses to blush and their mother to fan her face and exclaim, "Aren't you naughty, Lord Randall?"

How easily he flirted. He just as easily charmed willing courtesans, actresses, and desperate spinsters to his bed. He was only sorry that he had chosen the wrong one last night. *A horrible mistake.* Isabella recalled all the "my loves" murmured with the same breezy ease as he moved inside her. She should have known Randall's words had no connection to his heart. The only thing occupying his blood pumper was his own ambition. *Accept your losses and save your bank.*

But when she looked at him, his bright gaze latched on to the young ladies, her throat burned. She itched to run her nails down the dearest darlings' gowns and then across Randall's smiling, handsome face.

Randall watched Isabella sit with her cheek pressed against the glass, hands clenched, rocking with the train's rhythm. Even though he knew it was safer to pretend not to know each other, he would have appreciated some conversational help. An hour into the miserable journey, he wanted to leap to his feet and shout, "Don't you understand? My reputation and honor are about to be destroyed. I'm falling in love with the wrong woman, abandoned children clutter London's doorsteps, and I'm having to talk about promenading in the damn park and praising bloody bonnets!"

Despondency weighed on him as he drew an analogy: *my whole life is about being trapped on a first-class train carriage, complimenting millinery, and making pleasant, mindless chatter.* He couldn't stem these gloomy thoughts; they kept swelling like water from a spring. He composed his face in a pleasant expression, he murmured the correct words, but inside his anxious mind, the ladies' banter was like the annoying buzz of a fly. Across the carriage, Isabella remained quiet, staring at the countryside. He could see the scenery reflecting off her lenses. Sometimes she moved her lips, biting the inner corner of one or rubbing them together. As much as she angered or frustrated or hurt him—he didn't know anymore—he wanted to feel the comfort of those lips again. At every stop, he hoped Lady Rexmore and her daughters would say their adieus, so he could hold Isabella. But in the end, the Tupping-on-the-Water station arrived first.

Isabella fled the carriage as if it were about to go up in flames. Meanwhile, Randall was delayed, accepting condolences for his sick friend and best wishes for every member of his extended family, promising to attend Lady Rexmore's debut ball for her daughter that spring, as well as to call on them when he was next in London. By the time the ladies were finished, he had to leap from the moving train. He scanned the platform; Isabella was nowhere to be seen.

Would it have killed her to wait for him?

He stomped into the station, muttering curses under his breath. Amid porters lugging trunks, muffin vendors calling out, and people coming to a dead halt in the middle of the busy hall to listen to the departures being announced, he spied her speaking to a porter by the door.

"Izzy May," he shouted across the room.

She shot him a look that would have sent the hounds of hell scurrying away, their tails between their legs. The situation was tense already; must she exacerbate it? He jogged to her.

"Mrs. Merckler lives in a manor house on the hill," the porter was explaining. "After leaving the station, turn to the left and follow the street a half mile out of the village gates."

"Are you sure it's only a half mile?" Isabella demanded. "Have you measured it?"

The young porter raised his brows, offended. "I walk past it every day, miss." Any injury Isabella may have inflicted was forgotten when she dropped a groat into his palm. "It's probably less, miss," he assured her. "And downhill part of the way."

"Thank you," she replied, and headed off as if Randall wasn't standing beside her, offering his arm.

He bit another curse back and caught up with her.

"Can we talk now?" he demanded, his voice harsher than he intended, as they stepped outside. The clouds were low and thick, and the air wet. Pastel town houses lined the street. Women clustered in the doorways, conversing while holding babies on their hips. At their hems, small children played.

"I said before that there is nothing to talk about."

"Of course there isn't," he said in mock agreement. He matched her strident pace, only causing her to walk faster. "You know you could have said a nice word to Lady Rexmore, instead of leaving me to do all the work."

"You looked like you were enjoying yourself," she fired back. "It's so hard to be adored and coddled. How did you manage it?"

"Well, I had to make up for your chilly demeanor," he said, his voice getting louder.

"As if she wanted to talk to me! The Irish rights-for-women advocate. She was just terrified that I would give her daughters some socially disfiguring disease before their debut ball."

He shook his palms before his face. "Woman, why do you assume everyone will think badly of you?"

"Previous experience."

"All of England's spinsters and widows are enamored of you."

"That's because they don't know the real me. And, as I recall, you don't think too highly of me either."

"What!" He could feel the veins in his neck bulge. He grabbed her arm. "We need to talk. Now."

"Very well!" she yelled, causing several of the

women gabbing in the doorways to turn their heads and stare. "If I talk, will you leave me alone? Then can we go about solving our real problems?" She didn't wait for his answer. "I don't belong in your world of polite teas, balls, gossip, old family glory, ravishing actress mistresses, and gently bred, giggling, dearest darling debutantes." His chest tightened as she said the words he didn't want to admit. "I'm a detriment to you in any capacity. So if you are thinking of some gentle way to tell me not to get too attached to you, that you could never lo—*like* me, well, save your breath. I was your, quote, 'horrible mistake.' I'm—"

"You're changing my words. I never said—"

"I'm clumsy and strange…and…and…I don't want you anyway. We're enemies, remember?" A fat teardrop rolled onto her lashes.

"Then why are you crying?"

"I'm not!" She wiped her eyes. "I don't cry unless something is blooming or…or there's hay about, or certain types of dogs can—"

"Dammit, if you keep denying how you truly feel, if you keep trying to push all your emotions into a tight, tiny ball, one day you're going to blow like a steam engine."

"Let's just hope I'm not in the poorhouse when that happens." She yanked her arm from his hold. "There, we have spoken. Are you satisfied?"

"Bloody hell no!"

Clearly, she was mollified, because she stomped away.

A tiny child tugged at his mother's dress. "Mama,

they weren't using polite words," he said, his eyes wide. "They're in trouble."

Randall hissed an extremely impolite word under his breath and hurried to catch his enemy. In silence, except for the swishing of their clothes, each tried to walk faster than the other. In this ridiculous manner, they exited the village gates and marched into the lush, sheep-dotted countryside.

Inside, he knew that he should leave the issue the hell alone. She recognized the situation and wasn't willing to get herself entangled. Rather than being relieved, it only drove his anger higher. She was supposed to say that she loved him against all rationality, that her longing was tearing her heart apart. He desired weepy-eyed pleas to find a way to make their love work in this cruel, unforgiving world. He needed bombastic passion, sobbing fireworks; he wanted her to want him so badly, so desperately that she would give up her heart, her life, her world for him.

But Isabella was too smart for that.

I don't want you anyway, she had said.

That's not what you cried last night when your thighs were trembling around my head.

Damn her.

They turned onto the drive of a newly built manor home, a rather pompous creation of towers and massive, arching windows. The white stone gleamed through the gray day. Shaggy shrubs grew up the sides, almost covering the ground-floor windows. Two hounds with large, floppy ears lay on their sides in the tall, unclipped grass of the front lawn. They raised their heads as Isabella and Randall stomped passed.

Uninterested in the silent, warring pair, the dogs returned to their afternoon snooze.

Isabella and Randall reached to pull the doorbell at the same time. She bumped him with her hip, trying to shove him out of the way. He only stepped ahead of her, keeping his hold tight on the bell.

"What do you think you are doing?" she cried, as she tried to pry his fingers off the metal.

"I'm pulling the damn doorbell," he hissed back.

They were caught in this childish exhibition when the door opened. A dour, severe-faced woman, all dressed in black, peered first at them, then the doorbell which they both clutched, with disapproving eyes. Behind her, the house was ablaze with activity. Children sang nursery rhymes, glass shattered, and feet shuffled. A young, exasperated female voice rang out above this cacophony. "No, Uncle Linus, don't try to repair the ceiling by yourself." Another crash, this time something wooden and splintering. "Uncle Linus!"

Randall released the doorbell and removed his hat. "Pardon me, I'm Mr. Randy and we desire an audience with Mrs. Merckler."

"That's me," cried the exasperated female voice.

The dour woman stepped aside to reveal a petite, pretty blond, who looked no more than twenty-two. Yet the intelligent, annoyed green eyes and peevish set to her mouth belonged on a weary forty-year-old. Her hair looked as if it had been pinned up in fifteen seconds and then hit with a blast of wind. Her fingers were slim and the nails bitten down.

"Oh goodness, a *man*!" Mrs. Merckler smoothed her black skirt and forced a dimpled smile, which appeared painfully at odds with the rest of her harried appearance. "Good afternoon," she said in a sugary tone.

Randall clasped Isabella's elbow. She sported that confused, dazed expression she had whenever there was too much activity around her.

"Hello, I'm Mr. Randy," he said again, bowing. "And this is Miss Izzy May, my…" He turned to his belligerent companion. What incarnation was she this time? A nasty devil pulled up a chair on his shoulder, and he drew Isabella closer. "My dearest, lovely fiancée."

"Fiancée!?" both Isabella and Mrs. Merckler echoed.

The widow's eyes rolled heavenward and her smile flattened back to an agitated line. She must be on the prowl for a new husband, he thought, and only a few months after her other one's death.

"We desire to discuss some business concerning Merckler Metalworks." He smiled through the pain Isabella was inflicting as she dug her fingers into his arm. "We are thinking of investing our future little Izzy's and Randy's education funds into your factory." He received a sharp jab in the ribs for that one. "We received such a lovely brochure from you."

Mrs. Merckler flicked her hand. "Well, I'm perfectly horrid with business. And—Uncle Linus, put that ladder away!" she shouted into a room on the left and then turned her attention back to Randall and his silently raging "fiancée." "I don't understand appreciations, depreciations, capital investments, and whatevers. You should go down to the factory and talk to Mr—"

"Look what we found, Aunt Evie." A small, towheaded boy in coats tugged Mrs. Merckler's skirt. Behind him were two adorable children, each holding a fat, wiggling black-and-white puppy. "Can we keep them?"

The widow began to tremble.

"No!" Mrs. Merckler wailed an agonizing, soul-strangled cry. "No more cute stray kitties or abandoned snuggly puppies, or birds with broken wings, or huge, hairy spiders that you found in the woods, or orphaned, sad-eyed children or homeless spinster aunts or general relations in any pathetic, needy predicament. No more anything. I'm putting my foot down."

The faces of the tiny children and the dour woman crumpled as they broke into shoulder-convulsing sobs.

Mrs. Merckler pressed her palm to her forehead. "Oh God," she whispered. "I'm sorry. I'm very sorry. I love you all. I do. With all my heart." She knelt down and wrapped her arms about the weeping children. However, the sobbing continued crescendo-ing until Mrs. Merckler rolled her eyes heavenward and conceded. "All right, all right, keep the puppies." Great cheers went up. Happiness was restored to everyone except Mrs. Merckler, who was taking quick, shallow breaths as if she might break down on the spot. She turned and looked at Randall and Isabella, who no longer had her fingernails deep in his arm, but gazed upon the scene with her jaw dropped.

"You see, I am truly horrid at business," the widow explained. "I simply can't help you. I'm so very, very, very sorry. Why don't you take a puppy instead? Everyone wants a puppy." Beneath the brittle, pleasant words was a tone that implied, *Why are you still here? Can't you see I'm breaking down?*

"We won't take very long," Randall said in a low, calming voice. "I see you have a great deal of responsibility. We wouldn't want to burden you. Maybe just a relaxing, warming glass of sherry or two?"

"I don't think I should... S-sherry? Did you say sherry?" A soft light broke through Mrs. Merckler's tense features. "Sherry is lovely. Yes, oh, yes. Just a glass, to relax." She beckoned them toward a room to the right.

Randall and Isabella looked at each other, the last hours of hostility and fear temporarily forgotten. They followed Mrs. Merckler like two nervous comrades headed into the smoke-filled battlefield.

They entered a paneled parlor, the walls crowded with crossed rifles and the heads of various beasts. In the center of the room, two matching brown leather sofas faced each other. In the space between lay a leopard rug, and over it stood a marble table decorated with two ivory tusks and stuffed elephants' feet.

"Do sit down." Mrs. Merckler closed the double doors, silencing all the noise beyond. She crossed to a table along the side wall that held an array of crystal decanters and tumblers.

"A nicely appointed room," Randall lied, drawing Isabella onto the sofa beside him. He had been in a hundred such manly chambers in his political career, but today, the dead eyes staring at him heightened his discomfort. Maybe because he felt like the hunted animal now, running, waiting for the gunfire, and then the eternal silence—his short political life snuffed.

He sat, drawing his pretend fiancée beside him. He needed her touch to give him strength.

"I hate it too." Mrs. Merckler poured a glass. She had perceived his true feelings; he had to be careful. Beneath her youthful, beleaguered appearance, he sensed a sharp mind. "It was my husband's," she explained. "I wasn't allowed in it when he was alive. But Uncle Linus will insist on destroying the ladies' parlor with his repairs."

She drank down her sherry and gazed at the dead animals decorating the walls. "The poor dears," she murmured. She poured more spirits into her glass and two other tumblers. After distributing the drinks to her guests, she took her own and eased into the deep cushions of the opposite sofa.

"You are lucky," she said, studying him and Isabella over the rim of her glass. "You are very much in love."

"What!" Isabella cried. "No!" He gave her a tiny nudge with his elbow. "I mean, yes! Yes, we are very, very much in…in…" Her lips and tongue formed the *L* and the *V*, but the vowels came out a gargled slur. "How can you tell?"

"By how he holds you, so tenderly," the widow answered. "And how neatly you fit next to him. As if you each weren't whole without the other." She fanned her hand across her face. "And in your eyes. You can always tell when people are in love by their eyes." She turned silent, her gaze stretching a thousand miles away from this room. "You are lucky," she whispered again.

"I'm sorry about your loss," Randall gently said. "You must have loved your husband a—"

"I didn't care for him at all," the widow replied matter-of-factly. "I probably shouldn't have said that. See how relaxing sherry is?" She gave a rueful laugh. "There are so many words that shouldn't have been said. But it really doesn't matter anymore."

Isabella lifted her eyes to Randall. He could feel her discomfort and the sympathy that she didn't know how to express.

"But you've come to talk to me about business." Mrs. Merckler steered the conversation to its proper course. "In the bureau behind me are many ledgers filled with numbers that I don't understand. Mr. Merckler told me not to worry my pretty little head about such matters, and they didn't teach widowhood and running a factory in ladies' seminary. I'm afraid I can't help you."

"Do you not have a man of business?" he asked.

"The factory manager visits every Tuesday and Thursday. He speaks in odd terms and numbers. When I ask him to clarify, he tells me that, as a woman, I wouldn't understand." She rested her elbow on the armrest and rubbed her forehead. "I shouldn't tell you this, but you're fine, honest people. Don't invest little Izzy's and Randy's futures into my factory. Something is wrong and I can't figure it out." She shrugged her shoulders, making a hysterical sound between a laugh and a whimper. "You see, I've resorted to having my uncle repair my home."

He didn't want to leave Isabella's side, but Mrs. Merckler's distress was written across her lovely face. Had she been stuck in this house for months of mourning, taking care of people with no one to confide in? He crossed to her. "My dear lady, how can we—"

"A metalworks company shouldn't be losing money when the entire country is mad to cover itself in railroad tracks," Isabella stated. She stared at the bureau, her brows flattened in concentration. He knew her mind was running miles ahead.

A kindred light sparked in the young widow's eyes. She leaned forward and set down her glass. "That's what I thought. I've been reading this book *From Poor to Prosperous*. It's by a lady who understands business. She writes about opportunity and market demand. That's what I keep telling Mr. Quimby. He's the factory manager."

"*From Poor to Prosperous* is a wonderful, meticulously researched tome on the subject of investing and business," Randall said with a straight face, not daring to glance at the author. "Miss St. Vincent is a brilliant woman, and passionate about her subject—albeit I've heard she can be excessively violent if you annoy her."

"I feel like I'm one of her pathetic examples," Mrs. Merckler quipped. "The widow with seven hungry children and a meager pension…except, in my case, it's five spinster sisters-in-law, two maternal uncles, three widowed aunts, four female stepchildren, seven nieces and nephews, and other destitute people who just showed up one day and claimed they were related."

"You should write Miss St. Vincent." He gave Isabella the most direct, not-to-be missed glare he could discretely manage while enunciating each word carefully. "I'm sure she would *love* to *help* you."

Isabella blinked. "M-may I see those ledgers, please?" By God in heaven, could the amazing lady finally read him after all these years? "Perhaps I can help," she said, coming to her feet. "My late father owned some factories, and I managed them when he was sick, but ultimately he sold them. Oh, don't bother getting up. I can manage."

"All the ledgers are arranged by years in the shelves," Mrs. Merckler told her. "This year's has only a few pages filled out before he died."

Isabella opened the glass cabinet of the bureau. Randall watched her run her fingers along the ledgers' dates, finding the one she wanted. She quickly flipped the pages, but he knew not a single misplaced decimal or comma escaped her notice.

"Come, Mrs. Merckler, my glass is empty," he said. "Let us have another drink, because I might as well not exist while my fiancée is enraptured by numbers. They are her true love. I'm a mere diversion." He poured the sherry into her glass and then his own. "You've been through a great deal recently. You're taking care of many people. I can tell that they love you and depend on you. Like my fiancée, you're a remarkable and wonderful lady." He aimed his words at Isabella, but she was deep in a ledger and didn't hear him. He winked at Mrs. Merckler, sharing the private joke. "Tell me about your husband."

"There isn't much to say." She shrugged. "He was twenty-six years older than I. I was an ornament, much like these beasts on the walls." She adopted a deep voice. "I shot that. I stabbed that. I married that."

Randall chortled in sympathy, encouraging her to continue talking.

"I thought I was doing the right thing." She stared at an empty spot on the wall between a buffalo head and an old blunderbuss. "I learned to dance, sew samplers, and sing. I tried so hard to do everything perfectly. I even won an award in ladies' seminary: the superlative young lady of the year. My parents were so proud. When I was sixteen, they told me that I must marry Mr. Merckler, that he was rich and would take care of me. They said I would forget about J-Jonathon." She turned silent for a beat. "But memories don't fade. They just grow stronger and more painful."

A cold shiver flowed down Randall's back as if her words were meant for him. He realized what happened last night wasn't going to fade away silently. No matter whom he married or how far his ambition took him, he would spend his last moments on his deathbed remembering Isabella's vulnerable face when she had whispered, *I never thought it would be you. Never in a million years.*

"Mrs. Merckler, these numbers that Mr. Quimby gave you," Isabella said from the bureau. Her hard business tone broke into his sad ruminations. "Do you remember any of them? Did he say something about quarterly profit?"

"He said we didn't make a profit last quarter," she replied. "There weren't enough orders and he had to let workers go."

Isabella tapped her finger on the ledger's cover. "In the quarter before your husband's death, he turned the lowest profit of his last five years. A mere one hundred and fifteen pounds. That was down almost eighty-two percent."

"Oh," Mrs. Merckler said. "I don't understand. He was wonderful at business. What happened?"

"Nothing unusual," Isabella replied. "He had retooled his factory. Before he died, he had some significant pending orders from the Hull and Leeds Railroad Company and another from the Great Southern Railroad Company." Isabella waved a missive. "This letter was wedged between the pages. It concerns partnering with the Great Southern Railroad Company. What became of those orders or this potential partnership?"

All George Harding's rivals, Randall thought. *Bloody hell.*

"I don't know." Mrs. Merckler pounded the sofa cushion with her tiny fist. "I was too busy knitting him stupid slippers."

"How long has Mr. Quimby been the manager?" Isabella asked.

"Just after my husband's death. The old manager, a dear man, said the board had released him and given his position to Mr. Quimby."

"Did anyone at all consult you about the replacing of the manager?" Isabella asked, her voice becoming sharp and heated. "In the ledger, your husband listed all the shareholders. You own forty-five percent of the company. You have a say in how the business is run."

Mrs. Merckler shook her head, her blond curls slapping her cheeks. "They taught me how to make a pretty French knot, not how to run a factory. I'm useless. I don't know what I'm doing."

"No, no, Mrs. Merckler, that's not true," Randall said, patting the woman's wrist. "Perhaps you could be a little more gentle, Isabella," he said, trying to sound pleasant while heavily emphasizing the "more" and "gentle" part. But she was in another world filled with cold logic, quarterly profits, and whatever else ticked in the clockwork of her brain.

"Do you know if a Mr. Anthony Powers called shortly after your husband's death," Isabella asked, closing the ledger and returning it to the correct place on the shelf. "He's a bachelor, rather handsome and eloquent—"

"He's about as eloquent as my big toe and a good deal uglier," Randall interjected. "He is prawn-like, and his eyes—"

"No unmarried man has visited me except for you," Mrs. Merckler answered in a flat voice that left no room for doubt. "And you're hopelessly smitten. I would have remembered a young marriage prospect, prawn-like or not. Marriage is my only way out of this messy predicament."

"No, it's not," Isabella disagreed. "You have a factory that is modernized in a country that's railroad mad. Someone is purposely deceiving you."

"W-what?" Mrs. Merckler's gaze darted between Isabella and Randall. She paused, her lips forming an O. "What is happening here?" she asked slowly.

"Mrs. Merckler," Randall began, "I fear we haven't been entirely honest with you. My real name is Lord Randall and this is…" Isabella's eyes grew wide. "Isabella St. Vincent, author of *From Poor to Prosperous*. We are bank partners at the Bank of Lord Hazelwood."

"What…" The widow leaped to her feet and approached Isabella, her head cocked, eyes suspicious. "You're really Miss St. Vincent?"

"Yes."

"Why didn't you tell me?"

Isabella bit the edge of her lip. "Well, we, I mean, I… So there was a gentleman and he…well…" Randall was ready to break in when Isabella stiffened her spine. "I'm afraid someone has been circulating false stock in your company, and my bank may have bought it."

Mrs. Merckler's shoulders began to quake. "Oh God. Oh God. I can't take any…any more. I just can't! Where is that damned sherry!"

Randall shot around the sofa. "Now, Mrs. Merckler, just sit down and take deep, calming breaths."

"Don't get emotional," Isabella supplied.

"You've got to help me." The widow grabbed Isabella's hands. "I don't know what to do."

"I promise I will. I promise… Well, unless I end up in the poorhouse."

"What!" Mrs. Merckler screamed, tears bursting from her eyes.

"Forget I said that," Isabella cried. "I didn't mean it. It just popped out."

"Isabella is awful about saying random scary things," Randall assured Mrs. Merckler. "They edited those parts out of her book. Just take us to your factory."

Nineteen

THEY WAITED FOR MRS. MERCKLER ON THE FRONT lawn, where the dogs still lay in the tall grass. For a moment, Isabella thought they were dead, but then one wagged the tip of its tail.

"I can't believe you," she snapped at Randall. "Your fiancée? That was perfectly horrid of you."

"We were quite convincing, darling. She immediately recognized that you weren't whole without me."

"And you're hopelessly smitten with me," she retorted, and rubbed her finger over the list of Merckler Metalworks shareholders that the widow let her have. "Can I really help her? I haven't managed a factory since those few months before my father died."

He drew away a stray lock of hair that blew across her nose. "Isabella, as your greatest enemy, you must believe me when I tell you that I have complete faith in you."

She gazed at him, his vivid blue eyes contrasted with the heavy, dull gray sky. The wind ruffled his cravat and the blond strands under his hat. She should say something biting to further distance him, but she couldn't summon her defenses. Instead, she whispered, "Thank you." They didn't speak again, but looked at each other, the space between them filled with unspoken, flailing words. Enemies, friends, lovers, business partners—their relationship was as tangled as a ball of yarn after her cat, Milton, had batted it around the house for a month.

Mrs. Merckler exited the house with a cape and an umbrella. The dogs shot to attention and bolted to her side. Isabella stuffed the shareholder list into her corset, and she and Randall followed the woman and hounds down the street lined with pastel town houses, and then along a canal. The heavy sky reflected in the water, and ducks shot across the surface. The beautiful countryside reminded her of home. She had only been away three days, but it seemed like weeks.

What would her life be like when she returned? Would she be selling her home to pay off debt and worrying about how to survive? If not, she would save the bank only to continue living near Randall, pretending that last night hadn't happened. When he finally popped the question to the right Tory daughter, would Isabella have the strength not to scratch the woman's eyes out at the wedding ceremony or wish that their beautiful babies were hers?

The metalworks factory stood beside the canal. She had expected to hear machines booming across the water, but the low brick building with dirty windows was eerily silent. They entered into a hall, the cream walls decorated with wainscoting and mechanical illustrations. The scent of oil, metal, sweat, and heat wafted down the corridor. She found this plain, masculine setting comforting. She remembered being a little girl, sitting on that old blanket her mama had laid out on the factory floor. Isabella had played whist with her dolls amid the rumble and pounding of her papa's machines.

Mrs. Merckler knocked on a door. "Mr. Quimby," she said, her voice soft and hesitant. After waiting several long moments, she knocked again. "Mr. Quimby?" She waited about half a minute and then turned. "I'm sorry, he seems to be—"

The door opened and a muscular, broad-shouldered man strolled out. He sported a headful of oily, black curls and sideburns on his wide face. Dark stubble peppered his jaw and chin. His blue coat was wrinkled, and his belly strained the bottom button of his waistcoat. He studied them with frank, dark brown eyes, his mouth twisting into a juicy smirk. The office behind him measured no more than ten by four feet. It wouldn't have taken him but a few seconds, not an entire minute, to get up and open the door.

He only said "yes" as a way of greeting the majority shareholder of the factory. Isabella's father would have upbraided him on the spot.

Mrs. Merckler began to make the introductions. "May I present—"

"Mr. Randy," the viscount interjected. A silent, hostile communication passed between the men when their hands met. Isabella didn't know what was not said, but she felt an uneasy twinge in her gut. Randall didn't introduce her.

"Mr. Randy is interested in touring the factory,"

Mrs. Merckler explained. "He has some ideas how to generate profit."

"I'm rather busy today," Quimby said.

With what? Isabella thought. *Drinking the dark spirits from the jar on your desk and reading the caricatures in the latest penny journal?* "Mr. Quimby," she began. Her own voice shocked her, the deep power which sounded so much like her papa's. "The majority shareholder of your factory just told you to give us a tour. If you haven't the time, I'll be glad to supply her with a list of competent, respectful managers to replace you."

The man's eyes turned black with his glower. Randall placed a hand on her arm, trying to draw her back, but Isabella would not be cowed. She stood her ground.

"Very well," the manager conceded with a smirk. He gestured to a set of double doors at the end of the hall.

They entered a large, flat, unventilated area. The belts running along the walls and across the room were still. Shiny new machinery sat about, most unused, some of it even covered with blankets. The windows in the ceiling were closed, coated in dust, letting no light in and keeping the same dust-laden, acrid air trapped. Isabella's eyes burned, and she pressed her hand on her chest, laboring to breathe. Slender adolescent boys stood about tables, hammering metal into submission. Their skin glistened with perspiration and was streaked with grease. In the corner, blackened children, no more than eight years old, shoveled coal into the mouth of a blazing furnace. Isabella didn't see any adult supervising the work.

"How old are those children?" Randall demanded, his lips thinned and tight.

Quimby shrugged. "I don't know."

"No child under nine is allowed to work," Randall said.

"Well then, they're nine," Quimby said, and spat on the floor.

Randall crossed to the table where the boys pounded metal with mallets. "How long do you work a day?" he asked the young workers.

The boys glanced at each other and shrugged. "From dark to dark, sir," one answered with an Irish lilt.

"From dark to dark?" Randall repeated.

Isabella watched the tendons in Randall's neck bulge as he approached the manager. She had an awful dropping sensation in her belly, knowing that something terrible was about to happen. She had spent most of her life plotting ways to make Randall angry, but she had never seen him so enraged.

"Last year, a hard-fought law was passed in Parliament limiting the labor of children between the ages of nine and thirteen to nine hours a day," he shouted at Mr. Quimby. "These boys aren't workers; they're slaves."

"Come," she said, terrified Randall was going to hit the manager, who was the bigger, thicker man. "There are other ways to deal with this matter."

"Mr. Quimby, is this true?" Mrs. Merckler demanded.

"You have an issue, then tell it to Parliament," Quimby said in that slow, chewy way that he talked.

"They repealed the Corn Laws, so now those lazy, potato-eating Irish don't think they have to get off their lazy arses to work."

Isabella gasped. "*I* am half-Irish."

The manager eyed her, his jaw working. "Like I said." The edge of his mouth lifted in a sneer which Randall's fist knocked off his face.

"No!" Isabella shouted.

The factory manager fell like a stone, and Randall pressed his heel into Quimby's throat. "The Irish are starving," Randall hissed. "They're dying by the thousands. You will apologize to the lady."

Quimby spat on Randall's trousers.

"Mr. Quimby!" Mrs. Merckler cried.

The viscount pressed harder, until Quimby was making raspy choking sounds and clawing at Randall's leg.

"I said apologize," Randall repeated, his voice low and hard.

"I'm sorry," Quimby choked, gripping Randall's ankle.

"I've seen enough." Randall withdrew his foot. He grabbed Isabella's hand and pulled her away.

"I didn't know," Mrs. Merckler cried behind them, tears streaming down her face. "I didn't know. I promise."

Isabella couldn't stop to talk to her. Randall held her wrist so tightly that it hurt. She could feel his anger coursing through him. He was muttering terrible curses as he marched her through the double doors and back to the entrance.

"I will send you the names of competent managers

very shortly," she called over her shoulder to Mrs. Merckler. "We can talk about what you can do. I promise, I'll help."

Randall marched her out the entrance and down the lane running by the canal, away from the village. He stared straight ahead, his jaw set. She had never seen this side of him—primitive and violent. If Quimby hadn't apologized, Randall might easily have killed him. He released her hand, strode to the bank, and stared into the drifting water.

She felt useless. She didn't know what to say to calm him. He was the one who always knew the soothing, right words, not her. But she had to do something. "I have to think that Quimby was—"

"I am not some mindless, handsome, silver-tongued pawn that people can play with." He kept his back to her.

She rested a tentative hand on his taut shoulder. "I know."

"Yes, I like power. Yes, I am vain. Yes, I want everyone to love me. I possess a whole host of deficiencies that you have long pointed out." He turned and gazed at her. His eyes were tensed and vulnerable and broke her heart. "But I put my entire career in jeopardy to stop the things I just witnessed."

"Oh, Randall." She smoothed his cravat. "You're not those things." In fact, the Randall she thought she knew had begun crumbling away about seventy-two hours ago. Before her was a different man: smart, passionate, complex, confusing, and dangerous. She desperately wanted the right words, something that would soothe his hurt.

"Why the hell do I even try?" He flung up his arms. "The people I help can't vote. They don't matter as far as politics are concerned. You want to stay in power, you have to give railroads away to scoundrels like Harding. You must marry for connections and influence."

He slumped onto a bench, his back hunched, his head down. No, this wasn't beautiful, confident Lord Randall. She couldn't let him feel so defeated. She sat beside him, taking his hand into her lap. "One day you will be an earl. You don't have to do anything. You already have power."

"And that's the issue," he said quietly. "I want to be a true politician who rises on his own merit, not his family name. I want to be adored at the same time that I want to be my own man. I want to be a powerful Tory, but I don't want to alter my opinions that go against my party's position." He raked his hands down his face and closed his eyes. "Pardon me. I'm having a little difficulty figuring out who I am at the present."

"I think I'm having the same problem," she cried. "Figuring you out, that is. But I can never figure out anyone. That is what you do—see inside them and understand them. That's why you're a good politician. You have these doubts because you can break apart everything, everyone, including yourself. You understand this enormous world. You're brilliant, Lord Randall."

He raised her hand to kiss her fingers and then brushed his cheek on her knuckles. It felt so wonderful to feel his intimate touch again. The last few hours had been awful.

"And what do you do, fair Isabella?" he whispered. "What kind of magic happens in your enigmatic mind?"

"Magic?" She laughed. The only thing she understood were numbers, supply and demand, calculated interest, stock prices—things that were quantifiable. "I have to believe that manager was intentionally placed there to make the company fail," she said, because it was the only thing she really knew at the moment. What else? There were ducks swimming down the canal, there was a sun somewhere behind those heavy clouds, and she had fallen in love with a man she could never have. "A huge power exists in the shadows with enough influence over the Merckler Metalworks board, but it keeps its tracks covered."

Randall laughed and tossed back his head. "I wonder who it is?"

"Probably George H—"

He placed his finger over her lips. "I know," he said softly. "I was being sarcastic."

Her throat burned with embarrassment. She gave up trying to say the right thing or understanding this man. She was hopeless.

"Isabella, I know you don't want to talk about last night and that you really don't like me, but kiss me. Please. I need you to kiss me."

His lips descended on hers, her hands rose up his back, pulling him closer. She let her body tell him everything she couldn't. She didn't care if anyone passing saw them. She was comforting a brave man who battled to keep children from slave labor, helped strike down Corn Laws to relieve the poor, and had just fought a man who had insulted her mama's Irish heritage. She followed his motion, giving him what he wanted, losing track of place and time until splats of rain fell from the skies.

❧

Randall tried to shield Isabella from the rain, but it was futile. The drops came down hard, soaking their clothes and splashing on their feet. By the time they reached the overhang protecting the benches outside the train station, her bonnet was a soggy mess, her glasses had steamed up, and strands of hair stuck to her face. All the same, she was as beautiful as ever and he wanted to kiss her again, let her touch soothe his anxious mind.

Damn this rain, he thought as he opened the station door, letting her pass. "We have half an hour before the train arrives. Let's find a quiet corner to figure out our next move."

"You mean start preparing for our graceful ruin." She tugged at her sleeves, trying to peel them off her skin. "We've been running for days. We haven't found Powers. We don't have a hard case against Harding. Oh God!" She pressed her hand to her mouth and began backing up, until her back hit the wall. "Oh God!"

"I swear by every bit of breath left in my body, I will let nothing happen to you." He reached for her. "If Harding does his worst, we will have each other." Splat! The dangerous words fell out. He felt exposed as he studied her face, searching for the tiniest flicker of love. Surely, it was there. He thought he had felt something stirring in her body as she kissed him by the canal.

"Lord save me," she whispered.

Damn that woman! His pride and heart took a

strong punch. "Is being with me so terrible? Do you realize that most unmarried ladies in society would—"

"It doesn't concern you. Look around!"

He pivoted. Ladies sporting large white ribbons that read "The Mary Wollstonecraft Society—Manchester Chapter" packed the station. They weren't the harsh, sour women who enjoyed tossing eggs and rotting vegetables at him, but ladies of all social spheres, smiling and chatting together, Isabella's book in their gloved hands. Again he felt that ugly sting of envy.

If only he had such passionate supporters. If only these women could vote.

If he were Isabella, he would be introducing himself, basking in their love. Instead, she had collapsed onto a bench, her face buried in her hands, trying as much as humanly possible to be invisible.

"They like you," he whispered, sitting next to her, bumping her shoulder with his. "Don't be scared. Go talk to them."

"I wish I hadn't written that book." She shook her head. "They think I'm someone I'm not. What will happen when my bank fails? They will see me for the fraud I am."

"You're not a fraud, Isabella." He rested his hand on her shoulder. "Why do you have such a low opinion of yourself?" Before the words had left his mouth, the ghosts of hundreds of mean insults he had uttered through the years and nasty pranks he had played came back to haunt his conscience.

"Can you ask the ticket master if a private carriage can be arranged?" she pleaded. "Please. I'll pay whatever I have to."

He rose. "Are you going to be all right?"

"No!" she cried, her arms wrapped at her waist as she rocked back and forth. "Not unless some stray bolt of lightning puts me out of my misery."

"Very well, then. Just stay huddled like a scared ball. I'll be quick as possible."

Ten minutes later, he returned with the grim news. "The train broke down. Everyone is trying to get on the next one, which arrives two hours from now. You go ahead to first class. I must go back."

"I'm sitting with you. You can't leave me."

Warmth flooded his heart, but still he said, "The rain is coming down like it's the end of the world. I don't want you to catch a chill."

"I don't care. I'm sitting with you."

Passengers were packed in second class, shoulder to shoulder. Isabella quivered as the damp wind blew through the open cabin as the train sped down the track. Under the spread of her skirt, she held Randall's hand. He didn't have a coat any longer, having lent it to cover a cold infant a row up.

The child's young mother chatted with her companion. "Well, it's been hard after Alfred went off to India. Months pass before he sends money. Of course, he has a problem with the bottle. But I'm not going to let one terrible mistake ruin my life. But like all the members in my chapter, I've started an account in Miss St. Vincent's bank and put what monies I have in it."

Oh God! Isabella's life was going to financial hell, and she was taking the entirety of the Wollstonecraft Society with her.

Twenty

By the time they reached London, it was dark. Randall kept a hand clamped to Isabella, afraid the human current would carry her away. Her brows were creased, lips slightly puckered, her eyes sharp but staring at a place in her own mind. She moved with the flow of foot traffic, but she wasn't present.

The crowded station was humid and steamy from rain and sweat. The stairs to the lobby were narrow, and when he let Isabella step ahead, another covey of ribboned Wollstonecraft zealots slipped between them and then invited more of their kindred along.

Randall stayed on their heels, trying to keep close to Isabella, but she was pushed further ahead. When he couldn't see the top of her bonnet anymore, his pulse quickened. "Izzy," he called, not wanting to alert the ladies that their patroness saint was among them, but his words were lost in the unintelligible cacophony of chatter, and the melodic sound of newspaper boys calling the headlines.

As he stepped into the main lobby, he heard the

female screams. "It can't be true!" a woman shrieked. Another cried, "No, it must be wrong!"

The first thought that rushed through his head was that Queen Victoria had died. Then he heard the newspaper boy ring out:

> "Examiner special edition! Examiner special edition!
> Fraudulent stocks Lord Randall and Miss St. Vincent did sell,
> Leaving the Bank of Lord Hazelwood to fail,
> Now lord and lady do fly,
> Without kissing their clients good-bye,
> Hazelwood, a name you can't trust,
> With your monies or your government."

Randall's heart thundered. What the hell? Now he and Isabella were the villains? They were the ones who sold the bad stock? He dug his fingers into his chest as pain shot down his left arm. They were being framed—and no prizes for guessing who was behind it.

Where was Isabella? He staggered forward, finding her amid a thick crowd of wailing Wollstonecraft Society members. Her hand was pressed to her mouth as she gulped panicked breaths. Her eyes latched on to his, her fear shooting through him.

"Izzy May!" he cried, trying to break into the crowd. A rather substantial society member in front of him fainted. Instinctively, he reached out to catch the woman before she slammed into the hard stone floor.

"Forget that old bird," a man hissed. "Where's Isabella?" In the strain and confusion, Randall thought he had uttered the words himself until, out of his periphery, he glimpsed a familiar, prawn-like body clad in dark clothes. Randall turned his head to find himself staring into the perspiring face of Anthony Powers.

"You," Randall hissed, almost dropping the woman. "Bloody hell, I'm going to kill you."

Isabella was falling apart a good twenty-five feet away from Randall, a huge supporter of the Mary Wollstonecraft Society was unconscious in his arms, and, worst of all, he had dressed so hastily that he had forgotten his gun, else he would have shot Powers between his vacant puppy eyes. Then Randall could complement his fraud allegations with murder.

"We have to get Isabella," Powers cried, grabbing Randall's elbow. "We haven't any time to lose."

"I'm a bit preoccupied at the moment," Randall hissed through his gritted teeth as he hefted the society member.

Powers scanned the crowd and panic darkened his features. "Oh, damn, they're here." He staggered backward, spun on his heel, and tore off, sprinting along the far wall.

"Cock," Randall muttered. Then, in the most spectacularly unchivalrous moment of his life, he rested the fainted woman on the floor. "I'm sorry," he told her companions, holding up his palms. "A thousand pardons and more." He broke into a run.

"Disrespectful male swine," he heard one of the society followers call after him.

Isabella, love, just keep it together for a few minutes, he thought, hoping that there was some mystic power in the universe that could plant his thoughts into her head.

He rushed after Powers, dodging through travelers, leaping over baggage, until both men were out of the station and into the night. The air was thick with drizzle. Huge, hazy orbs circled the gaslights lining the entrance where the black hackneys were sitting in a line. The swollen moon glowed behind the low clouds. Several yards ahead, Powers's coattails were flapping off his hindquarters as his feet slapped the pavement. At the corner, he turned and stopped. Randall dove into the air, catching the man's shoulders in a hostile embrace. Both men fell to the ground.

"What the hell are you doing?" Powers shouted.

Randall's knees slammed the pavers, but he didn't register any pain. He wrapped his hands around the rapscallion's neck. "I don't know yet. I'm making it up as I go."

"Get Isabella," Powers choked.

"You are not going to touch Isabella ever again. Do you understand me?"

"Harding…w-wants…h-her." Powers clawed at Randall's hands. "That's why he…is…here. To…t-trap her. He…suspected you…were…coming."

"How? How did he know?"

"Harding…tipped…papers…police. They said… you left…with no bags…this…morning. Round… tr…trip."

Oh, damn. Isabella was alone and vulnerable in the station with Harding and police converging.

Again Randall regretted leaving his gun at his flat. He didn't have the time to neatly kill Powers with his bare hands; plus he was bound to be seen by those policemen rounding the corner in the distance. He released the cove, rose, and wiped his mouth with the back of his hand. "I'm going to find you and you're going to pay for everything you took from us, and if you don't have enough, I'm selling your fresh, steaming, prawn-like body."

Randall started to sprint back, muttering a stream of violent curses. In front of the station, people clustered about carriages as porters loaded or removed trunks. A shiny black clarence crossed the street and pulled up to the walk. The door opened.

Two of Harding's flash men broke through the crowd that waited for hackneys. In between them, their hands clamped on her arms, was Isabella.

"Stop those men!" Randall roared as he flew down the pavement. "She's being held against her will. Help her."

She turned her head, searching the night, her eyes finding his. "Rand—" She was lifted by the waist and tossed into the open carriage. Something flew over her head, sparking in the lamplight and then falling into the gutter. The two men jumped inside as the clarence rolled away.

Hot, dizzying terror shot through every vein, muscle, and internal organ in Randall's body. The entire street turned to black silence in his head, except for his scream. "Isabella!" His mind burst with a dozen different scenes of her hurt, crying out for him. Not his precious, beautiful Isabella. Take anything from him, but not her.

"You bloody bugger!" he shouted, sprinting down the street after the carriage. As he passed, he scooped her glasses from the muddy gutter. "Fuck! Fucker! Fuckery! You let her go, you goddamned bloody cove."

The gifted orator, the smooth, silver-tongued politician, launched into a detailed description, interlaced with colorful profanity, of exactly how he planned to remove Harding's genitals and in which of the man's orifices he would shove them, if the scoundrel dared to touch her.

All around him, he could hear the echoes of shocked gasps. In his periphery, two policemen bolted from the station. "Stop, Lord Randall!"

"He took my woman!" Randall yelled back. "That railroad pile of shit kidnapped my woman."

A four-wheeler pulled up beside him. The door opened, slamming Randall in the cheek. "Dammit!"

Powers leaned out. "Get in the carriage."

Up ahead, Harding's clarence rounded the corner. The walks were crowded and the street thick with muck. Behind him, the policemen continued ordering him to stop.

Randall grabbed on to the carriage. "Follow the shiny black clarence seven carriages up," he growled at the driver, and leaped inside.

He seized Powers by the cravat. "What the hell is going on?"

"I'm not talking unless you unhand me."

The carriage turned and both gentlemen crashed into the door.

"I'm trying to help you," Powers hissed, pulling himself onto the seat.

"Where have you been?"

"The scoundrel wants Isabella. He's wild for her."

"Answer my damn question." Anger edged Randall's voice.

"Harding's house. I've been there the entire time. He had me working like some damn stone mason."

"Harding kidnapped you too?"

"What? No! Look, I had some problems…some monetary problems…"

Randall drew back his fist, ready to improve Powers's ugly face. "And now Isabella is paying. What did she ever do to you? All she wanted was to marry you, and this was how you've treated her."

Powers's nostrils flared. "I said I was trying to help you. I escaped. Harding doesn't know I'm gone."

"And how did you get out?"

"I—I don't want to talk about it."

Randall shook his head, muttered a curse. He opened the coach door. Peering over the top of the carriage's roof, across lines of congested traffic, he spotted Harding's clarence. The carriage turned in the direction of the man's home and disappeared from view. The viscount glanced back at Powers, the man he had been chasing for the last week. *Bloody hell with it all.* If Harding touched Isabella, Randall would lose his mind. "May you rot in hell, Powers," he growled, and jumped.

"Wait, you don't know what you're doing," the man called out. "You're going to need my help. Harding is ruthless. He will destroy you."

His warning only made Randall run faster.

❧

Isabella slammed onto the carriage floor. She could see nothing but blurs of gray and black. "Randall!" she screamed. "Randall!"

"Boys, that's not how you treat a lady," a baritone barked. Harding! "My sincerest apologies, Miss St. Vincent." His large, warm hands clasped her arms, his gold ring pressed into her skin.

"I can't see," she cried. "Where's Randall?" She was lifted onto a warm leather cushion. Harding's honed, muscular body leaned against her arm. His exotic sweet and musky scent clogged her nose.

The carriage lurched forward. "No!" She beat at the window with her hand. "You said you would wait for Lord Randall. You must stop. Stop!"

"Boys, did you tell Miss St. Vincent that you were retrieving Lord Randall? You shouldn't have misled her like that. You apologize immediately for that and for pushing her in the carriage. I am appalled at you both and considering letting you go."

"We're sorry, Miss St. Vincent," the men said in the singsong voices of recalcitrant school boys.

"I want out now." She continued to pound the glass. "I won't speak without Randall present."

"Calm down," Harding said, anchoring her back against his chest. "I hope you don't think I'm going to harm you. I would never hurt a hair on your beautiful head, even though I'm a bit put out by your deception, calling yourself Izzy May and an unattached courtesan."

"Well, I didn't kidnap you! I'm a little put out myself."

"Kidnapped? No, no, I'm saving you, Miss Isabella.

All those police in the station were searching for you. There are dangerous rumors flying around London tonight that you and Lord Randall committed fraud. I'm trying to protect you, my chickadee."

"So, you left Lord Randall to be arrested?"

"Arrested?" Isabella felt the man's chest rumble with quiet laughter. "My little dove, you should know that he's not like you or me. We made our fortunes by our own talents and hard work. He's a handsome viscount who, I'm sure, will charm the magistrate just as he charms those empty heads in Parliament who don't know better."

"My father made a fortune. I did not."

He clicked his tongue. "I never like to contradict a lady, but I asked my friends around the exchange about the enigmatic Isabella St. Vincent—by all accounts an old, withered spinster. But I knew better. She likes to play games and confound expectations. To tantalize." He stroked her cheek, letting his finger trace her jawline.

She swatted his roving fingers. "I think you are confused. I'm not the lady from last night. I really *am* an old, withered spinster. I usually wear frumpy clothes, and I own an ornery black cat named Milton. Sometimes I cradle him like a baby, but then he gets cross and scratches me. Not very tantalizing."

The other occupants of the carriage snickered.

"More games." Harding chuckled, a dark, intimate sound. "Well, my stunning spinster, I put together a few numbers here and there, and figured out that you had tripled your inheritance and expanded a tiny rural bank into a large, profitable institution. I even read your book. Very clever, my sparrow, except for the examples; rather melodramatic claptrap."

"I thought so too," she said absently, twisting to look out the back window, but she couldn't see anything but the haze of glass, lights, and night. Where was Randall? *I need you desperately*, she beckoned with her mind, making a childlike wish that he could hear her silent plea.

"How clever of you to cater to the weak and easily influenced minds of your female readers," Harding continued. "But we both know that you are not moved by emotions, but calculated risk. You are just brilliant. Brilliant! For a woman, that is."

Isabella gave Harding—or whatever that fleshy blur was beside her—a leveled glare. "And you are treacherous, regardless of sex, that is."

"I'm sorry if that is the impression I gave you." He raised her hand and kissed it. She snatched it back. "You must give me another chance. I can change your mind. I think you will find I'm quite easy to work with."

Again, the other passengers snickered.

"How did you figure out who I was?" she asked.

"A regrettable acquaintance named Mr. Anthony Powers informed me."

She sucked in her breath. Her panicked train of thought suddenly switched rails. Randall was correct all along: Harding had a direct link to Powers. The railroad baron was the maestro of this adagio in ruin. "Do—do you know where I might find this Mr. Powers?"

"All in good time, my starling," the railroad baron said.

She put her nose a mere inch from his, until she could see his dark eyes from under the brim of his hat. "No, I want answers right now," she demanded. "This instant. *This* is the good time. My life has been sinking through the nine circles of hell for a week. I've got to save my bank, and Mr. Powers... He..." She paused. She didn't know how to play this new game. What cards should she show and which ones should she keep to her chest?

"Let me guess, that rascal Powers sold you fraudulent stock and then ran away with the money, and now you're taking the blame. So you're panicking because you fear a run on your bank. And, if I may be so bold as to suggest, you may not be making the best decisions."

The memory of her quivering legs wrapped around Randall's thighs blew up in her brain, as well as when he bound her in the silk ribbons and gave her a proper wiggle; and then there was that strange position in which she hung from the canopy frame. "Y-yes," she admitted.

Harding laughed, a lazy, relaxed sound. She slid across the carriage, wrapped her arms about her, and debated.

A few minutes before, she would have contemplated leaping blindly from the carriage. But now he had someone she needed. Today was Friday. The bank had closed several hours ago, hopefully before the news broke. Tomorrow the bank was closed. If she found Powers, she would have two days to perform a miracle—try to recoup what money she could from

the man and then give him over to the police in order
to clear hers and Randall's names.

"You're being too emotional," Harding said.
"Allow me to think for you, my ravishing dear. I have
a business plan for you to consider that might solve all
your little problems."

Across the carriage, the men snickered yet again.
For God's sake, could they just all-out laugh or
chuckle? The snickers chafed her nerves.

"But for now, have a grape, my lark," Harding said.
"Boys, reach into the basket and get out the grapes."

Seconds later, Isabella felt a cold, tiny grape being
pressed against her mouth. She parted her lips,
chewed, and swallowed.

∽

A bundle of force-fed grapes later, the carriage veered
and stopped. The door creaked open, and she could
hear the shuffling of feet and feel the sway of the carriage as the men disembarked.

"Come, my swan." Harding clasped her hand. She
wanted to slap him, perhaps give his finger a good bite,
but she had to play along until she knew the particulars
about Powers. "Randall," she whispered like a prayer
and allowed Harding to help her down.

"Here we are." He slid his hands to her waist and
turned her around. "If you look about the scaffolding
covering the home, you can make out my architectural insanity."

All she could discern were large orbs of lamplight
and smudgy black lines amid something deep red. "I
can't see anything. Please tell me about Powers."

"In my early career, I spent a great deal of time in China," the railroad baron continued as if she hadn't spoken. "I've modeled it after the great Oriental homes and pagodas I saw there, but added some English flavor with the stone walls and turrets."

"Oh" was all Isabella could manage. There were times when being nearly blind had its advantages.

"When I was in China with my opium business, I missed the dreary, damp England of my childhood," he explained. "When I moved back to dreary, damp England, I missed the exotic, limitless beauty of the China of my early manhood. But I'm beginning to find England as warm and inviting as the look in your eyes."

"I'm not looking at you warm and invitingly. In fact, I'm not sure I'm looking at you at all."

Harding broke into laughter, the long, exaggerated kind. "Beauty, brains, the ability to spin hay into gold, and wit. My God, woman, you are lethal. Allow me to escort you inside."

"I prefer to stay out here. Please tell me where I may find Mr. Powers."

"Well, you just might find him in my home."

"I'm not going into your home. But I would be delighted to discuss any business arrangement out here."

"Boys, go inside," Harding said in a low, authoritative voice. Feet crunched on pavers and a heavy door opened and closed. "Miss St. Vincent, you have my word as a gentleman that no harm will come to you. I ask simply that you listen to my offer. And if you decide not to take it, you can walk away."

He drew a finger down her cheek. "But I think we have an extraordinary opportunity here, business and otherwise."

Just what did "otherwise" encompass? That's what concerned her. "Is—is Powers inside?"

"Yes."

"And I can walk away at any time?" *Provided I can find the door.*

"I gave you my word as a gentleman."

He bumped his arm against hers. She slowly wound her fingers around his elbow. A terrible, sinking sensation filled her gut, the kind that usually occurred when making a dreadful mistake. At this point, though, every move was a mistake

And if Randall were taken by the police, the only way she could quickly free him was by giving them one of the true villains—Mr. Powers.

Twenty-one

SHE CROSSED A THRESHOLD, THE HUMID NIGHT GIVING way to a dry, airy space, which smelled of wood, sawdust, and paint. "Now, let me be your eyes." Harding slowly slipped off one of her gloves, and then the other. He guided her bare fingers along the door. "Carved in the wood are the house gods Qin Shubao and Yuchi Jingde. They are fierce warriors from the Tang dynasty who guard the house from evil."

They aren't doing such a great job, Isabella thought, since the evil twins Harding and Powers were wandering about the corridors.

"How lovely," she muttered, retracting her hand. "Now may I see Mr. Powers? And I would like my gloves back."

He didn't give them to her. "You are too impatient. Watch your step as I lead you into the great hall. We are still working on the mosaic on the floor. Ah, here we are. You can hear my voice echo. Miss St. Vincent intoxicates me!" She jumped. His words echoed around her, as if he had called across a mountain range.

"Before you is a grand hall as one would expect in a great English castle of yore, with exposed beams and huge fireplaces. But instead of tapestries, I have installed silk—"

"I'm sorry," she cut in, too anxious to be polite. "I'm not one for architecture, even when I'm not desperately trying to save my bank. If you could take me to Mr. Powers without the tour."

Another one of his expansive belly laughs. "Come, my nightingale, up the stairs to where I do business. Hold on to me. Not all the balustrades have arrived from Hong Kong. So, tell me what amuses you if not architecture, Isabella—I hope you don't mind my calling you by your name—"

"Not as much as I minded being kidnapped."

"—and I shall produce it. Surely, you have passions outside of trading or banking?"

Lord Randall is my passion, she wanted to answer. *Can you produce him immediately?* She said a hasty silent prayer that he had escaped the police and was safe. "All I do, every day, is think about stocks, interest rates, and investments. A very dull existence." That is, until the viscount had taken her into his arms and given her a glimpse of a new, wondrous world in a single night. She wished she were back in his sheltering arms, and that the last twelve hours hadn't happened.

From an open balcony, also scarily missing balustrades, the railroad baron led her down a corridor. The air was tinged with the acrid scent of tarnish and metal. Silver glimmered from the walls. "These are ancient Chinese weapons," he said. "Mostly Fu and Ji—ornate weapons of the Imperial guards. Follow me into this chamber, and I shall show you a rather interesting curiosity."

He drew her into a room—a blur of red, wood, and more metal. Releasing her, he pulled something from the wall. "This was fired at me during the opium war—an ancient and amazing crossbow of sorts, capable of rapidly firing ten arrows in a matter of seconds." He held it so close to her face that she could see the taut bow.

"W-what happened to the man who fired it?"

"We were at war, Isabella," he replied darkly. "Oh, but you are shivering. Have I made you nervous?"

She began backing toward the general vicinity of the door. "I—I would like to see Mr. Powers this instant."

"Come now, you are too impatient." In a quick move, he slipped behind her. His hands rested on her shoulders. His hot breath tickled her neck. "Let me take this cloak off you, my robin."

"I prefer to keep it on."

"I prefer that you don't." He whisked it off in a graceful motion. "Very nice," he said, his chin hovering over her shoulder, his eyes gazing down her bodice. "Now come make yourself comfortable."

He led her to a strange piece of furniture, a long, flat, red pad resting on a carved frame. "Is this a Chinese sofa?" she asked as he reclined beside her. He was so close that she could just make out the disconcerting smile on his lean face.

"A bed from the early years of the Qing dynasty," he replied.

"A b—" She leaped up and rushed toward something

silver—and hopefully deadly—gleaming on the wall. She ripped it from its moorings, cutting her finger in the process. "I don't care if it was built the first year in…in whatever the first dynasty was—"

"Xia."

"—I want to see Powers now, or I'm exercising my right to walk away."

She saw the motion of him rising to his feet. His lean body, shiny bronzed head, and hot eyes came into focus as he planted himself just inches from her. "Ah, that is a highly decorative Fu from the guards of the Imperial palace," he said, running his finger down the blade. "More ornamental than useful."

Nonetheless, she shook her useless, decorative Fu threateningly. "You spoke about a business deal."

"I just adore negotiating at knifepoint. Let me speak in terms we both understand. In return for Powers and my help in saving your bank, I'm putting futures on your mind and your body with a call for three months from now." He leaned down and kissed the blade, letting his lips linger. "I think we will both profit."

"M-my body? Mr. Harding, you have confused me for someone else. I'm not the courtesan I said I was last night. I'm not exotic or graceful or elegant. Maybe the excitement of the moment has blinded you to my true appearance and nature. I truly am a boring, homely old spinster. No one has asked me for a single dance at the spring assembly in the last three years. So if you would be so kind as to produce Mr. Powers."

"I disagree. I think you are an untapped resource, a virgin land, so to say, and I have the delight of discovering you."

"I have actually been discovered." *Four times last night.* She stepped back, keeping her adorned Fu in position.

"Many men may walk across the land—"

"What! J-just one."

"—never suspecting the diamond mine beneath. Do you know my talent? It's the same as yours. I see opportunity that no one has before, and, like you, I aggressively chase it until it is mine. I turn it into profit. You are my new opportunity, my new opium, my new railroad."

She paused to assimilate the information, slowly spinning the Fu as she thought. "So, let me see if I understand. I get to be your…your…concubine, your diamond mine to excavate, your opium, and in exchange, I avoid the poorhouse. Is that your offer?"

He laughed. "Now those aren't very good terms, are they?" She heard him pace away. "Here's my plan. We turn Powers over to the police, I repay some of the stock he stole, and I become a visible partner and investor in your bank to help reestablish any confidence that may have been lost. I'll have my boys at *The Examiner* write an article making you the heroine of the story. You know that everyone loves a good story, and all perceived sins will be forgiven. In fact, you may have more business and can give up this silly Wollstonecraft Society." He scoffed and shook his head. "Women investors with their penny stocks."

"All this for three months in your Qing dynasty bed?"

"Oh, my sweet canary, I want more than your body." He strode closer. "I want your succulent, unwomanly mind. We can make intellectual love for three months as business partners—three months to prove how well I can treat you, pamper you, and seduce you with stocks, companies, options, consuls, mortgages, and other lucrative foreign investments on which you can work your magic." He stopped before her. He was so tall, she found herself staring at the shape of his black cravat. "Care to play, or are the stakes too high for you?"

She swallowed, loosening her grip on her Fu. Harding had the international resources she never possessed. He moved in global markets. But why was he giving it away so easily? "Why do you need my so-called magic? Are you overextended?"

"I'm certainly not on the brink of financial ruin the way you are. There's just a temporary imposition caused by your bank partner, Lord Randall. He embarrassed me, causing a few of my less-than-loyal investors to back out. You know I cannot allow that to happen. I—"

"You must project confidence in the market," she finished.

"Exactly. You see, we are brilliant together." He slipped behind her, his dark, sweet scent wafting around her. "At the end of the three months, we total up what we've made and decide either to sell high or low or…" He kissed her neck. She sucked in her breath. She had to admit his touch wasn't unpleasant, but it wasn't Randall. It wasn't sweet enough to melt her heart or soft enough to reach her soul. But she could never keep the viscount. He didn't belong to her. She had just been lucky enough to know him for one devastating, life-altering night.

"Or?" she prompted Harding to finish his thought.

"I hit that sweet multiplier just right and buy in. I double my investment in you. Marriage, family if the numbers are right." He grasped the handle of the ornamental ax, his large hands—so like her papa's—covering hers. He withdrew the weapon from her grasp. "I keep your body and mind; you keep your bank. You honor your father's legacy while making even more money." He stepped back. Cold air chilled her neck. "Or you can walk away right now. I won't stop you."

Her throat burned. She began to pace, thinking of all those desperate women who had placed their paltry but vital savings in her bank. They depended on her. How far was she willing to go for them, to save her father's bank? She had never been the daughter he wanted, but she had managed to keep the bank. It was all she had left. If it went away, she wouldn't know who she was. She wouldn't be anything. And if she saved it, she might protect Randall's political career.

Randall.

Tears filled the corners of her eyes. She quickly wiped them away before they had a chance to swell. *He was never yours. If you truly love him, you will let him go and save his reputation.*

"My stunning kingfisher, your silence destroys me," he said. "I must use other means to persuade you." He drew her close, his lips descending on hers.

She pressed her palm against his chest.

"If—if I am to agree to this…this intimate investment, there is something more I want."

"Tell me."

Tears began to form in her eyes again. *Be strong*, she reminded herself and blinked them away. "Lord Randall."

❧

Randall slipped through Harding's open back gate. The gaslight about the mews shone on the stableboys who were unhitching the carriage and discussing which London actresses were the most beautiful as influenced by breast size. Randall edged into the darkness along the brick wall. His heart pounded, and his jaw hurt from grinding his teeth together. If that miscreant Harding touched Isabella, Randall would tear off every limb, eyeball, and tiny testicle on the man's body.

But he had to find him first, before he could dismantle him.

Harding's architectural nightmare was lost in the shadows of scaffolding running along the walls and up to the pagoda-like turrets, above which the massive moon rested.

Light spilled in rectangles from the ground- and second-floor windows. He snuck around a small kitchen garden, ready to climb up the scaffolding and smash his way in, when he almost toppled a maid. She was holding a mop and coming out the kitchen door.

"Good heavens, you nearly frightened me out of me poor wits," she cried. Her pretty features relaxed as she studied him in the low light. "Oh, my, you're a handsome fella," she purred.

A dim idea—a flicker of a desperate hunch—lit in his distraught mind.

"Am I now, my pretty little bit?" he said. "I'm Mr.

Randy Powers, Anthony Powers's dear cousin. What times we had as boys."

She giggled. "I wager you were quite naughty."

Oh, yes! He flashed a smile, hoping to hell it was seductive and boyish, not as panicked and murderous as he felt. "Tell me, dearie, do you like to play the Who's Papa's Naughty Pussycat game?"

"Meow," she said, and giggled again.

"Aye, everyone likes a wicked game of naughty pussy." He winked. "You see, it's a bit of a family game. Me papa played it with me mama and then came me. We Powerses are pranksters. Aye, in fact, I have got a fine prank I want to play on ol' Tony tonight. He ain't seen me in a while and I wants to surprise 'im. Can you be a sweet luv, and show me the servant stairs?"

≈

A minute later, Randall opened the back stairs door onto the second-story corridor. He gripped the maid's mop and a meat fork he had lifted from a kitchen table as he passed. He cursed his lack of a gun, all the while formulating graphic, barbaric uses for that meat fork.

Then, when he peered down the hall, hundreds of shining, exotic swords and axes flickered in the sconce lights. At that moment, any doubts Randall had about the existence of God were silenced.

"Oh, hell yes," he whispered, exchanging his mop and fork for a fearsome ax and a strange two-bladed sword, just perfect for making a bloody, unrecognizable mess of Harding…when he found him.

If he found him.

He edged down the corridor, weapons poised. Then he heard Isabella's voice. "If—if I am to agree to this…this intimate investment, there is something more I want." He paused, his ax ready to break through the wooden door.

"Tell me," Harding said. Randall raised his axe and then stopped.

"Lord Randall." Her voice was tight and high. "I know you are trying to destroy his career with the election happening in a few months. He's a good, honorable politician. He helps the poor and power-less. You must leave him alone. You or your cronies mustn't criticize him for your own political gain. You can take these terms, or I will walk away."

Bloody hell! She was sacrificing herself for him. Well, Randall had a few terms of his own.

He took two large steps, leaped into the air, and twisted to kick his leg out. *Bam!* The door flew back, slamming the wall. He saw her, her head tilted back, her lips underneath Harding's even as her hand pushed against his chest. An ornate silver weapon of sorts dangled from Harding's hand. Randall released a wild, high shriek, half-human, half–barn owl, and raced in, his sword in his left hand and his ax in the right, thirsty to inflict bodily harm.

Harding leaped back, his eyes widening and then sharpening within a fraction of a second. In Randall's head, he was shouting, *Get your goddamn hands off her*, but all that streamed out was another wild, primal shriek. He lashed out with his sword as Harding raised his fancy weapon. In an easy swipe, Randall ousted the blade from the railroad baron's hands, sending it sailing, turning end over end before slicing into a faded silk painting on the wall.

Isabella screamed Randall's name at the same time Harding spat, "Dammit, that was from the Tang dynasty!"

With quick, catlike grace, Harding drew what looked like folded wooden bars from the wall, each segment connected with a chain, like a medieval flail. He began weaving the weapon around his body, almost erotically, as if he were dancing with it. "You know what this is?" he asked, spinning a wooden bar.

"I don't give a damn." Black rage burned in Randall's muscles. "You're never going to touch Isabella again. Understand?" He jabbed his sword. One segment of the wooden flail whipped up and popped the sword. Randall felt the reverberations down to his bones. He cried out in shock and pain.

"It's a *sanjiegun* from the Song dynasty," Harding continued, his voice smooth, his eyes glittering. He lashed out again with the spinning wood and smacked Randall's sword, knocking it away. *Dammit!* The railroad man spun like a lithe ballerina and then the bottom bar of wood smashed behind Randall's knee. *Ah! That bloody arse!* He sank to the ground.

"Randall!" Isabella cried out. "Say something."

Randall raised his head. Before his face, Harding spun a length of the *sanjiegun*, the man's eyes shiny and wide, as if hypnotized by the circling flail.

"You can't have her," Randall hissed through his pain, and raised his ax.

"Just try to take her away," Harding baited him.

"Stop!" Isabella screamed. Four arrows shot into the high ceiling in quick succession. *Whew. Whew. Whew. Whew.* Both men froze and slowly turned to find her gripping an old and rather vicious-looking crossbow. She squinted, as if trying to see them. "Drop everything now," she ordered. Another arrow flew, and she leaped back. Across the room, a stone statue on a pedestal tumbled over and shattered.

"Oh Hades, that wasn't supposed to happen," she said. "What did I hit? I hope it wasn't a very valuable dynasty."

"Isabella, my exciting, dangerous dove," Harding began calmly, carefully. "Let's just put down the *chu-ke nu.*" He folded the *sanjiegun* under his arm. "You have to understand that Lord Randall came at me with a sword…so full of his misplaced chivalry. I had to defend myself in the restrained manner of combat that I learned in the East, so as to easily disarm Lord Randall without wounding or killing him."

"Isabella, my dearest African lappet-faced vulture, let me give you your glasses so that you might take better aim next time." Randall fished her glasses from his coat. He tried to rise to his feet, but the back of his knee was throbbing and Harding stepped in front of him, swinging that damned *sanjiegun* like a pendulum before his face.

"She's almost blind, man," the viscount hissed. "Or maybe you want her weakened and dependent on you. That's how you play, isn't it? First the wound, then the kill."

The man's lips twitched. "Give her the glasses. Let her see the real man among us."

"Love, I'm approaching." Randall raised his palms. "Just point the crossbow a little to the right?" He gently clasped her free hand, brushing his fingers against hers as he handed her the glasses.

She sniffed and her lids fluttered. She slid the spectacles on her nose and took in the room, her gaze stopping on the bed. Her gray eyes were enormous and wet, her chin trembling.

"Oh, Isabella," he whispered.

"D–don't look at me like that," she whispered, her voice cracking. She stared at where his hand rested on her sleeve. "He is going to save the bank…your political career. You're a good politician, no matter what I've said to you."

"Isabella has asked that I respectfully refrain from commenting on your activities in Parliament," Harding explained. "In fact, I might be able to help you. With a few words from me in the right ears, you could run uncontested. You'll just need to learn to keep quiet when it's good for you."

"You mean look the other way and let you and your cronies run the country." Randall didn't give a damn about his political career anymore. All he knew, all that played over and over in his head, was Isabella being thrown into a carriage, ripped away from him. And now she stood beside him, trembling, scared, but so brave in her sacrifice. He wanted to draw her close, feel the tickle of her hair on his chin again, and keep her locked to his protective heart for the remainder of her life. The entirety of the British Empire could sink to hell for all he cared. He just wanted her.

"This nation needs you more than me," he replied gently. He had to be careful. "Women are clamoring for you to help them. You give something more than hope; you give them power and respect. Don't leave them now."

"I think they would prefer that our bank remains solvent and keeps their money safe than whatever advice I can give them." He could hear the unshed tears darkening her words. "Don't make this any harder. Just—just leave. Please."

Randall felt as though the air had been punched from his lungs. Harding, that bumhole, clapped. "A wise woman."

She closed her eyes. A tear streamed down her cheek. *She doesn't mean it*, he told himself, trying to rein in his own emotions. *She's acting out of fear and misplaced loyalty.* Harding was playing games that she understood—numbers and risk. But Randall had a few games of his own. And they were ruthless and cut to the heart. He dropped his ax, letting it thud on the lush red carpet. In the fight of his life, he chose a much sharper, much deadlier weapon: words.

He began, in a whisper, "Very well, my love, if that's what you wish. But before I go, I want you to answer one question for me."

"Save the dramatics for Parliament," Harding said. "She asked you to leave. It's over."

"I'm not talking to you," Randall thundered.

Her head jerked up. The tears now glistening on the beautiful face of the woman who never cried sliced apart his soul. His voice cracked as he asked her, "What do you truly want in your heart?"

"To—to save t-the bank," she choked. "Our customers... My father's..."

"Legacy," Harding finished. "You are saving all
that he gave you."

"The question was for her," Randall reminded the
bumhole. Randall's heart pounded. He hesitated for
a moment, knowing his words and the pain he was
about to cause could never be taken back. "Isabella,
your father is gone. He isn't here to care anymore. His
legacy shouldn't be about a stupid bank."

Her lips parted, her eyes were wide and disbelieving
as if he had physically slapped her. "Don't say that,"
she screamed.

"You wanted to marry Powers because you desired
a warm, loving family, one that you have never
known." Randall began to circle her as he would
an opponent in a debate, keeping the other guessing and off balance, wearing him down. Except she
wasn't his adversary but his lover. What he was doing
was destroying his heart. He struggled to continue.
"You've felt so alone and alienated all your life, as if
everyone understood a special joke that you didn't.
You felt different, but you couldn't understand why."

"Please stop," she begged. "Please."

Forgive me, he silently pleaded as he pushed his
sword deeper into her ancient wounds. "You were
lonely growing up because your father was always
preoccupied with business. It was the most important
thing in his life. More than his own daughter. When
your mother died, you weren't allowed to grieve for
her. Your father told you to be strong. And you've
always been strong, haven't you? So strong."

"But I w-wasn't strong enough." He leaned in, trying to hear her halting words. "Look what has happened."

"Stop playing your games," Harding warned Randall, that damn flail swinging again. The man was feeling threatened.

"You thought when you moved to the country, things would be different between you and your father." Randall continued down his treacherous course. "Then he became friends with my father and started a bank. You were left alone again, except for me, who insulted you and pushed you away, and Judith. And your father liked me, doted on me, while he found you odd and gawky, not graceful like your mother. My life appeared so golden while yours was so cold and empty. No wonder you hated me." Randall raised a finger. "But what you could do was make money, better than your father. That was the one thing you could do to impress him. So that's what you did to try and make him love you." He stopped before her. Her head was bowed, tears dripping from her chin. He wanted so badly to draw her into his arms, pull all his words from her heart. "But he is gone," he whispered, "and your unfulfilled dreams remain—that love you wanted, never returned. So tell me what you want. Tell me the truth."

"Careful, Isabella." Harding was changing tactics now, attacking her fears. "If your bank fails, you will have nothing but your charms to recommend you in the poorhouse. Don't fall for this man's sentimental rubbish."

"Don't listen to him," the viscount said gently. "You have the power here. What do you want? This is so important now. Don't become defensive and shut me out. Tell me the truth."

"I want my bank…and someone…someone who will…" She faltered.

"Say it," Randall encouraged. "Show me that brave, fearless heart of yours."

"L-love me as I-I love him." The words burst as if they had been dammed up for ages. "Dedicated and loyal and forever. Who will be there for me and not make me feel different or odd. Who will give me children who hug with smudgy, dirty fingers and a home where people laugh and leave shoes on the stairs and journals strewn about and jam stains on the tablecloths. I want a man…I want y…" She stared at him, her eyes saying what she couldn't utter.

"I want you," Randall said. "I will give you that love, home, and children." Peace washed over him, even as he knew his life would never be the same. His old, ambitious, empty dreams were all falling away. "I love you so much."

Her face crumpled. "I—"

"Lord Randall, you only love yourself," Harding cut in, taking the moment away.

Randall had had enough of the man. "I know you're behind this bank failure. I know you've been plotting my downfall because I dared to cross you. Well, go ahead," he shouted, stepping into Harding's face. "Take my seat in the house, take my honor, take my integrity, my money, take everything from me but Isabella. She's mine."

"Oh, Randall!" Isabella cried.

"Isabella is too wise to fall for your dramatics,"

Harding said. "Your love-conquers-all philosophy is so touching, but wholly ineffective."

She raised the *chu-ke nu*, tears streaming down her cheeks. "B-be q-quiet."

"My darling, at this moment, you are a suspect in fraud. Not only could you lose all your money; you could go to Newgate." Harding was sinking to threats. Men like him didn't build railroads or turn a nation into opium addicts by conceding; he would try to win against all reason. "I don't need to tell you that if you leave, Powers will be free to skip the country."

Randall tried so hard to keep from smiling as he set his trap. "Let me guess, you led her here in exchange for Powers. Well, go fetch him. Why not get all the men in Isabella's life in one room, place all the cards on the table, and let her choose."

"Very well." Harding crossed to the door and bellowed down the corridor. "Someone bring Powers immediately."

Isabella remained still, her eyes focused on the floor.

"Isabella," Randall whispered. His heart ached. "Tell me you love me too."

Say it, Isabella told herself. *Tell him how much you when love him. Tell him how you've never felt more perfect than when in his arms. Tell him that sharing a home with him would be more than you dared dream in this life.* How easy it would be to say it. But she couldn't. She couldn't ruin his life.

"Isabella, please," Randall entreated again.

Harding laughed. The corridor thundered with heavy footfalls. Just outside the threshold appeared the two men who had tossed her into the carriage and another hulking, bearded man. The smell of gin wafted off him. He was dressed in the same dark pantaloons and coat as the other flash men, but he sported a sheer nightshirt of sorts on top of his garments and a long, fluffy white tail dangled between his legs.

"What the hell are you wearing, Ralph?" the railroad baron demanded. "Where is Powers? You were supposed to be watching him night and day."

Ralph glanced at the other men and rocked on his feet. "So he, um, said that pretty maid wanted to play a little game with me, Naughty Pussycat Likes a Big Tail. That we were all going to be curious, frolicking kitties...and...and then he tied me up and, well, that pretty little maid never came." He scratched his beard. "Do you think she doesn't desire me?"

"Be quiet!" Harding boomed. "Goddammit." He slammed the wall with his flail, knocking a nasty hole in the plaster. "Search the entire house," he yelled. "Find that blasted Powers! I should have killed that annoying cully one of the thousand times that I felt like it."

Enough of this madness, she thought. She had to get Randall out of here. Clutching her crossbow and keeping her eyes on the viscount, trying to transmit her idea to his mind, she edged closer to the long windows that faced onto the back courtyard and mews. A fat moon, partially concealed by clouds, sat practically on top of the neighbor's roof. She opened a window, sending a blast of humid night air through the room.

"What are you doing?" Harding demanded.

"Good evening, Mr. Harding. I only bargain in good faith. Now I'm exercising my option to walk away. Come, Randall."

She slipped out the window and grabbed on to the scaffolding.

Twenty-two

"Boys!" Harding shouted. He rushed forward, his *sanjiegun* spinning, but was too late. Randall had already dived outside and now dangled from a pole. Isabella shut the window behind him and rushed down a long plank as Harding's flail slammed the glass, shattering it.

"Isabella, don't be foolish," Harding called, his head poking through the broken window. "You're making a terrible mistake. If you come back, all will be forgiven. You're just being a flighty, mindless female."

"I've calculated your risk," she replied. "And I've decided against your offer. Let's go, Randall." She set down the ancient crossbow and jumped, her skirts flying up like wings as she descended down into the courtyard.

"You come back inside, or I'll put you in Newgate," Harding shouted. "Boys, catch her!"

Out of the darkness, three stable hands scampered toward her.

"Oh, hell," she heard Randall hiss from above.

Then his body crashed from the sky onto the men, knocking them to the ground. "Run!" he told Isabella.

She wouldn't dare leave him, not while she had breath in her body. She grabbed his hand, yanking him from the ground. One of the servants charged toward her. Randall brushed him off with a hard elbow as they rushed through the alley and into the street.

Her petticoats beat around her legs. Behind her, she could hear feet pounding. Glancing over her shoulder, she could see three of Harding's fleet-footed men, including the one with a white fluffy tail bouncing off his thighs, closing the distance. Randall held her tight as they veered onto a park lane. The walks were littered with the lovely people who loitered about Hyde Park at night. They tugged her dress. "Ey, got a fine necklace 'ere, just for me pretty lady." "Want a reticule for yer lovely gown? Doesn't cost 'ardly anything." Meanwhile, Randall received more illicit solicitations.

A heavy hand landed on her shoulder. "Got 'er!" a man shouted in her ear. She screamed and was jerked sideways, freed from the man's hold. She felt as if she were hurtling through the air, toward a four-wheeled black carriage that had pulled onto the curb.

The carriage door opened and Powers leaned out.

"You!" Isabella screamed.

"I knew you would need me," Powers shouted.

"Jump inside," Randall cried, and lifted her.

For the second time that night, she was tossed into a strange carriage. Randall leaped in behind her, his arms open and ready to embrace her. He was yanked back, falling half-in and half-out of the carriage. Outside, one of Harding's triplets held on to the viscount's leg, even as the carriage lurched forward.

"You let go of him, you filthy, hideous parasite," she shouted, and latched on to Randall's underarms. She would not let them be separated again. Randall gave a sharp kick. A black shoe arced into the air as Harding's foot soldier fell face-first onto the pavers. Isabella tugged, helping Randall scramble inside.

He collapsed against her. "I have you, my love. I have you," he whispered. She closed her eyes and rocked in his arms, drawing in his scent, the heat of his muscles, his damp perspiration.

"Randall, my darling, I—"

Powers cleared his voice. She opened her eyes to see her former object of devotion across the carriage, hunched over a satchel. Disgust washed over her. How could she have been attracted to this…this… "Rat!" she yelled. "Do you know how much trouble you caused? How dare you sell the bank false stock? And… and…I was going to name my first child after you."

"I think you've misunderstood my good intentions." Powers's hand slid from behind the satchel. He gripped a shiny silver and ivory gun. Etched on the side were the words "*La Diablo.*" She burst out in laughter, not the funny, mirth-filled sort, but the scary hysterical, murderous kind born of anxiety and terror.

"What's so damn funny?" Powers hissed.

"Don't you mean *el diablo*?" Isabella explained. "Your devil gun has a gender problem."

"What?" He looked at his gun. "Bloody hell! That cheap rogue inscribed the wrong words. I never get a break." His face darkened to a deep crimson and its lines hardened. Even through her fear, Isabella cringed in embarrassment for ever finding him attractive.

"I assure you, the bullets in it aren't so funny," Powers hissed.

"Don't point the gun at her, point it at me, you flea-witted bugger."

"Shut your hole, and sit yer arse down."

Randall muttered violent curses as he tried to tuck her behind him. Powers wagged his gun. His features relaxed as he enjoyed the power *la diablo* afforded him. "I'm going to tell a little story."

"Great, because I would love to hear it," Randall retorted, scaring Isabella. The small aperture pointed at his chest didn't seem to affect him except to make him more annoyed and arrogant. Meanwhile, she was terrified that with one slip of Powers's finger, Randall might be taken from her. She would have lost her mother, father, and then Randall. Not him. She didn't want to be in the world without him, even if he married another and she became the scary, old spinster Isabella who forgot the sexes of his children and bought beautiful frocks and ribbons for the boys and swords for the girls.

She felt the burn of tears coming back, and she didn't blink them away. Her father's injunctions to be strong were useless. Randall had chased them away. She felt as if her heart were outside her body, raw and exposed.

Powers's nostrils dilated with his fast breath. "You see, I was in love with Isabella and had suspicions that Harding was going to try and destroy her bank… and…your political career. And I was going to stop him because we're all partners, see?"

"So you became Harding's houseguest," Randall said. "Like a spy."

"Like a spy, that's it. I spied on him and learned some things." He patted his satchel. "Things that can get him in trouble. So, that's what you have to tell the police. Then Isabella and I can get married."

"Go ahead and shoot me!" she cried.

"Marriage proposal by gunpoint," Randall said. "You're such a romantic. Clearly this is true love."

"Look, this ain't what it seems!" Powers barked. "I'm helping both of you! And I, um, loved Isabella since I first saw her. And more than just for her money."

"Well, aren't you the chivalrous hero?" Randall said. "I'm glad you cleared everything up with your little explanation. Because here's the story I was going to tell the police; it's about a young man who has a little gambling problem and gets fleeced by an unsavory dealer in a situation set up by Harding."

"How did you know about that?" Powers yelled. His knuckles turned white, his fingers trembled on the gun. Isabella held Randall tighter.

Randall continued in a smooth, unruffled manner. "Oh, we know all about you. Your old tutor Busby, the naughty pussycat game, your semi-literate lovers, and the drawerful of hideous chemises."

Powers's ears reddened. "Be quiet. That's none of your business."

"Well, your future wife Isabella might be interested," Randall pointed out. "Especially that part where Harding convinced you to sell stock to her bank in return for help with a particular gambling debt. So when Isabella readily sees that the stock is fraudulent, you go running back to Harding like a scared little boy, accusing him of setting you up."

Powers's lower lip protruded. "He said that he didn't know the stocks were fraudulent."

"And you believed him?" Randall chuckled.

"No," Powers protested. "Like you said, I was a spy. That scoundrel said he would find out what had gone wrong. He said he would protect me. In the meantime, he made me work on that ugly house of his. All those little stones in the mosaic—I did those. Then he sees Isabella…and…" The man trailed off, unable to navigate through the numerous lies he had spun.

"Harding didn't know about Isabella, and when he found out about her, he fell in greedy *amour*. She changed his game and you were going to take the fall for the crime after all. Ah, but you out-wiled Harding, didn't you? You and your naughty pussycat. You escaped. I say, I'm quite fond of my story. It possesses that nice ring of plausibility that the police so enjoy."

"I want everyone to just be quiet, goddammit," Powers shouted. Fire spewed from the mouth of the gun, and a huge hole gaped in the top of the carriage.

Isabella screamed and pressed her hand into Randall's chest, feeling his heartbeat.

"Oh, damn," Powers yelled, staring at his gun, eyes wide with shock, sweat dripping down his flushed forehead. "Oh damn, oh damn, oh damn."

The carriage rocked to a stop. Powers banged the ceiling. "Keep going to where I told you. Or I'll…I'll shoot you too…and your horses. I'll bloody well shoot everyone." He carefully rotated the gun barrel.

Isabella heard the driver click his tongue, and the carriage lurched forward again.

"I'm not going to talk anymore," Powers announced, keeping his gun trained on them.

Isabella clutched Randall. He whispered calming "shhhs," caressing her arm with the back of his fingers. The carriage rambled on, weaving through the streets. They reached a wretched, unlit neighborhood where dark, scary eyes peered at the passing carriage. People huddled together on the doorsteps of falling, timbered homes, trying to sleep. Drunks wandered about, wild-eyed and talking to themselves. The reek of rot and human waste steamed up from the open gutter.

The carriage stopped in front of a building, the windowpanes grimy and almost impossible to see through. The torch beside the door lit the red letters painted over the window: Richard and Son's Pawn. The mouth of a murky alley gaped beside the shop.

Sweat slicked Powers's hair and beaded on his brow. "All right—all right, I'm getting out, and then you're following me. And don't try anything or your brains will be ornamenting the pavement." Randall exited first and then turned to help Isabella down, quickly putting her behind him.

Powers set down the satchel, keeping the gun trained on them, and tossed up some coins to the driver. "That's extra for the accident. I'm really sorry about that." He picked up his bag again, hugged it to his chest, and waved his gun. "Walk deep into the alley where no one can see you."

Isabella kept Randall's fingers laced through hers.

They would die together, she thought as they moved slowly into the darkness. How many years had she wasted? So many happy memories they could have made. But it all came down to this slimy and wet alley, which smelled like the mass grave of thousands of decomposing rats. The rhythmic drip of water echoed in her ears.

Randall walked slightly ahead of her, limping with only one shoe. "We can't go any farther," he said, halting her. "We're at the wall."

"Keep your backs to me and get on your knees," Powers said.

"If we just discuss things, we might be able to work out an agreement," Randall suggested.

"I said get on your knees!"

Isabella sank down onto the slimy stones, Randall beside her. "I love you," she cried. She couldn't let him go to the grave without knowing the truth. "I love you with all my being. I probably always have. I'm sorry." Tears fell again. "I'm so sorry."

"Count to forty," Powers barked.

"I wasted so many years." She wept, feeling those years coming back like restless ghosts, thousands and thousands of memories and unhealed wounds. "I refused to see you for who you were because…I was afraid you wouldn't like me. And now it's about to end and—"

"Love, he isn't going to kill us," Randall whispered. "He's trying to make a getaway. Just remain calm."

"No, I'm going to kill you," Powers said. "Now count to forty. Aloud. Start."

"You were right about me," she cried. "You saw

through me as you do with everyone. I loved my father so much. I loved him. And he didn't love me."

"That's not counting!" their captive yelled.

"He did, love." The viscount raised her hand to his lips, kissing each of her fingers and the inside of her palm. "He adored you. He just didn't know how to show it."

"Judith is right. I keep all this inside me, and it's been so hard for so long."

"I know, love. I know." Randall drew her close, pressing her to his racing heart.

"This is very touching, but can you stop making love and count?" Powers sounded exasperated. "One…two…three…and so forth."

"I never thought—" Her words fell out in starts and stops. "I never thought… Do you really love me? Did you really mean those words?"

"I didn't want to love you. Maybe I've been fighting it for years and I refused to admit it, because I knew…I knew it would change everything for me— who I saw myself as, who I wanted to be. When I saw you being pushed into that carriage, none of that mattered anymore. It was meaningless. The only true thing in my life is you."

"There's that bloody bugger," a gruff voice shouted.

"Oh, damn it," Powers cried.

Isabella turned to see two men in dark clothes and another with a white tail appended to his crotch at the alley's opening. A dark, large object flew through the air, hit the wall, and then a gun fired, raining mortar and brick down on them.

Randall's mouth latched on to hers as he pushed her

to the ground. Was he shot? She could feel the hard thrum of his heart as his arms tightened around her. His lips were stiff and his body taut. She was jammed in that filthy, reeking place between the wall and the slimy ground with something hard, square, and with a metal point that lodged under the small of her back. Another gunshot rang out.

"Get him," a man ordered. "I'll check the alley."

Footsteps crunched on the cobblestones, coming nearer and nearer. Randall clutched her tighter. She didn't breathe; her head rushed with black heat. The footfalls stopped just inches from where they lay. Randall's heart pounded against her breasts. For several seconds, no one moved. She heard the scraping sound of the man turning on his heel. He walked to the left and then the right. "Well, bloody hell," he muttered, and then broke into a jog, the steps becoming fainter and fainter as he sprinted down the street.

Randall's lips moved against hers. His tongue delved deep in her mouth. She knotted his hair in her fingers and returned his frantic kisses, tears streaming down the sides of her face. The worst was coming to bear. The bank would fail and a political career would be destroyed, but that didn't matter at the moment. The man she loved was alive and in her arms. She kissed his jaw, his eyelids, his nose, whispering over and over, "I love you," until his lips silenced her.

She kissed him until it was safe enough to leave, and then a few minutes more.

"Come," he whispered, and lifted her up.

She sniffed. "I've turned into a watering pot."

In the darkness, he gently wiped her eyes. "You have years of tears built up."

As she stepped closer to him, her foot hit the leathery hard thing she had been lying on. She bent and felt Powers's satchel. "My love, I think we have a parting gift."

Under the torchlight of Richard and Son's Pawn, they opened the bag and peered inside—three slim, brown books. Isabella withdrew one and opened it to the front page. "Good Lord!" she cried. "That rat stole Harding's ledgers."

Twenty-three

RANDALL KEPT ISABELLA LOCKED BY HIS SIDE AND Powers's satchel in his grip as he limped along the sidewalk. Aside from the missing shoe issue, his knee throbbed from Harding's spinning stick of pain. They were easy prey if any pickpocket dared ply his trade, but the wild, distraught, ready-to-kill expressions on their faces sent passing pedestrians in a wide arc to avoid them. Randall gazed up, finding St. Paul's dome rising above the chimney tops. He headed toward it. He had to be careful and keep to the dark, scary neighborhoods around the Thames. They couldn't amble along the well-patrolled, lit streets around Mayfair, since they were wanted by the police.

In a matter of hours, their lives had changed. Growing up, he had envisioned himself the powerful politician and, yes, even the prime minister. His life was to be a long, straight road leading to a golden end of greatness. Now, he didn't know what he would do in the next minute, let alone the next day or week or year. It was all new. His old life had fallen

away. He needed time to think, see what Powers had
given them, and in truth, he desired to hold Isabella
again, skin to skin, finding strength in her kisses
before the rising sun and the storm of newspaper
headlines, angry customers, accusations, swarming
solicitors, police interrogation, and bailiffs descended
upon them.

Near the Temple Bar, they found an inn with a
light in the window. A lanky man stretched on the
torn sofa in the squat front parlor, his thin chest rising
like a mountain and falling like a valley with his
rattling snores. In the back corner, a serious young
musician was hunched over a piano, drunkenly singing about a lover who had left him, oblivious to the
starry-eyed servant sitting beside him.

"Ey, pardon me," Randall said in his Mr. Randy
voice. "Do you 'ave a room for me and the missus this
fine evening?"

The sleeping man jolted up with a grunt, and stared
about, confused. As his world came back into focus,
grim lines set in around his mouth. He ruffled his wild,
greasy hair. Holding his knee, he came to his feet and
stretched his back with a groan. "Are you or have you
ever been hired by the police or the legal profession
in any capacity?" he asked them. Sewers smelled more
pleasant than his breath. "Or are you related to or
know a policeman, a former Bow Street Runner, or
member of the judicial system?"

"You means outside of that time I was sent to
prison?" Mr. Randy asked for clarification.

"Well, then, I've only got the garret room tonight,"
the innkeeper said. "It's a shilling even if you ain't

planning to stay the entire night. Two shillings if ye're wantin' clean water, four if ye're wantin' clean sheets, and six if ye're wantin' three lumps of coal."

"We'll take everything." Randall flipped a half sovereign in the air. The innkeeper caught it in his palm and jerked his head at the lovelorn servant, who scurried from the room.

"Come this way." The innkeeper beckoned them toward a dark, narrow, steep staircase.

They climbed to a small landing with closed doors on either side. From the left door Randall heard a mattress furiously creaking and a woman repeatedly beseeching her "God in heaven." Behind the other, a strident female voice asked, "Who ate mumsy-wumsy's last bit of plum pudding?" A whip cracked and a man yelped. "You've been a very, very bad boy and must be punished."

The innkeeper banged his fist on the right door. "Wot did I say about whips? You stop that business this instant." Then he yelled at the occupants of the left room, "Keep it down."

Isabella leaned into Randall, giving him a questioning, nervous look. "I'll show you later," he said, and wrapped a protective arm around her.

"We got rules 'ere, we do," the innkeeper said as they ascended another flight. "No smoking in bed, no speaking above a whisper, no exchanging stolen goods or government secrets, no women putting on men's clothes and vice versa—there's a place down the street for that—no eating Mrs. Garfield's mushroom pies, climbing onto the roof naked and singing 'Winds Today Are Large and Free' until the watch comes."

He shrugged at their confused faces. "It 'appens more often than you think."

At the top of the stairs, the landlord stopped. The servant was leaving a room, and the corridor was so narrow that everyone had to turn to let her pass. Randall let Isabella enter before him, into a low, tiny chamber. He had to duck to keep his head from hitting the exposed rafters. Shoved in the corner was a small, slumping bed—only big enough for one person—with a slanting canopy protecting it from the open ceiling where the attic rafters were exposed. Beside the bed sat a plain oak table holding a yellowed wash basin, two folded cloths, and a burning lamp. There weren't any windows in the room, save the one in the roof, where the gorgeous, lush moon glowed down. At least the sheets appeared to be clean and the water clear.

"Always keep it down," the innkeeper reminded, and left, closing the door behind him.

Isabella folded into Randall and raised her lips to his. She still couldn't believe the words that he'd said, that he loved her and wanted to give her a loving, warm home. It wasn't possible. In the morning, he would awake clearheaded and regret them. But for now, it was enough that he had said them. And tomorrow, she would face the scary knowledge that she wouldn't have Randall…or a home.

But that was hours away.

The pressure of his mouth increased, his tongue caressing hers. His fingers untied the ribbons of her bonnet, letting it fall away. She reached for his cravat, releasing the knot, and then pushed back his coat, undoing the buttons of his waistcoat, desperate to get to his bare skin.

"You have too many pieces." She laughed, nervous with anticipation.

"Bathe me, darling."

Her hands were shaking as she squeezed the linen, letting the water drip on his bare chest, streaming down the planes of his muscles. He was a beautiful dream that she intended to love as best she could before the nightmare descended. He released his trousers, and she sucked in her breath as he sprang up. She cleansed him, gently stroking him with the towel and then her hand, before kneeling down and taking him into her mouth. His breath was hoarse, his eyes closed, head bowed, lost in her touch.

"Oh God," he groaned. He gently pushed her away. "Your turn." He lifted her to her feet and spun her around, his fingers flying down the column of buttons, ripping at the laces, pulling her from their confines. All the while, she fantasized ways she would pleasure him in these last hours. She had to create memories she could hold forever. He reached around her, cupping her breasts in his hand, kissing her ear. His fingers plucked, teased, flicked her nipples, and his erection pressed against the small of her back.

She moaned. Then she was being lifted from the ground. She clasped her arms around his neck and pressed her ear to his chest, listening to his heart pounding away.

He released her onto the mattress. She sank down and down and down. "Help! It's swallowing me!"

"I'm coming in after you." He chuckled as he dived

on top of her. The mattress engulfed them. Face to face, she could see the tender light in his eyes. She smiled to herself. She could finally read him. Her fingers roved over the sandy stubble on his cheeks and the small wrinkles under his eyes.

"I love touching you," she said.

"You can touch me whenever you like."

Until we are put in Newgate, a vile little voice in her head said. She didn't want to think those scary thoughts. She closed her eyes and let him sink between her thighs.

Deep in their kiss, he entered her. Not the frantic, wild motion that characterized last evening, but a slow, gentle tempo. He released her mouth to whisper, "Say you love me again, Isabella. Please."

"I love you." She looked directly in his vivid eyes. "How could I not? But, Randall, you don't need to give up your life for me."

"Hush." His lips brushed hers.

The moon shined through the dormer window, casting shadows on his face. She knew she couldn't marry him. How could she demand that he give up his beautiful life for her? It was selfish. But she had him for tonight. She pulled him closer and raised her hips to heighten his pleasure. She released her mind, letting his touch, energy, and scent wrap her in a safe cocoon, away from the world. She softly whimpered with his rhythm until her back arched, her body rigid against his quick thrusts. Tiny, dazzling fireworks burst in her body. She writhed and, digging her nails into his forearms, she pushed harder and harder against him. He cried out, a mangled, desperate sound, then shuddered, releasing deep inside her pristine vessel where the babies were made.

He lowered his chest onto hers, kissing her neck.

She let her fingers drift like feathers down his back, over the top of his buttocks, and up again. The moon gazed down on their spent bodies.

"I love you," he murmured.

A small root of anger took hold in her heart as she stared at the moon, feeling Randall's heartbeat against her breast. He shouldn't have to give up his Parliament seat for trying to be a good man. His honor shouldn't be torn apart for trying to be honorable. Her anger rose higher as she considered everyone Harding would hurt because he didn't get what he wanted. Mrs. Merckler shouldn't be financially destroyed for taking care of people, and the Wollstonecraft women shouldn't lose their savings for trying to have some control over their lives.

"Excuse me." She shifted from under Randall.

"What?" he whispered, drowsy from lovemaking.

"I need to get out for a moment."

"No, stay here." He hugged her tight. "Mmm, it's warm and you're so soft and I have plans."

"I'll come back. Please let me out."

"You can try." He rolled against the wall. She tugged her limbs free and crawled over the mattress edge. Leaning down, she patted about for her glasses until she found them and slid them in place, only to see Randall staring at her with a strange smile. "Very nice. Can you do that again?"

She jerked her head back. "Put on my glasses?"

"No, bend over to pick them up."

"Like this, love?"

His smile turned upside down when he realized she was retrieving Harding's ledgers. "Oh no, no, no, you don't. You are not making love to me and then reading boring numbers. Was it that terrible for you?"

"It was wonderful." She kissed his forehead and raked her fingers through his hair. "You're wonderful." Then she offered him a ledger. "Look for something unusual."

He yanked it from her hands and quipped, "I hope when we are poor and huddled in my estate with the roof leaking and everything that isn't entailed sold off that you don't plan to spend the nights reading ledgers in our marital bed."

She gave him a flustered smile and crawled over him, turned her back against the wall, and raised her legs over the edge of the mattress.

"There isn't enough room in this bed for two ledgers," he announced and looked on with her, letting his finger draw little circles around one of her rosy tips.

The numbers and names were written in a short-hand code. Some she could decipher, others she couldn't. If there was any damning evidence here, it would take days to track down. Randall had given up before her, mumbling something about going to the police tomorrow and enjoying each other's bodies while there was still time. Now his tongue flicked across her nipple. She whimpered, about to give in to the pleasure, when she saw the name Merckler.

"Fudge!" she cried, reading the lines. "He has options in Merckler." She sat up, accidentally slamming Randall's nose.

"Ouch! Why did you do that?"

"Harding has hundreds of pounds in low options on Merckler. I have to think." She beat her forehead with the heel of her palm. "Think! Think! Think!"

"Don't hurt yourself thinking."

She was about to shoot Randall a smirk when the meaning fell over her. "Oh God! Oh God! The man is evil." She pounded the wall with her fist. "I want to make him suffer. I want him to feel our pain!"

"Keep it down," the muffled inn innkeeper's yelled up. "And you better not have a whip in there."

She struggled over the mattress and reached for her clothes. "I have to go back to Mrs. Merckler's."

"Now? In the middle of the night?"

"I might be able to turn this problem around. I'll take a carriage out of London until I find a train heading to Tupping-on-the-Water. I just have to…have to be back to speak to the Wollstonecraft meeting. I have to tell them the truth but reassure them, build confidence in the market. Oh God!" She squeezed her eyes closed and clenched her hands. "This won't work. I can't make that speech."

"Yes, you can." Randall crawled out of the bed and kissed her forehead, her nose, her chin. He stroked his fingers over her balled fists until they unfurled. "I'm not quite sure what you're talking about, but I have all the faith in the world in you. I'll help. I'll be there with you."

She shook her head. "You can't."

"Even though I won't be standing next to you," he assured her, leaning down until they were eye to eye. "I'll be in the audience—"

"No, I mean you must go to my stockbroker and explain to him that you're not the footman *d'amour*, and ask him to buy one hundred shares in Merckler Metalworks as soon as possible."

"What?"

"We're backed into a corner. We are going to go down if we do nothing. Now is the time to gamble boldly." She smiled to herself. *That's right, Mr. Harding.* "I see a way out. We have to try it."

"I'm not leaving you again. I almost had a heart attack when I saw you being tossed into Harding's carriage."

She fished the folded list of Merckler Metalworks' shareholders from under her corset on the floor. "Take this to Harker. See if any names on this list hold shares in Harding's companies. This is paramount. Vital. And you need to get to Judith at the Copenhagen and reassure her that I'm going to be at the Wollstonecraft meeting."

He ran his finger along the edge of the document. "I won't leave you."

"You have to," she whispered. "We might be able to save you, us, the bank, and Mrs. Merckler. You have to let me try. Please."

He studied her for a long time. His eyes were shining. Was he crying? "Oh, Randall." She hugged him.

"You promise that you'll come back to me," he said. "That you won't let anything happen to you."

"I would come back to you if I had to crawl on my knees all the way from Siam." She kissed his lips, and at first he didn't respond. She coaxed and caressed until she let him inside. "Let me go," she whispered.

He rested his head on her shoulder. "Very well," he said so quietly she almost didn't hear.

Then he squeezed her bottom. "I'm going to fetch Mrs. Perdita to accompany you."

"I don't have time to—"

"You're not going to convince anyone of anything in a dress that smells like rats vomited on it," he aptly pointed out. "And I need a shoe."

Twenty-four

IN ISABELLA'S TIRED, OVERWROUGHT MIND, THE LAST nineteen hours were an angst-filled haze of changing carriages and trains and worries about being spotted. Now Isabella and Mrs. Perdita hid around the corner from the Wollstonecraft Society meeting. That is, if Isabella could truly *hide* in a flowing blond wig, huge straw bonnet, and a gauzy pale gray dress that was once used in the death scene of a production of *The Vicar's Ruined Daughter*. But it was nothing compared to the shiny rainbow brilliance of Mrs. Perdita's painted face and revealing costume.

"Hee-hee," Mrs. Perdita giggled. "It's just like in *The Merry Cuckold*." She patted her ringlets, jingling her numerous necklaces and bracelets. "I played the devious Madame De Saucy, one of my most famous parts."

When Isabella and Mrs. Perdita had arrived back in London, the housekeeper had insisted that Isabella needed to disguise herself, so Isabella had wasted an hour in the moldy costume shop at the bottom of an ancient theater, sneezing. Now they were late.

The sun sat low behind the gray coal clouds. The evening portion of the meeting had started forty-five minutes ago, the police were waiting for her at the door, and she couldn't find Lord Randall anywhere. She panicked.

Meanwhile, Mrs. Perdita had her own problems. "Good heavens, my beauty mark fell off again. Oh, where did it go?" She bent over. "Here it is. No, that's a tiny beetle."

Isabella removed the long strands of blond hair from her eyes and peered around the corner again, hoping in the thirty seconds since she had last checked, the six policemen guarding the building and Harding's men by the entrance had decided to wander off for a nice spot of tea.

No such luck.

"We were supposed to meet Lord Randall an hour ago. He's not here. Why, why, why did I think this was a good idea? If anything happened to him, I'll—"

"Oh, there's that wicked little beauty mark! It's fallen onto my bosom. Hmm, I quite like it there, rather naughty." She patted it in place, jiggling her ample mantel of flesh. "Now, don't you worry, dearie. You need to give your husband a little due."

Isabella and Randall had met Mrs. Perdita in the early hours of the morning. Randall had been beside himself with worry. Clutching Isabella as if she might float away on the sidewalk and drown in the street, he had ordered the housekeeper to take excellent care of his betrothed all the way to Tupping-on-the-Water and back. If he were to lose Isabella again, he told them, he would take a no-return ticket to Bedlam…or Newgate for murder of a powerful railroad baron.

"He's not my husband," Isabella corrected. "If I truly loved him, I wouldn't let him marry me. I've just got to save his career and dreams." Unfortunately, her master plan hadn't included breaking into the heavily guarded society meeting. She groaned and pressed her forehead to the wall, crumpling the bonnet brim. "We can't get in that building. Those women will never learn the truth. We're sunk."

"Now you listen to me." Mrs. Perdita seized her by the shoulders and whirled her around. "We are strong women, like in your book. And a woman has to do what a woman has to do." She tugged at her bodice, exposing even more of her voluptuous breasts. "Now take those glasses off before anyone recognizes you. I'm going to get Miss St. Vincent on that stage."

The large feather poking from the housekeeper's bright blue hat was a crimson blur against the dull gray sky. Isabella followed the red splotch, trying not to stumble over the sidewalk, potholes, and her flowing hem. Her heart was light and racy, making her dizzy. All she could think was *Save Randall, save the bank, save its clients, save the Mary Wollstonecraft Society, save Mrs. Merckler, save my father's legacy, save my home…* Good God, why not just save the entirety of civilization while she was at it?

"Hallo there, my pretty boys," Mrs. Perdita called, drawing Isabella closer. "Is this that naughty Wollstonecraft meeting?" Isabella kept her head low, letting the brim of her straw bonnet and long stringy wig conceal her face.

"Yes, my colorful totty," a deep voice responded. "But you don't look like the type."

"Ohh, we Wollstonecraft women come in all types, and we can be awfully wicked when we want." Mrs. Perdita giggled and crashed into Isabella as if she had stumbled, shoving Isabella toward what might be a door. Isabella rushed through a threshold into a darkened corridor filled with large splotches of flesh and black.

She slipped her glasses from her sleeve and took a quick peek. Men in dark clothes and police uniforms were rushing toward her. She panicked. *Sorry, Randall! I'm so sorry I failed you.* She hunched down, drawing her arms to her chest, waiting for one to arrest her. But they dashed past as if she wasn't there.

"Oh, good 'eavens," she heard Mrs. Perdita say. "I fell so 'ard, me titties almost popped out. You gentlemen are so kind to 'elp me up. Let me give each of you a nice kiss on the cheek."

By the double doors into the auditorium stood a policeman, his legs spread, hands clasped over his male regions. Two dour women wearing ribbons across their chests that read "Mary Wollstonecraft Society" sat behind a long wooden table. Behind them waited a squat yet muscled second policeman.

Isabella had the urge to run away and hide. But the housekeeper's words echoed in her head. *A woman has to do what a woman has to do.* And she had to get into that meeting. She returned her glasses to her sleeve.

With her floppy bonnet low on her face and her heart pounding loud enough to lead soldiers into battle, she edged toward the two dark, smudgy female shapes at the table. "I would like to attend the meeting," she muttered, keeping her eyes low.

"May I see your ticket?" one of the ladies replied.

A ticket? *Oh Hades!* "May—may I purchase one?"

"I'm sorry. We have none left. You must understand, we've had a great deal of controversy surrounding this meeting."

"But it's extremely important that I attend," she said, her voice turning tight and thin, tittering on the edge of hysteria.

"And it's extremely important for you to have a ticket," a husky male voice mocked. She assumed it emitted from the muscle-bound policeman standing behind the women.

Now what? She pressed her hand to her mouth.

Think, Isabella. Think!

The only thought that bubbled up was: *Must save entirety of civilization.*

That is not helpful!

Beside her, she could see the shape of the huge wooden double doors and the policeman guarding it. Beyond its wood, she could hear Judith, in a muffled voice, saying, "I assure you that my cousin is innocent."

"I really, really need to attend this meeting." Isabella pressed her hands together, praying to the human smudges. "My life depends—"

"I knew yer were a-lyin' to me, devil woman!"

Mr. Randy!

Isabella wheeled around to see an approaching shape in shades of brown and green. She forced herself to remain still and not give in to the urge to rush into Randall's arms and melt away.

❧

Randall struggled to keep his character and not break into a relieved, thank-God-you're-alive-and-not-held-prisoner-or-hit-by-a-train-or-the-thousands-of-horrible-scenarios-I-imagined grin as he gazed upon blond Isabella in her rather doleful gown. He had been terrified since sending her off with Mrs. Perdita. The last hour—three thousand and six hundred slow, torturous seconds—when she hadn't arrived on time had been akin to seeing her shoved into Harding's carriage over and over. Randall had managed to loiter about the building undetected for two hours thanks in part to having dyed his hair, but mostly from sporting two swelling bruises on his face. One nasty blue contusion swelled just below his eye where Judith had bashed him with a poker when he snuck into her hotel room at the Copenhagen, and another welt throbbed on his jaw where she had hit him with a lamp after he told her he was marrying Isabella.

"Now, I'm taking your sad likes 'ome and giving yer a spankin' to remember what for," he told Isabella. "Then I'm burning that book of yours. That will teach yer for getting ideas and tryin' to teach yer bird-witted self to read. Now get yer bit of arse 'ome and clean my chamber pot up good."

❧

Isabella stared in his general vicinity with the shiny-eyed terror of a cornered, feral cat.

"Sir, do not speak to your wife thus." One of the reverent women taking tickets rose and placed a hand on her heart, her nostrils quivering. "Our society was formed in order to protest men such as you—low, brutish reptiles."

"Why, thank you, ma'am, for those kind words." Randall belched and scratched his bollocks. "But don't you listen to 'er," he told Isabella with eyes that pleaded *play along*, although she couldn't see anyway. "You're mine. If yer don't start behaving and knowing your place, I might just sells you. You 'ad better 'ope whoever buys yer is as nice as I am to yer."

Then a miracle occurred. "You…you treat yer… dog better than me," Isabella cried in an uneven, panic-infused cockney.

One of the dour Wollstonecraft Society matrons drew herself tall in righteous indignation and marched around the table to Isabella, linking their arms together. "Ma'am, it would be my honor to escort you inside so that you might hear the liberating truth spoken from the mouths of our sisters." The policeman guarding the door stepped aside.

"Don't yer let that devil woman in!" Randall rushed forward, pretending to be trying to prevent the ladies from entering. But instead he used his body to form a barricade behind them. "Get to your companion," he whispered to Isabella.

She bounded forward in a large, open space, but everything was a dark blur. "Judith, I'm here!" On that note, she tripped, hitting the floor. *Fudge! Fudge! Fudge!* She jammed on her glasses and ripped off her bonnet, taking her stupid wig with it. She jumped to her feet and rushed down the aisle.

On a stage in wooden chairs sat four ladies in

somber clothes and sporting Mary Wollstonecraft ribbons. Behind them, the society's emblem hung on a rope. Judith, with tears flowing from her eyes, stood behind a podium where a large gold bust of their fearless leader sat, gazing at the audience. "Oh, Isabella, my brave child."

The audience sucked a collective breath, bolting to their feet.

A great rumble echoed from the back of the theater and then a man's voice thundered through the huge space. "She's inside. Someone let her inside, dammit!"

Isabella glanced over her shoulder. Randall's beautiful face was bruised, his arms wide, trying to hold back the tide of men pushing to get in. "Randall!" she screamed.

"Keep going, love!" he shouted. "Don't worry about me." He was shoved to the ground by police officers and his arm wrenched behind his back. "You want me. Not her. You leave her alone." His words were muffled as his face was pushed to the floor, men trampling over him as they poured down the aisle.

"He's innocent," she cried. "Let me speak. I will tell you." She rushed along the front of the stage. Hands were reaching out, but none tried to grasp or seize her. They just wanted to touch her, she registered. She dashed for the narrow stairs leading to the stage, the police closing the gap behind her.

Judith leaped forward, yanking Isabella onto the stage and then spreading her arms and legs wide, ready to use her body to block the stairs.

The women in the front rows joined her effort,

barricading the police. "Let her speak!" they cried, starting a chant that spread over the crowd.

"Let her speak! Let her speak!"

Women spilled from their seats, clasping hands, forming human chains to further impede the police. "Let her speak!"

"You women are out of line," a strident male voice barked. "Do your husbands, fathers, or brothers know what you're doing?"

"Let her speak!"

Isabella sidled along the podium, searching the audience for Randall, but he was lost in the trample.

"Let her speak!"

Oh God! What was she going to say? What had she done? She reached for the head of Mary Wollstonecraft and cradled it, like an upset child seeking comfort in a favorite blanket or beloved toy.

The room fell to a hush. Her mouth moved, but no words came. She couldn't remember her speech or Judith's notes. She just held the gold plaster bust and swayed. "Ummm…ummm…ummm."

Say something! Say something! Save the civilized world!

"Promising openings," she blurted.

No, no, not that! Anything but that.

The women glanced at each other. Oh God, it was like Isabella always knew: she would let them down. She wasn't the powerful, charismatic leader they had imagined.

A man's rich belly laughter filled the space. "You are wise, Miss St. Vincent, not to incriminate yourself any further," Mr. Harding boomed. "Let the lord mayor of London through before he has all you women arrested." Harding used his powerful body to ram through the lines. Behind him was a smaller, graying man sporting a neatly knotted green cravat and tan plaid waistcoat. Huge lamb chop whiskers grew along his cheeks.

"Now, my little finch, just come down and cooperate, like a good girl," Harding called. "A gentleman who may be of interest to you has been returned to my safekeeping. Someone whom you thought you once loved until he betrayed you. He could be very useful now."

"I don't trust you." Isabella kept the bust against her chest like armor. "I have done nothing wrong."

"Tell me a story, darling," she heard Randall say.

"Randall! I can't see you!" she cried, coming to the lip of the stage, searching the audience. "Where are you?"

"I'm here," he called.

The ladies parted, revealing the viscount pressed to the floor. He struggled against his captors, coming to his knees. A ruddy and sweating policeman punched him straight in the mouth.

Isabella shrieked. "No! Lord Randall is innocent!" she shouted to the officer who was now massaging his fist in his palm.

The large man flinched. "I just punched Lord Randall?!" He began bowing. "I'm sorry, my lord. I didn't know—men, get your hands off him."

Randall rose to his feet and hissed through his clenched teeth. "Just—just tell me a story. Our story," he said, edging down the aisle, keeping his voice calm and controlled even as blood dribbled from the side of his mouth and the police followed closely behind him. "Just look at me, forget about the others, and tell me a story."

"Tell him the story about how you will go to Newgate," Harding barked.

"Don't listen to him, darling." Randall's eyes held hers, safety and acceptance in their depths. "Tell me about your father and his bank. Tell me."

"I—I loved my father." Her voice creaked like a tight, unoiled hinge. She didn't know what she was doing except that she trusted Randall, the great and determined orator. "His share of the Bank of Lord Hazelwood was the only thing I had, because I didn't have a husband or children—none of my own dreams had materialized. I clung so strongly to that bank and told myself to be strong, as my father had done. I wasn't supposed to show when I was scared but…" She glanced at all the women staring up at her. Her eyes watered. "At this moment, I'm very scared."

"Then just step down before you make another mistake," Harding barked. He jerked his head to the policemen. "Somebody get her off that stage. She's embarrassing herself."

"Don't listen to him," Randall countered. "It's natural to be scared." His swollen lip blurred his words. "We've all been terrified, haven't we? We understand."

"I was scared and had nowhere to go," a woman called out. "And then I read your book and you gave me strength." The audience clapped.

Every fiber in her body shouted for her to run and hide, but she remained, feeling terrified and vulnerable before the audience. For her beloved Randall, she had to keep going, pushing through her fears.

"Tell them about us," Randall prompted. "Tell them how we fell in love."

The female audience released an "aww." Isabella even heard some deeper male voices joining in.

"Growing up, I despised Lord Randall." She released a nervous bark of laughter. "I mean, how can you compete with someone everybody loves and who is as charming as the devil?" The audience's laughter made her jump with surprise. Were they laughing at her or something she said?

"Well, I was jealous of her too, and she didn't know it," Randall said. He talked to the ladies as if they were old friends. "In truth, I was probably in love with her then. You know how thick we men are."

"Oh, but I was bitterly jealous of you," she replied, not even seeing the audience anymore. "Because I'm so odd and different."

"Why does she think that?" he asked the ladies, shaking his head, his palms out. "I've told her a thousand times that she's beautiful and she won't believe me."

"Yes, she's simply stunning," Harding agreed. "It would be a shame if such loveliness wasted away in Newgate."

Anger surged through Isabella. "But then, Lord Randall dared to stand up to one of the most powerful men in England—our unwelcome visitor Mr. George Harding—justly questioning Mr. Harding's proposed rail line and financial stability, as a good politician should, humiliating Mr. Harding before his investors." She gazed directly into the eyes of the women. "This entire false stock debacle involving our bank was Mr.

Harding's attempt to destroy Lord Randall's honor and integrity in the face of a pending election."

"Just like men." A lady laughed. "Always dragging women into their petty battles." The woman's comment elicited a tiny eruption of clapping.

Isabella giggled despite the tension. The women began to gather beneath her. She leaned down to talk to them. "So Mr. Harding set up our bank partner to sell us false stock in a company called Merckler Metalworks. When we realized the problem, I was terrified there would be a run on the bank. I would lose everything. Lord Randall's political career would fall. And you"—she made a sweeping gesture to the audience—"our clients, would lose your savings and perhaps more. I couldn't let that happen."

"And if you want them to keep any of it, you'll stop talking this instant," Harding said, stalking down the aisle only to be stopped by a crowd of sturdy, hard-faced women with ribbons that read "Mary Wollstonecraft Society—Liverpool Chapter."

One of their more assertive members shook her fist in his face. "She ain't finished speaking."

"Tell them what we did, my love," Randall said.

Isabella blushed. "I can't say that aloud!"

"I meant to investigate."

She clutched Mary Wollstonecraft's head tighter and began to pace, her mind sharpening. She told the society members about Powers's gambling problem, her and Lord Randall's visit to Mrs. Merckler and all her numerous dependents, and the deplorable conditions at Merckler Metalworks under the new manager.

As she spoke, she felt a deep power blossom in

her belly, rising through her lungs and resonating in her throat. Her voice echoed back to her—not the timid one she heard in her head, but a strong, assured, and passionate tone. The stage was hers, and she looked her audience members in the eyes as she spoke. "So, you ask, why would Harding falsify stock in Merckler Metalworks to bring down Lord Randall and our bank? Because he wanted to hasten the company's demise anyway. Remember my chapter on futures?"

"That's the one where Fiona, the spinster, was left caring for her eight younger sisters, all dying of typhoid," a female voice rang out. "And she invested most of their inheritance in safe consuls but put ten percent in futures on a gas company and then sold those options as the company's stock rose—"

"Making enough profit to hire that handsome physician from London to save her sisters," a lady from the Birmingham chapter finished.

"I loved that chapter, especially when Fiona married the doctor," gushed a Manchester member.

"Exactly," Isabella said. "Except, in this case, George Harding has low futures on Merckler Metalworks. He stands to make a fortune if the company fails. And not content to do research like dear Fiona, he is going to make sure Merckler goes down, even if that means creating false stock and putting an incompetent manager in place."

The audience booed at Harding, calling him an "untrustworthy scoundrel" and "lying blackguard." The Liverpool chapter had more colorful and profane insults that they complemented by throwing objects from their reticules at him, but Judith quickly interceded, saying, "Ladies, remember your dignity."

"These are desperate accusations to cover your own guilt," Harding hissed at Isabella, shielding his face from the last of the flying hairpins and powder puffs. "How could I possibly influence Merckler's board if I own no stock in the company?"

Isabella opened her mouth, but Randall was already answering the question. "If you look at the shareholders in Merckler Metalworks, Lord Mayor, you will find some hold shares in Harding's companies as well, including the more obscure ones."

"If you look even harder," Isabella said, "I'll wager you will see that these people actually don't exist. They are all Harding. It's a standard fraudulent practice."

The lord mayor raised an alarmed brow, putting a little distance between himself and the railroad baron.

"We were all supposed to fall like dominoes, weren't we?" she said, looking Harding dead in the eye. She wasn't scared anymore. "It was a brilliant plan. But"—she clutched her Mary Wollstonecraft head and carefully enunciated each word, letting them thunder around her—"I will not fall!"

"I thought you were different from the others," Harding hissed, "but you're just another ridiculous woman."

"You think I'm ridiculous?" She drew the stock certificates from her corset and held them over Mary Wollstonecraft's head. "These are real stocks in Merckler Metalworks. Early this morning, Mrs. Merckler gave me half of her shares. Together, we two *ridiculous women* are going to make the company profitable, giving decent pay to the poor Irishmen and -women teeming into this country, and without having to employ child labor. My stockbroker has instructions to buy more of Merckler Metalworks on Monday morning. I will control the board. I will make the decisions. Your futures will be worthless, Mr. Harding."

"Quite a bold gamble." Harding's voice was a purr of deep menace. The tenacious man refused to admit defeat. "I approve. But it's all more the magistrate will take from you when your bank fails." An ugly smile twisted his lips.

"I have one hundred pounds in Miss St. Vincent's bank and it's staying there," a woman shouted.

"I have fifty pounds in Miss St. Vincent's bank and it's staying there."

"I have three pounds in Miss St. Vincent's bank and it's staying there."

"I have forty thousand pounds in Miss St. Vincent's bank and plan to add the ten thousand more that I have made following her sage advice," a shaky elderly female voice called. "And then I'll invest another five thousand in this Merckler Metalworks. You don't scare an old, rich, ridiculous woman, Mr. Harding."

"Sir, I would like a few words with you," the lord mayor said to Mr. Harding, and then beckoned to the police.

The ladies clapped, their hands high in the air, and cheers ringing out. Isabella stared at the audience, stunned at the applause; even some of the policemen were joining in. "Thank you," she cried. "Oh, thank you."

Judith hugged her. "I knew you would be a great leader. I always knew it."

Isabella's muscles turned goosey, so many days of tension flowing from her. She gazed down at Randall and pressed her hand to her trembling mouth as tears streamed down her cheeks. She didn't try to check them.

&

My God, Randall thought, *my amazing lady did it*. The crowd was on its feet, cheering, but his mind was a silent place as he stared at his beloved—her shoulders were shaking, her eyes large and wet beneath her lenses. He was so humbled by the power that he and Judith always knew she possessed but she could never see until this stunning moment.

He leaped onto the stage, getting to her before the others. "You were brilliant," he told her. "I'm so proud of you."

"I couldn't have done it if you weren't there."

"I will always be there for you. You are never leaving my side again." He tried to take her into his arms, gaudy plaster bust and all. But she stepped back, lowered her head.

"What—what is it, darling?"

"I love you, Randall," she told the floor. "I love you so much and I always will. But you are free now. You can be the politician you always wanted to be."

Randall's heart contracted. "What are you saying?"

The audience, sensing something was wrong, began to hush each other.

Isabella gripped her Mary Wollstonecraft head, running her fingers over the grooves of its hairline. "If I really cared for you, I should set you free to be the man you need to be. The politician, the viscount." She released a high, soft cry, and raised her head. "I-I set you free because I love you."

His first reaction was rage. He wanted to shake her. *Who are you to determine my life and what I want?* Why would she not believe that all the man he wanted to be was her husband? But as tears dripped off her chin, his heart softened. He could stand here and argue with the shrew. But she thought she was doing the right thing and she wouldn't relent, no matter how many times he told her that he wanted to give his old life away for her.

He turned and studied the society members, their faces tensed in worry for their leader. These women had rallied for the most basic rights afforded to men, overlooked their own safety to barricade the police, and let his beloved speak. Not so many days ago, Harding had said to him, "The world is about to change. You need to decide which side you're on." At that moment, Randall knew his side. He belonged with the voiceless, fighting to be heard. He would give them his voice, letting it thunder in the halls of power.

He had never felt more certain and at peace as when he said, "Hello, ladies, Lord Mayor, police officers, and reporters. I know I look a little different today, but I'm Lord Randall. Some of you may know me from greeting me at the bank or reading about my politics in journals, and others know me from

decorating my robes with various rotting vegetation."
Nervous laughter rippled across the room and then
died under Randall's serious face. "But I swear, by my
undying love for Isabella, I'll continue to be a staunch
Tory, and I will argue for the expansion of voting
rights for all British men and women."

The auditorium stared in shocked silence, exchanging glances that, if transposed to English would be,
Did he just say what I think he said? At the back of the
room, a familiar woman with a faux beauty spot on
her left breast stood on a chair with the aid of several
admiring gentlemen. She wagged her finger over her
head. "Miss St. Vincent, you had better marry that
nice young viscount!"

The ladies broke out into a chant again, their words
amplified to a deafening volume in the high ceiling.
"Marry him! Marry him! Marry him!"

Randall shot Isabella a self-satisfied smile.

"Oh, you bothersome man, you've bested me
again." She gave him a gentle swat. But she didn't
complain when he drew her into his arms and then
lifted her into the air.

"I am honored to accept Lord Randall," she cried
to the crowd and then raised the gold bust. "And the
Mary Wollstonecraft award."

Epilogue

1848

"Be nice," Randall told his mama, and gently inched her forward.

"Good evening, Lady Randall," she told his wife through a tight smile. "You look lovely this evening."

Randall agreed. For the annual house party ball, Mrs. Perdita, Isabella's closest advisor, had styled Isabella's hair in intricate loops and attached tiny, gleaming gemstones that matched her champagne silk gown. The effect was stunning, of course. But there was something different about Isabella tonight, something he couldn't put his finger on—a shining in her eyes, a radiant flushing of her skin.

"Aye, a regular vista of 'eavenly splendor she is." Mr. Randy winked.

"Why do you insist on speaking in that ridiculous, cant-like voice?" his mother demanded. "Ah, I see Lord Hazelwood beckoning. Pardon me."

Randall thought it best not to point out that Mama had never answered to her husband's summons before and the earl wasn't beckoning, but sipping wine and casually chatting with the prime minister, one of those unfortunate Whigs.

"Well, my sweet Izzy May," Mr. Randy said, and then switched back to his normal voice. "That conversation went better than I had imagined. Next year we are going to work up to a 'how are you doing?' and perhaps in another decade's time, you and Mama will have an entire civil conversation."

"She believes I've ruined her family."

He scanned the assorted house party guests. "I'll say, you would think it's the Vandals and Visigoths versus the Romans tonight. We've invited both the right and wrong kind of Tories, as well as some of those barbaric Whigs and chartists. Cousin Judith is running about with a raucous gaggle of Wollstonecraft members. And various merchants are eyeing the crowd nervously from the corners." All the people who had helped Randall narrowly win back his seat. No longer was he the golden boy who followed the party lines, but the influential Tory maverick who was married to that famous rights-for-women campaigner.

"Next year will be easier," he promised, and kissed the back of her hand. "We will spend less time in court and more time in the privacy of our favorite chamber."

They had spent their honeymoon in the lovely British judicial system. Powers's trial was brief, but Harding's dragged on as more evidence against the man was amassed. Harding was penniless by the end, and significant amounts of his investors' monies were confiscated to pay his debts. Both Harding and Powers had been sent to Newgate. Meanwhile, the Bank of Lord Hazelwood continued to expand and Merckler Metalworks, under Isabella's guidance, became a significant supplier of machinery to Britain and Europe.

"No, it won't," she said. "You'll be busy with your other wife—Parliament. And…" She didn't finish but flashed him an enigmatic smile. Again he pondered what was different about her tonight. She was a beautiful mystery. And he was pretty sure that to figure it out, he would have to remove all her clothes.

The violins began to strum a lively song. "The quadrille," the leader called out.

His wife's entrancing smile vanished. "The quadrille! I thought you told your mother to have a waltz for the first dance."

"Calm down." He wrapped her fingers around his elbow. "It will be just the way we practiced."

"Just as we practiced? I think the guests might be a little taken aback if we did a few turns and then made mad, passionate love on the floor…and sofa…and the table now holding the beef and mustard." She covered her nose with her hand. "Oh, that mustard is quite strong. I can smell it from here."

The dancers assumed their starting positions. Isabella wore the same expression as she had when they had danced the quadrille a year ago—as if something large was hurtling from the skies and about to hit her between the eyes. She tugged at his arm. "I suddenly feel sick. I don't think I should dance."

"You can do it." He patted her hand. "Don't be nervous. I'm here."

"No, I'm really going to be illsy."

"'Illsy'?"

"It's that mustard!" She pressed her palm to her mouth, muffling a heaving sound, and fled the dance floor. The male dancers glanced about, alarmed, but the women shared knowing smiles.

Randall chased his wife, finding her on the lawn, where she had located a convenient potted plant in which to remove the contents of her stomach. Milton was perched on the roof overhead, wailing amorous intentions to a wandering calico cat.

Randall knelt beside his wife and placed a hand between her shoulder blades. "I'll call a physician. You don't have to dance."

"No," she wailed into the plant. "I'm not sick." Taking three gulping breaths, she sat back on the grass. The perspiration on her face glistened in the light falling from the swollen full moon. She wiped her mouth with her wrist. "Randall, my love, I think we've made a baby."

Acknowledgements

I would like to acknowledge the wonderful Nancy Mayer, who suggested I purchase a book on nineteenth-century female bankers. To the ladies of the Mojito Literary Society: Laura Valeri, Tina Whittle, and Katrina Murphy, for laughter, writing advice, and listening to me as I struggled to weave the story threads together.

To my fabulous agent, Paige Wheeler, for her advice and guidance. To my excellent editor, Deb Werksman, for her vision and sense of humor. I truly appreciate my friend Abigail Carlton for her patience and willingness to join me in over-the-phone theatrical improvisation as I try to hash through dialogue. And finally, I want to thank my family for their love, support, and unending supply of comic material.

About the Author

Susanna Ives started writing when she left her job as a multimedia training developer to stay home with her family. Now she keeps busy driving her children to various classes, writing books, and maintaining websites. She often follows her husband on business trips around Europe and blogs about the misadventures of touring with children. She lives in Atlanta.

Wicked Little Secrets

by Susanna Ives

— ❧ —

It's not easy being good...

Vivacious Vivienne Taylor has finally won her family's approval by getting engaged to the wealthy and upright John Vandergrift. But when threatened by a vicious blackmail scheme, it is to her childhood friend that Vivienne turns: the deliciously wicked Viscount Dashiell.

When being wicked is so much more exciting...

Lord Dashiell promised himself long ago that his friendship with Vivienne would be the one relationship with a woman that he wouldn't ruin. He agrees to help her just to keep the little hothead safe, but soon finds that Vivienne has grown up to be very, very dangerous to all of Dash's best intentions.

— ❧ —

"With *Wicked Little Secrets*' intriguing plot, quirky characters, witty escapades, and heartfelt dialogue, Ives has created a read that's as thought-provoking as it is romantic." —*RT Book Reviews*, 4½ Stars

"If you love historical romances, this book is a must!" —*Long and Short Reviews*

For more Susanna Ives, visit:

www.sourcebooks.com

Lady Elinor's Wicked Adventures
by Lillian Marek

———— ∽ ————

Lady Elinor is searching for treasure

The intrepid Lady Elinor Tremaine is caught up in the Victorian fervor for exploring distant lands. Her travels throw her back in the company of an old friend—this time, far from the security of polite society.

And uncovering the secrets of her own heart

Harry de Vaux, Viscount Tunbury, has loved Lady Elinor for as long as he can remember—but his family's sordid background put her completely out of his reach. Prowling through Etruscan ruins in Italy with Elinor is exquisite torture. She is so close, and so forbidden…

———— ∽ ————

"This lively Victorian adventure…is sure to charm readers with the quick pace, mystery, and likable characters." —*RT Book Reviews*

"A simply delightful tale of love, passion, lies, and family life set against a wonderfully historical backdrop." —*Fresh Fiction*

For more Lillian Marek, visit:

www.sourcebooks.com

The Bridegroom Wore Plaid
by Grace Burrowes
New York Times and *USA Today* Bestselling Author

---❦---

His family or his heart—one of them will be betrayed...

Ian MacGregor is wooing a woman who's wrong for him in every way. As the new Earl of Balfour, though, he must marry an English heiress to repair the family fortunes.

But in his intended's penniless chaperone, Augusta, Ian is finding everything he's ever wanted in a wife.

---❦---

Praise for *The Bridegroom Wore Plaid*:

"Memorable heroes. Intelligent, sensual love stories. This author knows what romance readers adore." —*RT Book Reviews*

"Historical details enrich Burrowes's intimate and erotic story, but the real stars are her vibrant characters and her masterful ear for dialogue. Burrowes is superb at creating connections that feel honest and real." —*Publishers Weekly* Starred Review

"Intimate and erotic." —*Publishers Weekly* Starred Review

For more Grace Burrowes, visit:
www.sourcebooks.com

What a Lady Needs for Christmas

The MacGregor Series

by Grace Burrowes

New York Times and *USA Today* Bestselling Author

---- ❧ ----

The best gifts are the unexpected ones…

To escape a scandal, Lady Joan Flynn flees to her family's estate in the Scottish Highlands. She needs a husband by Christmas, or the holidays will ring in nothing but ruin.

Practical, ambitious mill owner Dante Hartwell offers to marry Joan, because a wellborn wife is his best chance of gaining access to aristocratic investors.

As Christmas—and trouble—draw nearer, Dante and Joan discover that true love often hides beneath the most unassuming holiday wrapping…

---- ❧ ----

Praise for Grace Burrowes:

"Burrowes is superb at creating connections that feel honest and real." —*Publishers Weekly*

For more Grace Burrowes, visit:

www.sourcebooks.com

Waltz with a Stranger
by Pamela Sherwood

❧

One dance would change her life forever...

Aurelia wasn't hiding exactly. She just needed to get out of the crush of the ballroom—away from the people staring at her scar, pitying her limp. She was still quite enjoying the music from the conservatory. And then a complete stranger—dashing, debonair, kind—asked her to waltz. In the strength of his arms, she felt she could do anything. But both would be leaving London soon...

When they meet again a year later, everything has changed. She's no longer a timid mouse. And he's now a titled gentleman—with a fiancée. Is the magic of one stolen moment, one undeniable connection enough to overcome a scandal that would set Society ablaze and tear their families apart?

❧

For more Pamela Sherwood, visit:

www.sourcebooks.com